DEMON FALL

ALSO BY
M.J. HAAG

FAIRY TALE RETELLINGS
(ALL IN THE SAME WORLD)

BEASTLY TALES

Depravity

Deceit

Devastation

TALES OF CINDER

Disowned (prequel)

Defiant

Disdain

Damnation

RESURRECTION CHRONICLES
(hottie demons!)

Demon Ember

Demon Flames

Demon Ash

Demon Escape

Demon Deception

Demon Night

Demon Dawn

Dmeon Disgrace

Demon Fall

M.J. Haag

ISBN 978-1-943051-63-2 (eBook Edition)

ISBN 978-1-63869-012-2 (Paperback Edition)

Editing by Ulva Eldridge
Cover design by Shattered Glass Publishing LLC
© Depositphotos.com

Version 2021.09.26

Demon Fall

Love isn't blind; it's devastating.

June had her future all planned out, and it never involved hiding in a bunker with her long-term boyfriend during what felt like the end of the world. In fact, surviving the zombie apocalypse never even entered the picture. Yet, that's exactly what fate gave her.

A game of survival. One horror after another. But, at least she's not alone. At least she has Adam…until she doesn't.

Heartbroken, June wishes she could face the apocalypse on her own, but she's seen what's out there. Infected that are smart enough to fake what they are, and the hellhounds are determined to kill every last human. If she wants to survive, she'll need help from the dark creatures who rescued her from the bunker.

She'll need a fey, and Tor is just the man for the job.

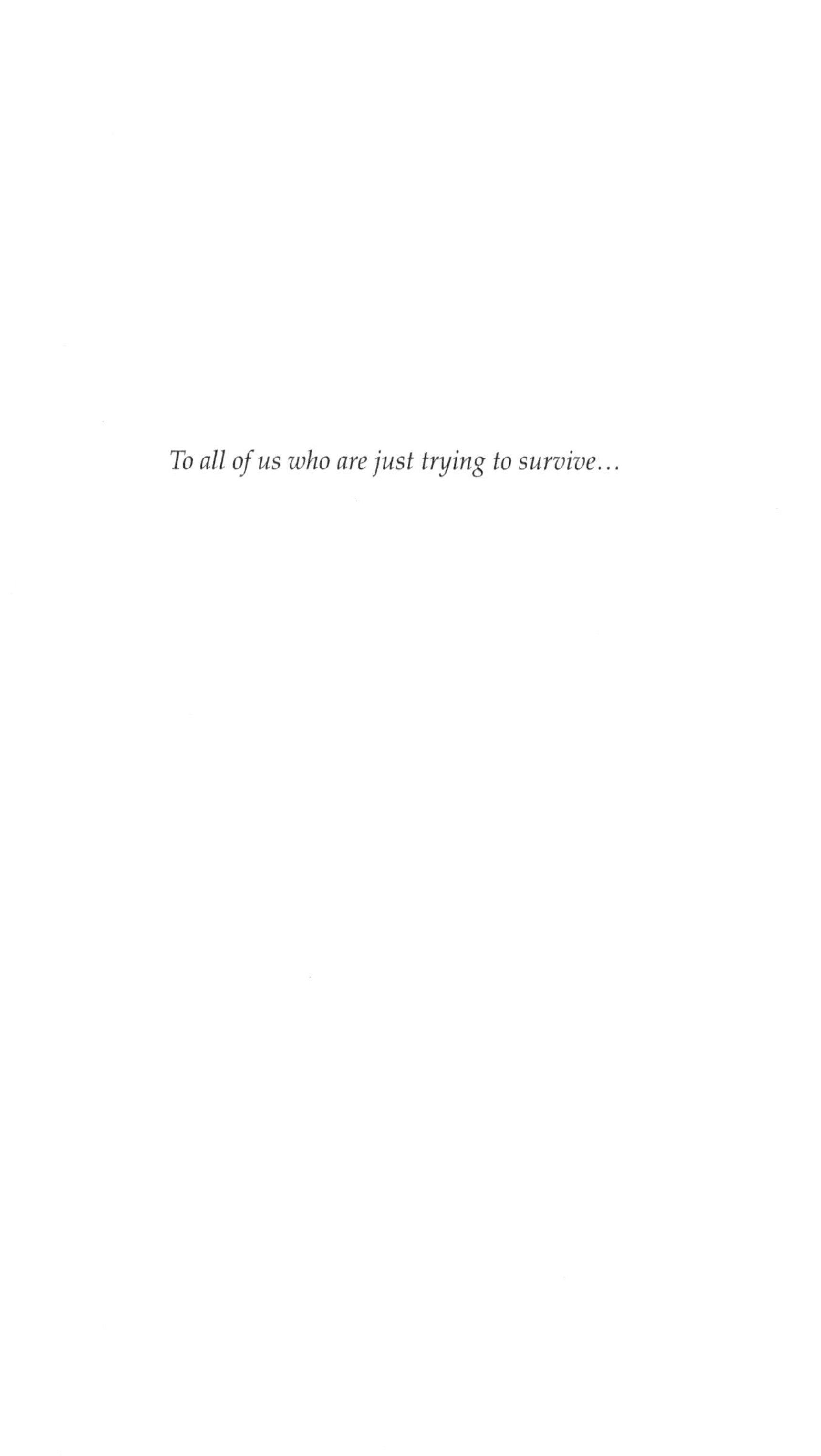

To all of us who are just trying to survive…

WHAT HAS HAPPENED BEFORE...

More than two months ago, earthquakes unleashed hellhounds on an unsuspecting mankind. The bite of a hound changes humans, turning people into flesh-craving infected.

The hellhounds weren't the only things to emerge from the earthen caverns. Demon men with grey skin and reptilian eyes have been trapped underground for thousands of years. They alone can kill the hellhounds and help bring a stop to the plague. They only ask for one thing in return: a chance to meet women who might be willing to love them as they are.

PROLOGUE

3 YEARS BEFORE THE QUAKES...

The first time they meet.

I TIGHTENED MY GRIP ON THE BOOKS I JUGGLED IN MY ARMS AND tried not to drop my fresh latte as I power-walked toward Building C's main door. Other students crossed the commons in their rush to get to their next classes. Or maybe, if they were anything like my roommates, they were escaping campus for a nap.

"Hey, June!" a girl shouted with a wave. "Great party last night."

I smiled in acknowledgement and caught the door with my foot as someone left the building. My latte jostled.

"Here, let me get that for you."

A hand reached around me and grabbed the door. I looked up into the bluest pair of eyes I'd ever seen. He was tall and broad-shouldered with short, sandy-blonde hair and an amazing smile.

"Thanks," I said after a stunned moment of silence on my part.

His gaze swept over my face, and I knew what he was seeing—facial features passed down to me from my Taiwanese grandmother, a heart-shaped face with dark eyes highlighted by darker lashes, smooth skin, and long black hair.

"Wow. You're so pretty."

His immediate blush stopped me from walking away because it showed his sincerity.

"That's nice of you to say so. I'm smart, too."

A devastating grin lit his face.

"Is there any chance you'd want to grab a coffee sometime?"

"Maybe. Write your number down for me."

He hurriedly dug in his backpack for a paper and pen. I walked away with a note that had his number and his name. Adam.

My pulse skipped at the thought of calling him. I probably wouldn't. I had a plan, a career to chase, a future laid out before me that didn't involve a relationship just yet. But I could dream.

3 YEARS BEFORE THE QUAKES...

The nudge of fate?

This paper was going to be the death of me. I'd thought taking Myth and Literature for my English credits would be fun because it was "fiction," obviously. But no, the professor was sucking all the joy out of what had once been my secret love.

I considered my laptop screen and shifted uncomfortably in my chair. Given the state of my room back at the house, I'd snuck away to the library for focus. It was quieter and much cleaner than what I'd left behind. However, my backside was far from cozy.

Smothering another yawn, I tried to concentrate on the words I'd written even as my mind wandered to last night's party my roommates had thrown. If not for that and the poor night's sleep, the paper would have already been done.

I really needed to find new roommates. A sigh escaped me.

"You," a voice said.

Cringing with the belief I was about to be scolded for the noise I'd made, I looked up and met a familiar set of blue eyes. My cringe disappeared, replaced by disbelief.

"I thought I'd never see you again," he said. "I can't tell you how many times I hung out by Building C's door in the last two months."

"Sounds a little creepy."

He grabbed a chair on the opposite side of the table, spun it around, and sat on it, facing me.

"Didn't have much of a choice. Someone never called me."

"Someone's busy." I lifted my laptop a little to emphasize the point.

"Fine. Tell me your name, and I'll go away."

"Still creepy."

"I'm going to have to get a lot creepier and start begging for your name at the top of my lungs in the middle of this library."

I looked around at the other mostly empty tables, met his gaze, and shrugged. He grinned in response, not even a little put off.

"You are a tough one. It's only going to make me more determined."

"Why? You're a good-looking guy. I'm sure you could find someone more willing."

He leaned back, studying me for a moment.

"Maybe," he said finally. "But I have a feeling, if I gave up now, I'd regret it for the rest of my life."

Oh, he was good. So good that I gave him what he wanted.

"My name's June."

"June. Will you meet me here again tomorrow night? Same time?"

"Maybe," I said, repeating his phrase.

3 YEARS BEFORE THE QUAKES…

He's all that

Adam dropped back and threw a twenty-five-yard pass. The crowd went wild when the receiver caught it and sprinted toward the end zone. I jumped up and down in the stands, cheering so hard that I knew I wouldn't be able to talk the next day.

The scoreboard updated. Thanks to Adam, we were decimating the other team. With only thirty seconds left on the clock, the game was over. Rather than waiting in the stands, I left my place and hurried toward our meet-up spot.

It took almost an hour for him to appear. When he did, the smile that lit his face was contagious.

"There's my beautiful lady." He picked me up and hugged me close as he spun us. Laughing, I wrapped my arms around his neck and hung on until he stopped.

"I like when you win," I said when he finally put me down.

"Not only win but win while a scout was watching. That's why I was late. He stopped me to talk. They're watching me, June. Two more years, and you'll be marketing me to all the major teams."

"I don't think you'll need any marketing. Now, the underwear you endorse, maybe."

He lightly kissed the tip of my nose and threaded his fingers through mine. My heart raced, and I hurried to follow him to his truck.

We were in his dorm room fifteen minutes later. Dropping his duffle by the door, he pulled my shirt off and kissed my collarbone with passion. This was the best part of a winning game night. Adam liked to ride the high of his wins with some of the best sex ever.

He walked me back to his bunk, already tearing at his pants. I laughed and fell onto the mattress, shimmying out of my clothes. He sidetracked for a second to grab a condom from the drawer beside his bed.

"We need to go shopping," he said. "I'll use up the two that are left before the night's over."

Any response to that evaporated when he kissed me hard and slid home. The first round was fast for him, but he changed condoms and started again. The second time was always for me. The third was just because he could.

Forty-five minutes later, we lay in a tangled, sweaty heap. The sound of our rapid breathing filled the room for a while, neither of us capable of speaking yet. Sex with Adam was amazing. My other two partners had been one and done types. Maybe it was the newness of this part of our relationship, but I sincerely hoped not.

"Hey, do you want to go fishing tomorrow or hiking?"

I shook my head and looked up at him.

"Why do you even ask when we both know you're going to talk me into both?"

He chuckled and kissed my forehead again.

"That's my girl."

1 YEAR BEFORE THE QUAKES...

Meet the parents

He rocked into me rhythmically, hitting my sweet spot again and again. I could feel myself climbing toward what I was sure would be the most mind-blowing orgasm to end all orgasms.

He paused.

"Hold on. Cramp."

The feeling started to fade no matter how much I tried to stay focused on where I'd been. By the time he'd stretched out his calf and started rocking once more, it was like starting over. For me, not for him. He twitched inside of me, and I knew he was getting close.

"You with me, babe?"

"I'm with you," I lied. If I didn't, he would try to keep going, probably get another leg cramp just as I was getting close again, and we'd both get frustrated. Then neither of us would be satisfied. This was the better option once he started cramping.

He finished with a few shallow thrusts while I kissed his shoulder. He groaned and lifted his head to look down at me.

"You didn't finish. It was the leg cramp, wasn't it?"

I grinned at him, and he playfully shook his head and started kissing his way down my neck like I'd known he would do once he realized I hadn't finished too.

"I knew I should have stretched first. You were too tempting lying there sleeping like that, though."

My smile widened when he reached my hips and gave me a little kiss.

"I'm glad you didn't resist. Your mouth on me is my favorite way to wake up." Sometimes though, like this morning, he left far too much spit behind. As if I didn't know what he was doing. But that extra lubrication so he could fast track to getting inside of me made me feel like a dog's chew toy. Not that I was complaining. Even a little bit of oral was worth it.

He chuckled and set his mouth on me again. In minutes, I was gasping and back to the place I'd been when he was inside of me.

"Almost there, babe?" he mumbled as he worked, knowing better than to remove his tongue.

"So close."

I shattered a minute later. He retreated from his spot between my legs and stood with a stretch.

"Almost had a tongue cramp, too. I better up my magnesium."

My bones were liquid and my brain too mellow to care what he was saying.

"Hey, what do you think about going out of town this weekend? I'm going home for a few days."

That caught my attention. In the two-and-a-half years we'd been together, I'd never met his parents in person. Sure, I'd said hi in the background when his mom called. Or managed to wave if they did a video call. But I hadn't been introduced, officially, in person.

"For real?" I asked, sitting up and looking at him.

"Yeah. It's about time, don't you think?" He grinned at me, his boyish smile melting my heart even as it raced.

"Yes. It is about time, and yes, I'd love to meet your parents."

We'd been living together since last May. Now, two weeks before our final year, I was finally going home with him. Excitement and anticipation filled me because I knew what meeting his parents meant. And I couldn't wait.

A few days later, I not only met his parents but also his aunts, uncles, cousins, and brother at a backyard cookout in Missouri.

I lost count of how many people hugged me and said, "Welcome to the family." My mind was already racing with when and how Adam would propose. He liked attention, so I fully expected it to happen at any moment as the evening wore on. But then, the first person left. And after that, the number of people slowly dwindled. Maybe Adam meant the moment to be private. The idea warmed me as I helped his mom with the clean-up.

When it was just his parents and us, he kissed my forehead, took my hand, and led me to the room we'd share. My heart was racing.

"They loved you. Uncle Jack even gave us an open invitation to come down and see his farm. I know that probably doesn't seem like a big deal, but trust me, it is."

"Everything about today was a big deal for me. Thank you for this."

"Just wait until tomorrow."

It took forever for me to fall asleep, but all those nerves were for nothing when the next day turned out to be a day hunting with his dad. I managed to keep my disappointment to myself through the remainder of the evening and the following morning when we packed up.

"You've been pretty quiet," Adam commented, thirty

minutes into the drive back to the university. "Did something happen?"

"No. Nothing happened. But I thought something was going to."

"What do you mean?"

"I thought you had another reason for taking me home this weekend."

"Something other than meeting my family, the thing you've been after me to do over a year now?" He glanced at me, his expression going from confused to "lightbulb."

"Oh. Oh, man, June. I'm sorry. I didn't know you were going to think that. I mean, we're still in school, you know? And we don't know where I'm going to end up and where your job is going to take you—"

"Whoa. Are you saying you don't think we're in a long-term relationship?"

"Of course not. We are. We both know that. I'm just saying I didn't think marriage was going to be something we'd think about for another five to ten years."

I stared at him for a long moment.

"Ten years? I'm going to be thirty-two in ten years, Adam. I thought we'd want to be married a few years before bringing kids into the equation."

"Kids?" He glanced at me again. "What if I sign with another team? Are you going to want to uproot a family like that?"

He knew me well enough to know living apart wouldn't be an option for me.

"Family is about the people in your life, not about the location. Yes, we'd move to be with you. You love football. It's who you are, and having kids won't hold your career back.

Kids mean you're giving me a little piece of yourself to love when you're away."

He shook his head and smiled at me.

"You are the best thing that has ever happened to me, June, and I'll be honest. I never saw myself with kids. But, with you, I can. One, though...maybe two if the first one's a girl who looks like you."

I smiled at him and reached out to set my hand on his leg, a familiar driving routine for us. I enjoyed touching, and he liked to be touched.

He threaded his fingers through mine.

"I'm sorry this weekend was a disappointment," he said sincerely. "I do want to marry you, June, and I promise not to make you wait ten years. Can we wait until after I'm signed?"

"I think I have enough patience for that."

"And a kid after a few years?"

"Just so you don't make me wait too long for the ring."

"You got it, babe."

THE DAY OF THE QUAKES...

For love of June

"June, get up. We have to go. Pack the essentials. We're leaving in five whether you're ready or not."

The rushed words and the panic in his voice penetrated my sleep-fogged brain.

"What?"

"Dad says we need to get home. Now." The rustling noise of Adam grabbing clothes from his dresser drawers brought me fully awake.

I flew out of bed and started grabbing things.

"What happened?" I asked as I quickly dressed and pulled out a bag of my own. "Is it your mom?"

"No. I'll explain on the way. Move."

His abruptness scared me, reminding me of the time we'd been hiking and a bear crossed our path. I scrambled to put what I'd need into the bag for a trip to his parents without knowing why.

"You won't need that," Adam said when he saw me grab my black dress. "Think warm. Jeans. Layers."

I pulled out the dress shoes I'd already shoved into the bag and put my hiking boots inside. We were out the door in five minutes. He wasn't kidding when he said that we needed to hurry. He ran all the way to the truck and tossed our stuff inside.

Then, he started up the truck and tore out of the parking lot.

"I need you to get the handgun out, June. Remember what I showed you?"

I nodded and started to shake as I reached under the seat. Warm clothes, and now he was talking about guns.

"What's going on, Adam?"

"I'm not exactly sure. Dad said there were weird reports from Europe before it went dark. It was just after a quake they had. A big quake was reported farther south in Texas. Dad found out from one of his old friends who still serves. The government was trying to keep it quiet, but Texas started going dark. Dad says something's coming our way. He doesn't know what, but we need to get to Uncle Gary's farm. They're going to meet us there."

As he spoke, he drove like crazy, missing stop signs and taking corners fast enough that I shook even harder.

"Adam, you're going to kill us trying to get there," I said.

"Right. Right." He slowed down a little more for the next corner.

I trusted Adam, and he trusted his dad. Whatever had them spooked, there had to be a good reason. Yet, I doubted it warranted Adam's current level of panic.

"I know you said the government is keeping things quiet," which I secretly found hard to believe, "but let's turn on the radio anyway."

He nodded, not relaxing his white-knuckled grip on the wheel. The local station I picked was playing music like I'd hoped, and we made it out of town in one piece just before ten p.m. Thankfully, the longer we went without anything happening, the more Adam began to show signs of calming down.

Until we passed a car driving at high speeds. Then another. Then another.

Adam began tapping the wheel.

"Turn the radio off, June," he said softly. "We need to listen."

I did as he asked, and we both remained quiet when we came across two cars, one in the ditch and another pulled over, likely to help. There was no one around, though, when he slowed to flash a light at both vehicles.

"Is the gun loaded?" he asked softly.

"Yeah."

I thought he was going to ask for it. Instead, he pulled away from the cars and kept going.

"You don't think we should check if someone needs help?" I asked, looking at the cars shrinking from view in my side mirror.

"No, I don't. My priority is getting you to Gary's where you'll be safe."

I reached over and set my hand on his leg.

"Everything will be okay."

He didn't glance at me or agree, and that worried me more than the empty highway around us. At the next exit, he got off the highway.

"I think we should stick to back roads," he said before I could ask.

We drove in silence for an hour before we saw another car pass. It flashed its lights at us rapidly and slowed.

The man behind the wheel only rolled his window down two inches to shout at us.

"Don't stop for nothing, you hear? Nothing!"

Then he took off with a squeal of tires.

Adam gunned it, too.

"Call my dad."

I tried his dad, his mom, and his brother, but no one answered.

The lights we saw ahead indicated a small town.

"My gut is telling me this is a bad idea," Adam said.

"Should we turn around?"

He tapped the steering wheel more rapidly, and the truck gained speed. I kept quiet as we hit the 25 miles per hour zone at 40. The streets were quiet but many of the houses were lit. I saw a curtain flutter out of one broken window. Adam did, too, because he didn't bother slowing for a stop sign.

Something big and black came running at us from the darkness. As the creature landed on the hood, its claws screeched over the metal surface, and our forward momentum caused it to crash into our windshield. The glass instantly shattered and bowed inward. Adam slammed on the brakes hard. The thing rolled off even as Adam jammed down on the gas.

In my near frozen state of shock, I registered two things beyond my racing heart and rapid breathing. The thing Adam just ran over had red eyes. Not just red, but glowing, as in illuminated from within. The second thing was that someone had screamed before we took off down the road.

My gaze slid to the side mirror, and I saw the thing get to its feet and bolt off in the direction it had been headed before we hit it. Or it hit us.

"What was that?" I rasped shakily.

"I don't know, babe. Our windshield can't take another hit like that, though."

I glanced at Adam, who was leaning toward the outside of the truck to see through the bits that had fewer cracks in them.

"I don't want to change vehicles if we don't have to," he

continued. "This one can take us through the fields if it comes down to that. Keep the handgun ready. Next time, we might need to use it."

Not far out of town, a station wagon idled in the middle of the road. Adam slowed down to take the shoulder on the opposite lane. As we passed, I glanced at the car. My breath caught as the little girl strapped into her car seat in the back turned her head to look at us with her milky white eyes.

"Babe, talk to me. What's wrong?"

It wasn't until he spoke that I realized I was making gasping noises.

"There's a little girl—"

Ahead, a woman appeared in our lights. She stood in the middle of the road, her back to us.

Adam slowed further.

The woman turned, and I started making more noises at the sight of her pink insides trailing from her eviscerated middle. Like the girl in the car, the woman had white eyes. Unlike the girl, the woman started moving, shuffling toward our truck.

"Nope."

Adam gunned the truck and clipped the woman. After that, he didn't slow down for anything.

It took fifteen minutes of his calmly delivered, "I swear I'll keep you safe, June," and the steady presence of his hand on my leg for my breathing to return to normal.

"This isn't real," I finally said. "Right?"

"Real or unreal, it doesn't matter. Okay? All that matters is that we're together, and I won't let anything happen to you. Do you understand? Focus on that, June. I'll keep you safe."

I nodded and watched the road for signs of trouble.

We made it to his uncle's farm in the middle of nowhere and

stopped in a spray of gravel in the driveway. Adam cut the engine and grabbed the gun from my lap.

"Get the rifle, June. Make sure it's loaded and ready. Safety off."

I hated the rifle. I hated the handgun. But I was far more terrified of why we needed either of them.

"We're going to leave the truck together. Quietly. Stay close and shoot anything that moves. Got it?"

I nodded and reached for the door when he did. Leaving the protection of the truck was the most terrifying thing I'd done in my life. The next most terrifying thing came a second later when Uncle Gary rounded the house.

Like the woman on the road, it looked like something had chewed him up, and his eyes had gone white.

I shivered as he shuffled toward us and jumped at the sharp report of Adam's gun. A red dot bloomed on his uncle's forehead before the man fell.

Nothing else moved. From the barn, I heard a faint mooing. Adam motioned toward the big building then pointed at me. The urge to throw up was strong. Swallowing hard, I started for the barn. The gravel crunched under my feet, sounding loud in the otherwise still night. I kept the rifle up and ready even though I knew my shaking would ensure I'd miss anything I aimed at.

Inside the barn, at least thirty cows milled about in their pen.

A few made noise when they saw us. Adam didn't stop to look at them. We moved farther into the building, and when we reached the end of the aisle, he led us left, through a narrow hall, and down a ramp.

"Watch our backs," he whispered.

I turned, walking sideways so I could see him as well as the hall behind us. A faint beep distracted me. I glanced at Adam as he opened a door that looked like it belonged to a bank vault. He motioned me into the lit hall beyond, and I hurried to comply.

The door closed with a rasp of air, and Adam turned to me.

"I'm so sorry, Adam."

He shook his head.

"That wasn't my uncle. My real uncle would have wanted me to do what I did."

"What about your parents?"

"If they're alive, they'll show up. Come on. I'll take you on a tour. Dad and Gary worked on this place together."

I turned around and looked down the long concrete hallway of the underground bunker.

"Welcome home, June," Adam said.

TWO WEEKS AFTER THE QUAKES...

Fun time's over

The never-ending sound of static crawled under my skin even in my sleep. The white noise bounced off the cement brick walls, echoing down the hall. There was no escaping it inside the compact bunker Adam's family had built.

Shifting on the narrow, lower bunk I'd claimed as my own, I forced my gaze to sweep the empty beds that Adam's parents, brother, and uncle were meant to occupy. The perfectly tucked in blankets and untouched, pristine white pillows were a reminder of why Adam still listened to the radio.

Even after all this time, he was hoping to hear something from his family. I held that same hope. But it was dying the longer we went without hearing from anyone.

When we'd first turned on the radio, it had filled the bunker with chatter, not the white noise of static. The voices we heard were from the other people holed up like us. When we'd been clueless, they'd been the ones who helped piece together what was happening.

Adam and I had listened to them talk about the hellhounds and the spreading zombie infection. It had been hard to believe it at first, despite seeing the woman on the road and Adam's uncle. The infection spread with a bite, killing and reanimating a person within minutes.

Then our radio friends started describing the other things running loose out there. Hearing about grey-skinned creatures that walked on two legs, hid from the light, and could rip the head off of a man in two seconds had terrified me. It still did.

Hell, so did the hounds with glowing red eyes and the idea that Adam and I were in a bunker riding out the apocalypse. None of it seemed real. But we'd both come to terms with just how real it was when the ground had shaken with the detonation of bombs in the nearest cities. The chatter said it was to stop the spread of the infection, but there'd also been speculation that it was meant to stop the grey creatures.

After the bombs, though, things didn't get better. They got far worse.

We'd all been unsure of what would be left after the dust settled, but hearing the voices had reassured Adam and me that we still weren't alone. Then "Chatty Kathy" had gone quiet. "Bitter man" had told the rest of us he was going to check on her since they'd known each other prior to the world going dark. He'd never reported back.

"Big Jonah" said he'd check on "Bitter man." A few hours later, we learned it wasn't a new threat but an old one.

The sound of the old man's tear-choked voice still haunted my dreams.

"The world isn't full of good people anymore. If it ever was. Don't tell anyone where you are. And if you leave, cover your tracks. Your shelter and your supplies are today's currency, and those who have are always damned by those who haven't. They killed Becky and Katie and took everything. I'm done, folks. I'm going to go bury my dogs and sit on my porch for a spell."

That was the last we'd heard from him.

After that, the radio had been silent except for the occasional emergency broadcast that talked about evacuee camps. Adam clung to the hope that his family had gone to one of them instead of heading here. I wanted to believe that New York was completely unscathed and that my parents were waiting for me there. But, all of the surrounding cities had been bombed. I doubted a place as big as New York had been spared. If it had been, that would have meant there was somewhere safe to go, and they would have come looking for survivors by now. But there'd been no broadcast, no sounds of vehicles or planes overhead, no sign of rescue.

Part of me was starting to wonder if Adam and I were all that remained of humanity. The fear that we were made it difficult every time Adam and I had to leave the safety of the bunker to clear away the dead, or rather, the undead, from the barn.

As soon as I had that thought, I started to panic, and I threw back my blankets. What if Adam had gone outside without me?

A brief moment of silence filled the bunker as Adam switched channels.

Breathing easier, I checked the time on my watch and saw it was past two in the morning. I shivered at the chill of the concrete and put on my slippers before leaving the bunk room.

Down the hall, the utilitarian bathroom with two toilet stalls, a urinal, two showers, and a sink was just another reminder of how many people were meant to be here. I gently knocked on the holding tank for the wash water and marked a new line to indicate the level.

In addition to the bathroom, the bunker housed an aquaponics room, an exercise room, a supply room, a kitchen, and finally the control room with the monitors. That was where I headed when I finished using the bathroom.

Adam sat in the chair before the monitors, keeping an eye on the livestock, which had somehow managed to escape the notice of the infected that roamed in occasionally. Well, escaping their notice wasn't quite accurate. The infected would look at the cows, seemingly understand that they were the source of the sounds that drew them in, then shamble around uninterested in them.

Adam figured, since the cows weren't human, the infected didn't care. It scared me to think he was right, since it showed the infected had some level of intelligence. I would prefer it if they were brainless zombies.

"Everything quiet?" I asked softly.

"Yeah. For now."

"Why don't you go to bed? I can watch for a while."

He nodded and stood. The weary set of his shoulders broke my heart, and I wrapped my arms around his waist to comfort him.

"I love you, Adam," I breathed against his chest. Considering everything we'd endured the past few weeks and our separate beds, sex had been the last thing on either of our minds. But maybe it was what we both needed.

I let my hand wander down to his butt.

He hugged me tightly, then lifted me and started walking. I grinned and looked up at him.

"I think the monitors will be fine without a few minutes of watching," he murmured before kissing me hard.

His lips didn't leave mine as we stripped in the bunk room. Things got a little awkward when we wedged ourselves on my bed, but we made it work. The feel of his hands on my skin helped make everything else seem unimportant. I touched him in return, greedy for the contact.

"Hold on." He pulled away, turned, then stopped. My chest ached again as I understood what had just happened. For a moment, he'd forgotten where we were and had been about to reach for a condom from his nightstand supply.

But there was no nightstand in the bunker.

"How's your birth control supply?" he asked.

I made a face. "I took my last one a few days ago."

He gave me a sad smile and leaned down to kiss me tenderly.

"I love you, June. So much that I know we can't do this without protection. I won't risk you like that."

"Risk?"

"We've cleaned out a dozen of the infected from the barn already in only a couple of weeks. We have to haul manure, feed, and do a million other things that jeopardize our well-being because of the state of the world. I won't add an accidental pregnancy to that list, babe. It's just you and me, and I'm no doctor. It's too dangerous."

I nodded, understanding. The world was in chaos.

"Then no sex. We can still hold each other."

We did a little more than holding, and I smiled at him after he groaned my name.

"Get some sleep," I said, standing. "I'll watch the monitors until you wake up."

"I love you, June. We're going to survive this. I promise I'll keep you safe."

I lightly kissed his cheek and left him to sleep in my bed.

CHAPTER ONE

PRESENT DAY...

A VAST EXPANSE OF NOTHINGNESS LOOMED ABOVE ME. I WAITED FOR my eyes to adjust and for the twinkling lights of the stars to pop into existence, but they didn't.

Even after all these weeks, or maybe it was months now, I still dreamt of the life Adam and I used to have. I missed fresh air and the stars. I missed my relationship with Adam.

Rolling to my side, I tried to make out his bunk in the darkness. It was unlikely he was in it since I was in mine. But just in case, I whispered his name softly.

"You awake, babe?" he called from somewhere else in the bunker.

"Yeah."

"We're low on juice. I had to turn off the non-essentials until sunrise."

"Okay." Knowing what that meant, I carefully got out of bed and felt my way to the shelves that held my clothes.

The battery bank handled the load we put on it reasonably

well, thanks to the small wind turbine behind the barn and the solar panels on the house. But the recent winter storm had hit us with a mix of snow and ice, and based on the depletion of power, the panels and turbine blades were still covered. We'd hoped the mess would've melted by now since I wasn't a fan of heights and Adam wasn't a fan of leaving me on the ground out in the open.

I dressed and felt my way down the hall to the bathroom. The complete silence inside the bunker registered as I reached my destination, and I realized Adam had not only turned off the lights but the aquaponics and the radio as well. Blind, yet familiar with the space after living here for so long, I used the bathroom then headed for the control room.

Adam had one monitor displaying four of the cameras his uncle had set up. My stomach twisted with worry.

"How much longer until sunrise?"

"Another forty minutes."

"Can we wait that long?"

"We're not going up there in the dark." He stood, kissed my forehead, and steered me into the chair. "I'm going to gear up. We'll be ready for first light. Let me know if the screen goes out."

I nodded, understanding what he wasn't saying. We were dangerously low on power.

As soon as I was seated, he left to prep our gear, and I focused on the monitor's split video images of the main barn door, side door, cattle pen, and the hall leading to the bunker. Had I not been staring, I would have missed the fingers that wrapped around the edge of the side door.

"We have a dead one on screen," I said.

Adam swore, and I heard him coming down the hall before

the beam of his flashlight flooded the control room. I pointed at the screen.

"It hasn't moved yet."

When it finally did move, I shivered at the creepy way it leaned in and peeked around the door. The woman's scalp was missing clumps of hair, and a bit of her chin was missing. Yet she moved fluidly, like she was alive.

"It's a runner," Adam said. "I don't like this, June."

"I don't either. But we both know we can't wait another day. Maybe we'll get lucky and it's just one scouting."

"Maybe." He squeezed my shoulder. "Keep watching."

He left the room, and I watched the dead woman peek into the barn twice more before its hand disappeared. The woman's hand reappeared several minutes later on the main door where she repeated her peeking move.

I switched the camera over from night to day as the sky lightened.

"She's a little less creepy in daylight," I called to Adam.

He chuckled. "Unless the patches filled in and she grew a new chin, I doubt that. You ready?"

I checked the hall camera one last time.

"Ready."

He had my boots and jacket waiting for me by the door. I quickly put both on and took the rifle from him.

"Run to the bunker if anything goes south," he said just before he released the latch.

The hiss of air was barely audible. We didn't hesitate, though, to see if the infected heard. Together, we moved forward, our steps quiet.

How many times had we done this? Hundreds of times because we needed to feed and water the livestock daily. We knew the hiding places. We knew the difference between normal cattle sounds and distressed sounds. And having a dead human in the barn definitely distressed them.

Thankfully, there were no distressed calls from the pen.

Slipping into the main area, we progressed down the aisle, and the heifers called out to us as we passed them. Adam paused at the exit door near the silo, the last place we'd seen the infected, and exchanged his gun for his hunting knife. I hated that we couldn't kill the runners at a safe distance but understood the need for silence.

When he opened the door, I was right behind him. The runner, who was still in the yard, charged at us. Trusting Adam's ability to deal with her, I scanned the area for additional threats. Only one set of tracks marred the thin layer of snow on the ground, though, and nothing else moved in the trees beyond.

The scuffle noises grew in volume before silencing. I glanced at him as he picked the body up. I hated this part. Not only did we need to move farther away from the safety of the bunker, but we were about to make some noise. It didn't matter that it was decoy noise to cover the sounds I'd make while clearing the panel. It was still noise.

My gaze didn't stop moving as we circled to the back of the house. Adam took over watching the area as I carefully removed the drop pit's cover. Silently, he tossed the woman inside then helped me lean the sheets of wood against the house.

There was a pattern to everything we did. Move, listen, watch, and repeat. That pattern ended the moment he untied the wind chime over the pit.

We hurried toward the front of the house. Together, we slid

the hidden ladder out from under the porch and got it into position.

He leaned in close. "Don't look down. Don't make a sound. You'll be fine."

Easy for him to say when he was the one on the ground.

With my rifle slung across my body, I grabbed the ladder and silently ascended. The black roof shingles were clear enough that the bottom of my boots scraped against them as I moved, and the sound carried through the air more than I would have liked. Focused on the task, I crossed to the solar panels and started brushing away the ice-covered snow as quietly as possible.

I did a rush job, knowing what little snow remained on the dark panels would finish melting, thanks to the clear skies. Walking carefully, I returned to the ladder. Trying to find that first rung without looking down was a death-defying bitch. I managed, though, and clinging to the rungs, I carefully descended.

With the wind chimes tinkling gently behind the house, we hid the ladder and crossed the yard to the open pasture beyond.

In the beginning, sound had attracted the infected. Then, at night, they'd been drawn in by light. Now, they were more advanced. Adam and I out in the open would be enough to attract them even if he and I were as quiet as church mice.

The movement of the windswept, long grass exposed by the melting snow made me twitchy. My gaze never stopped scanning for hidden infected. By the time we reached the old windmill base, I was wound so tight I wondered how I'd ever make it up those rungs.

Adam tapped my shoulder to gain my attention. When I

glanced at him, he made a heart with his hands. I knew he was asking for my love and trust. He had both. It was the infected I didn't love or trust.

Still, I nodded and took a calming breath. His lips tilted in the same boyish grin that I'd fallen in love with the first day we'd met. In my mind, I could hear him say, "There's my girl," before he returned his attention to the trees lining the field.

Grabbing the lowest rung of the built-in ladder, I glanced down to place my foot. Something else caught my gaze, though.

Blood dotted some of the long brown grass poking through the snow within the base support. I looked up and saw something wedged between the rotor, turbine housing, and tower.

Trap.

My heart pounded, but I didn't let panic set in. Instead, I scrambled up the ladder because there was no "right" choice anymore. We needed the power. If Adam saw the blood, he'd rush us back to the barn.

So I climbed fast, and when I saw the arm haphazardly tied to the turbine housing with a shirt, I didn't even hesitate to grab the material. Within seconds, I knocked the arm free and was monkeying back down. The frozen limb landed with a thud below, and I heard Adam softly swear.

In my head, I pictured infected pouring from the trees. I was so terrified that I didn't even stop to think of the height when I dropped the last few feet.

Adam grabbed my arm and started running. We made it to the side door and hauled ass to the bunker. The door barely closed behind us when he grabbed me by the arms.

"What were you thinking? An arm doesn't accidentally fall into a turbine."

"But we both know I did what had to be done. We need the power for the lights and to watch all the cameras. How many infected do you think there were?"

He gave me a long look.

"None that I saw. Don't take risks like that again, June. It's not worth it."

I gave him a sad smile, understanding what he was implying. He couldn't live without me.

"I love you too, Adam."

Since Adam was covered in the woman's blood, I went to the control room to check the monitors.

"Everything's still clear. Go shower. We can feed the cattle when you're done then reset the wind chimes."

He shook his head, his expression troubled. "It doesn't make sense. That arm was a trap. Where are they?"

"The turbine's been out since the storm. Maybe they got bored waiting and moved away."

"Maybe. Turn on the radio when the bank's at five percent."

I never got a chance. Adam returned from his shower just before it reached the mark.

"Everything still clear?"

"Yep. Nothing's moving."

"I think we should wait to feed," he said, watching the empty screens.

We didn't feed on a set schedule since we weren't sure if the infected were smart enough to notice that kind of pattern. And the whole excursion to clear the solar panels and turbine hadn't taken more than twenty minutes, so it was still early. Yet, I hesitated to wait any longer with the wind chimes still down.

They didn't make more sound than the cattle, but it was a human-type noise that seemed to draw in any nearby infected. We used them whenever we had to do anything topside to help cover our noise.

"Let's get the feeding done. It's earlier than usual, which is a good thing. Afterward, we can have a relaxing day with nothing else to worry about."

He gave me a considering look.

"I'd feel better if we waited. That arm..." He shook his head.

I walked to him and hugged him close.

"Adam, you know we don't have the luxury of hiding down here. This is our world. Risks and all."

He pulled me closer and kissed the top of my head.

"Run if I say run."

"Always."

It took longer to make sure the yard was clear than it did to feed the livestock and barn cats. We worked in silence then reset the wind chimes and hurried back to the bunker. While Adam went to the control room, I cleaned up and started breakfast.

A crackle of static filled the bunker. I sighed at the familiar sound and started the kettle. The water came to a boil just before a pause in the static. Adam always gave each channel a few minutes before moving to the next.

While he scanned the frequencies for any sign of life beyond our bunker, I added the water to the dehydrated potatoes and opened a can of spam. We had plenty of both, thanks to his family. Not a lot of variety, though.

The supply room was filled with those little cartons of dehydrated potatoes, bags of rice, cans of spam, cans of peas, and more cans of green beans. We also had several big totes filled with bags of flour and sugar and a smaller one of baking soda and powder. The powdered eggs made it possible to whip up pancakes for something different, too. Rows of jarred maple syrup, something his uncle made every spring, lined a shelf along the ceiling.

According to the portion charts Gary had made, there was enough to feed eight people for six months. With two of us, it would last much longer. But after that, things would get iffy.

Hunting obviously wasn't an option. Not only would the gunfire draw infected, but according to the other preppers who'd gone silent weeks ago, there also wasn't any game to be found out there. What hadn't gotten killed by the hellhounds had run off.

That was why Adam and I took care of the livestock even though there was a risk every time we left the bunker. If we wanted meat when the canned goods ran out, we needed every animal on the farm.

I plated our portions and went to the control room. Adam stood as soon as I entered.

"The cattle are acting up, but there's nothing on screen yet."

I watched the screens while Adam geared up and got our weapons ready. The cattle seemed more agitated than usual, shuffling into a tight bunch in the corner, which worried me. Typically, they only acted up when something was in the barn.

"Still nothing on any of the monitors," I called.

"Check the turbine power. Maybe the infected are messing with that again."

"No, the numbers are still climbing. I don't think that's it."

"I'm ready. Let's go find out."

I hated leaving the bunker blindly but vacated the chair and got ready to go topside again.

The barn was far from quiet this time. The cattle were making enough noise to cover the sound of our feet on the concrete as we checked around then peeked outside. We could hear the infected's moans coming from the other side of the house. A fair number of them. More than we could hope to face on our own.

We both withdrew to the barn again and hurried back to the bunker.

"They'll get bored and wander away. They always do. We'll be fine." He pulled me into his arms and hugged me close.

I wasn't comforted.

If the dead didn't wander away and, instead, entered the barn, we'd need to clear them out. So far, we'd been lucky only having to deal with one or two at a time since they didn't seem to travel in packs. In my gut, I knew the number outside the house wasn't something that we'd survive. And I was pretty sure Adam knew it, too, based on the way he was holding me.

"It'll be okay, June. You'll see."

I nodded, and he released me. Together, we watched the cameras for the next several minutes.

A dead one finally found its way into the barn. Based on its shuffling movements, it wasn't a runner, which I thought odd given the state of his tattered blue jacket. Usually, the ones that showed signs of being dead longer were faster.

Adam said nothing about going to clear the barn out, which confirmed my suspicion that he knew we couldn't handle the number of dead people out there. Thankfully, it wandered out again without going after any of the livestock.

Adam turned to me with a grin.

"See? Nothing to it. Why don't you go relax for a bit?"

Behind him, the same blue-jacketed dead man reentered the barn. He didn't shamble this time. He moved fluidly as did the woman at his side.

Something must have shown in my expression because Adam swiveled back to the screen. When he swore softly under his breath, I knew he'd realized the same thing I just had. These infected were now smart enough to pretend not to be smart.

The pair considered the cattle then moved to the doorway by the silo. One of the new barn kittens dashed out from the enclosure, and the woman's head cocked as she stared after it.

"Look at her eyes," Adam said.

I did and felt like throwing up. They weren't cloudy white. At least, not entirely. They looked dingier, almost a red-brown.

"I don't like this," I murmured.

Adam held out his hand, not taking his gaze from the monitors for even a second. I grabbed hold of the lifeline he offered, and we watched as the pair finished their inspection of the barn and left.

It took another thirty minutes for the cattle to settle down and for Adam and me to breathe easier.

"Maybe the sound of the chimes brought them here," Adam said finally. "We won't use them when we feed tonight."

That didn't help me feel any better about the situation, but there wasn't much either of us could do about what was happening outside the bunker. Yes, I feared the infected. But slower or faster, smarter or lacking any shred of sense, none of that changed the fact that Adam and I still needed to eat, rest, and care for the livestock. The endless cycle didn't stop for weird infected behavior. And I couldn't let my fears rule my thoughts and actions. It didn't matter if there were now more undead roaming the surface than living people. It didn't even matter if the infected were evolving into something the living would have no chance of surviving.

What mattered was what I could control. What mattered was that Adam and I were doing the best we could to survive. Whatever it took, we would survive. So, I left the control room and focused on my routine.

When I finished loading the washer, I took another turn in the monitor seat so Adam could sharpen his knife. Mostly, it allowed his eyes a break. I didn't mind watching the cattle. The way they wandered around their pen was almost as soothing as watching the tilapia swim in the aquaponics tanks. I did feel bad for them sometimes, though, and wondered if they missed roaming the pasture as much as I missed the sun. Probably. But we were all safer this way.

That thought fled between one breath and the next as two men strode into the barn. The tan leather pants they wore looked like nothing I'd seen before. Yet, a normal black t-shirt stretched across the broad chest of the first man, and a large jacket covered the other. The men themselves were far from normal, though. I frowned at the exposed arms then looked at their faces.

Grey skin.

Pointed ears.

These weren't men but the things we'd heard about from other survivors. The things that killed people with simple ease.

My blood ran cold as I noted how much bigger they were than Adam. How would he and I stand a chance against them? First, the arm in the turbine, then the "smart" dead nosing around, and now these guys? Fate had to have taken my thoughts about surviving as a challenge.

I watched the pair enter the pen. The one wearing the jacket patted a heifer then hooked his arms under it and lifted. My eyes almost popped out of my head when I saw the animal come off the ground. He set it down again and shrugged at the other one.

"Adam," I called, finding my voice. "We have a problem."

He hurried into the control room. When he saw what I was watching, he swore.

We watched the grey men survey the barn. One pointed to the hay we'd just forked down, and the other ran his hand over the cow he'd picked up. The speculation on the pair's faces was unmistakable.

The infected never wondered how the livestock were still alive. They just ignored them and moved on, usually. Except for the two this morning.

The grey man in the black shirt saw the camera hidden on top of a barn beam and stared directly at it. At us. There was something very weird about his eyes, and I leaned closer to the screen in an attempt to pinpoint what.

He spoke to his companion, who also looked at the camera.

"They know we're here," Adam said. His hand immediately settled on one of my shoulders. "It doesn't matter. They can't get to us in here. We'll be fine, June."

He wasn't saying it to reassure himself. He was reassuring me. Just like he had since the moment we packed our bags. I reached up, set my hand over his, and gave his fingers a squeeze.

The kitten that had run from the infected strolled up to these creatures and rubbed against the jacketed one's leg. They both looked down at it. Then the other one smiled broadly.

"Do you see his teeth?" I breathed. The sight of those sharp canines set my insides trembling.

The one in the black shirt picked up the cat and scratched it under the chin. They gave the space one last glance then left. With the cat.

"Do you think they're going to eat it?" I whispered.

"I hope not."

"What are we going to do?"

"We're going to wait and see if they come back."

We watched the cameras together after that. I took a quick break to make us lunch and returned to the control room. Everything remained normal, but after the morning we had, I didn't trust it.

With each passing hour, the knot in my stomach grew. We were going to have to go out there again to feed the cattle at some point.

Adam ran a hand through his hair and leaned back in his chair.

"I can't decide if we should go feed now, wait a little longer, or just forget it tonight."

"The cows will get loud enough to draw the dead if they don't get fed. And given how many infected we heard this morning, I don't want to risk that if they're still close."

He exhaled heavily.

"Okay. We go now, and we work quickly. Just the cattle."

I nodded and stayed to watch the monitors while he prepped our gear. When he called for me, he had two homemade knife harnesses for both of us. Adam's kill speed was better when he could abandon the knife and grab a new one. I didn't know my kill speed and didn't want to.

"Just in case," he said when he saw my hesitation.

I nodded, and he helped me into mine. My hands swept over the knife handles—four in total. The grey things had spooked him. Me too. But I didn't think more knives would help us if they were still out there.

Rather than voice my doubts, I gave him a smile that earned me a quick kiss on the forehead. Everything I knew about survival, I knew because of Adam. I hadn't been a fan of guns, but he'd convinced me that not liking something wasn't an excuse not to understand it. Learning to use the knives had happened once we were in the bunker. But only as a backup to him.

As soon as he opened the door, we were on the move. I didn't need to be told what to do and hurried toward the grain silo. While I worked, Adam watched the doors.

When I finished unloading the grain, I moved to the drop ladder for the hayloft. Dust danced in the beams of sunlight, peeking through the gaps in the barn boards, as I hurriedly forked enough hay down to feed the cows for the rest of the day.

Adam was watching the doors when I climbed down and signaled everything was quiet. I didn't slow, though. After replacing and latching the ladder, I started shuffling the hay over to the cows.

Before I finished, a sound reached my ears. The tinkling of the chimes. My eyes widened, and I looked at Adam.

He didn't look at me, but motioned for the bunker as he backed away from the main door. Outside, an infected moaned.

Heart hammering, I hurried down the aisle. We made it to the bunker hall just as the cattle called out in fear.

Neither of us stripped from our gear once we were inside.

Instead, we hurried to the control room. The cattle were once again crowded into a corner.

"I know we tied the chimes," Adam said. He checked the turbine numbers. "It's not windy enough for it to have blown loose."

We watched the main door open, and two infected strode in. Seeing infected and not the grey men brought us no sense of relief. Especially since a black beast with glowing red eyes kept pace between them.

My fear reached a whole new level.

The trio moved to the grain silo door and disappeared inside. Seconds later, the dead man from this morning entered the barn. He studied the cows for a moment before opening his mouth. I could imagine the awful moaning sound he made.

He edged closer to the silo, his attention not on his companions who'd disappeared within but on the main barn doors.

Two horses raced inside, making me jump. The whites of their eyes and the way they reared when they saw the dead man in the doorway fully displayed their terror. They didn't want to get near him. Yet, they couldn't go back out due to the wave of infected following them in.

Several of the dead went to the cow pen. I watched in horror as they attacked one of the cows and dragged it outside. The blood trail left in their wake didn't give me any hope.

My mind struggled to process what was happening.

"What are they doing?" I whispered.

Adam was quiet for several moments.

"This reminds me of how Dad and I put out corn and apples to bait the deer. I think the grey things weren't the only ones to notice we were caring for the livestock. Blue-jacket is baiting us."

"But why bring in horses then kill a cow?"

"We can't stick around to find out. At first light, we're leaving."

After the day we'd had and the hound now hidden in the silo, I wasn't sure we'd see first light.

CHAPTER TWO

WE SLEPT IN SHIFTS OF TWO HOURS. MY FIRST SHIFT WASN'T pleasant. The infected carried pigs through the barn and out the back. I didn't know what that meant, other than they'd noticed the hallway leading down to the bunker. One of the smarter infected stationed a few of the slower, new ones there. Before it left, though, it studied the door and tried the latch. It was locked tight, but I didn't like that the infected knew to try it. Or the way it had looked around afterward. I'd nearly peed myself when it angled its head up and gazed straight at the camera.

Adam cursed a blue streak after I woke him for his shift and told him what I'd observed. Then he'd kissed my forehead and told me to sleep.

My second shift wasn't as bad as the first. The infected had settled down, hiding in various spots in the main area of the barn. If they were waiting for us to emerge, they were going to be sorely disappointed. The cattle were our future, but we weren't dumb enough to sacrifice ourselves for them. We had the supplies necessary to hole up in the bunker and wait them out for months if needed.

They'd get bored and wander away.

However, when Adam woke me up at first light, he was still determined to leave.

"I'll clear them out then come back for you."

"That isn't going to work," I said, watching the monitors with him. "There are four right outside the door. Three in the silo. Seven just standing in the middle aisle of the barn, and who knows how many out back or in the yard."

"They were carrying pigs out there, June. Why? And the horses. My gut's telling me this isn't something we can wait out. You said one of them looked right at the camera. The one in the blue coat came back in and looked at each of the cameras during my shift. Then, they slowly killed more cows right where I'd see them. They're too smart. We need to go."

"How? If you go out there, you'll die, and I'll be alone. Our chance of surviving improves if I go with you." But we both knew he didn't want that any more than I wanted him to go without me. "There's two of us and more than a dozen of them. We need help, Adam."

"From who?"

We both looked at the radio. The static crackled like it always did, but we knew there were people out there, listening. Good and bad people.

"Your plan is just as dangerous, June."

"Is it? We know what those dogs with the glowing red eyes can do. That's why you wanted to leave at first light, right?"

With a sigh, he turned to check frequencies.

"I'll make us something light to eat."

He nodded, and I went to the kitchen. Ten minutes later, I was scooping the oatmeal into bowls when the static disappeared.

"End message."

The words filled the bunker, followed by Adam shouting my name.

"Begin message."

Grabbing the bowls, I hurried down the hall as I listened.

"This message needs to make it to the east coast. I repeat, this message needs to make it to the east coast. I'm broadcasting this message on all frequencies for twenty-four hours. The western barrier has been compromised. I repeat, the western barrier has been compromised. I'm relaying the message word for word as it was broadcast. End message."

Adam's shocked expression met mine as only silence came from the radio. Then, the man started talking again.

"Is it a recording?" I asked.

Adam spun in his chair, waited for the break, then responded.

"We hear you. What's the western barrier?"

We waited, both of us barely breathing.

"I don't know," the man said. "I was told to pass it on by someone else who didn't know. Honestly, I'm just doing it because I thought I was alone until I heard the message. We're not the last ones. At least, not yet. And before you ask…no, I'm not telling you where I am. Stay safe and pass the message on. You're the only one who's answered on this frequency."

"Has anyone answered on any of the others?"

"Two. They didn't give locations, and I didn't ask. Make sure you do the same if anyone answers you."

Adam hesitated and met my gaze before speaking over the radio again.

"Friend, we're in a bit of a bind and looking for help. Our place is full of infected and one of those dogs."

There was a long moment of silence.

"You don't need help. You need a miracle. Sorry, friend. Good luck. Switching to another channel to repeat the message."

I felt sick to my stomach. Adam didn't glance at me as he replied.

"Understood. I'll do the same."

He sat for a quiet moment then looked up at me with a faint smile.

"Well, we know we're not alone."

"And we know that no one is likely to help us," I said, facing the truth.

"Likely not. Even if we broadcast our location without saying anything about the infected or the dog, anyone who hears it will think it's a trap."

I studied the infected on the monitors as I thought over the message.

"There's a barrier out there that was compromised. By what? The runners? Those black dogs? The grey men? Probably all three. Add in some humans who kill for supplies, and what chance do those of us who've managed to survive have? How long until you and I are truly alone?"

Adam took one of the bowls from me and gave my hand a squeeze.

"That won't happen if those of us who are left start working together instead of robbing each other." He set the bowl aside and started writing down the man's words and the channel. "We might not trust each other enough to share locations, but we can start talking. That's a start. Maybe we'll be able to band together eventually."

"Maybe we will," I said, his false optimism not fooling me.

Filled with fear and desperation, the end of the world hadn't brought the best out of people. It had brought out the worst.

"The message changes the plan, for the moment. I'll check the other channels. Maybe we'll get lucky."

"And if we don't?"

"We need to be out of here before dark, June. The only thing that'll keep us safe is the light." He changed channels, listened for a minute, then started broadcasting the man's message.

I left him to work and considered the information we'd been given. Where and what was the western barrier? Who was the originator of the message, and who was that person trying to reach in the east? Was that where those evacuee camps were? How long ago had we stopped receiving those occasional emergency broadcasts? I'd thought that had meant the evacuee camps were overrun. Now I wasn't sure.

More importantly, why send something now, after all this time? If there had been an evacuee camp to the west, why hadn't we heard messages from that location before now?

I returned to the kitchen and sat at the table, listening to Adam as he cycled through the frequencies every few minutes. I hoped for both our sakes someone would answer us.

About an hour later, while I was feeding the fish, Adam swore loudly.

"What?" I called, hurrying to the control room.

He pointed to the hallway camera. It was no longer positioned to a view of the door and the hallway.

"One of the infected suddenly looked up and moved it."

"A new one?"

"No. One that's been standing there this whole time."

I stared at the screen, understanding what that meant. We

were blind and trapped by infected smart enough to play stupid.

"Why move the camera now?" I asked.

"I think this is all a big trap. They let us see the dog, have been methodically killing the animals, and brought in new ones. They're baiting us out and know we're more likely to emerge when the red-eyed dog can't come out."

"Full daylight," I said, understanding.

"Exactly."

"So we stay and we wait. We have enough supplies to last for months."

We both knew that wasn't an actual option. Before the others on the radio went silent, we'd heard stories about how the dogs would claw and chew their way through anything, if given enough time, to get to a human. The dog would try to get through that door tonight, and we couldn't be here waiting for it.

I shivered and knew that was why Adam wanted to leave before dark. The door wouldn't hold for very long.

There was a flurry of movement on the screen for the barn. The infected grabbed another heifer and dragged it out of the main door, eviscerating it on the way. I could see Adam's jaw clench.

"We're as good as dead either way. If we stay and do nothing, we lose our future source of food. If we go out there, we die."

I set my hand on his shoulder and gave it a comforting squeeze.

"Keep trying the radio. We're not out of livestock yet."

Another hour passed, and I made Adam take a break from the radio. He willingly let me watch the monitors and went to double-check our bug-out bags. Since he was meticulous about checking them once a week, I knew it was more than an inspection. He was getting us ready.

The infected in the main barn started to move, and the blue coat guy slipped out the side door.

"Something is happening," I called to Adam.

As he entered the room, several more infected merged with the larger group.

"Where'd they come from?" he asked.

"Not the side door or the silo. The hallway, maybe?"

Neither of us looked away from the screens as the infected herd moved toward the main doors, which were shut, and waited there.

"The blue coat guy went out the side door. This might be another trap to bait us out," I said, already knowing what Adam would be thinking.

"Trap or opportunity, I'm not sure it's safe to keep playing the waiting game."

"I'll suit up." I swallowed hard, feeling sick to my stomach.

"Everything's by the door. Let me know when you're ready."

Nodding, I hurried to the hall where our bags and jackets waited along with an insane knife arsenal. The jacket was warm but not too bulky, which meant the knife harness Adam had made for me fit comfortably and I could move freely. Once I had everything on, including the bag, I called out.

"I'm ready."

"I don't think it's a trap," he said, emerging from the room. "It's like they're waiting for something to come through those main doors. I don't want to be here to find out what."

He picked up his bag and settled it on his back.

"You open the door and stand behind it. I'll clear the hall."

I nodded and got into position. Adam stood a few steps back, giving himself room to fight whatever was out there.

"We've got this, June. I'll keep you safe."

We both knew there was no guarantee for that anymore, so I said the only thing that was still certain.

"I love you. Ready?"

At his signal, I pulled the latch and yanked the door open.

Noise flooded the bunker.

Infected moans. Shouting. Cattle crying out.

"Shut it!" Adam yelled as three infected rushed into the room.

I tried to slam the door shut, but a hand stopped it from closing all the way. Bracing my weight, I leaned back against the door as I drew my knife. As I'd expected, one of the three inside the room had heard the commotion and turned my way, hands outstretched.

While Adam continued to fight the other two, I remained focused on the one coming at me. The dead man moved smoothly, reaching for my arm pressed against the jostling door. Its milky eyes never dipped to the knife in my other hand. My sweat-slicked palm slipped on the grip as I drove my knife up under his jaw. He dropped like a stone, taking the knife with him.

Lifting my gaze, I saw Adam shove one infected into the other one. It stumbled a step back, closer to me. I fumbled for my second knife. The door heaved hard behind me, and the blade clattered to the floor.

The infected turned toward me. Adam grabbed it by the back of the shirt and swung it around. The door jostled harder, opening a good inch before it crashed shut. I glanced to the side, saw the hand was gone, and slammed the latch into place.

When I faced Adam, it was in time to see the single, remaining infected knock Adam back into the wall. Adam's face went slack, and his knees buckled.

The infected stood over him and let out a moan.

I grabbed the knife from the ground.

"Asshole."

It turned at the sound of my voice, giving me the perfect target.

It dropped in a heap beside Adam, who had his eyes closed.

"Shit, shit, shit."

I ran to the kitchen and washed my hands before returning to him and tapping his cheeks.

"Come on, Adam. Wake up."

He didn't respond. I checked his pulse then the back of his head. There was a considerable lump already forming, but no blood.

As much as I wanted to keep trying to help him, I knew I didn't have that luxury.

Leaving Adam where he was, I ran back to the control room and absorbed what was happening on the monitors. What I saw made my heart stop.

The grey men were back, and they weren't alone. There was a young, human man with them. He was walking in their midst, looking around the barn. An infected dropped from the trap door in the ceiling. The closest grey man ripped its head clean off and tossed it aside. The human said something and smiled. The grey man returned the expression as another used the ladder to climb up to the hayloft.

More of the grey men came in and began picking up the

heads and bodies piled by the main doors. The infected. The grey men had killed them all.

The human in the middle pointed, and grey men started moving as if the human was directing them.

What in the hell was happening?

The man then left the barn, along with most of the other grey men. I stared at the empty space for a minute.

Those grey men had picked up a cow and hadn't hurt it. They'd returned and brought a human with them. He smiled. He talked to them. And they listened.

I hurried out to the hallway and tried to wake Adam. He still wasn't responding.

His words about working together echoed in my head, along with all of the stories we'd heard from people on the radio about grey men on a human killing spree.

Easing the pack off my back, I went to the door and hoped that the grey men were the miracle they seemed to be.

The moment I lifted the latch, something shoved against the door. Decaying fingers once again appeared and wrapped around its edge.

"Help!" I didn't stop leaning into the door as I screamed again and again.

Suddenly, the pushing stopped. I looked over at the fingers, which now loosely curled around the door, no longer holding it.

A knock startled me.

"Anyone home in there?"

"Yeah," I answered. "There's still an infected holding the door."

"Uh, that's just what's left of him. The rest is gone."

I'd seen the human on camera. I knew he was real, but I was

still terrified to open the door. Too many people had died by being stupid about so-called friendly company.

"Why are you here?" I asked instead of opening the door.

"A few friends of mine saw the cattle yesterday. They thought the herd had been abandoned. We came to take them back to Tolerance."

"Where's that?"

"Out in the middle of nothing, a few hours from here. It's a town my friends made. It's protected by a wall to keep the infected out."

"Your friends with the pointy ears?"

"The very same," he said without hesitation.

Taking a steadying breath, I opened the door.

Not a speck of blood dotted the dark hair or pale skin of the younger man who stood in front of eight of those grey-skinned men.

After everything I'd witnessed in the last twenty-four hours, seeing those grey-skinned men in person shattered any remaining hope I had left of a stable world. I started shaking hard. I knew it was a mixture of adrenaline and shock.

"You shouldn't need the knife anymore," the man said, not moving to enter. "The fey will get any infected that are still hiding. I'd keep it close, though."

Fey? My gaze shifted to the creatures behind him. They were huge. The guy in front of me, who was tall, barely came up to their shoulders. Their arms were thicker than my head and their legs even bigger. If the grey skin, pointed ears, and sharp teeth didn't give away that they weren't human, their eyes did. Green with a vertical slit for a pupil.

"Are you hurt?" the man asked.

I shook my head, dragging my gaze to his.

"What about the guy behind you? Was he bitten?"

"I don't think so. The infected pushed him into the wall. He has a lump on the back of his head."

"Has he opened his eyes?"

"No."

"I'm going to be straight with you. You had a great setup, but the infected know you're here. It's not safe to stay, and he could probably use a doctor."

"You have a doctor?"

"As close as we can get to one. She was a nursing student but has treated her fair share of injuries since the quakes."

"What's the catch?" I asked. "People don't help people anymore."

"You're right. Most don't. That's why my sister made friends with these guys." He jerked a thumb at the men behind him. "They help humans and don't ask for much in return."

"Much?"

"Just a chance to prove they aren't what everyone thinks they are. Monsters. Demons. Grey-devils. They've been called a lot of things."

I exhaled a shaky breath, doing my best to keep it together as I put the knife away. The guy didn't make a rush for me.

"What's your name?" I asked.

"Ryan." He held out his hand, and I cautiously took it.

"I'm June. That's Adam."

Ryan nodded and released my hand.

"It's not smart to stay too long in one place. If you're okay with it, one of these guys can take Adam out to the truck."

"You have a truck?"

"Several. For the cattle and any supplies we find along the

way. We don't waste the gas. When we leave Tolerance, we scavenge what we can to keep everyone fed."

"What are the chances Adam and I will be coming back here?"

"We're not kidnapping you if that's what you mean. You'll be able to leave whenever you want."

"And if that's not what I meant?"

Ryan studied me for a minute. "If you've been here all along, you might have missed what's been happening. The infected are getting smarter. It won't take them long to figure out there are humans keeping the cattle alive."

I nodded, thinking of the one in the blue coat who'd left.

"Then we have a lot of supplies to take with us." I moved away from the door and motioned for Ryan to enter.

"Fallor and Etri, can you dispose of the infected?" He looked at me. "June, do you mind if the rest of the fey come in?"

"No. It's fine." In reality, it was anything but fine. But what were my choices?

I watched the pair of them pick up the infected with ease and head out as the rest crowded into the hall.

"Would you mind closing the door?" I asked. "It feels wrong to leave it open."

One of the fey shut it but didn't let it latch. I guessed that was better than nothing.

Motioning for Ryan to follow me, I stepped over Adam, showed Ryan the supplies in the kitchen, and then led him farther back to the aquaponics. He didn't hide his excitement.

"This is amazing, June. You have no idea how starved people are for greens. Did you and Adam make this?"

"No. His uncle did."

He started studying all the components.

"I think we could replicate this in Tolerance."

"Ryan."

One of the fey stopped in the doorway and tilted his head.

"What is it?" Ryan asked.

"I think someone yelled hellhound."

"There was one in the silo," I said, standing. "We can check the cameras."

By the time we reached the control room, though, the monitor showed an empty barn.

"Hellhound or not, let's hurry up," Ryan said. "Grab what you can."

He looked at me. "We'll need to leave the fish. I don't know any way of moving them. But I promise the fey will come back and try to save them."

I turned off the monitors and reduced what energy consumption I could so the tank would be fine for a few days. Then, I watched the fey load up their arms with the supplies Adam's family had gathered. When the grey men had what they could carry, one of them carefully picked up Adam from one of the bunks he'd been moved to.

On some level, I was terrified I was making the wrong choice. But mostly, everything felt surreal. The infected laying a trap and killing our cattle...the grey men and how they killed the infected.

When we reached the main barn, I glanced at the opening to the silo. There were no infected or a hellhound there. Just a lot of blood.

Surrounded by the fey, I stepped out into the yard. One of them was spraying off at the milk house. He wasn't wearing a shirt. Nearby, a blonde stood next to a dead infected, but she wasn't looking at it. She was watching the bathing fey.

The truck Ryan mentioned waited in the driveway. There was another human man behind the wheel and a woman standing, with bow ready, on top of the cab. The young girl, her dark, curly hair pulled back into a poof at the top of her head, watched us with a serious expression.

Four humans in a sea of grey men. Each of those four looked free, but were they really?

I wished Adam was awake. His insight had saved us so many times.

"Did someone yell hellhound?" Ryan asked, pausing to look at the washing fey.

"YES," the blonde said angrily. "And not enough fey came running. If not for Brenna, I'd be dead."

She glared at all the grey men.

"You guys are shit for protection. I understand finding new people is amazing, but don't sacrifice the ones you already have."

I REALIZED she was talking about me when Ryan apologized and said, "We were under a lot of concrete and couldn't hear."

"THE FEY by the trucks heard. Am I that useless? That much of a bitch that I'm not worth saving?"

The grey men—*fey,* I reminded myself—shifted restlessly

around me. I wasn't sure if that was because of the packages they carried or the guilt the woman was piling on.

"They were told not to leave the trucks under any circumstances," Ryan said. "We've been tricked before. Infected bait them away from the trucks then try to disable our only means of escape. I'm truly sorry, Hannah. It was my order. Usually, there are fey assigned to each human. We weren't prepared for how hard it would be to load the animals, let alone hear a yell for help."

"I'M SO SORRY," I said when she looked at me.

"It's not your fault. It's theirs. If they want to keep us alive, they need to plan better."

THE FEY who'd been washing by the milk house tossed the hose aside and pulled the girl against his chest.

"Forgive me," he said. "Because I will never forgive myself for what almost happened."

SHE HUGGED HIM IN RETURN, and it looked far from a platonic embrace.

"As you can see," Ryan said to me, "we get along with the fey, which is a good thing. They have the speed and strength necessary to kill the infected quickly."

"AND THE DOG THINGS? Can they kill those?" I asked.

. . .

"YES. It's not as easy, but the fey are the only ones who can kill the hellhounds."

"FINE. WE'LL GO WITH YOU."

"I don't think you'll regret it. But, if you change your mind after a few days, we can always come back here with the fey to see if I'm right about the infected returning."

I had no doubt he was right. I'd seen the way the infected had acted. The farm was no longer a safe haven.

Whether or not Tolerance was remained to be seen.

CHAPTER THREE

WHILE THE OTHERS LOADED THE CATTLE AND SUPPLIES, I WAITED IN the back of a truck with Adam and the fey who held him. The fey studied me far too closely.

"You can put him down," I said. "He can rest his head in my lap."

"I will hold him. He smells of infected and blood."

"Yeah, he killed a few before I yelled for help."

The fey continued to stare at me with his weird eyes. Even while freaking out on the inside, I wanted to ask questions. What was he? Where did he come from? Was it true that he and his kind killed humans? But until Adam was out of his hold, I'd rather not risk asking something that might upset him. I'd seen the aftermath of their destruction. Heads didn't just pop off of bodies on their own.

I heard a flurry of low voices just outside, and a minute later, three fey rounded the corner, carrying another.

"June, please sit by Adam," one of them said. "Uan was attacked by a hellhound and is covered with contaminated blood."

I scrambled to my feet and changed sides of the truck.

Uan moaned as they gently placed him on the floor. It looked like the dog had chewed his neck and shoulder and torn open his insides. Blood glistened wetly with each of his gurgling breaths. If death had a sound, it was that.

"Be well, Uan. Nancy needs you," one of the fey said before the group walked away.

I glanced at the fey holding Adam.

"Isn't someone going to help him?"

"Cassie will."

The engines started, and a fey jogged to the back of the truck. He hesitated at the doors, though. His gaze shifted between me and the fey holding Adam.

"Do you want a light?" the new fey asked me.

"I have one. We'll be fine."

He grunted and closed the door. In the dark, I shrugged off my backpack and pulled out the flashlight. It reflected off the netted supplies that jostled as the truck started to move and gave enough light that I could see the hurt fey was going into shock.

Digging through the items in my bag, I found the space blanket packet. The fey said nothing as I tore it open but stopped me when I moved to put it over the injured fey.

"It's not safe to touch him."

"I've had plenty of infected blood on me and haven't turned yet. I promise I'm not going to roll in it. I just want to cover him."

He grunted, which I took as a go-ahead. Uan's shaking didn't ease up.

"How far until that town Ryan talked about?"

"Many miles. Rest."

With a sigh, I pulled up my hood and leaned against the truck's cold wall.

"YOU ARE SAFE."

The words startled me from an unintended doze.

"What?" I asked.

"June?"

The sounds of Adam's voice had me scrambling to my knees. He looked pale in the dim light, and his pupils were messed up.

"You hit your head, Adam. What's the last thing you remember?"

He frowned, his gaze flicking to the fey holding him.

"I don't know. Am I dreaming?"

"No. He's real. The infected attacked the bunker, and one knocked you into the wall. These guys helped us."

"Oh. Okay."

He started to close his eyes.

"Adam, I don't think you should go back to sleep."

"June?" His eyes popped open, and he glanced at the fey. "Am I dreaming?"

I knew it was a concussion, but understanding that didn't make it any easier to see Adam's confusion and complete dependence. After answering him again, I did my best to keep him alert for a while. His continued memory reset was upsetting, but I counted us lucky that we hadn't suffered worse as Uan struggled to breathe with each mile.

When the trucks finally rolled to a stop, I was relieved.

The doors opened, letting in a blast of colder air. I shivered lightly and looked over at Uan. His grey skin looked waxen with a green undertone.

"He needs a doctor fast," I said.

The fey at the door grunted and jumped into the truck with a few of his friends. They tried gently lifting Uan, but he groaned.

"It might be easier if you set him on the blanket then lift the blanket. It's strong. It'll hold."

The fey immediately listened, working together to move the injured fey and carry him out of the truck.

When the one holding Adam stood, Adam opened his eyes.

"What in the hell are you?"

"Adam, you hit your head," I said yet again. "He's helping you."

"June? Am I seeing things?"

"If you're seeing a guy with grey skin and pointy ears, then no, you aren't."

"Did you give me something? My head is pounding like a bitch."

It wasn't the first time he mentioned it.

"No. I didn't give you anything. I wanted to wait until you were a little more with it. Does anything else hurt?"

"No. Just my head."

The fey jumped out with Adam, and another was there to offer me a hand, which was way more than a hand. He lightly gripped my waist and lifted me down.

"I'm going to throw up," Adam said a minute before he heaved. Thankfully, not on the fey who carried him but to the side.

I barely noted his suffering, though. Our surroundings had caught my attention. We stood near a wall of smashed-together vehicles. That feat of repurposed metal stretched as far as I could see in either direction. In front of us, two huge metal gates slowly opened.

"Come," the fey said. "Matt will help you."

I followed the fey with Adam through the door. Another man was hurrying to meet us. I had a hard time staying focused as I tried to take in everything. The wall surrounded what looked like an entire subdivision of houses. There were people everywhere. Human people.

"He's hurt but talking," the fey holding Adam said. "Uan met with a hellhound and will need Cassie's attention."

"I understand," the new human said, his gaze shifting to me. "When the fey left this morning, they weren't expecting to find people, but I'm sure glad they did. My name's Matt, and I'm in charge of Tenacity. Let's get you two settled in somewhere and take a look at him." Matt glanced at the fey. "Do you mind tagging along, Brog?"

The fey grunted and fell into step behind Matt. I followed as we walked farther into the maze of houses.

A set of young boys ran between the houses in front of us.

"Caleb. Connor. Go help unload and organize."

"Okay, Matt," they yelled at the same time, not slowing but veering back the way we'd come.

"How are you all alive?" I asked, too stunned by the kids to filter.

"Perseverance, a whole lot of luck, and even more help. We wouldn't be here today if it weren't for the fey."

"How many people live here?"

"Three hundred and thirty-three, including you two. To save on heating and other resources, I've had to assign shared housing. It's two or three people per bedroom, depending on the home's size. But since you're new, you'll get a house to yourself for a bit to let you settle in."

"How many of those three hundred and thirty-three people are fey?"

"Here? None, unfortunately. Over in Tolerance, there's about two hundred fey and maybe seventy-five humans now? That sound about right, Brog?"

"Yes."

Matt deviated up an unshoveled driveway.

"This will be your place," he said.

It felt weird walking straight into a house. No hesitation. No listening for infected. Nothing. Open the door and go right in. I hesitated, and Matt gave me an encouraging smile as he waited for me to enter.

"You'll get used to it," he said.

"I hope not," I said, reluctantly walking in.

"Any chance this guy can put me down?" Adam asked, sounding more lucid than he had during the whole trip here.

"That might not be the best idea," Matt said. "You're covered in infected blood. It would be better if Brog carried you to the bathroom."

"Fine."

The two of them disappeared into the bathroom. A moment passed as we listened to low murmured conversation. Then the door shut.

"Is he going to be okay in there?" I asked.

"Yeah, he'll be fine."

I looked down at myself. My sleeves were dirty, but the rest of me was okay. Setting my bag to the side, I shrugged out of my jacket and went to rewash my hands.

"Where did the fey come from?" I finally asked. "Adam and

I heard a lot of stories that painted those…" I looked at the door. "Fey. Is that what they really are?" I shook my head. "What we heard painted them in a very unfriendly light. Why are they here? Here as in on this planet and here as in helping us."

Matt chuckled behind me.

"Before I answer all of that, can you tell me where you came from?"

"A bunker Adam's family had."

"Adam's the one in the bathroom?"

"Yeah, sorry. I'm June. It's been a bizarre twenty-four hours."

"I'd like to hear about it. But to answer your question, those earthquakes a few months back created an opening to an underground cave system that had been sealed away for thousands of years. The dogs with the glowing red eyes? We call them hellhounds. They came out first. They're the cause of all the infected undead running around."

"And the fey?"

"They were down in those caves all that time. They have no memory of humans or women and children. When the fey came to the surface, they were met with fear and gunfire. Did they kill some of us? Yes. Can't say that I blame them, though. We had to be just as unusual to them as they were to us. I would say terrifying, but I doubt that. Not when they'd lived in those caves with the hellhounds for thousands of years."

I tried to wrap my head around what Matt was saying, but it sounded like a bunch of fictional nonsense. Yet, I had no other explanation for their existence.

"And to answer the second part of your question, they're helping us for two reasons. They know they're our only chance of survival, and there's nothing for them in those caves. Now, tell me how you ended up here."

I'd just gotten to the part where the infected drove the horses into the barn when the door to the bathroom suddenly opened, and a very wet Adam strode out with a towel around his waist. Brog followed him toward us.

"He was repeating everything you two said while the door was closed and the water was running," Adam said. "Caves? Hellhounds? Is that true?"

Matt nodded, and Adam looked back at Brog.

"Impressive."

Brog looked at Matt.

"He has no bites."

"Yeah, he checked," Adam said. "That's a little invasive."

Matt chuckled, thanked Brog, and waited for the fey to leave before speaking again.

"The fey don't have our same hang-ups about privacy. Keep that in mind if you ever go out on a supply run with them. They'll strip down whenever and wherever to clean up. They know how few of us humans are left and don't want to accidentally contaminate us with infected blood."

"I appreciate the consideration," Adam said, coming to wrap his arms around me. I could tell by the way he moved that he was hurting badly.

He pressed a kiss to my forehead and turned to look at Matt.

"Before we tell you anything else, I'd like to know what happened to all our supplies."

"They're unloading them now," Matt said.

Adam looked at the door and raised an eyebrow.

"We have a storage shed for all supplies the fey bring back

each run. We keep thirty percent, and they take seventy for doing all the hard work."

"Those were our supplies. The hard work was ours. I'm not heartless. I was out when the work was being done to clear our place, and I'm willing to share a little for the help we were given, but thirty percent is out of the question."

Matt exhaled heavily.

"You misunderstand. Thirty percent goes to our community. That gets divided and rationed out to feed the three hundred plus people I'm trying to keep alive."

"The hell it does."

"I get it. You prepared. It should be yours. But there are three hundred and thirty-three starving people in our little community. If they see you carry all the supplies here? They will rebel. I wish I could offer you more than an equal share. But if I do, I'd be painting a target on your back. You're in no position to want that," Matt said, his gaze flicking to me.

Adam's hold on me tightened fractionally.

"Some rescue. You're telling me that the infected and hellhounds won't kill us, but starvation will after my family spent years prepping."

"You won't starve. The fey go out looking for supplies every day. You have a chance to go out and bring back your own share that doesn't get divided."

Adam snorted.

"Can you tell me more about the infected who seemed to be coordinating everything?" Matt asked, going back to what I'd explained.

"Not really," Adam said. "His eyes, like his partner's, weren't the normal milky white. They had a hint of red. And he was smart enough to act stupid and bait a trap. What June didn't get to was the part where we received a message. The western barrier has fallen. The sender said it needed to reach the east coast."

Matt frowned and asked, "What does that mean?"

"No idea," Adam said. "I can't even tell you where it originated. We stopped sharing locations when people started killing each other for the supplies some of us were smart enough to stockpile."

Matt nodded.

"The world's a changed place and not for the better. But I haven't lost hope yet that we can turn it around. If we want."

He stood and moved to the door.

"I'm grateful you're both alive. Each one of us matters. I'll have someone bring over your share of the supplies. I am sorry."

He let himself out, and Adam swore.

"A share of our own damn supplies."

"I'm sorry, Adam. I didn't have much choice. We needed the help."

He changed his hold on me, hugging me close.

"I'm not mad at you. They took advantage." A shiver stole through him. "Let's check out what we traded the bunker and supplies for."

Several hours later, Adam was swearing again. We had a wood stove, but no wood. There were solar panels, but they barely had enough juice to keep the appliances going. He unplugged the ones we weren't using and vented that these people were stupid enough to waste energy on running a refrigerator that didn't have anything in it to cool.

Our supply box consisted of a cup of dried beans, a box of dehydrated potatoes, and a can of corn. Adam was dangerously quiet as we ate the potatoes and corn and soaked the beans for breakfast.

"We'll pull through," I said. "We always do."

He kissed my temple, apologizing for being an ass.

"You're right. We will pull through. The rules have changed, and we have a lot to learn. Especially about the fey."

I knew what he was thinking without having to ask. He wanted to get to know the fey better to see what type of people they were. Sure, the fey had the strength we lacked, but a person's character mattered to Adam. He'd want to know they were willing to work hard to survive. He didn't have any use for people too lazy or full of excuses to help themselves.

Adam was a team player and had already discounted the residents of Tenacity. But he'd hold out hope for the fey. If they disappointed him too, I wondered how long it would take before Adam talked about going back to the bunker.

Worried about what would happen to us both then, I curled up against him and let him hold me until we fell asleep.

"June, I made you breakfast."

I peeled open my eyes and gave Adam a sleepy smile.

"God, you're beautiful," he said softly.

Groaning, I rolled away from him.

"Don't make fun of my bed head."

"It's part of your charm. Get up. We have work to do today. It's going to be a long day if we want to eat again."

Accepting the proffered cup of beans, I sat up and started spooning them into my mouth. When Adam was driven, it meant there was a time crunch. He proved me right by tossing my freshly laundered clothes on the bed.

"What are we doing today?" I asked.

"We're going on one of the supply runs."

My stomach lurched.

"Adam, you have a concussion. Let's wait a day."

"I'm not going to watch you starve, even for a day. Besides, it makes sense to get the lay of the land and figure out how honest that guy was being about the supply division."

"His name is Matt."

"I don't care what his name is. He's the one responsible for this place and these people, and I mean to find out why our food needed to be doled out in the first place."

The determination in his tone and gaze left no room for protest or reason. But I still tried.

"It's dangerous out there. You've told me that repeatedly. How many times did we wait out snow or ice on the solar panels just so we wouldn't have to go out? You hated having to leave the bunker."

He exhaled heavily and tweaked my chin.

"I hated you going out there. This is different. The wall will keep us safe enough while we check out what this supply run is about. And if the supply run is what I think it is, we'll be safe enough to leave."

I finished eating and passed him the cup.

"And what do you think it is?" I asked, tugging on my pants.

"You said the fey had that barn cleared in the time it took us to kill three infected. I think those big grey guys are exactly what you speculated. Inhumanly strong and fast. Matt says they're here to keep us safe, and I believe him. Why else would there be so many humans alive in one loud, lit-up place?"

The shirt cleared my head, and I gave Adam a long look.

"And if it's not safe?" I asked.

"You don't go."

I sighed, having already guessed that would be his answer.

The sky was just lightening when we stepped outside, fully dressed and equipped with our knives. The neighborhood was eerily quiet.

"This gives me the creeps," I whispered.

"Me too. I need to find out who has my guns."

That was one of the many questions he'd asked me last night after I'd gone through everything that happened since running out to clear the solars. He remembered most of the events between that point and hitting his head, but there were some foggy areas.

"Any headache this morning?" I asked.

"A mild one and general soreness in my neck and the back of my head. I've been stretching it. If we find some pain relievers while we're out there, I'm keeping them."

When we reached the wall, Matt was already talking to a few other people. He excused himself and headed our way when he saw us.

"Are you sure you should be going out?" he asked.

"We don't have a choice when we were only given enough food for two meals from our supplies that would have fed us for a year."

A few of the gathered people shot Adam a look. I wasn't sure if it was due to his volume or the insinuation that they were thieves.

"These are the people who will be helping bring back more

supplies to feed everyone," Matt said. "They're trying to pull their weight."

Adam's flat glance at the group conveyed his disregard.

"How much of what we find do we keep?" he asked.

"Thirty percent of whatever you gather goes to your house to share with your housemates."

I could feel the anger radiating off of Adam at Matt's answer. We both understood what Matt was saying. We were living on our own, temporarily, and once we were assigned group living, we'd need to share with everyone in our house.

"Screw that."

"Waves are the last thing you need right now," Matt said quietly. "You're new, and people are watching."

"So am I," Adam said, finally lowering his voice. "You said there are over three hundred people here. If even a third of those are able-bodied, there should be a hell of a lot more people standing here, waiting to leave for a supply run."

"People are afraid."

"So afraid to leave that they're willing to starve?" Adam shook his head. "You need to wake your people up."

"That's what I've been hoping will happen when they see people like you going out for supplies and getting extra for the effort."

"Not when you're still giving them the majority."

"Trust me. Once it's divided out, it's not much."

As Matt said the last word, a fey jumped over the wall, landing neatly inside.

"Holy shit," Adam breathed.

Matt turned to look. "They're impressive. Wait until you see them in action."

Another fey jumped over the wall. He carried Ryan, the

man who'd been with them the day before. As soon as the man was on his own feet, he jogged our way, the fey sticking close.

"Hey, Matt."

"Morning, Ryan. How's Mya?"

"Good. She's getting out of the house more and has threatened to make Drav sleep on the couch if he tells her she needs to rest one more time." Ryan grinned. "You can imagine how that went over."

Matt chuckled then grew more serious.

"How's Uan?" he asked.

"Cassie said it's a miracle he made it home. He's stitched up as best as Kerr could manage, and now it's a waiting game."

They were both silent for a moment before Ryan looked at Adam.

"It's good to see you on your own two feet. I'm Ryan. I'm the voluntold leader of these supply runs." He stuck out his hand, and Adam immediately shook it.

"How old are you?" Adam asked.

Ryan chuckled. "At the time of the quakes, I was seventeen. But I think the months since then are like dog years, you know? I feel more like twenty-five."

Adam actually cracked a smile.

"I think you're right," he agreed. "How long have you been doing these supply runs?"

Ryan looked at Matt and shrugged. "You keep better track of the passing days than I do."

"Almost since the beginning," Matt said, clapping Ryan's shoulder. "Back when it was a lot more dangerous."

"It's safer with the fey here to clear the houses and protect the convoy," Ryan said before his gaze shifted to me. "Are you both going?"

I glanced at Adam, and he nodded.

"I'm guessing, based on the supplies you had," Ryan said, "you didn't need to leave that bunker much. Stay close to your assigned fey. They'll keep you safe and let you know what to do. Glad you're coming with us. Tenacity needs all the help it can get."

Neither of us said anything as we followed the rest of the humans to the trucks. We climbed into the back of one and settled in for a long ride. No one talked. Still tired, I leaned against Adam's shoulder and dozed until the truck stopped.

When the doors finally opened, there were dozens of fey waiting just outside.

"You know the drill," Ryan said. "One human to six fey. Be smart. Be quiet. Be careful. If anything looks or feels wrong, tell your fey and get out of there."

A shiver of fear worked its way down my spine.

People started moving away, and without a word, fey protectively surrounded them. Adam took my hand and followed their lead.

"We stick together," he said to me as the fey fell in around us.

I nodded. He glanced at the fey to his left, who was looking at our hands.

"We're new to this. Any advice you can give us would be much appreciated, friend."

The fey smiled at Adam, showing his pointed teeth.

"What's your name?" he asked.

"Adam. This is June, my girlfriend. What's your name?"

"Tor." His gaze flicked to me then to my hand locked with Adam's. "You tell us which house to clear. Three of us will check for infected. The rest will wait outside with you. If there are no infected, you can come inside and gather supplies."

Adam and I shared a glance. Nothing was ever that easy anymore.

"Okay. Let's look for the houses that have signs of kids having lived there," I said. "Those are more likely to hold more food."

For the next hour, it was as easy as they'd said it would be. Easy didn't mean less scary, though. While the fey did their best to kill any infected they found, some of the more intelligent infected proved better at hiding and managed to avoid detection. But that was why the fey stuck close to us humans while we collected supplies.

Adam was thorough and took everything he thought would be useful. From the obvious, like food, to the less obvious, like space heaters. Whatever we found went into a tote that someone from our assigned group of fey ran back to the trucks.

Tor stuck to us like our personal bodyguard and guide as we worked our way through the rooms.

"Check this out," Adam called.

I left the master bathroom, my assigned fey trailing behind me, to find Adam in the walk-in closet.

"Someone was prepped for stuffing stockings." He passed down a plastic bag. "We're almost done here," he said, looking at my assigned fey. "Would you mind scouting for another house with toys in the garage?"

While he left, I peeked inside at the Christmas candy. Tor leaned over my shoulder and studied the colorfully wrapped confections.

It was weird being this close to one of the fey, but I was slowly getting used to it. Their size might have made them intimidating at first, but the more time I spent around them, the more I saw beyond their appearances. They were quietly curious about everything and observed closely.

"What is it?" Tor asked.

"You've never had candy?" I asked.

He shook his head.

While Adam kept digging, I opened a bag and handed Tor a piece, taking one for myself. I showed him how to unwrap it then popped mine into my mouth. It was one of those taffy mints I used to like as a kid.

Tor mimicked what I did until he chewed. His neutral expression shifted to disgust before he started coughing and sputtering. I giggled a little and patted his arm.

"It's okay. It's not for everyone. Adam doesn't like them either."

"Did she give you one of those crappy mints?" he asked. "That's just cruel, June."

"He might have liked it," I said, bending down to tuck the bag into the waiting tote. As I did, I noticed something hanging under the bed and took a rapid step back.

"Tor," I said, pointing.

A second later, I stood in the corner, staring at Tor's broad back. He'd moved faster than I could register to get me there.

"We may have missed one," Tor said.

Adam swore, and I leaned around Tor just enough to see him come out of the closet with his knife drawn. He glanced at me, saw I was safe, then looked at the bed where I pointed once more.

"Something was hanging down under the bed. It looked like a hand."

Tor nudged my arm behind him again, and an insane part of

me almost laughed. The situation was far from funny, but in all the craziness we'd endured over the last few days, the fey's level of protectiveness, which rivaled Adam's, struck me as surreal.

Another fey strode into the room, grabbed the end of the bed, and flipped it to the side. Two infected tumbled out of the bottom of the bed. Before they could make it to their feet, they lost their heads.

"They cut the backing and hid in it," Adam said, moving closer. He plucked a knife from inside the material and showed it to Tor.

"We need to be more careful. Especially with June. I don't want to do anything that'll put her in danger more than she already is."

Tor grunted as he straightened.

"We will do better," he promised.

I shot Adam a look.

"Don't blame them. We'd both be dead already if not for their help. And you're the one who sent the other fey away."

Adam flushed and apologized to Tor for sounding like he was blaming him. But as I returned to the bathroom with another fey, I heard Adam say, "Stick close to her. She's all that matters."

CHAPTER FOUR

ADAM WAS GIDDY WHEN WE WALKED OUT OF THE SUPPLY SHED WITH enough food for a week. It was hard to feel the same. People stared at our boxes laden with food. Some with envy and more than a few with anger.

We'd been smart about what we'd taken. Dried foods, stuff that would require more work to prepare but would stretch further. We'd also taken the space heater he'd found, which was what I carried.

A man stepped in front of us.

"You took more than your share."

"Nope," Adam said, keeping his tone friendly. "We filled twenty totes. Fourteen went to the fey. Six came here. Two totes worth is thirty percent. That's our take for risking our lives to feed able-bodied people too afraid to fend for themselves. It's what happens when you put some effort into surviving. You might want to give it a try tomorrow."

He stepped around the man, and I hurried to follow, looking back in time to see the man spit on the ground in our wake.

"You shouldn't goad them," I said.

"They need goading. Until more people man up, no offense, and head out to get their own supplies, we're going to be busting our asses on their behalf."

I couldn't disagree with him, but I also remembered Matt's warning about painting a target on our backs. However, once we reached our house, everything was quiet. Adam put away the supplies, and I started dinner.

Rather than sit around after we finished eating, Adam went out to talk to Matt about his missing weapons. A day spent searching for hiding infected made me jumpy in the house by myself. I kept busy by sorting through the clothes that had been on our front step when we got home. The pile of clothing made me feel guilty that Adam had been so rude about our share of the food.

The door closed downstairs.

"June?" Adam called out.

"Here," I answered.

He entered carrying his uncle's shotgun and rifle.

"Matt wouldn't give me the handgun yet," he said. "He's worried I'm going to cause trouble."

Considering the way Adam grinned at me, Matt was absolutely right in that assessment.

Adam set the guns aside and came up behind me, wrapping his arms around my waist.

"Guess what I found when we were out?" he whispered close to my ear.

"What?"

He held up a line of five condoms.

"Tell me you're as ready to use one of these as I am." He kissed the side of my neck, and I turned in his arms to smile at him. The oral sex had tapered off after the first few weeks.

Neither of us had ever said no to the other. We'd just gotten caught up in the day-to-day worry of surviving.

"I've missed you," I admitted.

He grinned, and the tender kiss he gave me quickly morphed into hunger as we both stripped out of our clothes and fell into bed. Adam immediately went down on me, and I groaned. It'd been far too long. Long enough that I didn't care what he was doing to get me ready in a hurry.

When I was wet enough, he kissed his way to my breast, nipped me, then entered slowly while watching my face. I let him see everything I felt.

"I love you, June," he whispered before kissing me again. I tasted myself on his lips as he picked up speed, building a fire within me. He groaned and broke away from our kiss, his rhythm not slowing.

"You feel so good, babe. I want to stay like this forever."

He changed the angle of his thrust, and I made a small sound. He swore and faltered before hammering into me faster. I could feel him coming and hid my disappointment.

"Sorry, June. I lost it. You have no idea how hot it is when you do that. It's been too long."

"It's fine. Don't worry about it."

He slowly withdrew and rolled to the side, sliding his leg between mine.

"I'll make it up to you," he whispered.

MY BREATH FOGGED in front of me as we approached the wall. Another dozen people were waiting, but no faces I recognized from the day before. Except for Matt. He broke away from the people he was talking to and approached us. His gaze flicked to the guns we carried.

"Are you sure you want to go back out again so soon?" he asked.

"How else do you plan on stocking up that storage shed?"

Matt looked like he was going to say something more, but the arrival of the fey distracted him. They jumped over the wall like the day before, but this time, there was a girl with Ryan. She hurried toward Matt as soon as the fey put her down.

"Just the person I was hoping to speak with," she said with a smile. "I have some new ideas I'd like to run by you." She looked at the fey who'd followed her. "Thanks for the ride, Tor. I should be fine on my own today."

Without her use of his name, I wouldn't have recognized the fey who had helped us the prior day, and I felt a little bad for it. Bad enough that I studied his features and did my best to commit them to memory. His bright yellow-green eyes with the vertical pupil, his strong nose with a slight bump in it that hinted at a past break, and his prominent cheekbones and brow. When I looked past the unusual shape of his ears and odd eyes, he was actually handsome.

"Hey, Tor," Adam said, sticking out his hand. "I'm glad to see a familiar face."

I couldn't help but notice the girl's shock as she glanced between Adam and Tor, who was accepting Adam's gesture of welcome. Considering how unwelcoming this place was, I wondered if common courtesy was so unusual.

"I'm June," I said to her. "That's Adam."

"New faces. You must be the couple they found out at the farm. Welcome."

Her welcome was the first we'd received outside of Matt's.

"Thank you," I said.

"We better go," Adam said, calling my attention to the mass exodus.

"It was nice meeting you," I said to the woman before jogging with Adam to catch up.

As we waited to get into the truck, Adam spoke softly to Tor.

"Think we can have the same group as yesterday?" he asked.

Tor's gaze shifted briefly to me before he nodded.

"Good. Thanks to your help, June and I had a good night."

I flushed and pretended not to hear as I climbed into the back of the truck.

The ride took a little longer than the previous day, and the people in the back with us started to get restless.

"Ryan didn't say this was going to be a long run," someone grumbled.

"He stopped telling us," someone else said.

"If it's bad, I'm not leaving the truck."

I leaned my head against Adam's shoulder to distract him from answering. It worked. He turned to kiss my forehead, and I played with the hair at the back of his neck.

When the truck finally stopped and we could get out, a few of the humans stayed behind.

"What's their deal?" Adam asked Tor as we walked away. The subdivision didn't look any different from the one we'd raided the day before.

"They like staying closer to Tenacity. It feels safer to them."

Adam shook his head and called them idiots, which made Tor grin. The fey's pointed canines looked much longer than the rest of his teeth. Like a dog, but not. He caught me looking and immediately stopped smiling. Adam noticed and shot me a look.

I flushed again and focused on the surrounding houses.

"Let's start with the ones at the end of the cul-de-sac over there," I said softly. "Bigger back yards usually mean kids."

While we moved off in that direction, away from the people sticking to the homes closer to the trucks, I did my best to shake off my slip. Pointed teeth did not define a man's character, but it sure could be startling when not expecting it.

Three fey cleared the first house and moved on to the one next door while the remaining nine came inside with us. Adam and I propped our guns close by and started in the kitchen.

"So you guys live in that other town, Tolerance, right? What's it like over there?" Adam asked, opening the first cupboard.

"Good," Tor said.

Adam laughed and used more specific questions as we moved the things we wanted to the countertops. Gradually, we learned that Tolerance didn't have the same supply issues that Tenacity had. People could go into the supply shed and take what they needed whenever they needed it.

"Why did we get stuck in Tenacity then?" Adam asked.

"New people go to Tenacity."

"Okay. How do people get to live in Tolerance?"

"Mya and the other women have to approve them."

"Could you let Mya and the other women know we're interested in switching?" Adam asked. "Living in Tenacity sucks sweaty jock balls."

Tor grunted, and I wondered if he knew what "sweaty jock balls" were.

When I turned to open the full-length pantry door, Adam caught my arm and shook his head.

"I will check," Tor said.

He waited until Adam and I stood a healthy distance away then opened it. There was nothing but shelves of dry goods and chips inside. My stomach rumbled at the sight of the chips.

Adam grabbed the bag, handed it to me, then lifted me to sit on the counter.

"You snack, and I'll sort."

I opened the bag and took a chip out.

"We'll get more if I work," I said before shoving the crisp bit of deliciousness into my mouth.

"Union lunch break. Eat."

I rolled my eyes at him but kept munching. When I caught Tor watching, I tipped the bag his way.

"I promise it tastes nothing like yesterday's candy. Give it a try."

Adam grinned back at me as Tor took a chip and crunched on it. The face the fey made had me laughing again.

"Come on," I said, taking another one. "It's sour cream and onion. It's a universally enjoyed flavor."

"Don't let her bully you, Tor," Adam piped in. "It's not my favorite either. Watch for anything with flames on it. That'll be better."

I snorted, already picturing Tor's reaction to that.

"Flames usually mean spicy," I warned him.

We worked our way through the rest of the house without incident and moved on to the next. There were fewer infected here than in the other place, which meant we moved faster. We'd almost cleared the third house when Tor stopped us.

"We need to leave."

"Why?" Adam asked even as he hopped down from the chair he was using to search the top shelf of yet another closet.

"A herd of infected was spotted moving this way."

Adam swore softly, and we hurried out the front door. The fey jogged with us, easily keeping pace. The neighborhood was quiet with a few fey standing watch on the rooftops. No one seemed overly anxious until we reached the trucks.

The back doors were already shut, and the people inside startled when we opened one to climb in. Today, numerous boxes were packed in toward the front.

"Good haul," Adam said, sitting beside me.

No one commented. In fact, before the doors closed and cut off all light, I could have sworn one man looked like he was about to throw up.

The truck's engine roared to life, and we started moving. After a few minutes of hearing nothing, I leaned my head against Adam's shoulder and relaxed enough to doze.

Neither of us realized how serious the situation had been until the doors opened again at Tenacity. Gore coated the fey, and one of our fellow passengers did throw up at the sight of them.

"What happened?" Adam asked the clean fey offering me a hand down.

"What the fuck do you think happened?" the barfer said. "The infected swarmed the trucks."

Ignoring that guy, Adam looked at the fey.

"Thanks for keeping us safe."

The fey glanced at me then Adam before nodding.

There was a lot more tension as the supplies were unloaded and divided. Adam and I had three boxes to carry this time.

"Few more runs like that, and I'll feel a little better about being stuck here," he said, not being overly loud.

It didn't matter. People heard. Instead of angry glares, people either avoided looking at us or smirked, which didn't make a lick of sense to me until we got home.

All of yesterday's supplies were gone.

Adam swore up a blue streak.

"Matt warned us," I said. "Use your eyes, Adam. People are desperate and afraid. That same combination led to the deaths we heard about on the radio."

Adam stopped swearing and hugged me.

"I'm sorry, June. I promised to keep you safe and am failing."

"I'm the one that brought us here, Adam. Not you. This isn't your fault. We just need to be more careful."

He nodded, but the next morning, he still insisted we leave on a supply run.

"Fine," I said. "But today we don't take our personal share."

Agreeing with me, he nudged me toward the door.

"Give me a few minutes," he said. "I'm going to make sure our stuff is still here when we get back."

I didn't have to wait outside long before he came out and taped a sign on the door. It read, "Do not enter. Trespassers will be shot on sight."

"Let's go," he said.

"They're going to see that as confrontational."

"I don't care. It's a warning. Plain and simple."

I didn't understand what he meant by that until after we returned from the supply run, and Matt was waiting for us at the wall.

"We need to talk," he said, looking seriously pissed.

"Don't worry, after yesterday's theft, we agreed to waive our share of today's take," Adam said loud enough for the people waiting at the supply shed to hear. "Don't want anyone getting too sore about all the effort we're putting in, risking our asses to help feed everyone."

Matt looked down at the ground for a minute.

"Why didn't you come to me?" he asked.

"About the theft? What could you have done? We weren't home to witness who did it. Hopefully, they left some clues today, though. Or a blood trail."

"A man died, Adam. Shot in the face."

My stomach churned, but I remained silent beside Adam.

"I'm guessing he ignored my sign," Adam said calmly.

Matt ran a hand through his hair. "You're used to looking out for yourselves. I understand. But that's not the way things work here. This is your only warning. No more traps."

Then Matt raised his voice.

"The penalty for stealing supplies is exile. No exceptions." He looked at Adam. "You lost your right to firearms."

I could feel Adam tense and set my hand on his arm.

"Without those, you know we're not safe," Adam said.

"In here, you are. I'll have the men patrolling the walls keep an extra eye on your house if you choose to go out again tomorrow."

Matt turned away from us and started working his way through the crowd, talking to people.

Adam was so angry he was shaking with it on our way back to the house. There was blood on the porch and blood all over the kitchen.

"This is my mess," he said when I saw it. "Go upstairs. I'll clean it up."

I didn't listen and worked beside him, washing down the cabinets and scrubbing the floor. When we finished, Adam went to the cabinet under the TV and pulled out what we needed to make dinner. Neither of us said much. I hated that someone had died because of us. But I was well aware that the man, whoever he'd been, hadn't been innocent. He'd ignored Adam's warning and entered the house with the intention of stealing food.

"I'll talk to Tor again about what it takes to get out of here," Adam said, holding me that night. "This place isn't safe."

I agreed but wondered how the other place would be any safer once the people here found out there was a surplus of supplies over there.

IT FELT like I'd barely closed my eyes when a hand over my mouth startled me awake. I didn't fight it, thinking it was Adam, until I opened my eyes and saw a masked head above me. I threaded my arm over the one pinning me and thrust downward, freeing my mouth as soft thuds and grunts echoed in the room.

The man swore and fell on top of me when I started to roll away. His weight pinned me to the mattress long enough for him to grab my hair and pull back. Hard. I opened my mouth to scream and choked on the sock he shoved in it.

That didn't stop me from doing everything possible to get free. Fear and adrenaline fueled my efforts.

"Help me," a voice said harshly.

Hands grabbed my feet. Another body weighed down my

lower half. Panic overrode common sense. I forgot everything and just struggled to draw in my next breath.

"Smart girl," a voice whispered next to my ear when I stopped moving. "This was for Wayne."

The noises silenced, and the weight left me. I lay for a minute, crying, before I carefully lifted myself from the mattress. When I made it to the light, I cried harder at the sight of Adam on the floor. His face was bleeding, and his eyes were closed.

Kneeling next to him, I set my shaking fingers to his neck and felt his thrumming pulse. A pained sound escaped me. He was alive but beaten so badly his face was already swelling. I stood and went for a cold, wet washcloth. He didn't make a sound when I set it over his eyes.

I dried my tears and stood, debating what to do. For all I knew, the men were still in the house, cleaning us out. Even if they weren't, I didn't trust them not to come back and finish what they'd started.

That decided me.

Our attackers had proven I posed no threat. I couldn't protect Adam, no matter how much I wanted to. Leaving him on the floor, I pulled on my pants and grabbed my knives before quietly making my way toward the front door. The house was quiet and everything untouched.

Trusting nothing, I ran as soon as I was outside. Adam had pointed out Matt's house the day before. I didn't stop until I was at the man's door, alternating between ringing the bell and pounding on the wooden surface.

The lights turned on inside.

"I'm coming," Matt yelled.

I could see him running through the window.

He jerked the door open, his gaze sweeping over me, and he swore.

"What happened?"

"They broke in and beat Adam. It's bad. He's bleeding, and he's breathing so shallowly I had to check for a pulse to make sure he's alive."

Matt swore again and waved for me to come in.

"I can't," I said. "He needs help."

"And I'm getting it for him. Don't move."

He hurried back into the house and turned on a radio.

"It's Matt. There's a problem. I need Cassie."

A voice immediately responded.

"We will send Kerr."

"Hurry."

Matt grabbed his jacket and jogged toward me. Instead of heading in the direction of our house, he veered toward the wall.

"We need to let the fey know where to go," he explained before I could ask. He yelled instructions to the guards then ran with me back to the house.

It was as quiet as it'd been when I'd left, and Adam lay in the same spot.

Matt knelt beside him and lifted the washcloth. Then he leaned down close, his ear near Adam's nose and mouth.

"Get more of these," he said, indicating the washcloth as he straightened.

For the next several minutes, Matt asked me questions as we worked. Did I see anyone or anything identifying? Would I recognize their voices? Was there anyone who stood out as overly angry when we'd returned? Nothing I could say helped solve who had attacked us, other than it was clearly in retaliation for the man who'd died because of Adam's trap.

Matt and I lapsed into silence, and I gently washed away the blood on Adam's face while Matt cushioned his head with a folded towel.

"Matt?"

The suddenly loud voice made me jump.

"Up here," Matt answered.

Feet echoed on the stairway, and I looked up as a woman with red hair entered.

"What happened?" she asked, already bending to run a hand along Adam's swelling right leg.

"A group of men broke in and beat him," Matt said.

The fey behind her grunted, crossing his arms. His gaze flicked to me as I moved out of the woman's way.

"Adam hit his head a few days ago," I said. "He was out for a while and asked the same questions over and over again for a few hours afterward. Threw up, too."

"Do you know if they hit his head?"

"I don't know. They held me down. I couldn't see anything."

The fey growled.

"Stay objective and focused, Kerr," the woman said.

"We haven't moved him," I said. "Based on the sounds, I'm guessing they were hitting and kicking. The area over his ribs is pretty red. I'm worried something might be broken."

"I don't like the idea of moving him, either."

The woman opened the bag she carried and pulled out scissors. Chewing my bottom lip and trying not to cry, I watched her cut away Adam's t-shirt, sleep shorts, and boxers. Bruises were already forming everywhere, including his hips and ribs. She eased the clothes free and gently started feeling everything.

"I'm not a doctor," she said as she looked up at me. "I'm a nursing student who has learned more in these last few months than I ever did in school. I want you to know that because everything I'm going to tell you is a guess."

I nodded.

"The cut over his eye should be fine without stitches. Chances are good that something's broken. If we're lucky, it's his nose and a cracked rib or collarbone. Those tend to fix themselves. Bruising means broken capillaries and blood rising to the surface. He's going to have a lot of that. Again, if we're lucky, outside bruising is the worst of it. Internal bleeding is beyond my skill set.

"The best we can do now is make him comfortable, keep using these cold washcloths, maybe even some bags with snow, and hope he wakes up within the next twenty-four hours." She stood and came close to where I was sitting on the bed.

"I'd like to talk to you alone for a minute if that's okay."

I nodded and stood.

"Kerr," she said. "Help Matt get Adam into bed. Move his limbs and joints, including his head and neck, as little as possible. If he makes any noise, stop what you're doing. Okay?"

The fey nodded and started bending down.

"Stay objective and focused," she said, touching the back of his head as we moved past them.

As soon as she closed the bathroom door behind us, I knew what she was going to ask.

"Did they sexually assault you?"

I shook my head even as tears started to fall. She opened

her arms, and I flew into her embrace, sobbing out my fear. Fear that they'd come back. Fear that Adam wouldn't wake up this time. Fear that I'd made the wrong decision. That we should have stayed in the bunker and waited for the infected to leave.

She let me cry for several minutes before easing away from me. Her eyes were wet, too, as she gave me a sad smile.

"I wish I could give you the assurances you need. What I can say is that he's young, in good shape, and not underfed. That all works to his advantage."

"I know. Thank you."

When we left the bathroom, Kerr was standing in the hallway. His expression was one of sheer anger.

"Is he okay?" I asked, already moving to the bed.

"Did something happen?" the woman asked from behind me.

I didn't look back at the pair but studied Adam's swollen face and gently ran my fingers along his throat.

"He was rolled up defensively," I said, talking to myself. "That means they missed his throat and hopefully his stomach and laid into his legs and back and…" I pictured the position in my head and gently ran my fingers along his forearms, feeling the bumps there. "He needs snow."

I stood and jumped slightly when I saw the redhead behind me.

"Sorry," I murmured.

"Don't be. It's understandable. Matt already went outside for snow."

Only a moment passed before I heard him in the hall.

"Got it," he said, stepping into the room. He held a bowl in one hand and a baggy in the other.

"Clean baggies only," the woman said. "No dirty snow on open wounds."

I nodded, already grabbing handfuls of snow and making bags for Adam's arms.

"Would you mind if one of my brothers stayed here with you?" Kerr asked, speaking for the first time.

I glanced up and gave him a small smile.

"Not at all. I'd feel a lot safer, actually."

He glanced at Matt.

"No argument here," Matt said.

CHAPTER FIVE

I JOLTED UPRIGHT, INSTANTLY AWAKE, AT THE SOUND OF ADAM'S groan.

"Adam?" I said softly. "It's June."

"Thirsty," he rasped.

"Okay. Hang on. I'll get you something."

I ran downstairs. The fey who'd stayed behind to watch over Adam and me didn't say anything when I whacked a towel full of ice cubes against the counter and emptied the shards into a cup. However, he did follow me back upstairs.

"Adam?" I said again as I approached the bed. "Are you still thirsty?

"Mmmhmm."

"I have some ice chips. We don't want you lifting your head yet. Okay? Just open your mouth, and I'll give you a few."

His lips parted, and I wanted to cry when I saw he was not only understanding my words but also responding to them. I fed him chips until his lips stayed closed and his breathing became deeper.

I wiped my eyes and glanced out the window at the

predawn light. It was hard to know how long he'd been out when I wasn't even sure how long we'd slept before the men had snuck in. But he had to have been unconscious longer than when he'd hit his head the first time, and that worried me. As did the bruising that colored his face.

"Would you mind getting more snow?" I asked the fey without looking away from Adam.

"I will fill two bowls from the roof."

"Thank you."

The fresh snow bags didn't get another response from Adam, and I tried not to be disappointed. Instead, I sat beside him and watched the sun slowly rise.

A knock on the front door startled me from my exhausted stupor.

I hurried downstairs just as the fey opened it. The new fey's familiar gaze flicked to me, and he lifted a box.

"I found a bag with flames for Adam."

"That is so sweet of you, Tor," I said, tears welling. "Thank you for thinking of him."

Both men stared at me for a long moment then shared a glance.

"Should I take them back?" Tor asked.

"No. When Adam wakes up, he's going to appreciate them. Come in."

He brought the box to the kitchen and set it on the counter.

"Cassie sent some other things. She said the chips might not be what he wants first." He held up several brown packets of instant oatmeal. "Adam and I liked the same things. These taste bad."

I laughed a little. "Oatmeal isn't his favorite. But he'll eat it just fine."

"Are you going out again today?" I asked Tor.

"No. I wanted to help Adam."

"Come on. I wouldn't mind some sleep if you're willing to watch him for me."

Tor looked at the other fey. "Did anyone come back?"

"No. It was quiet. Should I stay?"

They both looked at me.

"I don't think both of you are necessary. Besides, I'm sure you're as tired as I am. Thank you for all your help last night."

He nodded and left. I stared at the closed door for a tired second.

"I forgot to ask his name."

"It is Brog."

Brog, the same fey who'd held Adam in the truck. I felt like an ass for not recognizing him. I needed to start paying more attention to them.

"I hope he doesn't think that I was being a snob. Everything's been..." I shook my head. "Will you tell him I'm sorry for not remembering his name?" I asked, looking up at Tor.

"He understands you are not a snob."

I nodded and led the way to the bedroom and quickly explained what happened to Adam, where his worst injuries were, and what I'd been doing to help him. Tor sat in the chair I'd occupied and watched me pull back the covers on the other side of the bed.

"If he makes a sound, I'll probably hear. But if I don't, please wake me up," I said, sliding under the covers.

Tor grunted, and I gave him a tired smile. This time, while looking at him, I noted the differences in Tor's features. His eyes were forest green around the edges and golden-yellow toward the middle. Paired with his dark, thick lashes, he had really pretty eyes, not that he would appreciate hearing that. His nose was just a bit broader than Brog's, too. And he had a thin scar running along the underside of his eyebrow. Almost unnoticeable…unless staring tiredly at the man.

I blinked and lightly rested my fingers on Adam's shoulder so I would feel him if he moved.

"Thank you for this, Tor. I'll sleep better knowing you're watching over both of us."

"Sleep, June. You are safe."

I looked at Adam one last time and closed my eyes.

The soft murmur of voices woke me sometime later. I lifted my head and looked at Adam. The hope that he'd woken withered when I saw his washcloth-covered eyes. Gently touching his cheek, I eased from the bed and followed the sound to the kitchen where Tor was at the door with the woman he'd carried to Tenacity a few days ago.

"Hi, June," she said with a sympathetic smile. "Tor was just saying you were resting. I'm sorry I woke you."

"It's okay. Can I help you?"

"I'm Emily. I live over in Tolerance. Mya, the unwilling leader of the human half of Tolerance, heard what happened to you and your boyfriend. She wants you to know you're both welcome in Tolerance once Adam is able to travel."

"That's great. Thank you," I said, trying to sound grateful. I knew Adam would be happy about the news. I just wished it would have happened a day sooner.

"You look like you could use a shower and maybe a little distraction. Why don't you let Tor keep an eye on Adam and go take care of yourself for a bit while I make you something to eat?"

I stared at her for a moment then glanced at Tor. What did it say about me that an offer of help from one of my own kind felt wrong?

"Sure. That sounds good," I forced myself to say.

Tor followed me to the master bedroom and sat with Adam while I grabbed a change of clothes and closed myself in the bathroom. I looked like hell. The dark circles under my eyes showed just how little sleep I'd had. The hot water helped revive me a bit as did the scent of the shampoo. It was sweet and reminded me of summer and better times.

Dressed in comfortable sweatpants, a sports bra, and a long-sleeved shirt, I left the bathroom.

"Did he wake up while I was sleeping?" I asked softly.

"He said he was thirsty once. I made the ice chips like you said. He ate a few and fell asleep again."

"That's good. Why didn't you wake me?"

He glanced at Adam. "Would he have woken you?"

I smiled slightly. "No, he would not. He would have wanted me to sleep."

"I felt the same," Tor said.

I reached out and gave his shoulder a light squeeze.

"Thank you."

He nodded, and I left the room to see what Emily was cooking that smelled so good.

"I smuggled in a box of cake mix," she said when she saw me. "Complete with frosting." She gestured for me to sit as she scooped something non-cake-like into a bowl.

"We found a stash of holiday candy when we were out there," I said. "We left it in the supply shed for someone else to fight over and opted for more practical items."

"That's smart. But sometimes cake is necessary."

I couldn't have agreed more.

She joined me at the kitchen island and slid a bowl of beef stew my way. I recognized it from the box that Tor had brought over.

"It's not exactly breakfast food, but food is food, right?" she said, noting my hesitation.

"I'm grateful Tor thought to bring it," I said. "It was really sweet for both of you to think of us."

"You seem surprisingly comfortable around Tor and the other fey. They terrified me the first time I saw them. While that wore off quickly, I was still pretty wary for the first few weeks."

"They're a lot nicer than the people here. Do you know you were the first one to welcome us? Matt showed us around, but there was no welcoming vibe. To be fair, Adam had to be carried here because of his concussion." I sighed deeply and played with the stew. "I guess there wasn't much of an opening for friendly introductions."

"Don't think you need to excuse them for my benefit. I had to live with these people on two occasions, and neither was pleasant."

"Fear and desperation are a toxic combination. Adam and I learned that early on from the people over the radio. They felt like family. People to talk to when we were otherwise cut-off from the world. Then they started going quiet, one by one. We learned that there were people using that feeling of community to learn the locations of those of us hidden away. They were killing our radio friends for supplies."

"And then you came here. Your supplies were taken. And Adam was beaten." She reached out and covered my hand with hers. "It shouldn't have happened that way. It should have been your choice to share what you had. It should have been your choice which community to live in."

"Why didn't we have those choices?" I wasn't angry with her but trying to learn the rules like Adam said.

"Because the humans here fling their hate at the fey while expecting them to risk everything to keep them safe. I know the fey look like they're big and strong and indestructible, and in a lot of ways they are. But, they also have a fatal weakness that the people here used relentlessly. The fey just want to belong. They want families of their own, but they're all men. They lived without sunlight for thousands of years. When they first came above ground, it hurt to go out during the day. It still does, but they ignore it. Do you know why? They're desperate to do more than exist. They want to be a part of something bigger. Our world, as crappy as it is, is better than what they had. Endless darkness and countless deaths and rebirths. Can you imagine? Dying again and again and coming back with all those memories. All they've known is pain."

Emily released my hand and shook herself.

"Sorry. I've made it my personal mission to find ways to integrate them into our lives. As you can tell, I'm passionate about it. They do so much for us and ask for so little in return. Anyway, my point was that we don't allow people to choose where they want to live because most will take advantage of the fey."

I glanced at the stairs, thinking of Tor and Brog, the fey who'd stayed with me before Tor.

"I don't want to take advantage of their generosity."

"Oh, you're not. Trust me. Tor told me all about the friendship Adam extended within minutes of meeting him. It made his day. The other fey in your group, too. Like I said, most of us have a freak out period."

"Adam and I saw the fey come into the barn before the infected attacked. There were two of them. One lifted a cow like it was no big deal. The other took a barn cat. They were scary-different, but the animals were fine with them.

"When they came back and cleared out the barn, protecting Ryan and following his lead, I figured they couldn't be the killers Adam and I heard about. I understand that they were, but they aren't anymore. Matt explained why the fey had that reputation. Fear is a powerful thing. I wonder what the fey's welcome would have been like if that first shot hadn't been fired."

"I'd like to think it would have been better; but in reality, someone always fires the first shot. We are a people who shun uniqueness and seem to crave conflict on any level, even to the point that we argue about conflict itself. I understand why. We're driven to stand up for our beliefs, whatever they may be."

What she was saying resonated deeply with me. Adam's beating had been retaliation for the trap, which had been due to the initial robbery.

"You look too young to have a degree in psychology."

Emily grinned.

"I pay attention to people. Most everyone is too busy focusing on their own lives and their own beliefs to put them aside long enough to look around and see things objectively. Losing my sister kind of slapped me out of my own headspace, I think. I started questioning things. A lot of whys, you know?"

"Yeah. I do know."

A knock on the door interrupted our conversation. The

redhead and the scowling fey from last night, Kerr, were on the step when I answered.

"I came by to check on the patient," she said. "May we come in?"

"Of course."

She said hello to Emily and asked about someone named Hannah while I took her jacket from her and hung it in the entry. The way they spoke to each other showed not only a level of familiarity but caring. Adam and I had absolutely been stuck on the wrong team.

Emily stayed in the kitchen, and the pair followed me upstairs to the bedroom.

"Hello, Cassie," Tor said, standing.

"Hi, Tor. Has he woken up yet?" she asked both of us.

"Once overnight," I answered, "and once while Tor was watching him this morning. Both times, he was thirsty. We gave him ice chips."

"Good," she said.

She moved closer to Adam and checked where we had the latest round of snow bags.

"Have you been keeping them on all night?" she asked.

"Yeah. Changing spots so nothing gets too cold. The washcloth I've kept on his eye more often, trying to get that swelling down."

"I'd say it's working," she said, lifting it. "The lid looks much better."

I wasn't seeing what she was. It still looked too puffy to open.

"Adam," she called. "It's Cassie. I'm here to look over your injuries. If anything hurts, I need you to tell me, okay?"

He didn't respond, but that didn't stop her from pulling

back the covers to his hips and gently feeling along his ribs and abdomen. When she touched his left side, he groaned.

"Adam," she repeated, "my name is Cassie. Can you tell me where you hurt?"

"Everywhere," he rasped.

"Focus on your abdomen. Does anything hurt inside?"

"Ribs," he breathed. This time, he tried to open his eyes.

Cassie leaned over so she would look right into them.

"Hi, Adam. How's the vision?"

"Shitty."

She chuckled. "I bet. It looks like you took a few hits to the face. The swelling is already going down."

"June?" he said, turning his head.

"June's right here," Cassie said. "She's fine. I'd like to stay focused on you. How does your neck feel? Did anything hurt when you moved it?"

"No."

"That's very good," she said, placing a hand on his shoulder. "I know everything is sore, but I'd like to look at your back. Do you think you can sit up with some help?" She motioned to Kerr, who immediately stepped forward.

Chewing my bottom lip, I watched the pair work with Adam. Cassie repeated several times that Adam needed to listen to the pain. That if anything hurt, he needed to stop. She managed to check over his back and wedged more pillows behind him.

"It's good to change positions. The elevation will help with the facial swelling. Keep going with the snow bags. Hopefully, it won't all melt in the next few days."

Adam, who'd been leaning back after all the movement,

opened his eyes again. His gaze swung around the room and landed on me.

"Babe. Thank God they didn't hurt you, too."

I went to his side, trying not to tear up, and gently kissed his cheek.

"They didn't. I'm fine. You'll be fine, too."

"How long was I out?" His eyes started to close, and I could see his determination to keep them open when they rolled a little before widening.

"Twelve hours maybe? I'm not sure what time they came."

"We can't stay here."

I gently took his hand, trying to soothe the notes of fear and worry I heard in his words. I knew Adam well enough to understand those emotions weren't for himself but for me.

"We're fine, Adam. I promise. Tor is staying with us."

I glanced back at Tor and waved him forward.

"Adam, I brought the flame chips for you," Tor said, leaning over my shoulder. "But Cassie says you have to eat the oatmeal first. I'm sorry."

The complete gravity of his words had Adam laughing and groaning.

"Thanks for having my back, Tor. Keep June safe for me, until I can do it myself, okay?"

"I will."

Adam's eyes rolled again. This time, they closed and didn't reopen.

"It looks like it's time for more rest," Cassie said. "Listen to your body, Adam. That's the best advice I can give you right now."

She looked at me. "Now that he's propped up, try to get

him to drink something next time he's alert. There are no IVs for us to use if he gets dehydrated."

I nodded, not letting go of Adam's hand.

Everyone left the room, and the house quieted. I continued to stroke his skin, my touch light. This wasn't the first injury I'd helped him through, but it was by far the most serious. There'd been twisted ankles and pulled muscles and strained ligaments, all of which had required rest and eventually physical therapy. Adam would know what he had to do once he was more himself. Until then, I needed to focus on what I could do to make him more comfortable. I moved his snow bags, changed out his washcloth for a colder one, and waited.

Eventually, I remembered Emily and got up to check on her. The cake was on the stovetop, cooling, with the canister of frosting beside it. Tor was sitting on the couch, watching a movie at a low volume.

"Did Emily leave?" I asked.

"Yes. She said she will come back tomorrow."

"Okay." I set my hand on the cake, which was still far too warm, and looked around the room.

"It's weird not having anything to do," I said. "At the farm, there were chores. The cattle to feed. Equipment to check. Monitors to watch. What does everyone do here to stay busy?"

"Here?"

I nodded.

"Most do nothing."

"That's probably part of the problem," I said.

He grunted, and I moved to join him on the couch.

"Do you want me to watch Adam?" he asked.

I gave him a small smile for that thoughtful offer.

"I think we wore him out with all the talking and moving.

He'll probably be out for a while longer. What are we watching?" I gestured at the TV.

"I don't know." He handed me the movie case, and I grinned.

"I wouldn't have pictured you as a mermaid fan, but I approve."

For the next hour, the classic film entertained us. It'd been years since I'd last watched it and could say I still loved it just as much.

"Did you eat any of the stew that Emily made?" I asked.

"No."

"Okay. I'll peek in on Adam then see if I can make us something for lunch."

Adam was the same as when I'd left him, but the snow bags had melted to warm water. I changed them out and checked his eyes. As soon as I lifted the cloth, he tiredly looked at me.

"I have to pee."

"Okay. Let me get Tor to help you."

His eyes shifted from me to the bathroom door.

"I could get a bottle or something if you're not up for it."

"Have Tor bring a bottle."

I nodded and crashed into Tor outside the bedroom. Thankfully, he caught me to prevent me from bouncing my face off his abs.

"Sorry," I mumbled, stepping back. "He has to go to the bathroom but hurts too much to get up. I'll find him something to pee in. He doesn't want me to help though. Would you mind?"

"I'll help."

I hurried to the kitchen and found two large, reusable water bottles in the cupboard. One I kept empty, the other I filled.

When I handed the empty one over to Tor, I also asked him to watch for blood in the urine.

"It can happen with hard hits to the kidneys."

He grunted, promised to make sure Adam drank, and went upstairs.

Distracting myself, I went to the TV and dug through the supplies Adam had hidden in the cabinet. By the time Tor returned, I had beans soaking for tomorrow and spaghetti boiling on the stove.

"His urine did not smell like blood." He announced before giving me a troubled look. "He did not like me smelling it."

I laughed. A real one because I could imagine Adam's face.

"I imagine not. It was for his own good, though. Is your sense of smell that enhanced? Could you have actually smelled blood?"

"Yes."

"That's impressive." I drained the noodles and poured the tomato sauce over them before excusing myself to check on Adam.

His eyes opened when he heard me entering the room.

"I heard you laugh," he said, a slight tip to the corner of his puffy lip.

"Bet you wish it would have been me pouring out your pee," I said, coming closer to fuss over his washcloth. Adam caught my hand and held it in his own. I didn't miss the wince in his expression.

"Are you doing things you shouldn't be doing?" I asked.

"Probably. I just needed to touch you. I'm sorry, June. Those men coming in here…that's on me."

"No. It's on them. But they're not our problem anymore. Once you're better, we're going to Tolerance."

"The fey place?"

"Yep."

I could tell by the way he slightly shifted under the covers that he was testing to see how much he hurt.

"You're not better yet. So don't even try to tell me you are. Brog, one of the fey, stayed with me last night, and I think Tor's going to stay until someone else comes to give him a break. There's no rush. We're safe."

Adam sighed heavily.

"I'd never forgive myself if something happened to you, June."

"I'm alive because of you, Adam. Countless times over. Please stop being so hard on yourself."

"That would be like me asking you not to worry about me right now." His grin turned into a wince.

"Are you hungry?" I asked instead of acknowledging he was right.

"A little. My jaw's sore."

"Oatmeal, coming right up."

Downstairs, I plated up our spaghetti and ate with Tor, giving Adam's oatmeal plenty of time to soften. When it was ready, I handed it to Tor.

"He won't want me to see how much eating that hurts him. Try to get him to eat it all."

"I will."

CHAPTER SIX

The bed moved. I lifted my head to look at Adam. He was still propped up, but based on the expression he wore, the pain relievers had worn off.

Beyond him, Tor slept in the chair. The way his chin rested on his chest was going to give him a neck ache. I smiled slightly to myself. Both of them needed a little fussing, and I imagined they'd react about the same to it.

Although I tried to ease from the bed without making a sound, Tor immediately lifted his head and looked at me.

"He needs another pain reliever. I'll be right back."

He grunted and focused on Adam.

Downstairs, Brog watched a movie, a cartoon, with no volume. I'd tried telling Tor he could go home to rest when Brog had shown up, but he asked to stay. After Emily's comment about his excitement over Adam's friendship, I'd agreed—on the condition he at least sleep while Brog watched over us all.

"Hey, Brog," I said softly. "Are you hungry? Do you need anything?"

"I'm fine, June. Do you need help?"

"No. Just getting more medicine for Adam."

He watched me fill a cold glass of water from the tap and shake out a pill that Cassie had left for us.

"Thank you for staying," I said before heading back upstairs.

Tor stood near one of the windows, peeking around the curtain when I entered. He immediately moved away from the window and focused on what I was doing.

"Adam, I think you need another pain reliever," I said, touching his shoulder.

"Yeah," he rasped, working to open his eyes. They opened a bit wider than they had for lunch.

"Bathroom too," he added.

"Bottle?" I handed him the glass and the pill and watched him take it.

"No. I want to try to move around. Would you mind going downstairs for a bit?"

"Nope. Not this time. I'm going to fluff your pillows and straighten the bed while you're gone. Plus, I plan to stare at your ass."

He made a sound that started out a snort and ended with a grunt.

"Careful. You're starting to sound like Tor."

Tor flashed his teeth at me, and I returned his smile this time.

"Would you like me to carry you, Adam? You can stand in the bathroom with the door closed."

"And deprive June of her peep-show? I wouldn't dream of it."

"He's just saying that because he'd feel weird if you carried him while he's naked," I said with a smirk.

"More pillow fluffing and less talking," Adam said before easing himself forward.

I watched his face closely. He noticed.

"It hurts, but it doesn't hurt more. I'm fine, June."

This time, I snorted.

He eased himself to the edge of the bed. However, when he tried to put pressure on his leg, he immediately sat back down.

"I'll need some shorts."

I hurried to get him a loose pair and knelt down so he wouldn't need to move more than necessary. As soon as his shorts were to his knees, he managed to shift his weight and pull them up. He was sweaty and shaking by the time he was done.

"What do you think, Tor?" Adam said. "Time for a ride?"

Tor answered by slowly sliding an arm under Adam's legs.

"Lean into me. Tell me when you're ready."

Each move they made was slow and careful and broke my heart. Adam's back had dark bruised patches all over. His arms weren't as bad. His thighs looked like they'd taken the brunt of it. I could see why he wouldn't have wanted to be carried, and it worried me that he'd changed his mind in the end.

I did my best not to hover and to keep all of what I was feeling from showing in my expression. As soon as they were in the bathroom, I started fixing the bed. Tor, the sweetheart, closed the door for Adam but stayed in there. I could hear the low murmur of voices and a burst of laughter that could have only been Tor due to its force.

Once I had the bed remade, I grabbed an extra blanket and

pillow for Tor. He wasn't using a reclining chair but, hopefully, both items would make him more comfortable.

The door opened, and Tor leaned against it, glancing out at me. I took that as an invitation to peek around the corner. Adam stood, leaning against the counter, carefully brushing his teeth.

"Are they all staying in?" I asked.

He carefully spit.

"So far. Lots of pink, though."

I didn't doubt it based on the bruise decorating his jaw.

He didn't take long, and I could see how much he hurt as he used Tor's arm to help him hobble back to the bed.

"I can't decide which hurt more," he panted. "Carrying or this."

As soon as he reached his side of the bed, he leaned forward into it, slowly collapsing and rolling into place with Tor's help.

"I need better meds," he said, the strain plain on his face. "Right now, I'm wishing I was dead."

For him to say something like that conveyed just how badly he hurt.

Worrying my bottom lip, I went downstairs and dug out a paper and something to write with.

"Brog, are you safe when you travel between the two towns at night?"

"Yes."

"Could you take this to Cassie? The pain relievers aren't enough. He needs something a little stronger. He won't be able to sleep without it."

Brog took the paper. Once he was gone, I asked Tor for more snow and packed the bags around Adam's knee.

"This is why I didn't want you to watch," he said, without anger.

"Ignorance isn't bliss. It's just more to worry about."

He caught my hand and brought it to his lips.

"I love you, June."

"I love you, too. Now where else do you need snow?"

By the time I had him iced up, Brog returned with a bottle, which he brought upstairs.

"Cassie said one now and one at first light. She will bring more."

"Thank you, Brog." I gave his arm a squeeze and shook out the first pill for Adam while Brog retreated downstairs once more.

"What are they?" Adam asked.

"Oxy."

"Dose?"

I told him.

"Two now, babe," he said.

I didn't argue.

He sighed the moment they kicked in and relaxed into the pillows. Tor stood by the bed, watching both him and me. I waited until Adam's breathing evened out.

"He's hurt more than he wants me to know," I said softly. "He hates those pills."

I continued to watch Adam, dreading what it meant that he'd wanted two.

"Thank you for the blanket and pillow."

Embracing the distraction, I sat on my side of the bed and turned toward Tor with Adam between us.

"You didn't look very comfortable when I woke up."

Tor shrugged and sat down.

"Emily said that you were in those caves for a long time. That you had many lives. Like reincarnation?"

"I have been reborn many times the same as I am now, but no hair and no injuries or scars."

"And all your memories?" I asked, thinking of what Emily had said.

"Yes."

He didn't look upset by it, but I could only imagine the trauma involved in dying. It wouldn't be something I would want to remember. If I would have known Tor better, I would have offered him a hug. Instead I gave him an understanding look and kept talking to him.

"What happened to your women?"

"We never had any. Not as we are. And we don't remember the ones from before the caves."

"Have you met any nice ones since coming up here?"

"Many."

I smiled. "Anyone special who interests you?"

"All the nice ones are already taken. But I still have hope. We all do. Rest, June. Adam will need you again in a few hours."

"Sleep sweet, Tor." I settled on my side and lightly rested my hand on Adam's shoulder so I would feel when he woke up.

A bit before dawn, Adam proved Tor's prediction correct. However, it wasn't with restless twitches. The soft rumble of conversation wormed its way into my awareness.

"She stopped me in my tracks the first time I saw her. She didn't want to give me the time of day. I can't imagine my life without June."

"Then why doesn't she wear your ring?"

I kept my eyes closed, fully awake now.

"It's complicated. I know she wants to." Adam sighed. "Have you ever heard of sports?"

"My brothers and I battled to the death in the caves. We can't do that here. Removing heads brings true death."

"Wait, you beheaded each other? For fun?"

"Sometimes."

"Well, sports up here test a person's athleticism without death. But they're extremely competitive. And addictive. If I'm honest with myself, I think football was my first love, and June was my second. It didn't feel fair to ask her to marry me when she wasn't my top priority, you know?"

"No. You are stupid. You should give her a ring."

It took everything I had to keep a straight face. Tor was completely right. Adam was being stupid. He put me first in so many ways. I never begrudged him his love of football. His passion was part of what attracted me.

"I know. I should have."

"I will find you one."

Adam chuckled.

"Thanks, Tor. But I think that ship has sailed."

"There are no ships."

"You're killing me, Tor."

"I am not touching you. Should I wake June? She will know how to save you."

Adam stopped laughing, and I felt him gently touch my hair.

"She already did save me."

"Does she show you her pussy?"

"Whoa. Man, we're friends but there are some things friends don't share."

"What do you mean? My brothers share what they learn about their females. How else will I become smart enough to win one of my own?"

"I guess you have a point. June doesn't show me anything. That sounds like porn. She's too high class for that."

"Eden says that porn rotted part of Ghua's brain. But she still lets him lick her pussy until she squeals. He likes the sounds she makes."

"I hear that."

"Yes. I just said it."

Adam chuckled again. "You're very literal."

"Emily tells me that, too. How can I win a female like June? She is nice and pretty and high class. She gave me a blanket and a pillow. You are a fool to not give her a ring."

"That I am, friend."

I could hear the weariness and pain creeping into Adam's tone and took a deep breath.

"We should stop talking about pussies," Tor said quietly. "Females do not like it."

"No, they do not," Adam agreed.

This time, I did grin slightly.

"It sounds like I should go downstairs and check on Brog," I said, lifting my head. "Let me know when the locker room talk is done." I leaned forward and lightly kissed Adam's cheek. "Do you want me to bring anything back for you?"

"Something light to eat and more Oxy if you can find some."

I nodded and shuffled out of the room. Downstairs, Brog crouched in front of the TV cabinet, looking at the food within.

"Are you hungry?" I asked softly. "I can make you something."

He stood smoothly and shook his head.

"I am not hungry. I was checking what supplies you needed."

"That's so sweet of you, Brog."

"Brog is not sweet," Tor called from upstairs. "Adam is."

I grinned and quietly promised Brog he was sweet, too. He grunted and glanced upstairs.

"I will go to Cassie and tell her Adam is awake and in pain."

"Let's let her sleep for a while longer. We already interrupted her sleep once tonight. What do you all do when you're hurt and in pain?"

"We heal. After we left the caves, a hellhound attacked Ghua. It took him many days to recover, and he was in much pain. Eden eased his suffering by letting him lick her pussy."

"I'm starting to see a theme here."

Brog looked around the room.

"I see no theme."

Amused, I shook my head and went to the kitchen for a glass of water. The fey were very literal. And significantly clueless about a lot of things. I was starting to understand how it would be easy for the people here to take advantage of them.

I refilled the glass for Adam and returned upstairs where Adam lay in bed with the covers pulled back. Water ran in the bathroom, giving away where Tor had gone.

"How you feeling?"

"Hurting," he said honestly.

Tor emerged from the bathroom. He set the empty water bottle on the floor beside the bed and gave Adam a hard look.

"I will speak to Brog." Tor glanced at me then left the room.

"What's going on?"

Adam gave me a tired smile and patted the spot beside him.

"Tor's upset that Brog mentioned Ghua's pussy-licking addiction in front of you."

Grinning, I curled up next to Adam, careful not to bump anything.

"They're very open, aren't they?"

"They are. Tor's great, though. It makes me feel better that he's here looking after you."

"He's looking after you, too, Adam."

He closed his eyes, not commenting. Why did men have such a hard time accepting help?

"I think it'll be better when we're in Tolerance," I said. "We'll be closer to Cassie and medicine."

"And what happens when the pills run out?" he asked.

"Hopefully, you won't need them any more by then."

"Yeah. Hopefully." He carefully lifted his arm and feathered his fingers across my cheek. "Go to sleep, June. You look like you haven't slept at all."

"I've had as much as you've had. I'm fine."

He watched me for a long moment.

"I love you, June."

"I know you do." I closed my eyes, grinning a little. "Maybe you should listen to Tor and put a ring on it."

He made an amused sound. "Sorry for the locker room talk."

"Don't worry about it. They're as clueless about us as we are about them. How else are we going to learn about each other if not by asking questions?"

"You're too smart for me."

Tor returned and sat in the chair.

"Brog will go for more medicine. He will ask Kerr so Cassie sleeps."

"Thanks, man" Adam said. "You're a good friend."

I peeked to see Tor's expression and caught his wide, toothy grin. Friendship meant a lot to them. And vaginas, apparently. The thought was more amusing than disturbing and kept me quietly entertained while I lay beside Adam.

They didn't start up another conversation. I wasn't sure if it was due to Adam's pain or the fact that they both suspected I was still awake. Either way, the quiet, long wait stretched my patience until I gave up and quietly left the room to wait downstairs for Brog's return.

While I waited, I made a big batch of pancakes. The familiar smell eased some of the tension I'd carried since leaving the bunker. It felt good to do something so normal. When I had two impressive stacks of cakes, I turned off the burner and plated a serving each for Adam and Tor.

Both looked up at me when I walked into the room.

"Breakfast is served, gentlemen," I said, offering them their plates.

"Thank you, June," Tor said, accepting his. "I will savor each bite."

Adam snorted. "Like you need girl help, Tor. You already have flattery down."

"That was not idle praise. It is an honor and privilege to eat what June spent time preparing for me." He met my gaze and gave me a grave nod.

"You need to get laid," Adam said under his breath.

Tor paused with his fork halfway to his mouth.

"I'm leaving the room for the explanation that turn of phrase is going to need," I said, smothering a grin.

The low murmur of Adam's voice followed me down the stairs. Adam wasn't the type to talk details, but I couldn't help but wonder what level that explanation would end up going to, considering the fey's curiosity.

I'd just finished my own breakfast when Tor came downstairs with their empty plates.

"Do either of you want more?" I asked, standing. "There's plenty left. I wasn't sure how many to make."

"Adam is full." He glanced at the stack of pancakes, and I could read his reluctance.

"It's okay if you don't want any. Brog probably hasn't eaten yet, either."

Tor's expression turned to a scowl. He took the whole plate and sat down at the counter with me. The hurried enthusiasm in which he devoured the food stunned me.

"Do you like pancakes?"

"I like the food you make."

I smiled slightly.

"That's an evasive answer to a yes or no question."

He swallowed and flashed his teeth at me.

"You are smart like Adam said."

"And you're still avoiding. Did you eat those pancakes so Brog wouldn't?"

The ends of Tor's ears turned a deep grey.

"Yes."

I leaned in, taking his plate, and kissed his cheek.

"You're a good friend to Adam, Tor. Thank you."

He stayed at the island and watched me wash the dishes. The intensity of his gaze had me wondering if I'd crossed some sort of boundary. He didn't seem mad, though.

"I'm going to go check on Adam," I said when I finished.

Tor grunted and stayed behind as I made my way upstairs.

Adam wasn't sleeping when I walked into the room. But he wasn't really with it either.

"Want more snow bags?"

"Please."

"I'll ask Tor to get some."

"Thanks, babe."

"I will get the snow," Tor called from downstairs. "Stay with your Adam."

Adam grunted a laugh.

"He's really hung up on guys calling dibs on girls," he said.

"No kidding. He ate the rest of the pancakes so Brog couldn't eat any. You should have seen Tor's face when I kissed his cheek to thank him for being so helpful."

Adam focused on me.

"You probably made his life. I would have died and gone to heaven if you'd kissed me after three days."

"It would have inflated your ego. That was the last thing you needed back then."

The smile he gave me was short-lived.

"I want to move today."

"What? No. You can't even walk to the bathroom, Adam."

He looked away from me for a minute.

"That's exactly why I want to move. We're trapped here just like we were trapped in the bunker. But you don't need to be. There are good people out there, June. People you can count on. Fey like Tor, who will keep you safe when the next batch of infected or a hellhound shows up. The people here have already shown us what they'll do to ensure they survive."

"They have," I agreed. "And we will move. But it doesn't need to be today or tomorrow or even this month. Give yourself time to heal."

He gave me a considering look but didn't argue further. He didn't fool me. He likely planned to work on Tor or maybe Cassie next. With Tor, Adam would play up my safety. Heck, he'd probably use the same angle on both of them.

"It's not going to work," I said. "My safety isn't more important than yours."

"We'll need to disagree on that."

"Why? Why do you think I'm so much more important than you?"

He shrugged and winced.

Tor came in before I could press him for an answer.

"Thank you." I started filling bags and placing them around Adam's leg. Tor worked with me. Adam exhaled deeply when we'd placed the last one.

"Try to rest," I said, grabbing Tor's hand and pulling him from the room.

"Should I stay with Adam to—"

"Nope. You can help me."

I waited until we were downstairs before rounding on him.

"Adam's hurt bad. You know that, right?"

"Yes."

"He can barely move. Watch him when he breathes, he's avoiding inhaling too deeply, which could lead to pneumonia. That's why he didn't want you to carry him to the bathroom this morning. Every time he uses the bottle instead of the bathroom, he's telling you without words that moving him would cause immeasurable pain."

With each word I said, Tor's frown grew.

"I don't want to hurt Adam."

"I know you don't. That's why I'm telling you this. Adam's so worried about my safety that he's going to try to convince you to move him to Tolerance before it's safe. We need to protect him from himself. Okay?"

Tor nodded. I smiled and leaned in to give him a quick hug. He twitched the moment my arms wrapped around his waist, which only drove me to give him the hug he deserved. Resting my head against his torso, I gave him a squeeze.

His large hand tentatively patted my back, and I laughed.

"It's a hug, Tor, not an attack."

"You like touching."

"I guess I do. It's another way to show appreciation and affection. Sometimes, even annoyance."

He grunted and gently wrapped his arms around me.

"This is appreciation and affection," he said. "I'm not annoyed with you."

I chuckled.

"I'm not annoyed with you, either. Want to pick out our movie selection for today?"

CHAPTER SEVEN

"It's time, June," Adam said when I walked into the bedroom with his breakfast two days later.

"Time for what?" I asked, feigning ignorance.

Thanks to Cassie and Tor's support, we'd managed to keep Adam in bed where he belonged. That didn't mean he'd stopped pestering me about moving to Tolerance.

I made myself comfortable on the bed beside him and handed him his plate.

"FYI, Tor is not a fan of mushrooms. But he swallowed them down like a champ because they were in the meal I cooked."

Adam glanced at his scrambled eggs and sighed.

"Distracting me with a topic change isn't going to work. Did Tor tell you that I walked to the bathroom this morning?"

"He did. He also said it looked very painful."

"Of course it's painful. It's going to be painful for weeks if not months. That's why it's time. When I almost collapsed and Tor caught me, it didn't hurt more than my damn leg. He can carry me now."

"Why are you so stuck on this?" I asked without rancor.

"Tor and Brog are here day and night. No one has tried anything. We're fine."

"Brog told me someone spit on him on his way in last night. One of the guards on the wall. Do you know what Brog did? He apologized to the woman and offered her a bag of chips. We're not being fair to Tor and Brog, June. It's time to go. I'll be fine."

Guilt hit me hard. Brog was so quiet and sweet. That anyone would want to spit at him angered me.

"Fine. I'll talk to Tor."

Adam gave me a tight, sad smile and picked up his fork as I left the room. Downstairs, both Tor and Brog warily watched my approach.

"Why didn't you tell me that people were being rude?"

"They are always rude, June," Tor said.

He was right. I'd seen and heard enough since coming here to understand the spitting last night wasn't a one-time only or new incident. It'd been happening since long before the fey helped create this town for these people. And the people here didn't like that two fey were staying in their no-fey-allowed town.

"Is Adam right?" I asked. "Is it time to move him? He has maybe three more days of Oxy left before he runs out. Maybe it is better to move him while he still has something to help with the pain for a few days afterward. What do you think?"

Tor considered me for a long moment.

"He will rest more comfortably when he knows you are truly safe."

"Will there be a place for us to stay?"

"You will live with me. Mya approved it."

"All right then. I'll pack up. You two should see if there's a way to carry him so his leg isn't jostled."

It took a bit of time and some consulting with Matt to come up with a stretcher for Adam. Adam didn't care how he was carried. He just wanted to get to Tolerance as soon as possible. However, he adamantly voiced his dislike that I was being left behind with the supplies while Tor and Brog transported him first.

"I'll be fine. The supplies and I will be with Matt."

"Yeah, he did a great job protecting you the first time. You were held down against your will and gagged to keep you silent while they forced you to listen to my beating." His gaze shifted to Tor. "Does that sound like protection to you?"

Tor's gaze swung to Matt. After the last few days we'd spent together, I knew him well enough to see the new tension in his shoulders.

"Adam, that's the medicine talking. Tor, I'm not the least bit worried. The people here are cowards. They're afraid of the infected, and they're afraid of the fey. They would never dream of doing anything in daylight that would result in being kicked out of here. Or worse, give the fey a real reason to come after them. Trust me. Please."

"I do trust you. I don't trust the people here." His gaze stayed locked with Matt's in heavy implication.

"Give me a chance to start earning your trust back," Matt said. "I'll keep her safe until you return."

Tor grunted and bent to pick up the stretcher from the bed.

"We will return soon."

I followed them from the room and watched how they carefully maneuvered the stretcher down the stairs. Matt saw my concern as I shut the front door behind them.

"Cassie will be waiting on the other side. She'll make sure he's comfortable." He exhaled heavily, and I could see the weary set to his shoulders. "I truly am sorry for what happened to you both. If there's anything you can do to help convince the fey of that, you need to try. The relationship between our two communities is rocky enough."

I moved to the island and sat on one of the stools.

"What I say isn't going to matter much, Matt. There's a bigger problem here. You're trying to save people, but some people don't want to be saved. They just want to hate until everyone is as angry and as hateful as they are. If you really want the communities to survive and mend the relationship between the two, everyone here needs to focus on the real enemy. The infected and the hellhounds, not the fey."

"Mya and I are trying to make that happen. Pushing these people to fend for themselves isn't doing any good. They're only growing more resentful of the abundance over in Tolerance. Emily's coming up with some great ideas to create small bridges between the two communities but is struggling to get people to participate. Like you said, there's a lot of hate."

"Then you need to weed out the haters before they destroy more than Adam's leg."

"And how do you propose to do that? We'd lose more than half our people if I kicked out everyone here with a fey-grudge."

"I'm not saying you kick out everyone. We both know that half the people here don't truly hate the fey. They're afraid of them. And some have biases because of the fey's past actions. Fear and bias can be overcome. But the people who hate solely for the sake of hating? They need to go, Matt. And you're smart enough to know who they are."

He gave a harsh laugh.

"I have hundreds of people here and am happy when I can

remember all their names. On top of that, I need to show the fey that same respect. That's a lot of people to know.

"I know you're angry and want to hold someone responsible for what happened, but it's not me, June. I'm doing my best to lead because no one else wanted the position. If you think you can do better, say the word, and Tenacity with all of its hate and problems is yours to fix however you see fit."

He ran a frustrated hand through his hair.

"When I took over, we still had some military left. Most of those men and women died defending the fences during the last Whiteman breach. The few who didn't die helped build this place, exhausting themselves during countless guard rotations no one else wanted. Meanwhile, the majority of people here don't lift a finger to help themselves. If I push, they'd push back twice as hard. I warned Adam not to push. I barely have any control here. What do you think will happen if I try sussing out the bad apples?"

I sighed and nodded. "Anarchy and chaos would ensue."

"Exactly."

He sat beside me, and I let the silence grow as I considered his situation. I wouldn't want to be in charge of this place and did give him credit for trying. It was unreasonable to expect that he knew everyone. But I had a feeling he also knew more than he was letting on. More than likely, he could name at least one troublemaker. Removing one without visible cause, though, would likely incite more anger from the rest. This place needed a clean sweep, and it needed to be done on a subtle level.

"You're right. It's not fair to expect one person to have all the answers and make all the decisions. I'll talk to Tor and try to get him to see it's not your fault."

"Thank you."

We sat in silence until the door opened a while later. Tor strode in first, his gaze sweeping the space until landing on me. I could see the relief in his eyes and smiled reassuringly as I stood and put on my boots and jacket.

"Is Adam all right?" I asked.

"Adam is fine. We were very careful."

Tor motioned Brog to the box of supplies and came to me.

"May I carry you, June?"

"Always," I said.

A startled squeak ripped from me when he picked me up faster than I could blink.

"I hope things go better for you, June," Matt said. "You're welcome back here any time."

I nodded and looped my arm around Tor's neck as he started for the door.

This wasn't my first fey ride, but it was by far the longest. My hands got cold before Tor cleared the wall, and I tucked them into his jacket along with my face.

"We are almost there, June. You will be warm soon," Tor said.

"It's okay," I mumbled into his chest. The guy was a complete furnace. Tucked in like this, most of me was fine. The exception was my butt and the backs of my thighs.

My stomach dipped a few minutes later when he cleared another wall and landed with a soft bounce. He slowed to a walk but didn't put me down. I lifted my head to see why.

A street lined with houses lay before us, and a few fey walked along the sidewalks. Somewhere nearby, kids squealed and laughed. There was distant mooing, too.

The immediate difference between Tolerance and Tenacity

was evident in seconds. This place was peaceful and relaxed. So I wasn't quite sure why Tor was still carrying me.

I glanced up at him. His gaze shifted around the area, scanning just like he would have been doing if we were outside the wall.

"Is it safe in here?"

He glanced down at me, putting our faces uncomfortably close together.

"Yes."

"You can put me down then."

He frowned slightly, and I could see it in his eyes that he was going to refuse.

"Please."

He grunted, and I found myself on my feet. Smiling, I tried to rub some feeling back into my butt. It didn't work.

"Which house is yours?" I asked.

He led the way, setting a moderate pace that I could comfortably keep up with. A few fey stopped to stare at me as we passed. I said a friendly hello to each one, which Tor immediately followed up with, "She belongs to the human, Adam."

"They aren't hitting on me, Tor. I'm a new face, and they're just curious."

He glanced at me, surprise lighting his features.

"None of my brothers would ever hit you."

"To hit on someone doesn't mean actually hitting. It's a phrase that means a person is flirting with another person in an attempt to establish a romantic relationship."

Tor grunted.

"Then they might hit on you. You are too beautiful, June.

And the jacket does not hide the bumps of your breasts. You need a better jacket."

I laughed so hard I had to stop walking.

Tor patiently waited for my fit to subside before leading me the rest of the way to his house where a promising curl of smoke drifted from the chimney. He opened the door for me, giving me the first view of the inside of our new home. There were so many windows at the back, and the curtains were all wide open to let in the light. And the heat hit me in the face with all the welcome of a grandma's embrace.

"Your home is wonderful, Tor," I said, removing my jacket as I took in the comfortably furnished living room and neat kitchen and dining room. The couch, positioned to face the fireplace, called to me. It looked so comfy.

Tor hung my jacket and pointed to a hall under a set of stairs to the left.

"Adam is down there."

I nodded and followed the hall to a small bedroom with a twin-sized bed. Adam lay on it, eyes closed, as Cassie gently felt along his leg. She looked up as I entered.

"The swelling has gone down nicely. Keep using the ice packs and the meds."

"Do you know what's wrong and how long it will take to heal?"

"I don't," she said honestly. "If the world were still up and running, a general practitioner would have likely done some x-rays to make sure it's not a break and then refer him to a specialist. I don't even have a best guess to give you. This is outside of anything I've had to deal with yet. But, Adam mentioned having an ACL injury before and that it felt similar.

Maybe that's it and, if it's not serious, will heal on its own. I really hate that I don't have a better answer."

"I understand. I was just hoping."

She nodded and gave my arm a sympathetic squeeze.

"I gave him another oxy when he got here. He'll be pretty comfortable for a while."

"Thank you."

After a last look at Adam, I followed her out of the room, partially closing Adam's door so we could hear him if he needed something. I thanked Cassie again and said a quiet goodbye.

Tor stood in the kitchen, doing nothing but watching me. Considering all our past interactions, I was betting that he had no idea what to do with me.

"Want to give me a tour of your home?" I asked.

"It's your home now, too, June."

I smiled and followed him through the house. It wasn't huge, but had a lovely open concept living area with a full guest bathroom across from Adam's room and a separate mudroom with a washer and dryer coming from the garage. Upstairs, there were two guest bedrooms, another bathroom, and a master suite. Only one of the bedrooms had a bed in it, though.

"What happened to all of the beds?" I asked.

"Some were dirty from clearing the houses."

"You mean bloody?"

He grunted. "Anything with infected blood on it was removed. Everything here is safe for you. I moved the extra bed downstairs so Adam won't need to be carried as far if he wants to watch a movie with us."

"That's very considerate of you. Thank you."

"It was Adam's idea. You can sleep here," he said, gesturing to the neatly made bed.

"Where are you going to sleep?"

"With Adam."

I did my best not to smirk. Although Tor didn't mean it the way it sounded, I was going to repeat his preference to Adam. He'd find it funny, too.

"We'll worry about sleeping arrangements later," I said. "Where did you put the backpack?"

"Adam told me to unpack it. Your clothes are over here." He strode toward the dresser and tapped a drawer. "Adam's clothes are in his room. There are towels in the bathroom closet, along with soaps and shampoos. Anything I have is yours."

He was so incredibly sweet and earnest. I could see in his expression that sharing his things wasn't putting him out in the least. He was genuinely excited to have us stay with him.

"Let's go look at the kitchen and see what I can make us for lunch."

He followed me downstairs and stood back while I explored his supplies. Cupboard after cupboard was crammed full of foodstuffs. Canned goods. Boxed items. Jars. Even spices. When he led me to a stocked chest freezer in his garage, I was shocked speechless for a moment. If anyone in Tenacity had an inkling of how much food was here, Matt's worst nightmare would become a reality.

"Do the fey share with each other here, or is this all yours?" I asked finally.

Tor's face took on an uncomfortable expression.

"If any of my brothers are hungry, I would share with them. But they know I hope to win a female soon. I collected this for her."

"Oh, Tor. I'm so sorry. Adam and I can stay somewhere else."

"No. I want you here."

Before I could blink, he wrapped me in a firm hug.

"Adam is my friend. Please stay. I can learn things from him."

I snaked my arms around Tor's waist and leaned into his hug.

"I won't take Adam away from you. We'll stay as long as you want us. But I'll make sure we help you restock before we go so your lucky lady will have plenty to eat."

He grunted and eased away from me.

"Adam shouldn't allow hugs of affection. I'll talk to him. I could feel your breasts."

"Well, that's not acceptable. Rather than bothering Adam with this, I'll talk to my boobs and let them know that they need to keep to themselves."

Tor gave a partial, and very confused, grunt. Trying not to grin, I grabbed a wrapped roast from the freezer to thaw for dinner and headed inside. While I warmed a can of soup, he sat at the counter and watched me work.

"How have you been trying to meet females if you don't mind me asking?"

"I help Emily when she goes to Tenacity to recruit volunteers for the dinner dates. The females tend not to look at me, though, and don't like when I look at them. Am I ugly to you?"

"Aw, Tor." The hesitancy in that question almost earned him another boob hug, which I knew he wouldn't appreciate. So I held myself back and relied on my words instead.

"No, you're not ugly. You are different. But if they stop

focusing on the differences, they would see the kindness in your eyes, your beautiful, wide smile that makes everyone want to smile back, the dimple in your cheek, those pretty flecks of orange in your eyes near the center—"

He grinned widely, and just as I'd said, I had a hard time not returning it.

"You're very handsome, Tor. And strong. Women like muscles. A lot."

"Brooke drew Solin's muscles. She likes looking at him naked. I want a female who likes looking at me."

I chuckled. "Hold out until you find one who does. The right female is out there."

He sighed gustily. "Emily says the same thing."

"Does Emily have a fey of her own?"

"No. Emily is waiting for the right one, too. She says she's not looking yet. She wants more of my brothers to find their women first. If she stays single, it gives all of us hope."

I wondered if it was really hope they were feeling or a mild form of torture, having a kind, single lady around that they couldn't have.

"Is there anything else you do to meet people?" I asked.

"We help with the supply runs, but there are not any single women on those."

"Yeah, probably not the best environment for hitting on a girl, either."

"Or touching. The infected blood gets everywhere."

I laughed.

"Yes, it does. You need to find a way to talk to women, Tor. You're funny and relaxing to be around."

I set our bowls of soup out on the counter and grabbed some crackers before joining him.

"Tell me more about these dinner dates that Emily is recruiting for. What are they about?"

"In exchange for a free meal, the female talks to us. There are rules. We can pull out her chair for her and can sniff her hair when we push in the chair, but only if she doesn't catch us. Emily says no looking at breasts or asking to see—never mind.

"I'm letting my brothers go first and learning from their mistakes. Sain's female asked to see his house when Hannah told her he had a supply of food. She lives with him now, but she hasn't yet shown him her—never mind."

I was starting to get the idea of what the never mind was for and couldn't believe they had come right out and asked to see that.

"I think I understand. You have dinner with a female, and she's supposed to make conversation with you while you eat. That seems simple enough. When is it your turn?"

He shrugged and played with his soup.

"Emily ran out of volunteers. Brooke is going to teach art to the females. She needs a male model. Solin said that Brooke likes sketching his cock, and the model will be able to show his cock to the women. Maybe one of them will like my cock if my name is drawn."

I realized I had my spoon partway to my mouth as I stared at him and slowly lowered it. Never in my life had I heard "cock" used conversationally, and he'd managed to drop it three times in a row.

"You're going to be a nude model?"

"Yes. If my name is drawn. Many of my brothers want to model, too. Solin says that Brooke's…special place gets hot and wet when she draws him."

"Oh, boy. You all really do information share, don't you?"

"Yes."

"Okay, here's some information for you. Make sure you share this with all your brothers, too. Women want to know that they are more than living sex toys. We want to be wanted for our thoughts and our humor and whatever we're good at—like Brooke's drawing. It's great to be physically attracted to a girl, but you have to wait until at least the third date before you start having the level of open conversation like we're having. So no talking about your brothers' sex lives or anything related to your genitals or female genitalia."

Tor nodded.

"That's why Emily made conversation cards. The females can ask us about our favorite colors and foods, and we can turn the question to them." He paused for a minute. "I like the word genitals."

"So, what's your favorite color?" I asked, steering the conversation in a safer direction.

"Blue like the sky when there are no clouds. It sometimes gets so bright it hurts to look at it, but it's beautiful. I like watching the clouds, too. I didn't know there was so much movement in a sky."

"I didn't realize how much I would miss just staring at the sky until I was shut away from it. Being in the bunker for a few months was tough. I couldn't imagine not seeing the sky for years. Or ever. It must have been breathtaking the first time you saw it."

"It took my breath and my vision. There was much pain."

I smiled.

"I meant awe-inspiring."

"Yes. It was." He considered me for a moment. "Females think we are odd for wanting one of them so badly. Angel said it shows our desperation, and no female likes that. But females are like the sky. We never saw one until we came here. They are awe-inspiring every time we look at one of them. But they don't act like the sky. We can't watch them and enjoy their beauty. They don't welcome our gaze. They shake with fear or spit at us."

"Wow. That's the prettiest and saddest thing I've ever heard."

"Sad? No. They are only angry."

"That's what makes it so sad. You only want to get to know us, and we're shooting you down before ever giving you a chance. I never thought of how unique and interesting I would be to someone who's never seen anything like me. Your interest in our physical differences makes so much more sense. I'm surprised you're still interested in any female after the way some have treated you."

"When the sky pours freezing rain on me, I don't think it's less beautiful. It's only angry. And the anger will calm, and it will show me its pretty colors again."

"That's a really nice way of looking at it. You need to figure out how to work that analogy into your dinner conversation. If it doesn't pull at her heartstrings, I don't know what will. It definitely tugged at mine."

CHAPTER EIGHT

"I LIKED THE MERMAID ONE BETTER," TOR SAID WHEN THE MOVIE ended.

"Why's that?"

"She liked him and was trying to get his attention. I wouldn't have been so stupid. I would have given it to her. This one didn't like how he looked or that he was different. He tried so hard, and she still refused to see how much he wanted her." Tor turned to look at me. "Do all women like books?"

"No, but I think many do."

"Farco's woman likes books. I will need to ask my brothers."

"Ask them what?"

"If their women like books."

"Are you thinking of building a library to lure women in?"

"Will that work?"

I couldn't stop my laugh.

"It might."

"Do you like books?"

"I used to. Reading for college kind of killed some of the joy

I used to find while reading. Probably because it wasn't what I wanted to read."

"What do you like to read?"

"I used to read whatever caught my eye. Usually romances. I think most women are romantics at heart. I haven't read anything in a really long while though."

He grunted, and I could tell he was heavily considering the book angle.

"I'm going to go check on Adam and see if he's up yet. Hopefully, he'll be hungry."

Leaving Tor on the couch, I went to Adam's room. We'd been careful to keep the TV turned low so we wouldn't disturb him. However, he was awake and staring at the ceiling when I walked in.

"Hey, hun. How are you feeling? Did you just wake up?" I gently kissed his cheek.

"I don't know how you can do that," he said.

"Do what?"

"Kiss me. I'm rank."

"You're not rank." He was a little, but I didn't care. "But sitting in some water might feel good on the leg. Do you want to try taking a bath?"

"A bath sounds good. But not you. Tor's already seen my balls more times than I can count. What's one more time?" A hint of bitterness lingered in his tone and his expression.

"Does anything hurt?"

"It all fucking hurts, June," he said sharply.

Adam didn't talk to me like that. Ever. The shock of it must have shown in my expression because he immediately exhaled and reached for my hand.

"I'm sorry. You didn't deserve that."

"No, she did not. June loves you, Adam. Stop being stupid," Tor said from the other room.

The corner of Adam's mouth tilted briefly.

"Yes, I'm in pain. No, there's nothing else we can do about it. I'd rather save what's left of the oxy so I can sleep at night."

"Okay. Maybe the bath will help."

He nodded, but I could see the strain around his mouth and the doubt in his eyes.

"I will help Adam," Tor said, setting a gentle hand on my shoulder.

"I think I'm going to go for a walk and give you two some quiet time."

"Thank you," Adam said. He gave my hand a light squeeze and let me go.

I wasn't running from the pain Adam would likely endure while cleaning up. I was leaving to find better medicine.

As soon as I had my coat and boots on, I was out the door and waving down the first fey I spotted.

"Hi. I'm new here and staying with Tor."

He stopped moving and looked around as if checking to make sure I was talking to him. I didn't let that stop me.

"I don't know my way around here yet and was wondering if you could tell me where Cassie lives."

"Yes. I will take you."

I held out my hand.

"I'm June."

He took my hand in his own, slightly caressing his way up my palm before gently clasping and shaking my hand.

"What's your name?" I prodded.

"Turik."

"I appreciate your help, Turik."

"May I carry you?" he asked as he reluctantly released my hand.

"Is it that far?"

"No."

My smile widened, and I hoped he didn't think I was mocking him.

"I think I'll walk if that's all right with you."

Turik grunted and fell into step beside me. He barely paid attention to where we walked, focusing mostly on me instead. After my talk with Tor, I wasn't offended or uncomfortable.

"The sky is a really pretty blue today," I commented, looking up. "Which do you like better? Watching the clouds or watching the stars?"

"The stars. They remind me of the caves."

"Do you miss the caves?"

"Sometimes. Mostly I miss my brothers."

"What do you mean? Are some of your kind still trapped?"

"The weakest of us stayed behind to guard our home."

"Oh. I'm so sorry. Does that mean you're planning on going back?"

He slowly shook his head. "None of us will want to return no matter what happened to Molev."

"Molev? Who's he?"

"Our leader. He left us a long time ago."

"Why?"

"We do not know. Cassie lives in that house," he said pointing down a side street. "But she is with Nancy and Uan."

The name sounded vaguely familiar.

"Uan? Is that someone I know?"

"He was the one who stopped the hellhound from killing

Hannah and Tasha when my brothers were collecting the cattle from your barn."

"Oh. How is he?"

"Not well."

Guilt wormed its way in even though I knew none of what had happened to the fey was my fault.

"Who is Nancy? Is that his wife?"

"Yes. And Tasha and Brenna are his daughters and Zach is his son. Uan has much to fight for."

As we neared a brown ranch, the front door opened and Cassie emerged with Kerr right behind her. They were speaking too softly for me to hear, but their expressions said enough. They were worried.

My steps slowed. Anyone with eyes could see that now wasn't the best time to—

Cassie looked up and saw me. Surprise lit her face then more worry.

"Is everything okay?" she asked.

"Yes and no," I said reluctantly. "How's Uan? I rode in the truck with him and was so caught up in Adam I never thought to ask."

"He's not healing like he should. But that's nothing you need to worry about. He's a strong man with a lot of people determined to pull him back to good health."

"I wish those infected would have never found our barn," I said, thinking of all the pain they'd caused.

"If wishes were fishes we would all be well-fed," Cassie said with a smirk. "It's funny how that saying has so much meaning in this world. Why don't you tell me why you're walking around town?"

"Adam's hurting. A lot. For the first time in three years, he snapped at me. He didn't even do that the night we ran or when he realized his family wouldn't be joining us."

"I've been using all the heavier hitting medication on Uan," she said. "There's not much of it, and honestly, he needs it more than Adam. I think it's the only thing that's helping him hold on."

"I understand. Is there anything I can do to help him or Nancy?"

"I wish there were."

I nodded and said goodbye before following my helpful escort back to Tor's. However, the distant cattle calls distracted me, and Turik happily led me to where the animals were now being kept. The majority of the cows roamed a large open lot, grazing on the dried grass poking through the snow. A few wandered between nearby houses.

Turik and I weren't the only ones checking out the livestock. More fey lingered in the area as well. The large, grey men walked among the cattle, running their hands over their hides and talking to them in low tones. When a cow went too far from the rest, a fey would gently redirect its attention to the mound of hay in the middle of the area.

The pigs and horses intermingled with the herd. Watching them, I felt a sense of relief and contentment. How often had I felt sorry for the trapped animals and wished we could let them out to graze? I was glad they were being well-cared for and finally able to go outside. And even more deeply, I was glad they were no longer our responsibility. We'd had far too many close calls with the infected due to them.

Back at the house, I quietly hung up my jacket and checked Adam's room. It was empty, and the door to the bathroom was tightly closed. Hopefully, that meant the bath was helping.

Rather than disturb Adam and Tor, I dug out an electric pressure cooker and set the partially thawed roast in it. Cooking in the bunker had taught me to lean on seasonings to change up the dishes. Thankfully, Tor had plenty of those. I seasoned the roast, set the pressure cooker, then went upstairs.

Since Tor and I hadn't officially resolved the sleeping arrangement, I collected a pillow and some blankets from the master bedroom and created a blanket bed in the spare room. Just in case. Tor was sweet to give up his bed for me, but I didn't want him forgoing sleep because of it. I only wished there was another mattress so one of us wouldn't end up on the floor or couch.

A door opened on the first floor. I hurried downstairs and saw Tor carry Adam to the bedroom. Adam's hair was still damp and his skin rosy as Tor helped him into bed. Except for Adam's expression, he looked worlds better.

"Feel like a new person?" I asked.

"A completely different person. One that lost his independence." Adam looked at Tor. "I really do appreciate the help."

"Friends help each other," Tor said simply.

"They do," Adam agreed, closing his eyes. "It's been a long day. I think I'll take my next pill now and try to sleep."

"Are you sure? I'm making a roast for dinner. It should be done in another hour."

"I think you spend too much time in bed," Tor said, backing me up. "Let me carry you to the couch. You will feel better."

"Says the guy with two working legs," Adam said with a hint of bitterness. "Fine. Carry me there."

Tor flashed me a look before leaving the room with Adam. I was glad Tor had said something. A change in scenery was good. But I also worried that we were aggravating whatever was hurt on Adam by moving him around so much. Yet, wasn't his mental health as important as his physical? I'd thought the move to Tolerance would help with that. Granted, it hadn't even been a full day and the journey probably hurt him more than he'd let on. But still, this move had been his idea, and he didn't seem any happier about it.

"I saw the cows when I was out," I said, following them. "They're grazing in an empty lot and seem really happy."

Tor settled Adam on the couch and dragged over a chair to prop the leg that seemed to hurt the most.

"That's good," Adam said. "I'm glad we didn't need to leave them behind."

"They have babies inside of them," Tor said.

"Yep," Adam said. "I think a few of them might be ready to give birth in the next month. With the rest following a few weeks from then. My uncle liked to breed for the summer fairs. It was a good place to sell the cattle. He didn't like the milking aspect, just the breeding. He'd always find the strongest bulls. Made better offspring."

Adam's breathing was getting shorter.

"How are your ribs?" I asked.

"Ribs are fine. It's the leg."

I grabbed a couch pillow and gently slid it under his knee. "Better?"

"I'd be better if the two of you stopped staring and hovering." He said it without anger, but that wasn't enough to take the sting out of his words.

"We're trying to help. We don't like seeing you in pain."

"Then close your eyes. This is my life now. Pain and dependency."

"You know that's not true," I said. "It's only been a week. You can open your eyes. You can eat without wincing. The bruising is starting to fade. Give yourself some more time to heal."

"While you're hoping time is the answer, I'm dealing with reality. Something's seriously wrong with my leg. I can't put any weight on it without shooting pain that makes me want to vomit." Anger and bitterness started to give his words volume. "There's no surgeon or physical therapist here. With time, I might be able to walk with a limp. I'll never be able to run. I sure as hell won't be able to go out for supplies. I don't even have a vagina to be useful."

He yelled the last bit, and I cringed, glancing at Tor. The fey did not look happy with Adam.

"I'm complete dead weight. Dead weight dies in this world."

I didn't know what to say or do to give him back the hope his injuries had stolen from him. No, not his injuries. The assholes from Tenacity.

"No yelling at June," Tor said, his voice a low growl.

Adam closed his eyes and sighed.

"I'm sorry for raising my voice, but not for speaking the truth. I'm next to useless and don't see that changing any time in the future."

"I think that's the pain talking," I said more for Tor's benefit than Adam's. "You were right. You need the next dose of oxy." I moved away to get it for him. "I saw Cassie when I was out. I asked her if there was anything stronger. There's not. Uan, the fey who was hurt stopping the hellhound hidden in the silo, is still in bad shape. She was using the heavier stuff on him.

Maybe Tor and I could go out on a supply run and look for more though."

"No," Adam said immediately. "I don't want you going out there."

"And I don't want you sitting in here, thinking your life's done."

"Tell her, Tor. Tell her how dangerous it is."

I made a derisive sound. "It wasn't dangerous a week ago. Why now?" My expression softened as I approached the couch again. "Because you won't be there, right? I trust Tor to keep me safe. And you do too or we wouldn't be here."

Adam made a face without opening his eyes.

"I couldn't live with myself if something happened to you because of me."

"And I can't live with myself if I sit by and do nothing while you're suffering. That's not what you do when you love someone. Here. Take this."

When he opened his eyes, I handed him the pill and a glass of water then sat next to him.

"We're in this together, Adam. We're a team. I'm not going to let you suffer when there's something I can do to help you."

"Let's give it a few more days," he said, threading his fingers through mine. "Maybe you're right. Maybe I'm being overly impatient."

However, his underlying despondency lingered even after the pill kicked in. He ate dinner quietly, listening to Tor's praise of my cooking skills without comment. He made it through half a movie before asking Tor to return him to his room.

It felt like he was withdrawing. From me. From life. From hope in general. And I didn't like it.

When Tor returned, I tried to keep the mood light and

continued my explanation of why the friendship between a hound and a fox would be so unusual. His curiosity and observations distracted me from my underlying worry. By the time the movie ended, I could talk about Adam more calmly.

"Adam's going to need more medicine," I said when Tor moved to put the movie away. "And I don't think it's going to be easy to find. I'd rather start looking before he runs out."

Tor studied me for a moment.

"Ryan can look for it."

I shook my head.

"Now you're being stubborn like Adam. There's no reason for me not to go out there." I stood and set my hand on Tor's bicep. "I trust you. Trust me enough to know what I'm capable of. I'm not reckless. I won't needlessly put myself at risk. I'm familiar with the supply runs and know to listen. Plus, I know you're strong enough to toss me onto a roof if the situation becomes questionable."

Tor glanced down to where my hand rested. He exhaled heavily.

"Adam shouldn't have yelled at you."

"I know. And I think he knows that, too, deep down. He's hurting, and it's messing with his thinking."

"Uan doesn't yell at Nancy, and his insides are outside."

I grimaced.

"Uan has stronger pain medicine. Please help me help Adam. He needs the medicine to help him think past the pain, too."

Tor grunted and gently lifted my hand from his arm. He turned it over, looking at my palm. He was so curious about everything that I didn't mind the intense scrutiny. I let him look his fill and waited patiently for his decision.

"I will help you help Adam."

"Thank you, Tor." I turned my hand in his, giving his a squeeze. "Do you think Brog would be willing to keep an eye on Adam tomorrow?"

"Tomorrow? Adam said we should wait a few days."

"And I said we shouldn't let him run out of medicine. You saw what happened when he missed a dose. His thinking got darker. He wasn't acting like himself."

Tor considered me for a long moment.

"Not tomorrow. The day after. I need to speak to Brog and talk to Cassie and Ryan."

"We agreed we'd wait a few days," Adam said angrily.

"No, you acknowledged you shouldn't be so impatient about your progress. I never said anything about waiting to get you more medicine. The pain is clouding your judgment."

"My judgment is fine. Yours is the one that's—."

"Adam," Tor said sharply. "No yelling at June."

Adam's face flushed, and he closed his eyes for a long moment.

"Ganging up on me is a low move," he said more calmly.

"That's not what we're doing, Adam," I said. "We both care about you and want to help."

"I don't want your help!"

Tor's hand closed over my shoulder.

"June, go for a walk. Adam and I need to talk."

"Get him to take his next pill. No more saving."

Tor grunted then gently steered me out of the room, and

closed the door in my face. But, I could still hear what was being said.

"If you cannot return June's kindness, do not speak. She is too good and too smart for you, remember? You are a lucky man. Stop being so stupid."

Smiling slightly, I put Adam's oatmeal on the counter and bundled up for an early morning walk. Hopefully after the oxy kicked in, Adam would eat and apologize for upsetting Tor. Tor's defense of me was sweet. He understood Adam was in pain, but in Tor's mind, that was no excuse for Adam to take out his frustration on me. And Tor was right. It wasn't a good reason. That didn't mean I didn't understand, though.

I nodded to the fey I passed and wandered to the cows, content to watch them graze.

"Good morning, June."

I glanced toward the fey approaching me and smiled in welcome.

"Good morning, Turik. What are you up to today?"

"Cow watching until Hannah and Eden start fighting."

"Uh…why are they fighting?"

"Eden fights to learn. Hannah fights because Merdon says it's good for her."

"Can I watch too?"

"Yes."

We walked together to the other end of the settlement. Other fey were already gathering around another semi-empty lot. The scarecrow dummy with all the holes in it made sense. It was obviously some kind of target. The colorful mound of melted plastic made no sense at all.

"Are those penises?" I asked.

"Yes. Pretend ones. Eden promised Ghua she would never shoot a real one. She is the only one who promised, though."

I coughed to cover up the laugh that had exploded from me at his deeply troubled words.

"I'm sure no one plans on shooting any real ones."

He grunted. "Hannah says that accidents have been known to happen."

"The new girl," a cheery voice called.

I turned to watch a fey approach. In his arms, a blonde grinned at me.

"I was going to come say hi if you didn't show up before long. I'm Angel." As soon as she was on her feet, she handed me a snack cake. "Welcome to feight club. Stands for fey fight club. There's only one rule. Nah, I'm kidding. There are no rules. Last week Eden punched Hannah in the baby box." The fey around us hissed out breaths. "It wasn't pretty, but Eden won the match."

"Eden fights dirty?"

"Don't we all?"

She ate a bite of cake and rolled her eyes at me when her fey wrapped his arms around her from behind and started groping her belly.

"How's your man holding up? I heard the assholes in Tenacity are starting to tip their hands."

"Adam's doing as well as can be expected. The swelling is down. He can see. But they messed up his leg. The pain is unbearable when he tries to put any weight on it. He's hurting even when he doesn't use it, too."

"I'm really sorry to hear that," Angel said sympathetically. "June, right?"

"Yeah."

"I think it's normal for all of us to ask ourselves if we're lucky to have made it this far or if we're cursed. Life is so different, but we're still holding ourselves to the same expectations of the past. He'll come around."

"I hope so."

"Are we ready to rumble?"

I turned toward the sound of the new voice. A young woman with brown hair pulled back in a ponytail jogged our way.

A fey jogged beside her, his gaze flicking to his partner.

"You want to rumble here?"

She snorted. "Wrong kind of rumble Ghua, and no, we're not doing that here."

"Hey, June. I'm Eden. Welcome to feight club."

"Nice to meet you, Eden."

"Hannah should be here soon," Angel said. "I think they went to check on the cows."

"Any idea if Brenna and Tasha will be here?"

Angel shook her head, looking sad. "Uan's not doing so well. I think they're starting to consider the caves."

Eden frowned, growing serious. "But I thought Cassie said…"

"Exactly."

"What's happening?" I asked, lost.

"The caves, where the fey came from, had special crystals," Eden explained. "The crystals changed the fey, making it impossible for them to truly die when they were down there."

"Each time their current life ended, they were reborn in the nearest resurrection pool," Angel added. Her fey grunted his agreement.

"Tor mentioned something about being reborn," I said.

"Yeah, it was a shock to them when they came up here and one of their own didn't come back." Eden gave Ghua a sympathetic pat. "They didn't understand what true death was."

"So they're taking Uan back to the caves?"

"They're thinking about it. They didn't at first because Cassie said she wasn't sure Uan would make the journey. Now…" Eden shrugged, and Angel took over.

"Now his family is thinking that might be his only chance."

The group grew quiet. I couldn't imagine having to make that kind of choice. I'd seen how badly Uan had been hurt. Turik saying his insides were outside hadn't been an exaggeration.

"When are they going to take him?" I asked.

"They're still trying to figure out how to do it in the safest way possible," Eden said. "The stretcher they used to bring Adam here gave them some ideas. They're hoping to rig something up in the back of a truck. Something to absorb most of the bumps. Garrett's been helping with that, and Ryan's been going out for the pieces they need."

"And once Uan's in the caves, they're going to bring him to the healing pools?" I asked.

The girls looked at their guys.

"No," Angel's fey said. "Once they are in the caves, they will tell Uan it is safe to die and hope he is reborn."

CHAPTER NINE

THE HOUSE WAS QUIET WHEN I LET MYSELF BACK IN AND HUNG UP my jacket. A door opened, and I turned to see Tor emerge from the hallway. He paused when he saw me, and his ears slowly turned a dark grey at the ends.

"Hey, Tor. Everything okay?"

"Yes."

"You sure? You look upset?"

"I am not upset. Adam was explaining females to me."

Given the way his cheeks started to darken, I could imagine what he was explaining.

"Ah. That was nice of him?"

"He wanted to apologize for being rude."

"Then, yes, that was nice of him. Are you hungry?"

Tor's eyes looked like they were going to pop out of his head as he gave a single, hesitant nod.

"I think there's some roast left. Let me see what I can whip up while you sit and tell me more about where you use to live." I moved toward the kitchen. "I was talking to Angel and Eden, and they told me that Uan's family is thinking of returning him to the caves. Do you think they can fully heal him that way even after he's been up here?"

Tor sat and watched me check the cupboards.

"What do you mean?"

"The girls said that the crystals changed you. Made it so you were reborn. Do you think being away from the crystals undid that change? What if they get there and he dies?"

"No. That is not how the crystal works. If he dies while wearing a crystal in the caves, he will be reborn, whole and healthy. He only needs to live long enough to make it to the caves."

"And what are his chances of that?"

"The hellhound hurt him badly. If we were in the caves, he would have already asked one of us to end his suffering."

A scrape of noise from the hall brought my head up. Adam stood in the hallway, clinging to a wall. Sweat beaded his forehead and he looked white as a sheet.

"Does it work on anyone?" he asked.

"Adam." I dropped the can to the counter and hurried to his side. "You shouldn't be walking. You said it hurt."

"It's fine," he said even as he leaned on me.

"Would it work on me, Tor?" he asked.

It took me a moment to understand what he was saying.

"Are you insane? You're not going to the caves so Tor can kill you. You do get that's what he's saying, right? They're either going to kill Uan or let him die and hope their magic works to bring him back."

"Yes. I fully understand what I'm asking."

I looked at Tor, who hadn't moved.

"I don't know, Adam. When Mya was in the caves, she grew very sick. We returned to the surface to save her, and she did get better. But when the infected bit her, she didn't become stupid. Mya believes the crystal began to change her, making her more like us. Drav believes it was sex with him that made her immune because Eden is also immune but did not go to the caves."

"Wait, what?" Adam asked. "The women sleeping with the fey are immune?"

"Cassie believes so since two of the women bitten did not turn stupid."

Adam looked down at the ground for a long moment, and I couldn't even begin to guess where his mind was going with all the new information. But I could feel him shaking.

"We should get you back in bed or you're going to hurt too much to sleep tonight."

Tor immediately came over to assist.

"I want to go," Adam said when he was once again settled on his bed. "When they take Uan, I want to go too."

"As your girlfriend, do I have any say in this decision? You're simply going to up and leave me?" I looked at Tor. "How long will it take to get there and back?"

Tor considered my question.

"The infected are smarter now," he said slowly. "The traps are more complex. It took many days and nights to get here from the caves. It would take almost twice that now. And twice that to return."

"So what are we saying?" I pressed. "Two weeks? Three?"

"Perhaps," Tor said.

I turned back to Adam.

"You didn't want to let me out of your sight for more than three seconds but you're willing to run off for three weeks to die and *maybe* be reborn without your injury? No. You're not allowed to ask me to sit here in a constant state of worry and fear for three weeks because you have a bum leg."

Adam studied me, his expression growing sadder by the moment.

"Don't do this to me," I said softly. "Don't risk yourself on a maybe when you don't know what time will do for your leg. I'll get you something better for the pain. You'll be fine."

"You still want to go tomorrow?

"Yes."

He glanced at Tor then back at me.

"They head out early. We'll need to make sure you're awake on time."

"Okay. Yeah, fine." I exhaled in relief that he was actually listening. I knew he was afraid his leg injury would result in a permanent limitation, but not as afraid as I was of him never coming back if he went to those caves.

"I'll go finish dinner. Want to watch another movie tonight?" I asked.

"Nah, I have a lot of thinking to do, and you need to get to bed early. It's not safe out there, and you need to be sharp." He looked at Tor. "Promise me, no matter what happens, you will always put her safety first."

"I swear," Tor said.

"I'll be fine, Adam. Just focus on yourself and getting better." I leaned down to brush his lips with a kiss. He surprised me by grabbing the back of my head and kissing me with a need I hadn't seen from him in weeks. It left me breathless and unsteady when he finally released me.

"I know you'll be fine," he said. "Tor will make sure of that."

Knees still weak, I nodded and left the room. I missed

Adam. It seemed far longer than a week ago since we'd been together. If I felt that way, did he? Maybe I was the distraction he needed from the pain. Sure, we couldn't have actual sex yet, but I was more than happy to use my mouth on him.

Heart lighter, I made dinner, only half-listening to Adam pull more promises from Tor to look after me. My mind toyed with several possible ploys to remove Tor from the house for a while, but I finally settled on simply asking him to leave for a bit once we were done with dinner.

However, my plan fell apart when Adam said he was tired after he finished eating.

"Are you sure? I was thinking you and I could spend a little alone time together," I said.

"I think alone time right now would only hurt us both in the long run," Adam said without looking at me.

It broke my heart that he was in so much pain that he was willing to pass on what I was offering. Especially after that kiss. The desperation he'd conveyed with his mouth hadn't been fake or fleeting. And it settled in my mind as I snuggled in Tor's bed.

It also fed my dreams in the best way possible.

Glimpses of Adam, whole and healthy, teased me endlessly. First, I dreamt of a romantic dinner that ended with his lips kissing a path along my neck. Then, a post-game celebration where he traced his way up my spine, his warm fingers sending shivers of need through me. Followed by a party at a friend's house that faded as Adam ground against me with my jean-clad legs around his waist.

By the time I dreamed we were in the back of his truck under the stars, I ached with need for him.

His weight settled between my legs, and his fingers hooked

the sides of the lacey underwear that left little to the imagination. He leaned in and brushed his nose against my mound as he gently worked the material down.

"I need to taste you, June. Let me taste you."

I willingly lifted my hips, letting him remove the barrier that was keeping him from what he wanted. What we both wanted.

His gaze held mine as he gently nudged my legs wider.

"Beautiful." The heat of his exhale sent a shiver through me, and my core clenched.

The first drag of a tongue parted my folds. A small sound escaped me, and he grinned. He loved when he did things that evoked noises from me. I'd give him all the noises he wanted if he just kept going. My clit throbbed with need.

I spread my knees wider, begging for more.

The flat stroke of a tongue, from entrance to clit, tugged at my consciousness.

Dream and reality overlapped for a confusing moment. My pulse sped as the tongue continued to stroke close to my sensitive nub, but never going where I needed it.

Warm and comfortable, I stayed in that place between sleep and awake, aware that Adam was trying to wake me up in my favorite way. His tongue danced around and around my clit, teasing me. Waiting for me to acknowledge I was awake enough to enjoy this treat.

With a sleeping smile, I drew my knees up and set them over his shoulders, giving him the access he wanted. His lips immediately closed over my clit, and he began his gentle suckling, occasionally flicking his tongue over the nub.

My breathing became ragged. I moaned and reached down to grab his head. Sometimes, I pushed him away when it became too much. Other times, I ground myself against his mouth until he shoved me over the edge. Today, he stole the choice from me by pinning my hands beneath his on my thighs.

He spread me wider, flicking faster than he'd ever managed before.

The orgasm came so hard and fast that I almost forgot to muffle the sound that wanted to rip from my throat. I arched, my channel squeezing hard around nothing in pulsing wave after wave. The suction from his mouth gentled but stayed with me as I rode out the best orgasm of my life until, depleted, I collapsed onto the bed.

He didn't try to touch my clit again but tongued me thoroughly. At first, I thought he was making me wetter and I smiled, too glad to have the old Adam back to complain. Then, I realized he wasn't leaving moisture behind. He was lapping up what he'd created.

I made a satisfied humming sound, and he lifted his head.

"Did I wake you up right, June?"

My eyes popped open at the sound of Tor's husky voice, and I jerked my head off the pillow to make sure my ears weren't lying.

Nope.

Tor lay between my legs, his lips glistening and his pupils dilated as he looked from my face to between my legs.

"You made the happy, squeaky noises," Tor said, tearing his gaze from my center and up to my face once more. "That means you liked it, right?"

My pulse, which had started to calm, began to race again with my panic. What had I done? I'd cheated on Adam. Shit. Had he heard us? Heard me? He knew exactly what I sounded like when I came.

I made a pained face and closed my eyes, struggling not to cry.

Tor immediately released me.

"Did I hurt you? Did I do it wrong? Was my tongue too rough? Adam said it would be okay if I licked inside you. Ghua says that's where the best taste is. He was right. But I didn't mean to hurt you."

Adam said it would be okay...

Those words rang like an angry gong in my head, killing my guilt and panic.

The happy, squeaking noises? That's what *Adam* called the noise I made. The way Tor had endlessly circled my clit before teasing it with his tongue? Adam had obviously told Tor about that, too. Why? Why would Adam send Tor to do this?

The panic in Tor's voice was the only thing that kept me from flying out of the bed and running downstairs.

Carefully concealing my rage, I sat up and clasped Tor's strong hands.

"You didn't hurt me. I promise."

He freed a hand to gently wipe away the moisture at the corner of my eye.

"You cried."

"Because you are very good at waking me up."

The panic didn't fade from his expression. Not completely.

A part of my brain whispered that this all might be a huge misunderstanding. Adam had told Tor things yesterday. Things that had made the dear fey blush. Maybe Tor had assumed he had permission because of that discussion.

"Tor, when did Adam tell you how to wake me up?"

"Last night while you were sleeping. He tried walking again and got angry. Talking about you made him less angry but really sad. He said waking you up would make you happy, and you deserved happiness."

I could see in Tor's expression that he was starting to realize Adam had lied to him somehow. After all the ways the other humans had mistreated the fey, I didn't want this to add to it.

"Tor," I said firmly. "You made me very happy. I haven't felt like that in a long time. Sometimes powerful orgasms can bring a woman to tears. I swear you didn't hurt me. I liked everything you did." Just not what my asshole boyfriend did, I added mentally.

Tor's gaze flicked down again.

"Does that mean I can wake you up tomorrow?"

"We'll see, okay?" I eased my legs off his bare back, trying not to show how embarrassed his intense focus was making me.

He grunted and reluctantly released me. I drew my legs together and reached for my very plain and borrowed underwear.

"Would you mind doing me a favor? Adam and I need to have a private conversation that I'd rather no one overhear. Could you leave the house for a few minutes?"

"Of course. I will make sure none of my brothers are nearby. Don't take too long, though," he said, glancing at the window. "We need to leave soon."

"Okay. Thanks, Tor."

He grunted and walked from the room. I stared at his impressively muscled back, and my core clenched again. The man was built like a beast but had the spirit of a lamb. Which only made what Adam had done even worse.

Angry and hurt beyond words, I quickly dressed.

Tor was already gone when I descended and marched into

Adam's room. There he lay, the man who'd loved me for years and had been at my side for months when the world went to hell, arms behind his head as he stared up at the ceiling. While he was trying to look all calm and collected, I knew him well enough to see his tension.

He knew why I was here and knew I was angry. Rather than attack, I played it cool.

"Did you send Tor to wake me up?" I asked calmly.

"Yeah. We talked about that last night."

"Right, but I don't remember the part where you told him how he should eat me out so I'd make the happy, squeaky sounds."

I waited, riding out his long silence until he sighed.

"I don't know what you want me to say."

"Start with an explanation for why you betrayed the trust of two people who care about you."

"Isn't it obvious? You need him, June. Sleeping with him will give you immunity."

I had to look away for a minute. If Adam wasn't already so hurt, I would have hit him myself.

"Can you even hear yourself?" I asked, letting my hurt show. "Are you honestly going to lie there and tell me you're okay with another man touching me? Because I sure as hell am not. And Tor? He freaked out when I started crying. Crying because I hadn't realized it wasn't my boyfriend between my legs until the deed was done. Crying because, for one horrible minute, I thought I'd accidentally cheated on you. Instead you pimped me out like some unwanted piece of garbage."

Adam closed his eyes and swallowed hard, saying nothing.

"You're lucky Tor has no idea what you did. That you used him. That you used us both. And why? Because you're suffering from some form of inadequacy? I don't give a fuck about some rumor regarding immunity, Adam. I care that my boyfriend hurt me in a way I'm not sure I can forgive."

I waited. When he spoke, his voice was rough.

"We don't live in the same world we did when we started dating. There aren't any white picket fences anymore. There are no happily-ever-afters." He opened his eyes and looked right at me. "If having him eat you out brings a smile to your face every morning and brings immunity, then let the man go to town. Turns out, eating out a girl is his lifelong dream. Who am I to deny you two a moment of happiness?"

His complete indifference to the gravity of what he'd done was too much. My hand lashed out, uncaring that he still carried lingering colors on his jaw. He deserved to feel the sting of my hand.

He caught my hand in his own, though.

"Who knows how many moments we have left, June? Don't waste them on anger."

"You should listen to your own advice, Adam. Get your head on straight while I'm gone. The world is a different place. I don't need a man who can make me immune from infection. I need one I can trust."

He exhaled heavily and released me.

"I'm sorry, June."

I shook my head, still too angry.

"We'll talk more when I'm back. Maybe I'll be in a calmer state of mind to accept your apology then."

I stalked out of the room without a backward glance and geared up by the front door. It wasn't the same, strapping on the knife holster without Adam there to help me. But, after the way I'd woken up, nothing had felt the same. Adam's pain was feeding his desperation to keep me safe. That was the only explanation I could come up with to explain his betrayal. Let Tor touch me and ensure his protection of me.

Heart heavy, I opened the door and spotted Tor and Brog speaking quietly across the street. Tor immediately looked up as I closed the door behind me.

"Are you done talking to Adam?"

"I am. Thank you for giving us some privacy."

"Of course." He flashed his teeth at me as I crossed the road, and I did my best to set aside what had happened between us. For both our sakes, I needed to stay focused on the task at hand.

I glanced at Brog. "Thanks for staying with Adam. He might be in a bit of a crabby mood. Please don't let anything he says upset you. He's not himself and is saying a lot of things he doesn't mean."

Brog grunted and started across the road.

"He will keep Adam safe," Tor said.

"I know he will. I'm more worried about Adam acting like a jackass and offending Brog."

"They will both be fine, June."

"I'm sure you're right," I said, walking with him. As the silence stretched between us, I watched the lights on the wall flick off one by one and the sky begin to lighten. Tor's repeated glances and slowing steps warned me that he was about to say something I might regret.

"I think Adam is right."

"Oh? About what?"

"It's not safe for you to go on a supply run."

I stopped walking and faced Tor.

"I'm angry with Adam for trying to control my life based on

what he thinks is right for me. I was born with a brain, Tor. I'm allowed to use it to think and decide things for myself. If you're going to start acting domineering like Adam, we're going to have a problem."

"I promised him that I would keep you safe."

"And you will, but not by keeping me locked up in a gilded cage. You'll keep me safe by sticking close to me and advising me. With or without you, I'm leaving and returning with more medicine."

He studied me for a long moment and nodded.

We didn't speak again until we reached Tenacity.

"Will you ride in the truck with Richard?" he asked. "It will be more comfortable than in the back."

"Sure."

Richard, as it turned out, was the "Dad" of Tolerance, and very kind. He kept me distracted with the history of the two settlements and the animosity that had grown between them. Considering that his first grandchild would be part fey, it was easy to see that he fully supported the efforts to integrate the two towns peacefully.

"Not sure how that will ever happen," I commented.

"I heard what they did to Adam and what you said to Matt. He knows you're right, by the way. Mya's been telling him the same things for ages. Until he removes the people who hate without cause, there will never be peace.

"The haters are clever about spreading their hate, though. And it doesn't help that there are women involved. The fey would have no problem kicking out men and letting them fend for themselves against the infected. A hateful woman? The fey would rather she spit in their eye every night just to keep her safe."

"That's messed up."

"Yes and no. They realize women are the key to their futures."

The topic rang too close to what Adam had said before I'd left.

"Is it true? That sleeping with one of them brings immunity?"

"Without a bunch of testing, there's no way to know that for sure, but it sure looks that way. It's a good thing, too."

"How so?"

"It gives us humans another reason to look at the fey more closely. How can they be bad when they hold all the keys to our continued survival? Immunity. The ability to kill the hellhounds. And patience. I've never seen people more patient than the fey. We're afraid and make all kinds of mistakes, but they rarely get angry."

"That only makes them easier targets for the people who want to use them."

"It does. But that's why they have people like us. We'll stand up for them when they won't stand up for themselves."

The trucks rolled to a stop on an overpass. Buildings stretched in the distance. While I knew this was a supply run for most, I also knew from the ride with Richard that Ryan and I had different objectives. They'd purposely chosen to stop this close to a city to find more medical supplies for Uan.

"This is a lot closer to a city than I'd like to be," he said, staring at the buildings with me. "You be careful out there."

"I will be. Tor will make sure of it."

My door opened, and the fey in question looked up at me.

"Are you ready, June?" he asked.

"Yep. Let's get in there and find what we need."

He lifted me down from the cab and gestured to the fey around us.

"Tell us what we're looking for."

"No playgrounds this time. We're looking for houses that might have had someone with medical needs. Like a ramp going up to a front door."

They grunted in understanding.

"May I carry you?" Tor asked.

I nodded, trying not to flush. He'd been tongue deep between my legs a few hours ago, yet somehow managed to act business as usual. I wasn't sure if I admired his casual attitude or worried that his life goal hadn't measured up to his standards.

As soon as I was in his arms, he ran with me, the other fey falling in around us. The leap from the bridge ripped a squeak from me. Tor dipped his head to mine and brushed his nose against my temple, saying nothing. He didn't need to. The gesture was reassuring in itself.

We ran in silence for several moments before I heard the first moan. Tor veered toward the nearest house and jumped to the roof while the others did the same on different houses. We watched from our rooftop positions as a herd of infected moved fluidly between the buildings a block away.

Tor's hold on me tightened fractionally, letting me know he didn't like what he was seeing, either.

The infected slowed and their calls stopped. The sound of my own breathing seemed too loud in the silence. One of the fey across the street looked at us and pointed straight down. I thought he was telling us to leave the roof until Tor quietly lay back against the outcropping of the dormer's wall. He kept me close to his side, holding me in place, face to face. His finger pressed against my lips, and I nodded.

While I wanted to believe the infected wouldn't get to me, that Tor and the other fey would keep me safe, I knew there was always a chance something could go wrong. My pulse began to race. Tor's finger moved from my mouth and traced from my temple to my jaw, like he was trying to comfort me. I gave him a weak smile, which widened when he flashed his teeth at me.

The suddenness of an infected call so close to us made me jump. Tor shook his head slightly and continued to stroke my cheek. I focused on his eyes and tried to breathe quietly. We stayed like that for several long minutes before he flashed his teeth again and picked me up.

I watched one of the fey jump lightly from roof to roof, following the infected. The rest leapt to the ground and started walking again.

CHAPTER TEN

We managed to find several houses with ramps and a house with an "oxygen in use" warning sign taped to the door. I didn't think Uan needed oxygen, but the tanks were too useful to pass up. Tor made me wait outside with him and the rest of the group while two fey went inside to collect everything. He said it smelled too bad to let me in.

Between all of our stops, we had morphine, which I figured Cassie might use on Uan; several prescription painkillers, which Adam could use; and two shotguns, which I could use if Adam's apology wasn't good enough.

"We should head back," I said softly.

Tor immediately picked me up and started jogging. We'd avoided two infected herds while scavenging and killed plenty more inside the houses. The fey were on edge.

When we arrived at the bridge, I saw they had a reason to be. Bodies littered the area around the overpass, and gore coated the sides of the trucks. Tor reluctantly let me stand on my own, but I could feel the heat of him radiating against my back. Given the number of times he'd had to jump on a roof with me, I didn't mind his hovering proximity.

"Trouble?" I asked Ryan as the fey stowed what we'd collected.

"You could say that. A herd of infected spotted us and started calling out. Every infected within hearing came running. It was a mess. Thankfully, the others were already back and in the trucks. We were about to send a party out for you."

"Sorry we took longer, but I think it was worthwhile. I found morphine."

"What? No way. A clinic?"

"No. Someone on hospice, I think. Tor didn't let me inside."

"It smelled too bad," Tor said, setting his hands on my shoulders.

"Death usually does," Ryan said solemnly. "But I'm glad everyone's okay and twice as glad you found some morphine. Uan needs it bad. Let's load up so we can get home. I'm hungry."

I glanced at all the nasty around us.

"You have a strong constitution if you're surrounded by this and still hungry."

He shrugged and smiled as he started walking backward to his own truck.

"It's the curse of my age. I'm always hungry."

Shaking my head, I jogged to the truck that Richard had driven here. Tor opened the passenger door and helped me up.

"Ready to go home?" Richard asked.

"More than ready. Did the Tenacity people get a lot of supplies?"

"Most of them came back after the first house. Honestly, it's a good thing too. Who knows how many we would have lost if they'd still been out there when the infected swarmed."

I wasn't exactly sure if I'd call it a good thing but was smart enough to know that was my bitterness influencing my opinions and kept that thought to myself.

The ride back to Tenacity was relatively quiet, and I used that time to think about how I felt regarding what Adam had done. Definitely still angry. Betrayed. Hurt.

Confused.

I didn't understand how Adam could think what he'd done was okay. And I couldn't imagine how upset Tor would be if he ever found out Adam had tricked him. After all, Tor politely asked each and every time he wanted to pick me up, barring life-threatening emergencies. I had no doubt that, eventually, someone would set him straight about pussy licking not being an acceptable way to wake up someone else's girlfriend. And then what? We'd lose our place in Tolerance because Adam had some dumb idea in his head that I was into a reverse harem lifestyle?

By the time we reached Tenacity, I still had no idea how I wanted to handle the conversation I knew Adam and I needed to have. My emotions were high, and I wasn't sure I was ready to face him yet.

Thankfully, there were supplies to unload and medicine to deliver. Ryan and Richard willingly handed over all the medicine to me while they worked to unload everything else. With the rattling shoe box in my arms, Tor ran me back to Tolerance with our group of fey. Although he didn't say anything on the way, I felt his repetitive questioning glance.

As soon as we were inside the wall and I was on my own two feet, I faced him.

"What's wrong?"

"I don't know. You're quiet and angry."

"I'm still upset about how Adam treated me this morning."

Tor frowned. "How did he treat you?"

"Not nice."

"I will talk to him."

I made a face. "As much as I would appreciate that, I think this is something Adam and I need to talk out on our own. Thanks, though."

He grunted and led the way to Cassie's. The fey we passed kept giving me weird looks. They'd done that before, but it'd felt more curious. Now it felt…confused. Like they were trying to figure out who I was.

I shrugged it off and waited for someone to answer Tor's knock.

Kerr, Cassie's husband, opened the door and glanced at us.

"We found some medicine," I said. "Is Cassie around?"

He nodded and let us in. A movie played in the background, showing a girl with red hair shooting a bow.

"I like this one," Tor said, nudging me. "We should watch it with Adam."

I smiled and agreed as we made our way to the kitchen where Cassie was at the stove, stirring something that smelled really good. My stomach growled, proving that I could have an appetite even after seeing all that infected goo.

"Hi, Cassie. I think we found some good stuff for you. The fey collected everything. Even the opened bottles. I figured we might not be able to afford to be picky, but will leave that up to you."

Cassie's eyes lit when she saw the morphine. She sorted through the bottles and pulled out one with thirteen Oxy in it.

"You can take these for Adam. Just don't leave them around where he can self-administer. As soon as dinner's done, I'll swing by to check on him."

"Maybe hold off on the check-in until the morning."

Cassie stopped sorting to look at me.

"Why?"

"Frankly, Adam's being an asshole, and he and I need to have a long talk because I'm struggling to forgive his behavior. He's not acting like the man I know."

Cassie nodded thoughtfully.

"He went through an emotionally and physically traumatic experience. Bruises fade with time, but the emotions take longer to process. I imagine his feelings of helplessness and fear for you aren't easy to sort through."

Part of me wanted to feel guilty for not being more forgiving. The other part of me knew his actions hadn't just teetered on the line of unforgivable. They'd stomped on it.

"I'll keep that in mind when I talk to him."

"Have Brog or Tor get me if Adam needs anything."

I nodded and left with Tor.

"Do you want to talk to Adam privately again?" Tor asked.

"Maybe. I don't know if I want to do it right away."

He grunted and walked beside me. I was starting to get the hang of Tolerance's layout. At least, the way between our house, Cassie's, and the meeting spot along the wall.

The house was dark when it came into sight, which I thought was a little odd. Did Brog think that having lights on would wake up Adam if he was resting?

I was quiet when I opened the door, but the house was more so. I flicked on a light.

"Brog?"

There was no answer.

Tor moved off to the bedroom while I removed my knife harness.

"Adam's not here," Tor called.

"What do you mean he's not there? Where else would he be?"

Tor emerged with a piece of paper in his hand.

June,

Brog has a gaming console at his place. I'm going to go hang out there. You two lovebirds have a cozy night. Make sure to tell Tor he can wake you up early again.

Adam

I STARED at the note and regretted taking off my knives. That Adam wasn't in his right mind was completely clear to me. How could he even think, after my reaction this morning, that I would be okay with inviting Tor's attention again?

Fisting my free hand, I tried to remember Cassie's perspective on Adam's behavior as I read the note again but just couldn't. Helplessness be damned. I'd been in that room too. I'd listened to the muffled beating while they held me down. I'd had no idea what was going to happen next and had feared the same beating or worse. But I wasn't pushing Adam away in response.

Adam was acting like a coward.

"Tor, do you know where Brog lives?"

"Yes."

"Take me there."

I folded the note and gripped it tightly as I followed Tor from the house. Brog's place wasn't too far away. Not far enough to stop shaking or to calm myself down. I still managed to knock politely and smile at Brog when he answered.

"Hi, Brog. Could I speak with Adam, please?"

"Not now," Adam called from inside. "We're in the middle of a game."

Any shred of patience evaporated. I stepped around Brog without invitation and stared at Adam, who sat in a recliner with his leg propped and a controller in his hands. He didn't even have the decency to look at me.

"I'm struggling to be understanding, Adam. I know you went through something terrible, but you're not the only one. I was there, too. Stop treating me like I don't matter to you."

Adam sighed, all the life seeming to drain from him as he looked at me.

"You're right. I'm not being fair to you. I'm sorry, June. I can't do this anymore."

My anger withered at the sight of his defeated expression, and a tight, sick ball settled into my stomach as he continued.

"It would be better for everyone if I stay with Brog until it's time to leave for the cave."

"What are you saying?" He couldn't be saying what I thought he was. Not now. Not after everything we'd been through.

"I'm saying we're done, June. I don't want you to worry about me when I'm gone, and I don't want to worry about you."

A numb state of shock blanketed me as he shifted his gaze to Tor, who stood behind me.

"I'm holding you to your promise. Keep her safe."

Gutted and bleeding from the inside, I couldn't move. I couldn't accept what he was saying.

"You don't mean that. You're hurt and afraid you can't keep me safe. Both will pass."

"No, June. They won't." His gaze shifted again. "Don't let her come back here. It's only going to hurt her more."

That sentiment snapped the fragile hold I'd maintained on my hope. Hope that he was only struggling as Cassie had said. Hope that he'd give himself some time to heal. Hope that he'd realize how much I loved him.

"Hurt me more? How can you possibly think anything can hurt more than how you've already hurt me?"

He flinched.

"Take her home, Tor, before she starts yelling."

Yelling? I dug the pill bottle out of my pocket and tossed it to him.

"There's the oxy I risked my life getting. For you. Let me know when you're ready to act like a decent human being."

He picked up the controller and started playing the game again, not acknowledging the pills that rested in his lap.

I turned and walked out the door. Everything started to shake. My hands. My arms. My legs. I stumbled a few steps and started to sniffle. A pained sound escaped me.

A moment later, I was up in Tor's arms. Tears started falling in earnest, and I tucked my face against his chest. While heartache was the prevalent emotion, others were bubbling beneath it. Disbelief and denial were at the forefront. Adam had never been such a complete ass to me. Ever. This had to be some kind of weird lack of confidence thing. He was doubting his ability to keep me safe and pushing me toward someone he thought was better for me.

That brought on more tears. How could he think a complete stranger was better for me? Three years. Talks about getting married. A family. All gone.

I barely registered the sound of a door opening. It was only when Tor put me down and started unzipping my jacket that I realized we were home. Home without Adam. What was I supposed to do now? Mooch off of Tor? Was my invitation to stay at Tolerance only good if Adam and I were a couple?

The importance of those questions collapsed under the weight of the bigger one. Were we really over? He would come to his senses. He had to. Yet, his comment to Tor about not letting me come back rang with a finality I couldn't ignore.

Tor's face swam into focus right before mine. Concern lit his green and gold eyes.

"Should I get Cassie?"

I shook my head, my throat too tight and aching to answer.

He grunted and smoothed a hand over my head. The comforting gesture only made me cry harder because it should have been Adam.

Tor immediately removed his hand and looked around the room before tugging on his ear.

Knowing my crying was making him uncomfortable, I hung up my jacket and went upstairs. The bed welcomed me back, and I burrowed under the covers.

Why hadn't I seen this coming? What could I have done differently? My mind raced as my insides hurt. I wished today had never happened. Maybe I shouldn't have gotten so mad about this morning's misunderstanding. Maybe I should have taken some time to talk to Adam about how he was feeling before I left. Maybe I should have been clear that I hadn't liked what Tor had done.

I barely had that thought when guilt gutted me because I had liked it. Far too much. Maybe that was why Adam left. Maybe he heard me.

My throat grew tighter and more painful as I continued to cry.

A whisper of noise almost muffled by the sounds I was making registered enough that I lowered the blanket from over my head. Tor paced nearby, tugging on his ear so hard it was turning dark grey. When he turned and saw me looking at him, he hurried to the bed and fell to his knees beside it.

"I don't know what to do."

Breath hitching, I tried to reassure him.

"Adam hurt my heart, Tor. Nothing but time will take that pain away." My face crumpled as I struggled under the weight of those words. Time. Time without Adam.

Tor made an angry sound.

"Adam is being stupid."

I nodded, tears falling faster. Tor picked me up and partially slid under me, hugging me to his chest.

"He should have married you," Tor said, sounding angry.

"He should have," I whispered brokenly. "We talked about it, but he never proposed. He wanted to wait until we were out of school and more settled in our careers."

I rubbed my face against Tor's hard chest, trying to soothe away some of the pain throbbing in my head.

"It wasn't supposed to be like this. He always worried about me. My safety. My happiness. How does that go away in a few days? How can he just decide not to love me anymore?"

The last words were choked, and I gave up speaking and let the tears fall in earnest.

Eventually, the tears dried up, and a numbness settled in. It pulled me into the welcome escape of sleep. The dreams were a mix of happy Adam moments and running for my life from infected. Both were easier to deal with than my current reality, which reinserted itself the moment I opened my eyes the next morning.

Adam isn't here. He's gone. He's left me.

A fresh torrent of tears washed over my puffy eyes. The same question I'd spoken out loud echoed in my head. After three years together, how could he suddenly decide we were done?

An arm slithered under my side. I didn't care who or why. It could have been an infected for all it mattered, and I wouldn't have moved. I hurt too much. Which is why I didn't fight when I was picked up, blankets and all.

Tor looked down at me, his expression deeply troubled. I closed my eyes, not wanting to see his concern, and didn't open them again when he started walking. I didn't care where he was taking me. I hurt so much nothing else mattered.

The world had ripped everything from me. My home. My family. My future. Adam was the only thing I'd had left. And now he was gone too.

A door opened, and fresh air cooled my overheated face. I didn't want the relief. I wanted Adam. Turning my head into Tor's chest, I cried harder. The cadence of his step increased and then stopped.

My head hurt almost as much as my heart.

"She won't stop crying," Tor said.

"Why?"

I barely registered the voice.

"Adam hurt her heart."

The sympathetic sound increased my tears.

"Bring her in and set her on the couch."

Tor did more than put me down, he stripped the blankets from me, revealing Angel's understanding face.

"Come here, you," she said, opening her arms.

I hugged her hard and continued to cry as she stroked my hair.

"Men are assholes," she murmured. "I'll teach you to use my bow so you can shoot him in the dick."

There were twin pained breaths in response to that comment.

"Angel, no dick shooting."

"Based on how she's crying, it's shooting or cutting it off."

I partially laughed through my tears at the absurdity of her comment. She heard it and pulled back enough to look me in the eye.

"You want to tell me about it?"

Something about the understanding in her expression hit me hard, and I realized that was exactly what I needed. Someone to listen. Someone to tell me what went wrong. Someone who would understand.

But I hesitated and glanced at the two fey watching me with matching concern. There were some things I couldn't say in front of them. Not without possibly jeopardizing Adam's and my place in Tolerance.

"Could I speak to Angel privately? With no one else listening?" A hitched breath interrupted every other word.

"Yes," Tor said, grabbing the other fey by the arm. "We will be outside."

"Wait, Angel needs—"

"Angel needs you to leave and not listen, like June said,"

she said interrupting the other fey. "Out. I'll give a yell when we're done."

Tor moved like his feet were on fire and dragged the other guy out the door. Angel didn't pay them any attention, though. She focused on me.

I wiped my face and swallowed thickly several times, doing my best to calm down enough to sound coherent.

"Adam and I were together for three years before the earthquakes. We talked about getting married. Having kids." Fresh tears welled up with the new wave of pain. "Everything was fine until he was hurt. His leg."

My lower lip trembled.

"He used to wake me up with oral. He said he loved the sounds I made." I broke down for a minute and cried. She rubbed my arm consolingly until I pulled myself together enough to speak again. "I was dreaming we were in the back of his truck. He was between my legs, tugging down my underwear. Only I wasn't dreaming. The mouth on me was real, and I was so happy Adam was trying. But it wasn't Adam."

"Oh, shit."

"It was Tor. Adam told him what to do."

"Tor is in so much trouble."

I shook my head and explained exactly what had happened. How Adam had twisted things around and manipulated Tor. And how I'd kept the truth of what Adam had done from Tor.

"Why would Adam do that?" she asked.

"I don't know. We were fine. Really fine. We had sex just before those men beat him up. Nothing was wrong, or if it was, I didn't see it."

Even as I said it, his words from yesterday morning rang in my heart.

"What?" Angel asked, watching me closely.

"When I confronted Adam, he said that I needed Tor. That sleeping with him would give me immunity. I went out to get Adam more medicine, and when I came back, there was a note. He said he was staying with Brog to play video games so we lovebirds would have alone time."

"Oh, June."

"I went to Brog's to demand an explanation. Adam wouldn't even look at me until I said he wasn't being fair. That's when he told me I was right and that we were done. He can't mean that, right? I mean, it doesn't make any sense. Who does that? Who gives their girlfriend away like some unwanted piece of—" A sob stole my words.

"Oh, sweetie." Angel hugged me again. "I don't know Adam, and I don't know you very well. But I do know the signs of a failing relationship. Letting another guy go down on your girl is at the top of the list. Adam isn't worth your tears, no matter what kind of history you have together. He willingly threw away what you had. The only thing you should be asking yourself is, 'now what?' Our lives are too precarious to waste energy on lost causes."

"So I'm supposed to give up on him and forget everything we've been through together?"

"Forget? No. Give up on the man who already gave up on you?"

She pulled back and looked me in the eye.

"You're still alive because you're a survivor. Surviving means moving forward, no matter what. Holding on to something that isn't there is dangerous."

The truth in her words severed that last thread of hope I'd been clinging to. The pain surged and settled deep in my chest even as my tears slowed.

Angel was right. I wouldn't forget, and I also wouldn't try holding onto a man who didn't want to be held.

"What am I supposed to do then? Mooch off of Tor until…what?"

"You don't need to decide your future today. In fact, I recommend not thinking about it for a little while. You need a distraction."

She nudged me to my feet, and I helped her stand.

"What kind of distraction?"

"I was serious about the dick shooting. Come on. It's exercise, and it's fun watching all the guys wince when we hit one."

CHAPTER ELEVEN

"ELBOW HIGHER," ANGEL SAID. "YEAH, THAT LOOKS RIGHT. DON'T release. Return to the starting position and draw again. You'll need to do that a hundred times once Brenna gets here."

"Why? My arm already hurts."

"Trust me, it'll hurt worse tomorrow. But it's a hurt you'll be able to rub and make feel better."

I nodded, understanding what she was saying, and drew again. Each time, it got harder, but she claimed I was getting better. When I heard someone shout hello, I quickly relaxed my stance, ready for a break.

"That's Eden," Angel said, helpfully reminding me.

"She's the one that promised not to shoot real dicks," I said, remembering a conversation I'd had with Tor.

Angel laughed.

"Yeah, Ghua was pretty worried. Shax is a little more relaxed about it."

"No real dick shooting," Shax said abruptly from where he and Tor were standing a safe distance away.

Angel grinned at me.

"What if real dick shooting helps the baby come out faster?"

The man looked truly torn, and Angel pealed with laughter.

"I'm kidding, babe. That wouldn't help. Your dick is safe with me."

Eden jogged up to us, a smile on her face.

"Obviously, everyone's dick is safe with me since I took an unbreakable oath."

The fey behind her grunted, dropped a kiss on the top of her head, then walked off to join the other two.

"Testicles are a completely different body part, though," Angel said. "We should try for that ballsack today."

I looked at the melted dildo blob and spotted the monstrously huge green scrotum protruding from the right side. There was a black lumpy strand right below it.

"Are those anal beads?"

"Shh. We don't talk about those," Eden said with a panicked look in her eyes.

"Most of the metal ones sunk when the fire was really going. There was so much smoke, and it smelled so bad that they put it out before everything melted into obscurity. You'll see a lot of nifty things in there."

"Stop. I'm begging you," Eden whispered.

"If you walk around to the back side, there's a plastic hand. You know what that's for, right?" Angel asked.

"He's listening," Eden hissed.

Angel grinned at her. "You've been together for months now. Don't you want some new ideas to spice things up?"

"I still have a hard time walking some mornings. We do not need to feed the machine more data. In fact, I think Ghua needs to be in the room when you deliver so he understands what he's trying to do to me."

"Yes," Ghua said. "I want to watch the baby come out."

"Sorry, Ghua. I promised the last spot would be a random drawing."

"How many people are going to watch you deliver?" I asked, trying to keep up with the conversation.

"Well, Shax is going to be there, obviously. Cassie and Kerr. Julie's going to be there, too, since she's been through it and will be able to keep Shax calm."

"I will be calm, Angel," Shax called.

"We need to start a pool," Eden said. "Put me down for fainting. Five candy bars."

"I'll get Garrett to put something together," Angel promised. "He wants to be at the house but not in the room. Solin will be the fifth. I heard he can draw and am hoping he can capture the moment to share with the other fey. That leaves one more spot. Julie and Cassie both agree that six will be crowded, but I know the fey will stand back and stay out of the way, so I'm not worried."

"When are you due?" I asked.

Angel shrugged. "Who knows. When it's time, it's time. Cassie says I'm looking more like I'm in the last few weeks, but I think that's the snack cakes they keep feeding me." She rubbed the side of her belly, not seeming upset by the extra treats. "I wouldn't mind if the ninja stayed put for a little longer. He's safe where he is."

"He will be safe out here, too, Angel, where I can hold him."

She looked at Shax, her expression grave.

"Babe, there's been something I've been meaning to tell you. We can't have sex for six weeks after the baby's born. It takes that long for my insides to heal."

His look of horror was mirrored on the faces of the other fey gathered.

Eden started laughing.

"Yeah, that's right. Babies break your favorite toy."

Although I managed to keep a smile on my face for all their playful banter, it hurt. I'd been so ready for that phase of my life.

"Sorry I'm late," a voice called, redirecting everyone's attention.

A young woman and another fey strode our way. The fey was huge and scarred and looked ready to tear someone's head off. The woman, while also very serious, didn't convey the same sense of danger. I recognized her as the one who'd been standing on top of the trucks the day Adam and I had been rescued. The reminder only caused me more pain.

"Hey, Brenna. How's Uan?" Angel asked.

"Not good. Instead of getting better, he seems to be slowly getting worse. Kerr checked him over, top to bottom, for embedded teeth or claws but couldn't find anything. He's sure that's the problem, but with Uan's insides so messed up..." She shook her head. "Kerr finally convinced Mom it was time. He's going to talk to Drav about taking Uan back to the caves."

"When?" Eden asked.

"Two days. Three days tops. They want to make sure he's in the caves and his crystal is glowing before anything happens."

The big man beside her reached out and set a hand on her shoulder. She glanced up at him, and her bottom lip trembled.

"You will not lose another father," he said, his voice a raspy rumble.

She nodded.

"I brought new blood for you to teach," Angel said, quickly changing the subject. "Her stance is a mess, though."

Brenna looked at Angel and smiled crookedly before looking at me.

"I hope you're ready to be my distraction," she said.

"As long as you're ready to be mine," I replied.

For the next hour, I worked hard to learn everything Brenna had to teach me. Then I watched Hannah, a girl with a bright smile, fight with Eden. They moved fast and fought rough. But neither one held a grudge and always offered the other a hand up.

I understood why the other women were getting together every day. They were honing their skills. Learning to fight so they'd have a better chance of surviving whatever was thrown their way. They were doing what Adam never wanted me to do because he was too busy trying to shelter me.

"You ready for a turn?" Hannah said, looking at me.

"I don't think June is ready to fight," Tor said, stepping forward.

After watching them, I knew I would get my butt handed to me, but I didn't want that to hold me back.

"I'd like to try anyway."

"Good, I'm taking a break," Eden said, collapsing on the frozen ground nearby.

Hannah waved me forward.

"We'll start simple and use Merdon's favorite move," she said. "I'm going to try to knock you to the ground. Make sure you land on your back and get your forearm up to my throat. If I'm an infected, that move keeps my teeth from getting to you. Brace your hand on my shoulder for support. Ready?"

I nodded but quickly learned how unready I was.

Despite all the time I had spent on the treadmill in the bunker, Hannah was faster and stronger. And, it didn't matter that they'd all been doing this longer, it still frustrated me to be the least able-bodied. Well, Angel was technically less able than me, but she was pregnant. I didn't even have that as an excuse.

"I know that face," Hannah said, offering me yet another hand up. "Don't let the voice in your head talk you down. You're doing great, and fighting with you is better than fighting with Eden. She bites."

"So do infected," Eden called out, not taking her eyes off of Brenna, who was working with her on the bow.

"Please don't quit and leave me with the biter," Hannah begged.

"I'm done after this," Brenna called.

"Me too," Angel said, letting an arrow fly. "My back's getting sore. Feet, too."

Hannah rolled her eyes. "You're only saying that so you get a massage."

"Yep," Angel said with an unrepentant grin. "You should try it some time."

Hannah snorted. "Merdon doesn't do manipulation."

"Does he know most massages have happy endings?"

"Angel, if you don't shut your mouth, I'm shoving a snack cake in it," Eden warned.

Hannah flashed a bright smile at me. "Looks like you're off the hook. You better be here tomorrow, though."

"She will be," Angel said. "I'll stop by and pick her up."

The group broke apart, still bantering as they went their own separate ways. Tor approached, his gaze seeing far too much as he studied me.

"Are you hungry?" he asked.

"A little," I admitted. All the exercise had reminded me I'd skipped breakfast. And dinner the night before.

We slowly walked back to the house. The hurt crept back in as I looked through the cupboards for something easy to make.

"Do you want to watch a movie?" Tor asked.

"Sure. A movie sounds good."

Except, I didn't really see the movie. My mind fixated on Adam and everything that had gone wrong. It would be easy to say it was the beating that had been the catalyst, but the beating would have never happened if the world was still the way it had been. If Adam and I were finishing up our senior years. If he was still talking to agents and scouts.

Tor laughed, drawing my attention. He glanced at me and flashed his teeth. I couldn't help but smile back and feel a twinge of guilt at my selfish thinking. Sure, without the earthquake, my life would probably still have been happily moving along. But then Tor would have been stuck in his caves, living endless lives with no hope for a future family whatsoever without women.

That thought caused a deeply painful epiphany that I didn't want to acknowledge.

Although I felt like my future had been ripped from me, that wasn't the reality. There were other men out there. Perhaps, one day, that would sound like a good thing. Just not today.

When the movie ended, I went upstairs and ran myself a hot bath. It'd been ages since I'd had one, and it felt good. Since Angel had been right about crying, I didn't waste any more tears on Adam. Instead, I let myself remember all the good things. The late nights laughing. The romantic moments. The heated looks. Cheering him on at his games. In each memory, I began to see what I loved most about him. His unshakable confidence, persistence, and his incredible smile.

Tenacity had taken that man from me.

Without a doubt, Cassie was right. Adam was dealing with some serious trauma. What had happened changed him. And Angel was right, too. There was no point clinging to a man who'd made it very clear we were done. Yet, I knew I was right, too. Adam did still love me. Why else would he demand Tor keep his promise to protect me after telling me we were through?

"ADAM SAID NOT TO COME BACK," Tor said, striding beside me.

"Yeah, Adam's been talking a lot of crap lately."

Tor stepped in front of me and gently clasped my arms to prevent a collision.

"No, June. He will hurt your heart again." He wrapped his arms around me, his heart thudding hard under his ribs as he pressed my head to the base of his sternum. "Let Adam be stupid. No more crying."

I sighed and patted Tor's back before extracting myself.

"I won't cry anymore."

His gaze swept over my face, and I clearly saw the doubt in his expression.

"I promise I won't cry again."

"You hurt my heart when you cry."

Why couldn't Adam be that sweet?

I offered Tor a sad smile.

"I'm sorry I cried so much. It takes time to understand why things happen. I think I now understand why Adam told me he didn't want me anymore. I also think he still plans on going to the caves with Uan. I want to talk to him before that happens. If I don't, I might have a lot of regrets that will haunt me for the rest of my life."

He considered me for a long moment before stepping aside.

"If Adam makes you cry again, more than his leg will need healing."

"You know what? Maybe I should talk to Adam alone."

Tor grunted but continued up the walkway with me. Brog opened the door on the second knock.

"Adam is busy, June. He said—"

I stepped around him like last time and strode into the living room. Adam was on the couch this time. He still held a controller in his hand, though. I plucked it from his grasp and tossed it across the room.

"Hey, you can't buy those anymore," he said, scowling at me.

Despite my sore legs, I knelt beside him so we were close to eye level.

"Uan's leaving soon. Two or three days tops."

Adam's expression became shuttered.

"I know."

"And you're still going?"

"I am."

"I hope it works for you, Adam. I really do. I'm not going to sit here waiting for you while you're gone. That was the whole point of the break-up, right?"

He swallowed hard.

"But I'm not going to move on like you want, either. I'll worry about you each day that you're gone whether you want me to or not. But, I want you to know you don't have to worry about me. I was fine before you, Adam, and I'll find a way to be fine without you." I leaned forward and kissed his cheek. "I will always love you," I said softly.

When I pulled back, his eyes were closed.

"Please just go, June. You're making this harder than it needs to be."

"No, Adam. You did that."

I stood and walked toward the two fey by the door.

"Thanks for taking care of him, Brog."

He grunted and glanced at Tor, who was watching me for any sign of a breakdown.

"Let's go," I said. "I have a lot I need to do."

Tor didn't ask what I meant. He simply followed me from the house.

I was fine without conversation. My mind was already racing. I'd meant every word I'd said to Adam. I hoped his trip to the caves would end with him healed, and I'd worry about him and probably wouldn't sleep well until he was back. Yet, I wasn't going to stop living while he was gone. I was also done foolishly hoping he'd change his mind and want me once he was healed. The reality was that he'd likely pull this again the next time something happened, and I refused to put myself through that kind of heartache more than once.

Understanding that didn't stop me from loving him though. It still hurt knowing that we were done. But I was determined to channel that into something useful.

"I'd like to meet Mya. Do you think that's possible?" I asked Tor.

"Yes."

We continued past our house toward the other side of Tolerance. I spotted the home I needed as soon as we turned onto the street. Fey were gathered before it, and a man stood on the porch.

"Ghua will lead the group. The infected have proven themselves smart. Nancy has agreed that we must keep the group small for the safety of the humans that remain. Twelve volunteers are needed. No more."

The gathered fey broke into groups and started talking in low voices. The fey on the porch went inside without waiting for the outcome of whatever the others discussed. My steps slowed with my uncertainty. Maybe this wasn't a good time to interrupt with my ideas.

Tor didn't notice my hesitation and marched right up to the door. His knock didn't silence the gathered men, but it did bring the speaker to the door.

"Tor," he said when the big fey saw us.

"Drav, June would like to meet Mya."

Drav grunted and opened the door for us to enter. The smell of some kind of baked sweets hit me, and I inhaled appreciatively.

"What is that?" I asked.

"Cake," a woman called from the kitchen. "Come in here and help me taste test it."

I shed my jacket as I moved toward the sound of her voice.

A young woman with dark hair moved around the kitchen. The cake in question rested on the stovetop as she melted some chocolate. She glanced at me when I entered the room.

"June?" she said. At my nod, she smiled. "I've heard a bit about you. I was going to give you another day to settle in then come for a visit. Eden mentioned that you were at their feight club this morning."

"Yeah. It was interesting."

"I bet. One of these mornings, I'll wake up early enough to check it out."

"They go until lunch."

She flashed a grin at me. "So no excuses for tomorrow, eh?"

I gave a small shrug, still trying to gauge what type of person Mya was. She was the gatekeeper for Tolerance. She was the reason Adam and I had gone to Tenacity in the first place. I couldn't decide what that made her in my eyes.

"Adam left me, thanks to the beating he received in Tenacity."

All humor left Mya. She exhaled heavily and fully faced me.

"I heard." Her gaze flicked to something over my shoulder, and I glanced back to find both Drav and Tor standing there. "Could you two give us a few minutes for some girl talk?"

They both left without another sound.

"How'd you hear?" I asked.

"News travels fast here. The fey like to share what they learn about humans. Seeing a man give up a perfectly good female blew their minds. They don't understand. To them, relationships are all or nothing from the start. There's no test period. No dating, you know?"

"Yes, I've been getting that impression." I moved to the table and took a seat. "The fey aren't the problem, though. It's the people in Tenacity. Your dad told me that you've been telling Matt he needs to remove the bad apples from Tenacity. Is that true?"

"Yeah. He and I have talked about it several times. It's not simple, though. If he removes people without having cause, he'll have a riot on his hands. Honestly, there are days I wouldn't care if that happens. Then, I look at all the fey still without females of their own and know we need to keep trying to find a peaceful way to bring the two communities together. The fey are counting on us. They need each human that remains. They've been alone for too long."

"I heard," I said. "And I feel bad for them. But not bad enough to keep doing nothing. The hate is festering. Whether Matt does something or not, he's going to end up with a riot. The mood is volatile over there and growing more so each day due to their desperation and fear."

She studied me for a moment.

"Matt's a reasonable person. If you have any ideas, I'm sure he'd listen."

I shook my head.

"I'm sure he wouldn't. The ideas I have aren't nice."

Mya's brows rose.

"Those people lived here, ransacked our supply shed, and spit on the fey. Even if Matt's not in the mood to listen to 'not nice,' I am." She joined me at the table as she spoke. "Tell me your ideas."

"We need to profile everyone in Tenacity."

"That's a lot of people."

"I know. But I have a lot of time on my hands."

"How do you want to profile them?"

I smiled at the interest in her expression.

"I'll need fey help. Emily and Tor told me a little about Emily's efforts to find ways to integrate humans and fey. Her lack of volunteers says a lot. People are afraid of the fey. Why wouldn't they be? The first time I saw two at our farm, one of them lifted a damn cow. Do you know how terrifying that show of strength was? The second time I saw the fey, they were covered in blood. Those encounters built a perception that they were dangerous. Of course, humans fear them. We need to change their perception, and in our attempt to change human perception, we'll watch. We'll profile."

"That sounds great, but how."

"You have food, and Tenacity needs it."

Mya was already shaking her head. "We've tried that. Giving those asshats food only made them feel more entitled to it. We're not going down that road again."

"We're not going to give it to them. We're going to soup-kitchen it. Fey prepared and served food in a common group area where we can watch how people react and take notes."

Mya leaned back in her chair, clearly considering the idea.

"That's brilliant. The haters will balk at the idea of having to eat fey food. The hungry people will see fey doing something mundane and domestic." Her smile grew. "That could work."

"Being hateful isn't enough to get kicked out of Tenacity, though," I said. "Stealing food is. We build a list of the haters, then we bait them to steal until each one is gone."

"How do we bait them?"

"The same way Adam did. I'll move back to Tenacity and go out on supply runs. I show off what I bring back and be vocal about everyone else's lack of initiative while eating like a queen."

"No," she said, shaking her head. "That's too dangerous. Look at what happened to Adam. The fey will never go for it."

"I want the people who beat Adam to be caught and exiled. In order to do that, I need to see faces and have witnesses. The bunker had cameras all over the place. I want to do something similar. And I don't plan on being alone. With your permission and Matt's agreement, I'd like a fey to watch over me while I'm in Tenacity. Whoever volunteers would need to stay hidden at all times and understand he's only there to observe. No violence under any circumstances."

Mya was silent for a long moment.

"Every decision I've made has come down to a simple question. Will this help protect the people I care about?" She sighed. "The short answer is yes in this case. But the long answer is more complicated. Who are we to tell other people what to think? Don't they have a right to their fears and biases just as we have a right to ours?"

"Everyone has a right to their own beliefs until those beliefs start harming people. If these people want to hate the fey, they can do it somewhere else. No violence."

"Then, I agree to your plan."

CHAPTER TWELVE

Mya talked my plan over with Drav. He didn't like it any more than she had. But his expression was nothing compared to Tor's.

"No. It's not safe," he said fiercely.

"It will be safe. A fey presence is all the deterrent the humans will need. They aren't stupid enough to try to attack me in front of a fey."

"I promised Adam that I would keep you safe."

"Think of it this way. If the troublemakers are removed, the relations between the two settlements will improve. That means more women will want to volunteer for those date nights and attend art classes."

"And the massage sessions," Mya added.

"There's massages?" I asked.

"Oh, yeah." Mya grinned. "Angel's been coaching Shax, and the others have been learning, too. They need human volunteers, though. Ryan and Garrett get a massage after every supply run."

"I might need to sign up for a few of those."

"No sign up needed. There's not much of a line." She looked at Tor. "If you're worried about her safety, you can volunteer to stay with her. I trust you'll stay hidden and not cause any issues. And, like June said, this is going to open up some opportunities for you and your brothers in the long run. You'll finally get your dinner date."

Drav and Tor shared a long, doubt-filled look.

"I won't be moving right away," I added. "First, we'll do the soup kitchen and take notes on how people react. We'll learn who's most likely to make trouble and also get a better idea of how many haters we're dealing with. Only when we have that information will we move on to the next phase. It could take weeks."

It could, but I knew it wouldn't.

"We agree to the soup kitchen and learning about the troublemakers. We will talk again about you moving to Tenacity afterward," Drav said.

"I'll talk to Ryan and Matt," Mya said. "Give me the rest of today to work on the logistics."

"I'd like to stay involved," I said.

"You will. I'll get Matt on board. Ryan will need to push for a bigger supply run in the next day or two so we have enough food to cook for the masses. Emily will need at least a day to make sure the fey will know what's expected of them in regard to cooking and serving the food."

I knew Mya was thinking out loud now and listened.

"Matt's going to need time to set up a temporary kitchen and tables." She frowned for a moment.

"I'm betting we can find some tables at some local parks. Does anyone know the area well?" I asked.

"We do," Drav said. "We will find tables."

The discussion went on for another thirty minutes until we had a fairly solid plan. Tomorrow, I'd go to feight club and let Angel know what was happening so she could recruit some fey to cook and serve. Afterward, I'd go to Emily's to help her come up with a training plan for the fey and for the food prep. Having a purpose and a goal felt good.

We left the house when the car lights already lit up the night sky. Tor was unusually quiet on the walk home.

"Are you mad?" I asked.

"No. I'm worried. Are you taking risks because Adam hurt your heart?"

The insightful question made me pause. Tor was more perceptive than I'd realized. He was smarter, too.

"I'm not taking any risk that I haven't already taken, Tor. I lived in Tenacity before coming here. And I'm going back because they hurt Adam, not because he hurt me. What those people did was wrong, and their actions are only going to get worse if someone doesn't step in and stop them."

"Matt can stop them."

"He would have already if he could. He needs someone else to take the lead. Someone to be the fall guy if things go wrong, so he can maintain what little control he has."

"I don't like this."

"I know, and I'm sorry for that. But this is important to me. The infected and hellhounds bring enough unrest to our lives. We shouldn't be adding to it by fighting with each other. That needs to stop, or we'll never have any peace."

He opened the door for me and turned on the entry light as I hung up my jacket and slipped off my shoes.

"And having something to focus on right now is good for me. It helps keep my mind distracted from Adam."

Tor shrugged out of his jacket and hung it beside mine.

"We could play games instead."

"Or we could find bigger shirts for you. That can't be comfortable," I said, noting the way his shirt seemed glued to his chest and only slightly looser on his abs. It stopped a little shy of the waist line of his leather pants. "Where'd the shirts that fit go?"

Tor glanced down at himself and ran a hand over his chest.

"They all fit like this."

"What? No way." I told myself I would have noticed that. Wouldn't I? I couldn't unnotice it now.

Instead of heading toward the kitchen like I'd intended, I went upstairs and started rummaging through drawers. Most of his shirts were extra large. I found two double X's.

"Try this one on," I said, tossing it to him. He caught it and reached back with one hand to pull his shirt off from the neckline.

I stared at the rolling flex of his muscles and felt a flush rise to my cheeks as he tugged the new shirt into place. It still hugged his shoulders and chest, showing off his bulk.

Frowning, I picked up the shirt he'd worn and looked at the tag. A double X.

"This feels the same," he said.

"Because it is. Sorry. When we go out for supplies, we'll watch for bigger shirts."

He grunted and tugged the new one off and made no move to put another one on.

"Mya said that we needed to wear shirts. Warmer clothes make us look more human. The shirts are not comfortable."

He scratched at his chest and rolled his shoulders.

"This is better. Thank you."

Crap. Had I just given him permission to walk around shirtless? My gaze swept over his torso before I hurried from the room.

"I'll start dinner."

"Do you want to watch a movie?" he asked, following behind me.

"Sure. A movie sounds good. While I don't mind the cartoons, maybe we could watch something a little more adult tonight?"

He grunted and went to the living room, giving me some space to collect my thoughts in the kitchen. So much had happened in the last forty-eight hours that I hadn't really had time to process what had transpired between Tor and me.

Seeing him shirtless had brought it all back home, though. The man was built. Chiseled and buffed to perfection. Any blindness I'd had to it before was now gone, and I didn't like that. It was safer to not see Tor and not remember how amazing he'd been when he'd—

Another wave of heat washed through me. My attempt to squash it proved futile and frustrated me to no end. I didn't want to feel any attraction to Tor based on principle. It would be like admitting that Adam was right, which I refused to do.

Adam had been wrong to send Tor to wake me up. He was disillusioned if he thought breaking up with me would force me into Tor's arms. I'd been fine without a man in my life before Adam came along. I'd be fine again.

"What are you in the mood for tonight?" I asked. "Ravioli sound good?"

"Is it in the red paste?"

"Is red paste bad?"

"Like sour cream and onion."

I laughed and shuffled through the cans.

"You have a lot of ravioli for a guy who doesn't like red paste. Which of these cans do you like?"

The sudden appearance of an arm reaching around me made me jump.

"Sorry," he murmured, setting a hand on my other shoulder as he took a can of spam from the top shelf. "I like these."

"Okay. I think I can work with that."

He sat at the island and watched me dice the spam while some rice boiled.

"Do you think my plan will work?" I asked. "Will the people at Tenacity stop seeing fey as a threat if some of you serve them meals?"

"Maybe. Wearing clothes made some of the humans like us more. Giving them things made some of them pretend to like us. I like when you cook for me."

I smiled at him, trying only to focus on his face.

"And I like that you're so appreciative of it. Hopefully, the people in Tenacity will feel the same appreciation."

He grunted.

"Do you want me to wake you up before Angel arrives tomorrow? She will want to know about your plan, too."

"Sure," I caught what I was agreeing to and quickly added, "But not in my favorite way. That was a one-time thing, okay?"

"Why only one time? I like your favorite way. It's my favorite way, too."

My insides went hot, and I turned away to find the can of peas and carrots.

"You said you liked it," he said, hesitation filling his words.

I mentally cringed and knew I needed to handle the situation with more care.

"I did like it, Tor. But it was weird doing that with someone who wasn't my boyfriend."

"I will be your boyfriend. Then it won't be weird."

Gripping the can, I faced him. He tilted his head as he studied me.

"Why are you red? Are you angry?"

"Nope. I'm embarrassed."

"Why?"

"I feel like Adam took advantage of you by asking you to wake me up like that. I think he knew how much you'd like it, and he believed it would endear me to you enough that you'd keep me safe when he left. And in a way, I took advantage, too. I shouldn't have let you do that when I was still with Adam. But I didn't know it was you until at the very end."

Tor said nothing for a long moment as his gaze held mine.

"You thought I was Adam," he said slowly.

"I did. I'm really sorry."

Tor looked down at the counter. The tips of his ears slowly darkened.

"I did something you didn't want me to do."

I shut off the stove and quickly rounded the counter. Heat radiated from his shoulder when I set my hand on him.

"Tor, you didn't do anything wrong."

"Adam asked you if you wanted me to wake you up. You said yes. I thought that was consent."

"I know. It was a misunderstanding. I'm not mad at you, Tor. You heard the sounds I made. I liked what you did. But that's why I'm embarrassed. I should have realized you weren't Adam. I should have been able to tell the difference. And I'm worried that what we did together is going to give you false hope."

He lifted his gaze to look at me.

"What do you mean?"

"I'm not ready for a new boyfriend and might not be for a very long time. Or ever."

He gently tweaked my chin.

"You don't need to love me, June. I will still keep you safe."

There was nothing I could say or do. He seemed to understand the situation perfectly, and he wasn't upset or hurt even though I'd just nicely told him I had no intention of jumping into a relationship with him. Why, then, did I feel so guilty about it?

"Thank you," I murmured before returning to the other side of the counter.

I worked in silence, very aware of the way he watched every move I made. When I set a plate of spam fried rice in front of him, he finally looked away to study the food.

"I haven't seen the meat made this way before." He picked up his fork and took a bite.

"Making it like that stretches the meat. The rice also picks up the saltiness of the pork. The peas and carrots give it texture and color. So it pleases your mouth as much as your eyes."

He glanced at me. "Yes. Pleasing to the mouth and eyes."

He said it innocently enough, but that's not where my mind took it. I rewound to yesterday morning and how he'd look down at my private parts with longing and hunger.

"Your face is turning red again. Why are you embarrassed?"

"Sorry. Hot flash." I fanned my face. "I think I might skip the movie and go to bed early."

"A flash of heat, like a fever? Are you sick? Should I get Cassie?"

"No, no. I'm fine. Hot flashes can happen for so many

different reasons. I'm not sick. But if I did get sick, you wouldn't need to panic. Humans often get colds. It's not the end of the world."

He studied me for a second then went back to eating.

"So what else do you not like besides red sauce foods."

"Peas taste bad, but not the way you make them. I like eating them this way."

"I'll keep that in mind. What else?"

We talked about human foods he'd tried through the rest of the meal. He noticed that Mya loved sweets, especially chocolate, and wanted to know if all women were like that. I gave another "not all, but most of them do" answer, which didn't seem to bother him.

Once we cleaned up the dishes, I wished him a good night and went upstairs. It wasn't until I was on the cusp of sleep that I realized I should have taken Adam's bed. I told myself one more night in Tor's large, comfy bed as I drifted off.

I should have relocated.

Instead, I woke up with my sweat-soaked tee-shirt sticking to my back in the middle of the night. The heat radiating off of Tor's chest, and the arm anchoring me against that broad expanse, complicated the problem.

"Tor," I said, pushing at his arm, "you're making me too hot."

He grunted out a tired sound and pulled the covers down before returning his arm to my waist.

"Tor."

"Shh. It's not time to wake up yet. Sleep sweet, June."

I almost snorted a laugh. Tor sounded half-drunk and the s's came out more lispy than crisp. Rather than laughing, I struggled to turn in his arms.

He made a growly noise, and I froze.

"Is that a bad sound?" I asked.

"No. I like when you wiggle against me. You can do more."

"Tor, wake up. I'm not trying to wiggle against you. I'm trying to understand why you're holding me in my sleep after I told you I didn't want a boyfriend."

He opened his eyes and frowned in confusion.

"You said hugs show appreciation and affection. You hugged me and patted my back."

"Right. But this isn't a hug."

"Yes. My arm is around you. The other one was too but my fingers started to tingle."

"Tor, you're over the top sometimes. Do you know that?"

"Is that bad?"

"For any other guy, I think it would be. But it's not for you."

"Good. Can we go back to sleep?"

I shook my head at him and said, "Sure."

"You're confusing," he said, closing his eyes. "All you need to do is tell me what you want, June. I will do anything for you."

His breathing evened out while I still stared at him in disbelief. I wasn't the only confusing one. He seemed so accepting of only a friendship with me most times, but then said things like that. Things that made me think he held onto a secret hope I'd fall into his arms like Adam had wanted.

Yet, as I watched Tor's sleep-relaxed face, I didn't want to move away and further support my earlier warning. I wanted to snuggle next to someone while I slept. It'd been so long.

Pillowing my cheek with my hand, I burrowed closer and closed my eyes.

The next time I roused, it was due to a hand clamping down on the leg I'd just moved.

"Hmm? What's wrong?" This time I was the one who sounded drunk.

I lifted my head, swiped the hair from my face, and tried to move my leg back to where it'd been.

"No," Tor rasped. "Wait. Don't move."

What he was saying didn't fully register. What I understood was that my leg was somehow a problem. So, of course, I tried to move it.

His fingers seized on my leg, and he groaned long and loud as his enormous cock spasmed against my inner thigh. I froze as I realized what I'd done. He didn't thrust against the weight of my leg but pressed it hard, keeping it in place as he came in shuddering waves.

I could hear the thundering race of his pulse under my ear.

"I didn't mean for that to happen," he said in a low rumble when he finally stopped twitching.

"I know," I croaked.

"It was almost time to wake you up, and I was remembering the last time. I—"

He didn't try to remove the hand I placed over his mouth.

"I understand. No need to explain anything further. Is it okay for me to move now?"

He nodded and slowly released my thigh. There was nowhere to go with my leg that didn't spread the mess. It was everywhere. Between my thighs. On his belly. On the sheets.

"I think we need to strip the bed and wash the sheets before we leave."

He grunted and got out of bed. Completely naked. I

inwardly slapped my forehead. Of course he was naked, he'd just come against my leg.

Then he turned.

"Oh my no…"

It had felt huge against my legs, but that was nothing like actually seeing it. Tor's cock, even semi-soft, was thicker than my wrist. I couldn't imagine its size when hard. As if hearing my thoughts, it twitched. My gaze flew to his.

Whatever he saw on my face had him slowly shielding himself with his hand. His hand wasn't big enough. The bulbous head of his cock dipped below his fingers.

Tor was a monster.

"No."

I clamped my mouth shut when I heard my second denial.

"I'll change the sheets," he said, watching me closely. "You should shower."

I bolted for the bathroom. Once safely inside, I pressed my back against the door and took several calming breaths. What was I doing? Tor was sweet. Nice. Good. And things kept happening that weren't fair to him. I shouldn't have slept in his bed. When I woke up in the middle of the night and realized he had joined me, I should have gotten up and gone downstairs. I wasn't being fair to Tor. What happened was on me.

Even my panicked overreaction at the end.

But holy shit he was huge.

Nothing had prepared me for that. I looked down at my leg and the sheen drying there. So much sheen.

Exhaling, I pushed away from the door and stripped out of my clothes. Tor and I would need to talk. Again. I needed to set boundaries and make my expectations clear then ask him to share his expectations. Based on how he'd snuggled up to me, I felt pretty certain our expectations weren't aligned, despite our conversation before going to bed.

Piling my hair on my head, I got in the shower and washed. It didn't take me long. When I was done, I groaned at my lack of forethought and wrapped the towel around my torso.

"Tor?" I called.

"Yes, I am here." There was movement on the other side of the door.

"Would you mind leaving the bedroom? I forgot my clothes."

"I will wait downstairs."

"Thank you."

The bedroom door closed, and I peeked out of the bathroom to make sure I was alone before emerging. The bed was already remade with fresh sheets, and my heart gave a pained squeeze. That was my fault. He'd asked me not to move, and I had.

As soon as I was dressed, I went downstairs and found Tor in the kitchen. He was making oatmeal at the stove.

"Tor, I'm really sorry about this morning. I wasn't fully awake when you told me not to move. I'll sleep downstairs tonight so you can have your bed back."

He glanced at me.

"I liked sharing the bed."

My heart gave another squeeze. I hated this part.

"I could tell you did. Maybe a little too much. You're so ready for a girlfriend, Tor. I'm not her."

He turned off the stove.

"Not yet. But maybe someday you will be. I can wait."

"What if you wait and it never happens? What if, by waiting, you miss your chance at a real girlfriend?"

"Why do you think you might never be mine? You said you

find me handsome and strong. You squealed when I licked your pussy and drank your sex juice."

"Oh, boy. Let's never use the phrase 'sex juice' again, okay?"

"Why? What do you call it?"

"Nothing?"

"Something that sweet and good needs a name. I could drink it all day."

A flush started in my face, and my core clenched.

"I think we got off topic," I managed.

He walked around the island, stalking closer to me.

"I like this topic."

CHAPTER THIRTEEN

PULSE HAMMERING, I RETREATED ONE STEP THEN ANOTHER. BUT I was slow. The way Tor moved, that unhurried prowl of a predator stalking its prey, sent my pulse thundering, and heat flooded my body. My brain was saying no when my body was saying yes. What did that say about me?

"I know you like it, Tor, but I don't. Letting one man lick me when I was dating another made me feel cheap."

"You are not cheap. You are smart and beautiful." He kept moving toward me, and I kept retreating.

"Tor, please. This isn't about what you feel for me or what I feel for you. This is about what I feel for myself. And if you keep pressing, it's going to fill me with more doubt and self-loathing over the mess I've already made of things."

He stopped and blinked at me.

"Self-loathing? Why do you hate yourself?"

I struggled to find the words to describe what I was feeling. How wrong it was to feel any attraction to him after only a few short days.

"It's not okay for a woman to jump from one man to the next."

"Why? Adam does not want you. I do."

"Ouch."

He frowned.

"What hurts?"

"The reminder that Adam doesn't want me anymore, Tor. I know this is all new to you. Can you please just be my friend for a while? I need time to let my heart heal and to make sure I'm ready. It hurts when you're wrong about someone. I don't want to hurt you like Adam hurt me."

He took another step toward me, and I quickly retreated. He sighed and tugged at his ear, showing his frustration.

"Come here, June. I wish to give you a hug of affection and friendship."

"Less touching would be better for a while."

"I like touching you."

My heart gave another squeeze, and I wished he wasn't making this so hard.

"Honestly, I like it too, Tor. But do I like it because it's you or because I'm hurt and want comfort from any source willing to give it? That's something I need to know. Otherwise, I might only be leading you on. I need time. I need to make sure I'm myself. Whole. Do you understand?"

He paused, his frown deepening as he slowly nodded.

"Yes. I understand." He looked up and met my gaze. "I will be your friend. When you want my touches again, you will tell me."

"Thank you."

He grunted and made his way back to the stove.

"Are you hungry? I made you oatmeal with strawberries."

"That sounds really good."

"It's not. I'm sorry."

The pity in his eyes when he passed the bowl to me was almost comical.

"I like oatmeal. Especially the kind with strawberries."

He made a face, and I relaxed a little more. The knock on the front door defused any remaining tension.

Angel was clearly a morning person, based on her bright smile and chipper hello. Shax, the fey, following her, seemed just as upbeat.

"Ready for another day of dick shooting?" Angel asked, joining me at the island.

Shax winced behind her.

"Maybe we should give it another name," I suggested.

"Yes," Shax said immediately.

"We could call it cuddle time, but then you'd start to wonder if I really meant cuddles or if I wanted to do violent things to your fun maker. Isn't it better to simply call it what it is?"

Shax gave her a disgruntled look even as he agreed. She grinned at me.

"A little birdy told me that you went to visit Mya yesterday. What did you think of our fearless leader?"

"She seems really nice."

"She is. And she isn't, when she needs to be. Brenna's not a fan, but I think she's coming around."

"You're really open, aren't you?"

"Yep. Clear communication makes life easier in the long run. The biggest mistake people make is assuming that everyone else can read their minds. Half the time, we're so caught up in our own heads we barely notice the people around us, never mind taking the time to try to figure out what they might be thinking or feeling."

She made a very valid point, and I wondered if that had been part of the problem with my relationship with Adam. He coddled me too much instead of giving me the straight truth.

I told her about my conversation with Mya, and Angel nodded along.

"Some of those people are real assholes. The rest aren't bad. Garrett, my brother from another mother, is one of the good ones. He got to stay after the breach."

I finished my breakfast as Angel filled me in on some of the history of the people in Tolerance. There were a fair number of human and fey couples already. And a few humans who'd been deemed friendly enough to coexist with the fey here. Everyone seemed to get along with only minor tension at times.

"I can't wait for you to meet James and Mary," Angel said. "They are the sweetest old couple and love the fey. They host the dinner dates if you're ever interested in some amazing cooking. I convinced them to let Shax and me do a test run. It was fun."

"You're already a couple." I moved to rinse my bowl. "Isn't the point of the dinner date to give a single fey some practice?"

"Yeah, but it also gives Mary and James something to do and look forward to. There's not a lot around here for entertainment. Why else would we be out practicing archery?"

"Survival?"

We walked toward the door, and I started to put my things on.

"Sure. There's that. But let's face it. Even with the skills we're learning, we wouldn't stand a chance out there without the fey."

"Adam and I managed pretty well."

"You were found in a bunker under a barn filled with infected, from what I heard. A few of the rest of us have also been lucky enough to survive until the fey found us. But let's face it. The infected are getting smarter. The luck for anyone else still out there is probably running out."

We left the house and walked down the street together. Angel's words rang in my head and in my heart. I hated that she was thinking like Adam as if validating his choice to leave me. Passing me off to someone else wasn't love. It was giving up.

I was glad when we reached the training grounds and there was something else to focus on. With a bow in hand, I listened to Brenna's instructions for the next hour. Then, I tumbled around with the other three while Angel cheered us on and ate her snacks.

After one brutal toss from Hannah, I tapped out and sat on the sidelines to rub my shoulder and neck.

"You should come to my house after this. I could have a fey massage lined up for you in three seconds flat," Angel said. "No strings attached. They're seriously only looking for a way to be useful."

"I can't. I'm supposed to go talk to Emily."

"Okay. I'll stop by later with that list of names, and if you want to take me up on the offer then, let me know."

The other women called me back in, and as the morning wore on, Angel's offer for a fey massage started to sound better and better. My legs and arms burned by the time the women signaled that we were done.

Winded and tired, I limped off to the side and sat on one of the tree stumps someone had set nearby.

"Are you okay, June?" Tor asked.

"Yeah, I'll be fine in a minute. Are you okay with going to Emily's house after this?"

"Yes."

I watched the other women walk off with their fey. They didn't look nearly as exhausted as I was.

"How are they not tired?" I asked.

"They have been practicing for many days. You haven't. You will get better."

"I don't see how. Hannah's wicked good. Eden, too."

Brenna was the only one who hadn't flipped me over repeatedly. That didn't mean she wasn't good, too. Only that she was being nicer about sparring with me.

"Hannah's good because Merdon spanks her hard at home."

My tiredness evaporated.

"What?"

Tor repeated himself.

"Yeah, I heard you the first time. I meant what do you mean by 'he spanks her hard?' Is he abusive?"

"He hurts her only enough to keep her from hurting herself. He does not like it, but he knows it will help her live."

I knew I'd need to ask Angel what the story was behind those comments the next time I saw her. My mind returned to her offer for a massage. I could get the scoop on Merdon and Hannah, plus relax at the same time.

My legs felt weak when I stood, affirming the idea.

"I hope Emily's place isn't too far away," I said.

"Do you want me to carry you?"

"No. Walking will be good for me. It'll help loosen everything up."

Emily answered the door when Tor knocked the second time.

"Hey, this probably isn't a good time," she said, the headphones on her head pushed back so one ear was exposed.

"Mya sent me to talk to you."

"Oh. Um."

In the background, I heard a rhythmic sound. Like something being hit.

"Is everything okay?" I asked.

"Yeah. It's just Merdon and Hannah."

My eyes went wide.

"Is he hitting her?"

Emily snorted.

"Not the way you're thinking. You're welcome to come in, but they'll get a lot louder before they get quiet."

As if they heard her, the thumping noise increased in frequency. There was a sharp female cry then a low rumble.

"I think Merdon heard we have company," Emily said, removing her headphones completely. "They should be down in a few minutes. Come on in."

Face flushed with understanding what the noise had been, I refused to look at Tor.

"I'm really sorry for coming over unannounced," I said as I followed Emily inside.

"Seriously, don't even worry about it. Everything is unannounced these days."

She had a point.

"What can I help you with?" She gestured to the couch, and I took a seat.

"Something needs to be done about Tenacity," I said bluntly.

"The fear and desperation are spreading, and it's only a matter of time before the situation explodes."

"I agree. I'm trying everything to get them to come over to Team Fey's side, but the people there are extremely stubborn."

"Mya and I came up with a plan to help with that. We both feel the stubbornness stems from a small group of people. The extreme fey haters. The ones who will continue to hate the fey no matter what gestures the fey make to amend past mistakes. Matt's afraid to start removing them one at a time, believing such a move will provoke the ones who remain. After what they did to Adam, I agree. So, we need to identify all the potential troublemakers before Matt can make a move. That's where you come in."

"Me?" She looked completely surprised.

"Yes. You've been the lead for the fey and human integrations. It won't look suspicious if you start something new over there."

"Like what?"

"A fey-run soup kitchen. Tolerance will provide the supplies and the fey to man the kitchen. The food will be cooked and served all by the fey. At the end of the day, anything that's left will be taken back here by the fey."

Emily's concern was plain on her face.

"It's going to cause trouble."

"We want it to lightly stir things up. The people who don't like the fey won't show up. Or they will show up and throw attitude about the fey presence. Either way, we'll have names on our list. But having a fey-run soup kitchen will do more than make a few people angry. It'll show the rest of the people at Tenacity that the fey have a gentle and compassionate side.

That they can do more than kill infected and hellhounds and gather supplies."

Emily slowly nodded.

"I like that. It's good."

"You're on board, then?"

"I am. How soon do we want to start this?"

"Angel's rounding up the names of some fey volunteers we'll need to train to cook for large numbers. Mya spoke with Ryan last night so he could plan for bigger supply runs for the next few days to accommodate for this. Drav has a crew out looking for tables. And Matt should be prepping an area where the fey can cook and serve the food. So, a few days from now, maybe?"

Emily nodded thoughtfully.

"That sounds good. I'll let Ryan know that we should plan on five hundred servings of whatever the fey will make each day. I don't expect we'll see everyone, especially not that first day. It's going to take a few days for word to spread through Tenacity. But those we do see will appreciate the opportunity for seconds. That'll really go a long way to paint the fey in a good light. And I'm guessing we'll need to continue this for at least a week. Maybe a little more.

"That's a lot of soup, even if it's soup kitchen style. It shouldn't be too hard to manage. The worst part is going to be the dishes. Yeah, I can coordinate it. No problem. I'm going to need help from someone who knows Tenacity, though."

Emily smiled widely as Hannah jogged downstairs just then, her curls bouncing with each step.

"Hey, June. Sorry about that. I didn't know you were planning on coming over."

Hannah looked completely fine and happy. Tor's comment still had me worried, though.

"No, I'm sorry. I didn't realize you and Emily were in the same house."

"It's okay. Merdon said you're here about the Tenacity assholes. How can I help?"

"You can help me," Emily said. "We need to talk to Taylor. I bet Caleb and Connor will help, too."

"Help how?" Hannah asked.

"We're going to throw the fey and the humans together and note the troublemakers," Emily said. "We'll need to recruit the boys and Taylor to take the notes since you and I don't know everyone."

Hannah made a face.

"That doesn't sound like a good idea. We call them the Tenacity assholes for a reason." She looked at me. "They beat the hell out of your man for having the balls to get his own food while they were too chicken shit to do it for themselves."

"I know. It won't be easy on the fey, which Angel is making clear to the volunteers." I quickly outlined for Hannah how we planned to keep the humans and the fey together while the humans ate. Then I went over the pros and cons of having the soup kitchen.

"And once Matt has a list of names? Then what? Having an attitude isn't a reason to die," Hannah said.

Emily reached out and took the other woman's hand in her own. Their shared look said more was behind Hannah's comment than she was letting on. Something personal.

"It's a watchlist," I said quickly, "not an exile list. Matt won't act until there's actual proof of wrongdoing."

"How are we going to get the proof?" Hannah asked.

"Matt will worry about that part later," I said, unsure how much of that Mya and Matt wanted me to share. "It'll take us a while to get this part going."

They both agreed to help and started to make plans to go to Tenacity right away.

"I'll do an inventory on what's in the supply shed after today's run and work with Mary on a menu plan," Emily said. "We'll keep it simple. Soups and stews will be easiest. Noodles and rice will help everything stretch. While we're over there recruiting for help, I'll check in with Matt and see what space he's prepping. We'll stop by later to give you an update."

"You can let Mya know," I said, standing with them.

"I will. But I don't mind stopping by and letting you know, too."

"She likes getting out of the house," Hannah said with a smile as Merdon descended the stairs. His hair was wet, hanging down his back. He didn't look at me or Tor. His gaze remained locked on Hannah as he crossed the room and stood beside her.

He looked angry even as she smiled up at him. I really needed to get their story.

"Then I won't mind the visit," I said agreeably.

We all left their house together. But, with a wave goodbye, they went their separate way to the wall.

My legs ached even worse now from the time I'd spent sitting. I tried to walk normally, but it was next to impossible. I was more than ready to agree to Angel's massage offer, even if it was some random fey petting my feet instead of actually rubbing out the aches. Anything would help. And afterward, I'd go home and take another soak in the tub. Hopefully, Emily wouldn't be back with an update until after dinner.

I glanced at Tor, who'd been silently following me since we left the house this morning, and wondered where he fit into my plans. Was it fair to ask him to show me the way to Angel's place? Although he said the fey didn't have much to do to occupy themselves, he had to be bored by now.

"If you want to go do your own thing for a while, I'm fine finding my own way to Angel's," I said, walking beside him.

"I can show you where Angel lives."

"Are you sure? Emily and Hannah are going to Tenacity, where all the single women are. Wouldn't you rather go with them?"

He gave me a considering look.

"Are you nicely telling me to go away?" Shock must have shown on my face because he hurried to add, "It's okay if you are. I can give you space. Emily says that females sometimes need space to be themselves."

"It sounds like Emily is giving you some sensible advice. But that's not what I was trying to say. I'm feeling guilty that you're spending all your time following me around. If you want to do something else, I would understand."

"I have nothing else to do, and I like following you."

I gave him a small smile and decided I needed to talk to Emily on Tor's behalf. He was everything I'd already told him. Handsome. Sweet. Kind. And I was a mess he had his eyes on simply because I'd been nice. Giving a guy a pillow and making him a meal wasn't grounds for the type of relationship he wanted. He deserved so much more and needed to see that there were better options than me out there. Hopefully, Emily would be able to hook him up on a dinner date.

Tor led me to Angel's house and knocked on the door. Shax answered after a few moments.

"Hi, Shax. Is Angel up for company?"

"Yes!" Angel yelled from inside.

Shax motioned for me to enter, and I quickly obliged. Angel walked toward us from the living room, absently rubbing her belly.

"I heard you interrupted fun time at Hannah's," Angel said with a smirk.

"How do you hear everything so fast?"

Her grin widened.

"The fey know I like hearing what's happening and trade news for baby feels."

"You must get groped a lot."

"Yep. The touching I don't mind. It's all the feeding that's starting to get to me. The baby's taking up too much inside space now to keep feeding me all the time."

Shax grunted, his gaze lingering on her belly.

"Don't even say it," she warned. "The baby is not ready to come out yet."

"The baby decides when the baby is ready," he said.

"Exactly."

"I will talk to the baby tonight."

She rolled her eyes at me.

"Gotta love their persistence. What brings you over?" Excitement lit her eyes. "You want a massage, right?"

"I think so."

She clapped her hands together and waved for me to follow her.

"I set up a room for practice. Shax found a table and everything. Come check it out. Let me know what you think. Shax, babe, see if you can find any willing apprentices, okay?"

A grunt followed us down the hall.

"Am I going to regret this?" I asked.

"Not likely. The fey have amazing hand strength. I'm so excited that someone female has finally volunteered. Ryan and Garrett have been great practice, but it's just not the same."

She opened the door to a nicely made-up room. A chair sat off to one side. A table filled with massage oils and lotions waited under one of the room's curtained windows. And the table itself took up the center of the room.

"Now, keep in mind that everything the fey know they learned from me, and I am not a licensed massage therapist. So if anything doesn't feel good to you, say something. And if something does feel good, definitely say something so they know to keep going. You're helping them learn what works and doesn't work."

"Okay."

"If it's all right with you, I'd like to be present to help coach whoever gives the massage."

"That actually makes me feel more comfortable."

"Perfect." She folded down the top sheet covering the table. "Strip down to your underwear and lie face down. I'll be right back with your volunteer. They're probably doing another lottery drawing."

"It's only been thirty seconds."

"You've seen how fast they move." She chuckled as she left, closing the door behind her.

CHAPTER FOURTEEN

I'd had massages before and quickly undressed, placing my neatly folded clothes on the chair. The linens covering the cushioned face-cradle smelled fresh and felt soft against my skin. The old familiarity struck a chord in me, and I took a deep, relaxing breath. I'd always enjoyed massages. And touching, as Tor had pointed out.

It was crazy how much I missed being touched. When my thoughts drifted to Adam, I quickly pushed them away and focused on the now. I'd get plenty of touching once my lucky fey winner got in here. I really hoped he'd use some of his strength and not spend an hour petting me.

I frowned, realizing I'd never asked Angel how long the massage would last.

A light tap sounded on the door.

"Are you ready?" Angel asked.

"Yep," I said loud enough to be heard.

The door opened.

"Always wait for the person's answer before entering. You

don't want to walk in on someone when they're undressing," Angel said.

A fey grunted in response.

"Do you mind if I put your clothes on the floor so I can sit?" Angel asked.

"Not at all. How long will the massage be?"

I heard a rustle as Angel moved my things.

"As long as you want. Or as long as my bladder will hold." She gave a sigh at the same time I heard the sound of lotion being dispensed.

"If it's cold, use your hands to warm it up a little before smoothing it on her. Usually, the person providing the massage would ask the client if they have any specific areas they want worked on."

The fey grunted again but didn't say anything. I could hear the amusement in Angel's voice when she spoke next.

"June, are there any specific areas that you'd like him to focus on today?"

"Everything hurts equally from head to toe," I said. "Both Eden and Hannah are brutal with their flips."

"Yeah, those two both have a competitive streak. That's why Shax won't let me join in again until after the ninja's born. Eden freaked him out when she pretended like she was going to flip me."

As Angel spoke, big warm hands started smoothing lotion over my back, and I struggled not to sigh at how good it felt. The pressure was firm enough that it didn't feel like petting, and he was going slowly like he was trying to feel the muscle structure under the skin.

More tension dissolved, and it was a struggle to remember

what Angel had said. Hannah and Eden and their wrestling skills. Right.

"How did they learn to do that?" I asked while the fey continued to work over my back.

"Merdon taught Hannah as part of her rehab. How's the pressure?"

"It could be a little harder," I said.

My volunteer grunted and applied more pressure. I almost groaned. This was magic. People were idiots not to line up for a massage. It felt so good I almost forgot that I was going to ask what she meant.

"Rehab?" I managed.

"Yeah, Hannah wasn't in a good place. She blamed herself for her sister's death and was drinking a lot. Not making many good choices. Hurting the people around her with the way she was acting. I think she'd pretty much given up on living. Merdon helped her see there was still something worth living for."

I groaned when the fey suddenly found the knot in my left shoulder.

"There. That is so good," I said.

"Seriously, June, you have no idea how amazing you are for stepping up and volunteering for this."

"This isn't any hardship. I can't believe more people aren't volunteering."

I almost drooled, so I stopped talking.

The fey continued to gently work the knot until it released then moved lower, checking for more along the shoulder blade.

"Trust me, a lot of us females wanted to volunteer, but our better halves threw fits. They don't mind information sharing but aren't keen on physically sharing with their brothers. So

I've directed a few massages for Ghua and Eden and Hannah and Merdon, but that's it. No actual hands-on practice for the fey who would be going to Tenacity to do this."

"Why can't the committed fey do massages? It might make the human volunteers more comfortable if not all the fey were single," I said.

"But that would defeat the purpose."

"Would it? The whole point is to make the people living at Tenacity comfortable around the fey. If the message you're sending always leads back to hooking up with a fey, they're going to keep resisting."

Angel made a disgruntled sound then admitted I might be right.

"Have Emily start putting the word out that it's a chaperoned massage with a fey already in a relationship. I bet you'd get a few nibbles."

"Okay."

The hands slicked over my shoulders one final time and worked their way down again. When he got to my lower back, I let out another groan.

"Oh, yeah. That's another good spot." He rubbed little circles that gradually grew, dipping a little further down into the tucked sheet than I was comfortable with. It still felt amazing, only a bit too personal. Before I could say anything, Angel did.

"Never below the underwear line unless requested."

He grunted, and his fingers immediately retreated.

"Unless requested?" I asked, wondering what she was teaching them.

"The fey aren't timid. If you want a butt rub, they'd be more than willing to accommodate."

"Good to know, and not requested today," I said quickly before the fey mistook that as a "Yes, please."

Angel chuckled, and silence lapsed for several long moments as he continued to work on my lower back.

"June, there's a spot on the outside of what I'd call the hip area that sometimes feels really good to have rubbed. Would you mind if he worked on that over the sheet?"

"Not at all."

"When starting on a new area, don't assume it should be the same pressure. Start light and ask how the pressure is. Once you get to know a client's preferences, you won't need to ask all the time. But for now, start light and ask."

Since he'd already started tentatively rubbing, I gave feedback right away.

"That's plenty firm. I didn't realize how sore that spot was until you started rubbing it."

"Yeah, it's hit and miss for some people. I love it when Shax rubs there, but Eden didn't like it. It was too tender. Hannah said she didn't trust Merdon's hand that close to his favorite spot." Angel chuckled to herself.

"Tor made a comment about Merdon and Hannah that worried me," I said as the fingers gently continued to work the tension from my outer butt cheeks. "He said Merdon only hurts Hannah enough so she doesn't hurt herself. Does Merdon hit Hannah?"

"Merdon trains Hannah. Part of that training is that flipping and avoiding being bitten like you've been doing. Fey teeth are sharper, so Merdon is careful, but yes, he will bite her to remind her that she needs to fight back to survive. While he would never truly hurt her, the infected won't hesitate. And part of his reminder also includes a sharp smack to her ass if he happens to get her to the mat. He promised Mary and James that he never leaves a lasting mark, though."

The fey set his hand in the center of my back for a moment then covered my top half before sliding his hand down my left leg and uncovering that.

"I guess that explains why Eden and Hannah keep it real with biting. I'm glad they didn't incorporate spanking."

Angel snorted.

"Eden put her foot down. She doesn't want to feed any of Ghua's fantasies."

"Ghua wants to spank her, too? Is it a fey thing?"

The hand smoothing lotion down my leg hesitated only a fraction, and Angel laughed.

"No, it's not a fey thing. If Eden was into spanking, Ghua would be into it too. Since she's not, he's not. But I bet he wouldn't mind trying. Ghua's a curious guy. Especially sexually. I think his openness to try anything and everything scares Eden a little. She doesn't need to worry, though. The fey are completely respectful of boundaries."

The fey rubbing me sure was. He never went too far up my thigh or too far toward the center to make me uncomfortable. Everything he touched, though, felt good. The perfect pressure, and he always seemed to sense what felt amazing since his fingers lingered longer in those spots.

"June, would you be comfortable with me stepping out for two minutes? Ninja just karate kicked me in the bladder."

"I'm completely okay with it."

The door closed, and there was nothing but relaxing silence and the firm, soothing touch on my calf. I groaned when he used his whole hand to kind of knead the entire muscle.

"That feels so good. I really hope more people volunteer for this. You're doing incredible."

He didn't respond, only continued his work, slowly moving down the calf to my heel.

"Foot rubs are hit and miss with me," I warned him. "If you keep your touch firm, we'll be okay. If you're too light, it won't be relaxing. My toes are ticklish."

He grunted in acknowledgment and firmly stroked his thumb over my arch again and again.

"Perfect," I said.

Angel reentered the room, asked how everything was while she was gone, and praised my fey for his good work after my report. When he finished my other leg and it was time for me to turn over, she was right there to make sure the fey stayed looking away and covered my eyes with a washcloth so I would remain focused on relaxing.

The fey worked on my neck, arms, and the front side of my legs again. And by the time he was done, I felt like a human puddle.

"I could fall asleep here," I mumbled as he left the room.

Angel patted my arm.

"If you want to, go for it. If you want another fey in here to do it all over again, I can make that happen too. It's all up to you."

"I think I'm good for now, but I might be back tomorrow. This was amazing."

"Take your time getting up. We'll be in the kitchen."

The door closed again, and I lay there for a moment. It had been one of the best massages I'd ever gotten. *Perhaps the most needed, too,* I thought, sitting up and removing the cloth covering my eyes. The one that had absorbed my tears during the last few minutes.

The world was hard to live in sometimes. It always had been.

Infected. Hellhounds. Fey. Those were new elements to deal with. Breakups. Heartache. Loneliness. Those hadn't gone away with the end of the world and likely never would.

I needed to figure out how to deal with them and keep living. Preferably before some fey got it in his head that I needed spank motivation. Wiping away the remnants of my tears, I smiled to myself and got dressed.

Angel had a glass of water waiting for me in the kitchen.

"Where'd Shax go?" I asked after I drank it down.

She chuckled. "Outside with all the rest of the fey to learn how the massage went. They're beyond excited to hear all the muscular details. If you're ever daring enough to ask for a boob massage, let me know how it goes. Shax is crazy good at them, and I'm interested to know how well the skills transfer by word of mouth."

"Considering the massage I just received, I'd say it works well. I can't believe that was your volunteer's first time giving a massage."

"He'd be happy to be your personal masseur. All you'd need to do is say the word."

I shook my head.

"I don't want to give anyone false hope. I already explained to Tor that I need time."

She nodded sympathetically.

"I understand."

"I'm not sure Tor does. I'm worried all the time he's spending with me is sending the wrong signals, especially after what's already happened. I've seen how people treat the fey and don't want to be another source of cruelty."

"It's sweet of you to worry about him. But you can't control his hopes, June. You know that, right? Besides, allowing a massage after the beating you took early this morning is hardly sending mixed signals. Every fey watching was wincing on your behalf."

"If Merdon taught Hannah to fight, does that mean the fey train like that? Now, that's something I wouldn't mind spectating."

A speculative look entered Angel's eyes.

"You're full of good ideas. I'm so glad you're here and can't wait until Tenacity's less fey-hostile. We're going to have so many ways for them to fall in love with the fey."

"Remember what I said about the love connections."

She waved away my concern with a sudden wince and a belly rub.

"I think I'm going to go lie down. The freeloader is all knees and elbows this afternoon. I'll stop by later with the list of names, though."

"No rush. Take it easy. Growing babies is hard work." I glanced wistfully at her belly and grabbed my things.

"If you see Shax out there, send him in, okay? I'm ready for my own back rub."

With a wave goodbye, I let myself out.

The mass of fey gathered in the front yard, their backs toward me, was a bit of a surprise. As soon as they heard the door open, the low rumble of the man speaking stopped, and the fey turned to look at me.

I offered a friendly smile to the group.

"Shax? Angel's back is hurting her. She's wondering if you could join her inside."

The fey parted, revealing Shax. He nodded and strode toward me, along with Tor, as the rest of the fey dispersed.

"I didn't mean to interrupt."

"You didn't. We were finished. Are you ready to go home?"

"I am. Thanks for waiting around."

Relaxed from the massage, I thought of little else but the long soak that I planned to have once we reached Tor's place. He seemed content with my silence, leaving me to disappear into the master bath in peace.

The lavender-infused water did wonders for my body, but not so much for my mind. Thoughts of Adam crept in, especially his plan to leave for the caves, and I found a certain irony in it all. Adam broke up with me so I wouldn't worry about him; yet, I couldn't stop it. I told Tor I wasn't ready for a boyfriend to prevent him from placing his hopes in a relationship with me; yet, he couldn't stop what he felt either. Angel was right. We couldn't control what someone else was feeling. I wondered if that meant Adam felt as guilty about causing me pain as I felt about potentially causing Tor pain.

Mentally cringing away from it all, I sank lower in the steaming water.

While I cared about Adam and knew he continued to care about me, our relationship was forever changed. The sooner I came to terms with that, the better off I would be. However, knowing that didn't turn off the tumultuous cycle of regrets, doubt, and self-recrimination.

Realizing my mistake in taking a bath, I quickly left the warm water and dried off. I needed to stay busy and keep my mind focused on something productive rather than my three-year failed attempt at a happily-ever-after.

Concentrating on clearing out the bad seeds from Tenacity was a perfect task for me. While it might prove physically dangerous, it was emotionally safer, by far. There were so many moving pieces, but I trusted everyone to do their parts. They wanted the same thing just as badly as I did, though for different reasons.

As soon as I was dressed, I opened the door and almost screamed at the sight of Tor right there in the hall.

"June, you are safe," he said quickly.

"Sorry," I said, pressing a hand over my heart. "I startled easily even before the infected showed up. Did you need to get into your bedroom?" As soon as I asked the question, I realized I needed to move my clothes downstairs.

"No. I wanted to tell you I made you something to eat."

"Oh, thank you. I'll be down in a minute."

He grunted and turned away while I went to the dresser to collect my clothes. There wasn't much in my arms when I was done.

From the kitchen, Tor watched me descend the stairs.

"Be right there," I said, hurrying into Adam's room. I stopped short at the sight of the bedless space and backtracked.

"Did you put the bed upstairs?" I asked.

He gave me a decidedly uncomfortable look and tugged at his ear, something he tended to do when he was upset.

"Brog and Turik came for Adam's things as well as the bed last night. I didn't know you wanted to keep it."

"N-no. I didn't." Of course, they'd come for Adam's things and needed the bed. Tor had told me there weren't a lot of spares. "That's completely fine, Tor. Don't even worry about it. I'll put my stuff in the other room upstairs."

"Please sleep in my bed. The sheets are clean." The tips of his ears darkened, and I knew he was thinking of this morning when he averted his gaze.

My mouth opened and closed twice as I almost said several stupid things. Reminding him that we were just friends would not only be hurtful but pointless as Angel had said. Asking him if he minded sharing was laughable, and insisting I could sleep on the floor was plain self-destructive after the workout I had today.

"Okay," I said finally. "I promise to try staying on my side of the bed."

He lifted his gaze to mine and nodded slowly, which made it hard to tell what he might be thinking. Probably hoping that I wouldn't and that he'd wake up with me on him again.

I gave him a reassuring smile, set my things on the steps, and joined him at the island where he had two bowls waiting.

"What's this?" I asked, sitting.

"Emily showed me how to make the noodle box meals. It has meat in it."

I took a bite and made an appreciative noise. It was far better than the dried foods I'd been fixing and more flavorful than the canned goods we'd had so far.

"Do you like it?" he asked.

"I do. It's been a long time since I had anything like this."

"What are your favorite foods?" he asked.

"I'm not even sure anymore. I miss salads the most, but I don't think they were my favorite. Maybe burgers? There were some good bars around campus that had the best grilled burgers." Those thoughts stirred some Adam memories, so I quickly changed the subject. "What about you? What foods do you miss most from your old life?"

"Aodibun. It is a water creature with a hard shell that had to be cracked open. I ate it right from the shell." He sighed slightly. "It was a good taste. Hard to find. I would swim for hours in some pools."

"Is your home pretty?" I asked.

"In many ways, yes. This is prettier, though."

He told me stories about the caves and his adventures in them while we ate. The animation in his expression and the way he described things pulled me in so thoroughly that I didn't notice the passing time. I loved listening to him, the sound of his voice, and the wry smile he flashed when he admitted past mistakes.

He talked me into playing games with him after dinner, and I heard his laugh for the first time when he crushed me at Go-Fish and I stuck my tongue out at him. The sound curled around me, wrapping me dangerously in his spell. I knew it was too soon and there were too many reasons why even these simple moments weren't fair to either of us. But I didn't have the heart to walk away. I liked spending time with Tor too much.

"We should bet on the next game," he said, shuffling the cards.

"Oh, like what?"

"If you win, I will find you a fresh salad."

I snorted. "You must be pretty confident I won't win. There's no way you'll find a salad."

He smirked at me. "I know where to find one."

"Okay. I'm interested. And what do you want if you win?"

"I want to be the one to stay with you when you go to Tenacity."

It was like he'd read my mind moments ago. I knew I should say no but decided to let fate make the choice for us.

One hand later, I said goodbye to my hope for a salad and shook my head at Tor.

"It's not going to be very fun for you in Tenacity."

"I am not concerned with fun. I'm concerned with you. I will keep you safe while you taunt the other humans. They will not hurt you like they hurt Adam. I promise."

CHAPTER FIFTEEN

A KNOCK ON THE DOOR SAVED ME FROM HAVING TO RESPOND. I jumped up from the table and hurried to answer it.

Emily waited in the encroaching dusk and smiled at me.

"Have a few minutes?" she asked.

"More than a few. Come on in."

I took her jacket for her and led her to the cozy couch.

"How did it go?" I asked, sitting with her. Behind us, Tor shuffled the cards and went to the kitchen.

"Better than I expected. Taylor, Caleb, and Connor are onboard. There are a lot of undercurrents they've already picked up on, and I've started a watchlist with a few names they've given me.

"Matt said he's ready to use their storage shed for the food kitchen. He also had some great ideas. Whiteman had a full cafeteria setup that they left behind when everyone evacuated. Tomorrow, some of the fey are going to go there for the supplies. Matt's asked them to sneak the things into Tenacity after dark. He doesn't want anyone to question what's going on until it's time to open the doors.

"The temporary kitchen will have a few simple camp stoves that they were using at Whiteman. And we won't have to worry about dishes or utensils. It sounds like he'll have everything we need for the setup. All we have to do is provide the fey and the food."

"That's great. Did you see Ryan after he returned from the supply run?"

"I did. And he had a sizable haul. The people who volunteered were less than happy about it."

"That makes no sense."

"The big hauls are riskier. He takes the fey into the cities for the bigger stores they can find. Two untouched chain stores could feed everyone well for several days. But they tend to be filled with infected and traps. The people in Tenacity would rather hit outlying homes that are less risky."

"And are probably already picked over," I said.

"True."

There was another knock on the door that Tor hurried to answer.

"Hi, Tor. Can I speak with June, please?" Angel asked, her gaze already searching for me. She smiled when she spotted Emily sitting with me, and I waved her in.

Shax, her shadow, followed behind her.

"I have good timing," she said.

She handed off her jacket to Shax and joined us on the couch. Tor and Shax lounged in the chairs nearby and listened to Emily repeat what she'd learned.

"How many volunteers do we have, and did you warn them that they might be spit at?" Emily asked when she finished.

My mouth dropped open a little, and my gaze shifted to Tor.

He flashed his teeth at me and shrugged, which made me sad for all the fey that this wasn't news to them.

"Usually, I'd say that every fey volunteered, regardless of the spitting. But tomorrow's the day that Uan is going back to the caves," Angel said.

A sick knot settled into my stomach at the news.

"There were a lot of volunteers for that," she continued, "and Drav's going to decide who goes in the morning, along with who's in the new group he's going to send out to look for Molev. I did get eight fey who are fully committed to doing this, though."

"Molev?" I asked as the name teased my memory.

"Our leader," Tor said. "He has been missing for a long time."

"Almost two months," Emily said. "Matt's been sending out the plane to look for him, along with signs of any other survivors, but it hasn't been very successful, and there's no fuel left. They switched to sending out scouting parties now." She looked at Angel. "And eight is perfect. I don't think we should need more fey than that."

"They'll report to your house in the morning," Angel said. "Do you need help showing them what to do? I'm more than willing."

"And skip feight club?" Emily asked.

Angel shrugged lightly.

"I think Brenna is going to stay with her mom tomorrow, and Merdon will probably train Hannah at home to avoid any potentially painful reminders."

Emily nodded slowly.

"Yeah, I think you're right. I might pull Hannah into helping train the fey to cook, too. She makes some amazing biscuits, which would be a good thing to learn. It'll be a crowded kitchen, though. Maybe we can split into two groups. Four in our house and four in yours. I could be the go-between."

With feight club canceled the next day and Emily training her fey volunteers, what was I going to do? I didn't want to sit around, thinking about Adam leaving for the caves.

"Do you have any menu ideas based on the supplies we have so far? Anything you still need?" I asked.

"I've been thinking about the menus and the overall goal for the plan. We want to draw the troublemakers out, right? I think the food on the first day needs to be pretty good. Enough to get people talking. Ryan's done an amazing job finding supplies. We have a lot of canned vegetables, noodles, and rice. Enough to throw together a decent soup for the first day, easily. But I'd like to up the game. Biscuits would do that. Bread would be even better. Meat even better than that.

"I'm figuring we'll need at least enough to serve two hundred the first day, three hundred the second day, and the full five hundred the third day. I think the third day is when most of the troublemakers will show up. So a lot more flour if we can find it. And meat. It doesn't need to be a ton of it. Just enough to have bits floating in the soup to show what Ryan's finding out there."

I thought of Tor's freezer and glanced at him. We would need to talk about that once we were alone.

"I'll go out with the supply group tomorrow and watch for both those things," I said.

We talked more about aspects of cooking for the large group and what issues we might face. After a while, I offered to cook dinner for everyone, which turned into an evening of cards with the group. I couldn't have asked for a better distraction and said a heartfelt thank you to the three of them when they finally said it was time to go.

Angel hugged me at the door, and based on the extra little squeeze, I knew she understood my reason for leaving tomorrow even if Emily didn't.

"I'll save you some biscuits," she promised before she left.

I turned to Tor once the door was closed and gave him a tired smile.

"How do you feel about donating a roast or two if we don't find any tomorrow?" I asked, moving toward the stairs.

"I will give whatever you need."

I knew he meant every word of it.

"Thank you, Tor."

Neither of us spoke as we made our way to the master bedroom. My stomach churned with nerves as I took my pajamas into the bathroom to change. When I emerged, the lights were off, and I could see Tor's shape already in the bed. On his side.

A glint of light reflected on his eyes, an indicator that he watched me as I pulled back the covers and got in on my side.

"Sleep sweet, June," he said softly.

"You too, Tor."

He exhaled deeply. Something about the sound said he was winding down for sleep. It helped me relax enough to close my eyes. Instead of thinking of how I'd screwed up this morning with Tor, my mind drifted to Adam leaving tomorrow.

I hurt for him and hoped he would find the answer he was looking for.

Bliss. Contentment. Those two feelings lingered with me as I slowly rose from the depths of the best night's sleep I'd had for a long time. I was warm, comfortable, and didn't feel an ounce of worry about anything.

I frowned slightly, my sleepy brain trying to remember why I needed to feel any worry.

The reality crash that followed could have been worse. However, *why* I was so content took center stage over all the other negative aspects of my life.

Tor's hand gently smoothed over my back. His chest rose and fell under me. I was laying on the man like he was my personal bed space. And based on the hard length pressing into my stomach, he was loving every second of it.

Unlike yesterday, I had the presence of mind not to move more than my head as I lifted it to look down at him. He watched me, his hand continuing its slow, soothing circle.

"I know I didn't climb up here myself."

"You were making a sad face in your sleep. I hugged you, and you seemed to like it, except for my arm under you. I think it hurt your side. I rolled over like this so I could continue hugging you and keep the sadness away without hurting you." He lifted his head and breathed in deeply near my neck, which sent a tingle of need through me.

"You smell good," he said in a husky rumble before lowering his head back to the pillow.

He didn't grind against me or move his hand to any area other than my back. What else could I think but that he was being completely honest about how and why I'd gotten into this position? Tor had truly only meant to soothe away the sadness Adam's departure had caused me, even in my sleep.

Curling my arms around Tor's sides, I set my head against his chest again.

"You smell good, too," I said softly. "Thank you for taking care of me."

His cock twitched against me.

"I will always care for you."

My pulse sped up, and for a moment, Tor was the focus of my thoughts. What would it be like if he and I were together? Would he hold me like this every night? I knew the answer to that would be yes. He would hold me like this when I wanted and do so much more when I was ready. My core clenched at the thought of doing more with Tor. The man was huge. Would I like it? I wasn't sure, and I definitely wasn't ready to find out. Yesterday had been enough of a shock to last me a while.

"Is it okay for me to move yet?" I asked softly.

"I won't release against you again. I apologize for yesterday. I should have released before bed but forgot. I made sure to use my hand after you fell asleep."

I jerked my head up to stare down at him and struggled with what to say. Did he just admit that he'd masturbated in bed? Next to me? Did I really want to ask and get more clarification? Absolutely not.

"I appreciate your honesty, Tor. I really do. But maybe you don't need to be so open about everything."

"What do you mean?"

"You shouldn't tell a girl that you masturbated in bed next to her."

"I didn't masturbate next to you. I went to the bathroom so I wouldn't make a mess on the sheets again. I know you didn't like that."

The twitch between us was even more noticeable than the

time before. He may know that I hadn't liked it, but he certainly had.

"I think I'm going to get up now. I don't want to be late for the supply run."

He grunted and released me. I carefully eased off of him and averted my gaze as I got out of bed.

"I will make you something to eat," he said before he got up and left the room.

I breathed a sigh of relief and quickly dressed. When I went downstairs, he was standing by the stove. A pair of shorts covered his hips, but his back was exposed for my perusal. His grey skin had stopped looking odd to me. Instead, the dusky color tempted me.

Swallowing hard, I sat on the stool and tried to understand what I was doing. I had no business feeling any attraction to Tor when I was still so caught up with Adam.

"But are you?" a little voice inside of me asked.

I paused, trying to decide what exactly I did feel. I was still hurt by the way Adam had left me and what he'd said. I missed him because he'd been a familiar part of my life for so long. And I loved him. But that love wasn't a burning passion. It was a flame of caring and devotion to someone who'd risked everything time and again to keep me safe.

Angel's words teased my mind again.

Adam had asked me to let him go. Why cling to someone who didn't ask for devotion?

"You look unhappy," Tor said. "What's wrong?"

"I'm struggling," I said honestly. "Adam is leaving today to go to the caves. I trust the fey to keep him safe until he gets there. But I understand what he means to do. He hopes that once he's in those caves, he'll be reborn without injuries like you guys are. That means he needs to die.

"What if it doesn't work? I don't know how to feel about him possibly heading to his death. I know he and I are not a couple anymore. But that doesn't simply erase three years of memories and feelings." I let out a frustrated breath.

"I don't know what I'm supposed to think or feel. And, honestly, waking up on you like I did this morning was amazing for so many of the wrong reasons. It was a good distraction. It made me feel safe and cared for. And none of that is fair to you because I know what you want from me, and I'm not sure it's something I can give."

He turned off the stove and prowled toward me. This time, I didn't back away or ask him not to touch me.

When he towered over me, he ran his fingers through my hair.

"You think so much. Thank you for telling me. But don't worry about what I feel for you. I understand how you feel. Let that be enough. I promised to respect the rules you put in place for us."

I gave him an exasperated look.

"Saying stuff like that isn't helping."

He flashed his teeth at me.

"It is. You only don't see how yet. I will keep helping you, my June. You will see."

He playfully tugged a strand of my hair.

"I think I will go shower and use my hand again while you eat." He sauntered away, calling, "You better hurry," over his shoulder as I stared after him with my mouth hanging open.

Did he not understand what I meant by not oversharing? I

did not need images in my head of Tor stroking his enormous cock while I ate my breakfast.

Yet, that was exactly what I had along with my strawberry oatmeal.

I'd barely managed my last bite when he strolled back downstairs dressed for the day.

"Are you ready to find flour for bread and biscuits? Is a biscuit like your strawberry oatmeal?"

The normal, non-sexual question put me at ease and helped banish some of the images plaguing my thoughts. The tight shirt he wore made up for them, though.

"It's better," I answered, joining him by the door.

He grunted, his doubt plain on his face, and I grinned. His expression didn't change even after I described a biscuit's buttery flakiness.

"Angel said she would save me one. I'll let you try a bite of mine. I think you'll be surprised." He helped me put on my knife harness and watched me tug on my boots.

"Surprises are not always good."

"True. Do you like sweet things? Like honey?"

"I don't know if I've tasted honey."

"Then I'm adding that to today's list. Flour, meat, shirts that fit you, and honey."

We continued talking as we made our way to the wall. Tor didn't mind chocolate, but it wasn't his favorite. In fact, meat of any kind beat any human food he'd tried so far, even the cake Emily had made us back in Tenacity.

"Biscuits and honey will be your new favorite food," I said. "Just wait and see."

He flashed his teeth at me and picked me up to jump over

the wall. Ryan was in another fey's arms, but he was the only other human I saw before tucking my face against Tor's chest.

"Were there any foods in the caves that were sweet?" I mumbled against his shirt.

"Many."

"You should have asked your brothers to bring some back."

"They will, along with seeds. I like when you talk against my nipple."

I jerked in his arms, and he rumbled with laughter.

"Were you just teasing me?"

"Yes."

I grinned.

"You're lucky I'm not like Eden or Hannah. If I were, I'd try to bite you in retribution."

"You should try. I might like it. Your blunt, little teeth aren't meant to bring pain."

I snorted against his chest, knowing he was fully teasing me now, and went ahead and playfully nipped him. It wasn't easy to find anything to nip. Not only was his shirt tight, everything underneath it was too. I ended up mouthing him more than biting. His arms twitched around me, and I immediately apologized.

"That didn't work well."

The rumble of his laughter shook through me.

"You may try that again later," he said, playfully tugging my hair.

I rolled my eyes and kept my face buried until he jumped over Tenacity's wall. Matt was already there waiting for us along with a very small group of people.

"Good morning," he called to Ryan as Tor set me down.

"We want to know where we're going today before we

commit to a run," one of the men shouted. The tension in Matt's face tightened as he shook Ryan's hand. I couldn't hear what he said to Mya's brother but did see his lips move and the way that Ryan's gaze swept to the waiting people.

"We're going to press closer to Columbia again. From the north this time. We're not expecting any more infected than usual. Depending on the number of people who decide to go, we can change up the size of the groups. I swear we won't take any unnecessary risks."

"We don't want to go to the city. We want to search houses."

"I understand. We can go back to some of the neighborhoods we've already hit, but we're likely to hit more infected and traps than we can deal with. If I had more fey, maybe I'd be willing to take that risk. You know what happened when we went back to the distribution center. They were waiting. It's better to avoid repeats. And as far as hitting somewhere new, we've tapped out everything that's close. We can go farther out, but we run a higher risk of being out after dark.

"This is the world we live in now. There are risks. We need to accept that. I'm studying the maps at night and doing my best to keep our supply runs as random as possible in case the infected are smart enough to see patterns. I'm also gambling on what cities have and haven't been bombed. Anyone who wants to take over leading supply runs is more than welcome to it. I'd be happy to hand over the maps. And the fey are more than willing to work with someone new."

No one volunteered. Two men walked away, leaving less than a dozen volunteers.

"All right then. If we're ready, let's load up."

"June," Matt called when I would have turned to follow everyone.

I paused as Matt jogged toward me.

"I wanted to check on you. How are you doing? How's Adam?" He said it perfectly loud enough to be overheard but not so loud as to be obvious.

"Adam can't walk, Matt. How do you think he's doing?"

Matt grew serious.

"I'm sorry to hear that."

I nodded as an engine started.

"Good luck out there," he said. "If you ever feel like rejoining Tenacity, we could use the help."

I made a disbelieving face, shook my head, and turned on my heel, walking away without a word. At least two people witnessed it.

That was good. I wanted word to spread that Adam was hurt, and I was carrying a grudge about it. It would make it a little easier to convince them I had a chip on my shoulder when I moved back.

Instead of leading me to the back of the truck, Tor led me to the cab of one where Richard waited. In the passenger seat.

"Hi, June. Looks like I'll be your copilot today, if you're willing?"

I raised my brows.

"You want me to drive?"

"We need drivers we can trust. If you're willing to learn, I'm willing to teach you."

For the next hour, I focused on driving. It wasn't easy at first, but it got easier. Richard was patient and laughed when I accidentally choked the engine during my first stop. He didn't seem worried about anything, which helped. By the time we reached the outer city limits, I had more confidence and pulled the truck around like he instructed without any problem.

"You did great, June. Not much of a difference between this and a pickup, right?"

I was too polite to disagree to his face. Driving the truck had been much harder. He grinned knowingly.

"Go on and find enough to fill up the back."

Tor opened my door and helped me down. Richard would wait with the trucks and his assigned fey. My usual group of fey gathered around me, and we listened to Ryan.

"We're looking for bigger stores. Stay close. Stay together. And signal if you spot any infected."

CHAPTER SIXTEEN

MOVING THROUGH THE CITY WAS A LOT DIFFERENT THAN MOVING through the suburbs. Some of the roofs weren't as accessible, so there was less cover. And there was a lot more tension.

Only two of the people from Tenacity had left the back of the truck after seeing where we'd stopped. It seemed stupid to come all this way and not at least try, but I understood their fear. I was so filled with it that I felt sick. The only thing holding me together was Tor's strong arms. I leaned more firmly into his chest, glad he was carrying me. The fey were far faster than any human could hope to be, and I knew he would bolt if any infected were spotted.

He gave me a comforting squeeze and continued jogging with the group.

Ryan lifted his arm and pointed to the left. The fey changed directions, turning down that street at the same time an infected called out close by. I lifted my head and looked behind us. Several of the fey peeled away from the main group, darting away to investigate the source of the sound. I hoped it wasn't a trap.

Tor turned again, and I saw we were heading straight for a chain store and grinned. Eight fey encircled each human-carrying fey while the rest went inside to do an initial sweep. I knew the store was full of infected when three ran out into the early morning light. The nearest fey broke away and killed the infected before they could make a sound.

Inside, though, several called out.

"I need lookouts on the roof," Ryan said softly. "We need to watch every direction to make sure more don't gather while we're inside."

His eight fey took running starts and climbed the vertical face of the store while the one carrying Ryan joined Tor in the center of my group.

"A store like this is how Mya almost died. Stay next to Tor at all times. Grabbing distance, no farther."

I didn't even want to leave Tor's arms.

The group of bloody fey emerged, their arms full of infected bodies.

"Did you check the tops of all the shelves?" Ryan asked.

"Yes. It looks like other humans have been here. Many of the cans are missing."

Ryan swore and glanced at me.

"It's still worth checking," I said.

We moved inside, thoroughly surrounded by fey. And it was a good thing, too. The easy-to-eat items were gone. The candy section was decimated. But, the baking aisle was almost untouched.

Fey with totes packed up what I indicated. It was a decent haul, including the overstock supplies we found in the back. When we had cleared everything we could, we went in search of another store. We got lucky and found one not far away.

Unlike the previous store, the new one hadn't been touched, and there were far fewer infected inside. We gathered as much as we could from that one as well. I even managed to spot a novelty t-shirt for the city in a triple X.

"This will give you more shoulder room," I said, holding up the soft grey shirt for Tor's inspection. He barely gave it a glance before his gaze went back to scanning everything around us. All the fey watched our surroundings as alertly as Tor. It made me feel more on edge but also well-guarded.

I tucked the shirt into my jacket along with a handful of candy bars and indicated I was ready to be picked up again. Tor relaxed slightly when I was in his arms and opening a candy bar. I eagerly took a bite and held it up to him. He only hesitated a moment before chomping off a portion.

Smirking, I watched him chew and swallow.

"Well?" I asked softly. "Was it good?"

"I like the peas you make better."

I snorted a laugh and ate the rest myself.

The runners who transported the supplies carefully varied their paths to and from the trucks. Despite their efforts, they still drew infected attention. More calls rang out as we left the store, and I could see concern on Ryan's face and pure panic on the other two human's faces.

I looked up at Tor. He winked at me. The gesture was so unexpected and shocking that any fear I'd been starting to feel vanished. With a small smile, I rested my head against his shoulder as he jogged with the rest.

The group slowed, and I lifted my head to see a fey on top of a nearby building. He was gesturing like we needed to back up. Tor and the other fey looked to Ryan, who was already looking behind us at another rooftop fey. That fey was gesturing to keep going.

Ryan swore.

"I knew you'd kill us one of these days," one of the men said far too calmly.

Nearby an infected called out.

Tor didn't wait for direction. He started running toward the nearest building. He grunted, shifting my weight.

"Hold me," he said a moment before he jumped. I clasped my arms around him and clung to him like a baby monkey. He moved fast, using his feet and one hand to propel himself upward. When he stopped, I had a three-story view of the surrounding area. Infected were flooding in from the indicated directions.

"Can we run along the roofs and avoid them?" I asked.

"It would be better to kill as many as we can," Tor said, setting me down. The other human-carrying fey joined us, and we all watched the scene unfold below.

It was complete carnage. For the infected. Heads flew, and bodies dropped as the fey methodically worked their way through the horde. I winced each time one of them disappeared under a wave of infected. Thankfully, the fey reemerged every time. A bit bloodier than before, but they emerged. When the infected saw they were losing, a call went out and their remaining number retreated. A few of the fey followed to pick off the ones they could.

"I think we can head down," Ryan said.

That was all the prompting Tor needed to pick me up, and my eyes went wide with understanding.

"You're not jumping, are you?"

"It'd be safer than trying to go down through the building,"

Ryan said as the first fey jumped over the ledge with his human.

I swallowed hard and looked up at Tor.

"Isn't it going to hurt your knees?"

He leaned in to press his forehead against mine.

"Only a little. I will be fine." He lightly rubbed his nose against mine. "No screaming, June. The infected will hear."

I closed my eyes and nodded, not pulling away from him. His forehead left mine, and I felt the briefest brush of his lips against my mouth before the world dropped out from under me. My stomach rose to my throat, but I didn't make a sound. Not even when Tor landed with a jarring jolt and grunted.

Heart hammering in my chest, I opened my eyes and pressed a palm against his cheek. He turned his head to brush his lips across the skin then took off running, hoisting me higher in his arms. It gave me a view of the fey trailing us and the massacre we were leaving behind.

There were so many bodies. I could only hope that meant we were leaving the city a slightly safer place to scavenge in the future.

As the bodies shrank from view, one of the infected stood. I frowned, trying to squint as Tor turned the corner. I could have sworn it didn't have a head. The shock of the confrontation and the ensuing scary drop to the street must have rattled me too much. That or I needed glasses.

Resting my head against Tor's chest, I watched the buildings fly past. It didn't take us long to reach the trucks where fey were still showing up with the final supplies.

"Looks like you ran into trouble," Richard said, surveying our group. "Maybe it'd be better if I drove home."

I was more than willing to let him take the wheel and

gratefully settled in the passenger seat. Thankfully, the ride home was as uneventful as the ride out, and we reached the safety of Tenacity's gate well before dusk.

"It was a good thing we didn't have a huge crowd with us today," Ryan said when Matt greeted him. "It left more room for the supplies we found."

"I'm glad to hear it."

Rather than waiting around for the haul to be divided, Tor and I returned to Tolerance. As soon as we cleared the wall, I insisted he let me walk.

"Your arms have to be screaming by now."

He frowned at me.

"It means they must be tired from carrying me most of the day."

"A little tired, but I could carry you longer," he said.

I wrapped my arm around his waist and gave him a side hug.

"Thank you for keeping me safe today. How about, to show my appreciation, I give you an arm massage after you take a nice relaxing shower?"

"Yes," he said immediately. "I like when you touch me. I'll shower afterward."

His pace increased, and a smile lifted the corners of my mouth at his eagerness. I doubted any massage I gave him would be as good as the one I'd received but didn't think that would matter to Tor. My heart gave a stuttering thump, which I did my best to ignore.

He opened the door for me and had his shirt and boots off before I managed to unzip my jacket. Laughing, I carried my candy bars and his new shirt to the counter.

"Which hand is your dominant hand?" I asked.

He gave me a perplexed look. "Both of them."

I knew they didn't have a written language that they could remember and wondered if he was unaware of a dominant hand because of that.

"Let's try something."

"Okay."

I tossed a candy bar to him, and he caught it with his right.

"I'd say that's your dominant hand."

"No. The candy bar was closer to my right side. I caught it with the hand that made the most sense."

I threw another candy bar to the left. He caught it easily with that hand, flashed his teeth at me, and sat on the couch.

"Wow. You really are ambidextrous?"

"Yes."

"Is that a common trait in your brothers?" I asked as I got us both a glass of water.

"Yes. We are all ambidextrous. You're not?"

"Nope. Right-handed. I was asking because I figured your dominant hand would be the arm that's most tired. Now I'm not sure which one to start on."

I offered him the glass. Instead of taking it, he clasped my hips and lifted me. I was so focused on not spilling the water I didn't realize what he was doing until I straddled his lap, one knee on each side.

"Now you can rub both at the same time." He grinned at me and took one of the cups, drinking the water in a few long pulls.

I watched his throat work with each swallow, too stunned to do anything else.

When he finished, he nudged my glass.

"Drink. My arms are tired and sore and need massaging."

Unable to help myself, I grinned at his teasing and drank my water. He helpfully set our empty glasses on the couch cushions beside him before leaning back. I couldn't stop my sweeping gaze from taking in the expanse of his chest before glancing at his equally impressive arms.

He flexed the one I was looking at, and a flush rose to my cheeks.

"Embarrassed?" he asked.

I nodded even though I wasn't entirely sure if I was more embarrassed or turned on.

"I think it would be easier if I was sitting next to you."

"How do you know when you haven't tried it this way?"

Giving in, I reached out both hands and gave his biceps a tentative squeeze. He made a pained face.

"What? I barely touched you, and you're ten times stronger than me. There's no way it hurt."

He reached between us and adjusted himself.

"There. The pain's gone. You can keep touching me."

I burst out laughing, and he grinned in return. He continued to tease me in the most ridiculous ways as I rubbed his arms, which was like rubbing cement. Only much smoother. Although my legs got tired, I didn't settle my weight on his lap like I was sure he wanted. However, he did complain that his shoulders hurt. And once I'd rubbed those, he complained that his chest ached.

A knock on the door saved me from having to wave the surrender flag. I scrambled off his lap and around the couch, listening to the echoing rumble of his chuckle.

Emily's brows rose when I flung the door wide. It was probably due to the flush staining my cheeks.

"Everything okay?" she asked.

"It's fine. Tor's enjoying tormenting me."

"Very much," Tor said, close enough to make me jump.

"Do you want to come in?" I asked quickly.

Emily shook her head.

"I wanted to stop by with a quick update and a biscuit." She handed me a folded napkin with a warm lump inside. "The fey are doing great, and the supplies you found today will keep us going for at least the three days we planned."

"Longer would be better."

"That's what she said," Emily said with a smirk.

I flushed crimson, remembering Tor's impressiveness.

"If you want to go for more supplies, Ryan is willing to go out for another bigger run. Not the city, though. I guess today was too close of a call."

"It was," I agreed. "But I trust Ryan's intuition and the fey to keep us safe."

"Sounds like you'll be going out again then."

"Yeah. Thanks for the biscuit."

"You're welcome." With a wave, she walked away.

I closed the door and turned to Tor, who was half a step behind me.

"Do you want to try the biscuit without honey?" I asked, holding up the napkin.

He studied me for a long minute, no playfulness in his hungry gaze. Before I could get too nervous, he flashed his teeth at me and moved to bite the napkin-wrapped biscuit in my hand.

"No, not like that," I said, dodging his attempt and hurrying to remove the paper. "Like this."

I showed him the biscuit and took a small bite. It was good. Really good.

Tor captured my hand and brought the food toward his mouth. His lips brushed my fingers as he took a bite, and I felt a new round of heat flood my face. My mouth went dry, making it twice as hard to swallow under the circumstances. Tor's thumb stroked the back of my hand before he released me.

"It's good when it tastes like you," he said, watching my face flush further.

I stepped around him and hurried to the kitchen to set the biscuit down and refill my glass.

"We didn't find any meat today," I said as I moved. "We should consider offering a few of the roasts in your freezer to the soup kitchen efforts. And it was fun having people over last night. What do you think of having your brothers who helped protect me over tomorrow night?"

I paused to gulp down some water, thinking that chaperones would be good. Safe.

"We could play some games, too," I added.

His hands settled on my shoulders, and my eyes nearly popped out of my head.

"You talk faster when you're nervous. Why are you nervous?"

When I didn't answer, he plucked the glass from my hand and turned me around. I stared at his chest until he nudged my chin. Whatever he saw in my eyes had him tugging at his ear briefly.

"Since coming to the surface and discovering females existed, I have spent all my moments learning. What do they like? How do they think? What makes a female happy? I still have much to learn, June. Help teach me."

I released a long shaky breath and tried to form a logical explanation that wouldn't embarrass the heck out of me.

"I spent the last while touching your arms and shoulders. And before Emily showed up, you wanted me to rub your chest as well. Then you gave me a look that seemed to say you were hungry for me and ate the biscuit from my hand."

"Yes," he said after a lengthy silence.

"I don't know how to explain what's going on in my head right now without sounding like an idiot."

He wrapped me in a hug and soothingly stroked my back. The comforting hold was too good to pass up. Especially in my current state of awkwardness. I wrapped my arms around his waist and returned the gesture, leaning on his calm strength.

"You cannot sound like an idiot. You are the smartest woman I know."

I almost laughed considering he didn't know many.

"I asked you for time, and you've been giving it to me. But you're also being incredibly sweet and nice. And you're very open about your interest in me. I'm trying to be fair to us both by making sure I have enough time to get over Adam. To find myself again. But instead of finding myself, I'm thinking indecent thoughts about you, and the things I'm feeling for you are…confusing? Conflicting?" I sighed and continued to snuggle against him, enjoying the feel of his hand on my back.

"Tell me what you feel for me," he said. "We can both try to understand then."

I immediately shook my head.

"No. If I did that, then we'd both be confused. I don't want to create any tension between us when things are comfortable the way they are." I lifted my head to look up at him. "I know I said you should touch me less, but I like that you hug me whenever you can. You always seem to know when I need one the most. I don't want that to go away."

He gave me an extra little squeeze.

"I will always hug you. I like the way your body feels against mine."

A laugh escaped me, and I started moving my hands over his bare back, giving in to the need to touch those strong, corded muscles.

"I like the way your body feels against mine, too, and I probably shouldn't."

"No, you should. I like the way it feels when you touch my skin. We should see if you like the same." He tugged playfully at my shirt, and I quickly pivoted out of his hold. The teeth he flashed at me told me I'd read the situation correctly. He was playfully teasing but willing to touch if I allowed it.

"If you choose meat from the freezer, I will run it to Emily's house tonight. You can tell my brothers tomorrow that they are invited to dinner."

The extra tasks and planning helped the evening slip by. While Tor ran the food to Emily's, I made a simple dinner for us. We ate together and watched a movie before I yawned and said I was headed for bed.

After a shower that should have relaxed me, I lay on the comfortable mattress, lost in thought. I wondered if being honest with Tor was the best route. He didn't understand that what I was feeling now might change with time. What if—

The sound of Tor's steps in the hall outside the door quieted the doubt in my mind. Relief flooded me instead, and I realized a part of me had been waiting for him to come to bed. Was his presence that comforting? Was I growing so used to him sleeping beside me that it was the only way I would find rest?

I closed my eyes, hiding from that potential truth.

The door brushed open, and I listened as Tor crossed the

room. I could feel him when he finally stood beside me. The need to open my eyes and see what he was doing burned within me.

"Sleep sweet, my June," he whispered before pressing a kiss to my forehead. I melted inside even as I started to panic. Did he know I was awake?

I knew he didn't when he straightened and moved away.

Peeking through my lashes, I watched him enter the bathroom. The door didn't quite close behind him, and I heard the rustle of his clothes followed by a long sigh. Then wet noises. My eyes went wide when he groaned softly.

He was masturbating. Just like he said.

I looked around the room, wondering what the hell I should do. Run? No. He'd hear me and would know that I heard him. I promptly squeezed my eyes shut and tried not to notice the increase in sound coming from the bathroom or the drawn-out groan that seemed to go on far too long…until I remembered the quantity of sheen when he'd come on my leg.

How had this not woken me up last night?

After a moment, the shower started. I took the opportunity to fan my face on the off chance he'd be able to see my flush in the dark.

"June?" Tor called, his dark fingers closing around the edge of the door.

I collapsed like I was pretending to be dead, not sleeping. The thunder of my pulse in my ears didn't cover the sound of his feet as he crossed the carpet.

"You are everything," he whispered. "I will distract you every day with my teasing until you no longer remember your hurt heart." His fingers whispered over my cheek. "How can such a peaceful face fill me with such need that my cock already aches again?" He sighed, and I could almost picture his disgruntled expression. "I will need to stroke myself many times so I don't release before morning."

The flush started creeping back into my cheeks. Thankfully, he didn't continue stroking my face and notice the heat. He returned to the bathroom so I could die peacefully in mortification as I listened to him come twice more before he finally showered.

If I were honest with myself, I was dying to slide my hand under the covers and do the same but too afraid of being caught. So I lay there, pretending to sleep and focusing on my breathing until he emerged from the bathroom and quietly got in on his side of the bed.

I almost jumped out of my skin when his arms slid around me and he pulled me close, dipping his head to the crook of my neck to breathe in deeply.

"No food will ever taste or smell as good as you do, June," he said softly, nuzzling slightly.

I thought for sure he would hear the way my pulse raced. Instead, he eased back and sighed gustily. While it only took him a few minutes to fall asleep, it took me much, much longer. Enough time for me to breathe him in like he'd done to me and think about what he'd said.

Tor had spent his day purposely distracting me from thinking of Adam. And it had worked. I couldn't remember thinking of him once. What did that say about me?

CHAPTER SEVENTEEN

I WOKE UP ON TOP OF TOR AGAIN. HIS HAND RUBBED MY BACK soothingly even as his hard length pressed against my stomach.

"This can't be comfortable for you," I mumbled against his chest.

"Why not? I like the feel of your body against mine. Each exhale teases my nipple. And sometimes you wiggle to get more comfortable." His massive cock twitched between us. "I like when you wiggle."

Opening my eyes, I sighed gustily. On purpose. The nipple near my mouth pebbled, and he twitched again.

My humor died when he growled low.

"Sorry. I shouldn't have teased you."

"I like when you tease me."

I lifted my head and looked down at him.

"If not for sour cream and onion chips and strawberry oatmeal, I'd think you liked everything."

"No. Only everything about you."

He said the sweetest things. My thoughts went back to last night and what he'd said when he thought I was asleep.

"Tor, I don't know what I'm doing when I'm with you."

"You can do anything you want. Lick me. Wiggle on me. Kiss me."

He flashed his teeth, and I knew he was at least slightly teasing. Though, I had no doubt he'd welcome any of those actions from me.

"I think sleeping on top of you and having you carry me around all day is enough touching for now."

He grunted, a speculative look coming onto his face.

"You might like it all, though. Give it a try like I tried your chips."

My initial smile faded as I stared down at him and thought through his suggestion. The urge to dip my head and lick his nipple was there. But so was the awareness that I'd probably like it. A lot.

"I don't think I should," I said.

Something in my tone robbed him of his playfulness. His hungry gaze swept over my face.

"Why not?"

"I don't think one taste of you will be enough."

His hips jerked underneath me, and his jaw clenched.

"The sun will rise soon," he said tightly. "Go dress for the supply run."

I eased off of him, and from the corner of my eye, I caught the way he palmed himself. My face flushed as I hurried to the bathroom. His groan echoed through the door while I brushed my teeth. When I emerged, the bedding was missing. That only made my flush deepen.

What was I doing? I wasn't purposely trying to torment Tor, but I still was because of my honesty. I didn't want to lie to him, though. Like he said, he was learning about women.

It wasn't fair to withhold what I was truly thinking and feeling.

Guilt plagued me as I made my way downstairs and found Tor at the stove, making me breakfast.

"I'm sorry, Tor. I shouldn't have said what I did this morning. It wasn't nice."

He turned off the stove and faced me. He wore the shirt I'd found for him yesterday. It hugged his shoulders and chest but hid his abs from my view, which was slightly disappointing.

"It was very nice. The only way it wouldn't be nice was if it were a lie. Did you lie to me, June?"

I swallowed hard and shook my head. He came around the counter and set his hands on my shoulders.

"I hope that, one day, you will sample me and never want to stop. That you are as addicted to my taste as I am to yours."

My core clenched at his words.

"But if that doesn't happen, I will not be angry. How can I? Thank you for allowing me to care for you, June. Know that is enough if that is all you will allow me." His fingers tangled with the ends of my hair and gave the strands a few gentle tugs. "Eat your breakfast."

Rather than doing what I was told, I slid my arms around his waist and hugged him. Another growl rumbled through his chest.

"Do you promise to tell me if you ever feel that I'm being unfair to you?" I asked.

"I promise," he said, his hands already smoothing over my back.

I nodded and pulled away to eat the breakfast he'd made for me.

If I was toying with Tor's heart, he was undoubtedly doing

the same with mine. I didn't feel like I was fresh out of a failed relationship. I felt like I was in the throes of a new one. It was terrifying and exciting, and I wasn't sure how I'd stay focused on the supply run.

When he carried me to Tenacity, I spent the entire time breathing him in. When I drove the truck, half my attention was on not killing the engine and the other half was watching Tor move. When it was time to search houses in the suburbs, I was busy resting my cold hand over Tor's steadily beating heart.

He only reluctantly set me down when it was time for me to search the cupboards, and he hovered close by. I could feel that something had shifted between us. Like we were standing on the edge of a cliff. Or maybe I was standing on the edge, and he was waiting below, ready to catch me.

Somehow, I managed to stay focused enough to coordinate my team's efforts and clear the house in a record amount of time. We moved from one place to the next, accumulating supplies. The people from Tenacity stopped around lunch to eat in the back of one of the trucks. Tor and I ate in a house with the rest of our team. I used the break to invite them over for dinner at dusk, which they all readily agreed to do.

As soon as I'd eaten enough, we continued gathering until another fey said we needed to move. A herd of infected was coming our way, and Ryan didn't want a repeat of the day before.

Richard drove us back, keeping me entertained with fey stories from when he first met them. My gaze kept straying to Tor as Mya's dad related how many times he'd overheard a fey asking his wife sexual questions. He even admitted to hitting one, which he didn't recommend since he only hurt himself and not the fey.

When we reached Tenacity, I didn't bother with claiming any supplies for myself. I went straight to Tor and breathed him in as he ran home with me. So many thoughts raced through my head, but the ones that kept playing on repeat were his groans of pleasure...because of me. Richard's story drove home what I already knew. The fey were starved for female attention in any form. Looking. Talking. Touching. All of it.

As soon as the door closed behind us, I turned to Tor.

"I feel like I'm taking advantage of you."

He paused from taking a boot off and straightened to give me a confused look.

"You've never had a woman do anything for you before me. Of course you're going to like me for being nice to you and sleeping next to you. It feels like Adam trick-started your interest in me when he sent you to wake me up. I'm not a mean person. I would never purposely hurt you. But that doesn't mean I'm the love of your life. Not when you haven't even been out there to play the field." I took a deep breath. "I think you need to see other women."

He blinked at me. That was it. A blink. Then, he returned to the task of removing his boots.

"I need some kind of verbal feedback here. I haven't yet perfected the art of reading minds."

"I think you're afraid. You're feeling too much for me too quickly, and I'm sorry I caused you to feel nervous and embarrassed and, now, afraid. If it will make you feel better if I look at other women, I will do that. I don't think playing in a field will make them any more appealing to me or me to them, though."

I stared at him for a moment. How did he manage to keep saying all the right things?

"You are lovable, Tor. I only want to make sure other women have a chance to see what I see."

"No one sees me the way you do." He snagged my zipper and eased it down. "When you look at me, my blood heats. My cock hardens." He slid his hands inside my jacket and over my shoulders, slipping it off of me. "I want to smile and laugh when I'm with you. You bring joy to my life where there was none." He hung my jacket and bent down to remove my boots. "I know you need more time, June. I will not rush you to make choices you are not ready to make."

He set my boots aside and stood to press his forehead against mine.

"I only ask that you don't push me away. Keep telling me I scare you. I will do everything I can to ease your fears."

"I have so many fears."

"Not too many for me. You are safe with me, June. Always."

I closed my eyes and nodded. He pulled away, brushing his lips against my forehead before wrapping me in one of his hugs.

"We should start dinner," he said against me.

It was just the distraction I needed. While the electric pressure cooker worked its magic on the large roast, I made a small side of vegetables and helped Tor find more chairs for the dining room table. I wanted us all to sit together, but seven would be a cozy fit. Tor assured me no one would mind.

When we finished setting the table, we went through Tor's supply of games.

The first knock on the door came just before the timer went off for the meat. Tor answered it so I could whip up the gravy. Something he said he hadn't yet tried.

I smiled at Noru and Ashkii then waved them over when I

saw them curiously watching what I was doing. It didn't take long for the rest of the team to show up. I laughed and talked to the fey who I'd been around enough to know by name. Scath teased me almost as much as Tor did. Fallor quietly observed everything, and Hasten's ears turned dark every time I spoke to him. He was easily the shyest of the group.

The gravy was a hit and disappeared just as quickly as the meat. However, the veggies, not so much. I finished those. When we were done, the fey thanked me for dinner and helped clean off the table, eager for the card games I'd mentioned. Two decks made Go-Fish interesting. The guys laughed and bantered with one another, and I loved the comradery.

When I broke out a bag of chips as the night wore on, Tor groaned and I could see a few of his friends grow curious. It turned into a round of making each fey try a chip. Not a single one of them liked the taste, but Scath said he would eat anything a female fed him without complaint.

The group got really quiet, and they all glanced at Tor.

"What?" I asked. "You're making me feel paranoid. What's Tor been telling you?"

Hasten's ears turned dark grey when I pinned him with my gaze.

"Tell me what you know about women."

"They are afraid to look at us."

I shook my head.

"Not true. I'm not afraid to look at you." I looked at Noru. "What about you?"

"They like different things."

My wide smile had him smiling in return.

"Exactly. Women are all different. If one doesn't want to

look at you, try another. Or try a different way to get her attention."

"Some women like when we don't wear a shirt," Tor said. "They will look at us for a very long time then."

I flushed scarlet at that one.

"What are other things we can do to get a woman's attention?" Ashkii asked.

"Stuff like this," I said. "Asking honest questions."

"Emily said that not all honest questions are good," Hasten said.

Scath nodded. "Asking to taste a woman's pussy is against date night rules. Emily said she would cancel date nights if we ask that."

I cleared my throat twice while they all waited expectantly for my opinion on that.

"We're private creatures by nature. We like clothes and coverings. Asking to see something we keep very hidden can be taken as an insult. It's something a woman would only share with someone she's very close with."

Understanding lit every male face at the table.

"Emily said we must get to know a woman first. But I didn't understand how we could know a woman when we couldn't ask all of our questions," Noru said.

"It's about getting to know a woman in the right order. First, you need to know her mind, then her heart. Once you think you know both, you might get away with asking questions about her body. But even then, you might get slapped."

They all nodded thoughtfully, and I hoped my explanation would give them a better chance with the ladies at Tenacity.

The group left with a lot of good nights and sleep sweets

and promises to see me in the morning. I couldn't stop yawning as Tor and I cleaned up the kitchen and started the dishwasher.

"This was a good night. Thank you for letting me invite them over," I said to Tor as he washed the counters.

"You showed us all that there is still hope."

"Hope for what?"

"For happiness. For a female of our own. For a life we want to live."

I went to him and wrapped my arms around his waist, and he hugged me in return.

"Go get ready for bed, June. I will come upstairs soon."

My heart gave a stuttering jolt at his words and what he'd likely do again tonight.

I RUBBED my face against Tor's chest and shifted a little in my half-asleep state, trying to get more comfortable on top of him. His hips arched against me ever so slightly a moment before his fingers ran through my hair.

A small sound of pleasure escaped me. I loved sleeping on top of Tor. He was warm and touched me non-stop. I didn't realize how much I craved being touched and didn't know if it was a new thing, a Tor thing, or a need that had always been hidden away, waiting to be discovered.

Moving my face again, I brushed my lips over his skin and felt his nipple. My tongue darted out.

The world flipped as Tor rolled us impossibly fast. One moment, I was on top; and the next, I was underneath him. He had my hands pinned above my head and leaned in, nuzzling the side of my neck. He inhaled deeply at the same time he slowly arched into me.

I gasped at the friction of his hot length against my folds, and my hips jerked in response.

He growled, the sound vibrating against my chest and filling my ears even as he nipped my neck.

"You are right, my June," he rasped. "It is difficult to stop." He licked me and groaned, pressing little kisses along my throat.

Then he was gone, the door to the master bath closing firmly behind his retreat.

I lay on the mattress, panting and very awake. It would have been easy to stay there until my heart stopped racing, but I knew what he was doing in the bathroom and didn't need to hear another throaty groan ripped from his lips because of me.

So, I grabbed my things and hurried downstairs to get ready for the day. It was a good thing, too, because I heard a knock on the front door just as I tugged my shirt over my head. Upstairs, the shower ran as I hurried to answer.

Emily stood on the stoop, bundled in her winter coat against the cold predawn air.

"Hey, June."

"Good morning. Come in."

I lightly shivered as I closed the door.

"I hear you," Emily said, noting my chill. "Spring cannot come soon enough. Sorry to stop by so early. I was going to stop by last night but saw you had a houseful."

"Tor and I hosted dinner and a game night for the fey who've been assigned to me on the supply runs. It was fun. I think they really enjoyed themselves."

"Trust me. They did. That whole 'get to know their mind and heart before their body' advice is a huge help."

"How do you know that already?" I asked before I could stop myself.

She chuckled. "They don't seem to need as much sleep as we do, and word spreads quickly. Which is why I wanted to talk to you. The fey cooks and servers are as ready as they can be for the simple meals we want them to make and serve. Matt's kitchen and dining area setup are too. I think we should start today before anyone notices the tables and starts asking Matt questions."

"Today sounds good," I said.

"Matt explained more of the plan to me. Are you sure you want to move back there?"

"I do. And I'm not worried. Tor will be there. I know he won't let anything bad happen to me."

"But will you make sure nothing happens to Tor?" Emily asked, not unkindly.

"I'll protect him as savagely as he protects me. I promise."

"I hoped you would say that. When are you moving out?"

"I'm not sure. I figured I would watch for an opportunity that wouldn't make it look suspicious. I mean, I can't imagine anyone believing I willingly left this place, having lived here themselves. The people are nice. There's food. Shelter. Protection. I need to make sure I sell it, you know?"

She nodded. "Just don't stay there too long. The girls are going to miss having a fourth at feight club."

I snorted. "You could always join in."

"No way. I'm a peacemaker, not a fighter."

She said goodbye just before Tor came downstairs. He

didn't say anything to me as he moved to the stove and started making oatmeal.

"Should we talk about what happened upstairs?" I asked hesitantly.

"Do you want to?"

"I don't know. Maybe, if you feel upset about any of it."

"I am not upset." He glanced back at me. "But I am very hungry for you."

"I could tell."

"Did it upset you?"

I slowly shook my head. "I think it should have, though."

"Why?"

"That's an excellent question. I think part of my brain is still trying to cling to things the way they were."

"What do you mean?"

"Before I met Adam, I was going to school to get my marketing degree. My dad used to say I was learning how to convince people they needed something they didn't want." I gave Tor a wry smile. "In a way, he was right.

"I had a plan for myself—degree, career, then a family. I saw men as a distraction I didn't need until I was ready. That changed a little when I met Adam. Through a thousand small acts, he won my heart and made me believe he needed me as much as I needed him."

I looked down at my hands, trying to sort through what I was thinking and feeling.

"I'm not mad at Adam for hurting my heart. I understand why he left. He felt like he couldn't protect me like you could, and he wanted me to be safe above all else. Even above our happiness together. But knowing his motivations doesn't change how hurt and sad I still am."

"Time will help with that."

I nodded in agreement.

"I know. It already has, and that's part of the problem. The way I'm feeling just seems like it's changing too fast. But that's based on how the old world worked. This new one's different. Yesterday's close call has me wondering so much. Am I moving too slowly for this world? Should I let go of the past more quickly? What if all I have is today?"

Tor came over and hugged me.

"You will have many, many days, my June. I will let nothing happen to you. Take all the time you need to know your head and your heart so I may know them, too."

The guy just kept melting me in all the right ways. I returned his hug and reluctantly released him to sit at the island, letting what he said turn over in my head.

After I'd eaten breakfast, we geared up and left the house. This time, when Tor picked me up at the wall, I let my fingers explore the wall of his chest. I could feel him glancing down at me and wasn't surprised when he stopped outside of Tenacity, set me on my feet, and hugged me to him.

"If you do not want the people here to know I crave you with every breath of my being, you will need to keep these perfect fingers to yourself," he murmured against my hair.

"Are you asking me to stop?"

"Never. I'm only making you aware of the consequences when you choose not to."

I didn't miss how he'd said "when" instead of "if."

"I'll keep my hands to myself," I said.

He grunted and breathed in deeply. I itched to go back to playing with his chest.

"Maybe someone else should carry me today?"

He jerked against me.

"To prevent temptation," I clarified. "And so it won't be so weird when I have to leave you behind at the house to go out for supplies."

He pulled back to study me, confusion on his face.

"The fey who stays with me needs to remain hidden at all times. That means you're stuck in the house until we're done. I'll still need to go on supply runs, though."

"I will ask Scath to carry you today."

Scath was more than willing to take on carry-duty. It didn't matter who vaulted over the wall with me or who carried me to and from the truck when we reached the neighborhood Ryan meant for us to clear out. Tor stayed close regardless. Always. And he still entertained me with his conversation and questions. Especially about the tote filled with tiny beheaded humans.

"Those are dolls," I explained. "A child plays with them."

"A child removed their heads," Tor asked, looking slightly worried.

"Seems so. Maybe she was switching heads with bodies."

I dug out a random head and put it on a body. Noru shivered.

"That is unnatural."

"From a guy who's removed more heads than this tote has dolls," I said with a laugh. "Let's take the tote with us. If there are kids in Tenacity, they might appreciate the playthings."

They grudgingly listened.

The day went fast like any other, and I was a little more boisterous about the haul when we were back at the trucks, loading the last of it.

"Hard work pays off," I said, trying to give one of the

Tenacity folks a high-five. He reluctantly caved when I waved my waiting hand. "You should seriously consider applying for Tolerance citizenship. You get to keep what you find. All of it. Not some stupid percentage."

He glanced at the fey, who'd moved farther away from me.

"Not sure I could deal with the change of scenery."

I shrugged. "Close the curtains. You can't see anything then."

"They're not making you live with one of them?" he asked.

"Pft. My assigned fey has a freezer full of meat. There was no making involved. I'd fight my way to the front of the steak-for-breakfast line. Who cares if I have to house share? Tenacity's the same way, only without the steak and a lot more stealing. My name's June, by the way."

"Bram. And I meant with a fey, but I can see your point. I wouldn't care who I had to live with to eat decently for a change. It's a little unnerving to watch them remove heads and then sleep in the same house as one of them, though, isn't it?"

"I've stabbed infected through the underside of their chins. Violently and bloody. Would you hesitate to room with me?"

He looked off thoughtfully for a moment. "I guess you have a point. Humans can be just as vicious. One of my past housemates was angry and an asshole to be around. But he didn't rip anyone's head off, you know? I think the idea that a fey could easily overpower me makes it harder to relax around them."

"Try being a woman in a room full of human men. I've lived with that kind of worry my whole life."

I walked away from him without another word.

CHAPTER EIGHTEEN

Often when we returned to Tenacity, people would be gathered, waiting to see the supplies we brought back. Then they would wait even longer in line for it all to be divided and doled out. Matt's rule of one box for each house kept things orderly. Everyone knew if they didn't keep things civil, there was a chance they'd forfeit their home's rations for that day.

However, nothing about Tenacity was orderly when the fey delivered us over the wall. Two groups of people stood outside the shed, both yelling at the other so loudly there was no possible way they could hear each other. We could hear them, though. Or at least, pieces of what was being said.

"You're betraying your own kind."

"We need food."

"Your hate will kill us all."

"Go fuck your mother."

"What the hell is going on?" Bram, the guy I'd high-fived, asked me as we both stared in confusion.

"No idea, but the mom threats are out, so it can't be good," I said.

My eyes swept over the area. I noted two young boys watching the group from a nearby house. With crayons in hand and coloring books on their laps, the pair sat on the steps. They didn't look like they were coloring, though. They looked like they were taking notes.

Clever.

Matt emerged from within the shed.

"This is your last warning. Break it up or I'm telling the fey to keep everything they collected today."

I could feel Bram bristle beside me. He took a step forward even as the groups started yelling at each other again. I clamped my hand over his arm.

"We don't know what's happening. It's better to wait and voice your objection after the groups threatening to kill each other leave."

"Of course you'd say that," he said quietly. "You have a freezer full of meat waiting for you. I risked my life for that food."

"And you'll be risking it again by bringing attention to yourself now." I released him. "But I get it. You worked hard for the food, and it's not fair to have it taken away because of some assholes. I've been in your shoes. And my ex-boyfriend was beaten so badly because of his objections that he can't walk now. Pick your battles carefully."

Bram didn't rush forward. He crossed his arms and waited next to me and the other humans who'd gone out for supplies. The fey who'd delivered us inside stood just behind us, watching and listening as well.

Matt's flushed face swung our way, then he cupped his hands to bellow to the fey. "Anyone who doesn't leave by the time I count to twenty, you have permission to throw over the wall!"

The guy next to me swore when Matt started counting.

Ashkii came forward and tapped my shoulder.

"Mya says it's not safe to throw humans. She will be upset if we throw them like Matt asks, right?"

The guy next to me did a double-take at the fey.

"Probably," I said. "But Matt's going to be upset if these humans start fighting." I pointed out the two boys across the street. "And it's likely innocent bystanders would get hurt in the process."

"These humans would hurt the children?" Noru asked.

The guy and I shared a look, and he gave me a clueless shrug like he had no idea how to answer. I faced my group of fey and answered honestly.

"Unintentionally, most likely. But yes."

Fortunately, none of the fey needed to worry about human-tossing. The group broke up rapidly when Matt reached twelve and kept counting. By the time he hit seventeen, the opening to the shed was clear.

A group of women hesitantly walked out. One of them was holding a kid's hand. The little girl couldn't have been more than two or three and had a tear-streaked face.

While the woman spoke in low tones to Matt, I turned and whispered to Noru.

"Get one of the dolls for the girl. Make sure it has a head and grab some clothes for it."

He leapt over the wall, and I strode forward.

"What's going on?" I asked, interrupting Matt's conversation with the woman. "Why was everyone yelling?"

"A few misaligned viewpoints. Nothing to worry about." He looked down at the little girl. "Did you like your soup?"

The little girl sidestepped behind her mother's leg, partially hiding instead of answering.

"She did. Thank you," the mom said, answering for her. "I'm worried people are going to act out against those of us who chose to eat here."

"You and Greyly have nothing to worry about, Abi. You did the right thing coming here. But, if you have any trouble, come find me."

There was a whisper of noise behind me. When everyone's attention shifted, I had no choice but to look too.

Noru knelt on the ground a few steps away. He was trying to put a dress on a naked doll and failing spectacularly. He looked up at the little girl.

"Something is wrong with her. I don't know how to fix it." He held out his hand with the Barbie and the dress in his palm.

The little girl stared at him. He stared back.

After a moment, she unlatched from her mom's leg and went to Noru. She took the doll from his hand, used her tiny fingers to straighten its backward head, and slipped on the dress. Holding Noru's gaze, she set it back in his hand.

He studied the doll closely.

"You fixed her," he said, looking up at the girl. "Now, how do I care for her?"

The girl started explaining about being gentle with the head in a childish voice. I glanced up at Abi. She was watching the pair, her expression slightly sad but not worried or filled with revulsion. None of the other women looked concerned, either. Proof that not all the humans here hated the fey and more motivation to finish what I'd started. Especially after the recent display of contention.

"Were you serious about sending away the supplies?" I asked Matt.

He lifted his gaze from the fey and child, meeting mine steadily.

"Absolutely."

Bram overheard Matt.

"If you're going to start pulling that shit, I'm done. I'm not going to risk my ass for food so you can get rid of it to pacify a few assholes."

"You would have kept your share. It's the community share I would have sent away. I won't ever bite the hand that feeds us. That includes the brave few like you," he said, looking at Bram and me, "and the fey."

"Good," Bram said, pacified.

"What set the crowd off?" I asked, needing Matt to spell it out.

"The fey recognized that some people aren't eating enough. To help, they offered to set up a soup kitchen of sorts. Anyone who wants to eat is welcome."

"That doesn't explain why some of the people were angry."

"The fey cook and serve the food," Abi said softly. "Some people don't like that. They would rather have the fey leave the food for Matt to split between the houses."

"This isn't my show. It's Emily's," Matt said. "Her terms were clear. Only the fey work in the kitchen. No takeout. No food left behind."

"So Emily found a new way to push her fey agenda," Bram said without malice. "Only this time she's dangling a carrot people can't ignore." The man shook his head and looked at Matt. "Good luck with that."

He walked away to help unload the supplies and grab his share.

"Thank you for agreeing to this, Matt," one of the other women said. "We know it's not going to be easy on you, but it's making more of a difference than you know."

"Danielle's right," Abi said before looking at her kid. "Two meals a day isn't enough for a growing child. It's time to go, Greyly."

The girl straightened the doll's arm and handed the doll back to Noru.

"Will you teach me more tomorrow?" Noru asked Greyly.

The girl nodded and returned to her mom's leg. Abi looked Noru in the eye, said thank you, and hurried away with her group. Noru slowly stood, his gaze tracking the woman and little girl. Abi probably didn't know it yet, but she and her child had just been fey-sighted and marked.

Shaking my head, I turned away from Matt and Noru. Tor waited by the wall, watching me as closely as Noru had watched his woman. Instead of going to Tor, I went to Ashkii and asked for a ride home. Tor didn't say anything. He understood what I was doing. Tomorrow, I'd ask a different member of our group to carry me.

As soon as we were inside Tolerance's walls, Ashkii left me with Tor.

"That looked a lot more hostile than I'd anticipated," I said as he walked with me. "Do you think the fey who were serving are all right?"

Tor's laughter rumbled from him.

"They are fine, June. They spent the day watching pretty

women. I saw seven women today, by the way. One met my gaze and smiled at me. How many more women do I need to see for you to believe I only want you?"

I glanced at him and shook my head.

"You're impossibly cute sometimes."

"I'd rather be impossibly handsome. Should I take my shirt off?"

A laugh escaped me, and I quickly shook my head.

"No. Leave it on at least until we get into the house. I don't care how well you're able to deal with the cold. Seeing you shirtless now would make *me* cold."

He grunted and continued walking with me.

"I'm worried," I said, growing serious. "If they're this angry about the soup kitchen, they're going to be even angrier about the next part of our plan."

"I agree. But I will keep you safe, June."

"I meant I was worried about you." I stopped walking and faced Tor. "They beat the last man I cared about so badly that he broke up with me and went to die."

"Those humans cannot hurt me." Tor gently ran his fingers along my jawline. "There is only one human who can hurt me. But, I trust her with my heart and my life. She is the smartest, bravest, most beautiful woman I have ever seen."

He winked playfully at me and dropped his hands to his side.

"If I am ever hurt, I will do as Uan has done. I will try to heal on my own and only return to the caves if I have no other choice. But I wouldn't break up with my female. I will ask my brothers to watch over her until I return.

"I will always come back to you, June."

I itched to step into his arms. To grab onto all that he offered with both hands. I thought I'd been giving myself time to heal, but I didn't think that was the case anymore. I was holding onto my heart, trying desperately not to let Tor steal it. But it was far too late for that.

"You say the best things sometimes," I said softly.

He grunted and fell into step with me.

My pulse was hammering when we walked into the house. I didn't know what I was going to do, but I knew I wanted to do something.

"What would you do if I kissed you right now?" I asked, hanging up my jacket.

"Hold still and hope you don't stop."

I grinned at him and waved at the couch. "Take a seat."

He had his boots off and was sitting where I'd indicated before I could blink. His enthusiasm did little to calm my racing heart.

I wasn't sure if I was making the right choice, but I was tired of waiting for the sake of waiting. More time wouldn't help me make this choice. The only way I'd know if we were right together was by trying.

Circling the couch, I studied him. His hands were loose at his sides, palms resting on the cushions. His sharp gaze tracked each move I made, though. He was a juxtaposition of calm and ready to pounce.

I stopped in front of him and moved his hands a little farther away from his thighs. Then, I straddled his lap like I had to give him his arm rub.

"I like this," he said, his voice all rumbly and filled with man satisfaction. "Can I touch you?"

I hesitated to say yes. If I did, there was every chance I'd lose myself too deeply. And Tor's earlier observation had been right. When I started to feel too much too quickly, it made me pull back.

"Will you be disappointed if I ask you to keep your hands on the couch?"

"No."

I stroked my fingers along his cheek and brow, learning the texture of his skin and the nuances of his facial features. His nose was strong and cheekbones high and prominent. They balanced his proud brow and square jaw. He twitched under me when I ran a finger along the edge of his ear.

"Sensitive?" I asked.

"Very."

"You tug on them when you're upset. It makes me want to pull your hands away and kiss the parts that you made dark. It can't feel good."

"It would feel very good if you kissed them when they are dark."

I grinned at his serious expression.

"I meant that it can't feel good to tug on them."

I leaned in until my chest rested against his and my mouth was close to the long edge of his ear.

"I like your ears."

He shivered under me. I smoothed my hands over his shoulders, using them as an anchor as I closed the distance and ran my tongue along the edge of an ear before kissing it. He kept his hands on the couch while I nibbled and kissed my way to his jaw and across his cheek. But he trembled, and his hips twitched non-stop.

"Allow me to touch you, June," he rasped when my lips finally hovered over his.

"Can you wait a little longer?"

His gaze swept over my face. I could read the absolute need there. A hunger so intense and consuming, I knew he would swallow me whole when I finally caved.

"I know I'm asking a lot. I just want to kiss you now. Nothing else. And I'm afraid, if I say yes to touching, this is going to turn into more than kissing."

He closed his eyes, but not before I saw the torment in them.

"Kiss me, June. I will not touch you."

Cradling his face between my palms, I smoothed my thumbs over his skin.

"Thank you, Tor," I said softly.

He groaned when I brushed my lips against his, and I felt him jerk beneath me. I pulled back to look at him, and his eyes snapped open.

"More," he growled.

I willingly dipped my head and nibbled at his firm bottom lip. Tor didn't play around there. He opened his mouth and nipped mine in return. The moment I gasped, his tongue invaded. He kissed me hungrily, devouring any hesitation and feeding my need for him.

His hand gripped my hips, seating me firmly on his erection. A whimper escaped me at the hard press of him through my clothes. He ground me down against his length in a slow rotation that robbed me of thought and air.

Tearing my mouth from his, I panted, pressing his face to my neck. He nipped and licked my skin, grinding against me for only a moment before nudging my head up and claiming my mouth again. My fingers twitched on the sides of his face, and I rocked against him.

This time he pulled back.

"Tell me your heart no longer hurts."

"It no longer hurts."

He growled low, his hand gripping the back of my neck as he gave me a hard kiss.

"Tell me I can touch you."

"You already are," I panted.

"Tell me," he repeated.

I knew what this would mean, and a knot formed in my stomach. I could feel what he wanted to do to me.

"We're moving too fast. Can we slow—"

He kissed me hard on the lips.

"Do you trust me?" he asked.

"I do."

"Then let me touch you."

Staring into his eyes, I saw a thread of doubt and hesitation there. He didn't believe I fully trusted him. And why should he? I'd been sending so many mixed signals. Snuggling him at night but asking him not to touch me too much. Acknowledging his interest and my own but saying I needed more time.

Hadn't I only seconds ago decided that time wasn't the answer? That trying was? I needed to stop hesitating. Tor wasn't Adam. He wouldn't walk away.

I smoothed my fingers lightly over Tor's cheeks.

"You can touch me."

The sound he made was pure triumph. He claimed my lips again, one hand on the back of my neck and one hand on my butt as he stood with me. He didn't give me a chance to ask what he intended. He moved. I felt him climb the stairs, and my heart started to hammer as I hungrily kissed him in return.

The mattress touched my back before I even realized we'd reached the bedroom. It jolted me, and I started to panic.

"Wait," I panted, tearing my lips from his. "I'm not ready."

"Shh. Show me your trust, June," he said, kissing and nipping his way down my neck. "Tonight, I only want to see you. That is all."

His words reassured me enough that I didn't fight him when he reached for the bottom of my shirt and gently tugged it up over my head. He tossed it aside as his gaze swept over my bra. I thought he'd reach for that next. Instead, he dipped his head, kissing and licking his way along my collarbone.

That he meant to take his time became abundantly clear when he moved to my shoulder. I relaxed and threaded my fingers through his hair. The heat that had started with the kiss on the couch continued to build with each press of his lips. I squirmed underneath him, and he whispered soothing non-human words against my skin.

A whimper escaped me when he moved to the other shoulder. How had I gone from worrying he wanted too much to needing him to take off my bra?

Releasing his hair, I reached underneath me and unclasped the hooks. Tor didn't hesitate to slide the straps down my arms and toss the bra away, like he had the shirt. His keen gaze swept over my breasts with a reverence that melted my heart further.

The flat of his tongue stroked over my nipple before he sucked it into his mouth. Another small sound escaped me as he flicked and drew on the tender peak. I didn't realize I'd threaded my fingers in his hair again until I tried tugging him over to the other side.

"Patience, my June," he whispered. "I will taste all of you. I promise."

My core clenched as images of the last time he'd tasted me rose to mind.

"Take my pants off then," I panted.

He ignored me and continued to suck and lick one breast before finally leaving it for the other. I gasped and panted when he gave the second one the same treatment. My skin tingled when he moved lower, kissing the undersides of my breasts then my sternum.

"Do you want me to stop?" he asked before he reached my navel.

"No. Not yet."

He growled low and swirled his tongue over my skin while finally touching the waist of my jeans. He eased them down over my legs, his lips never leaving me. I burned with need. I wanted his mouth between my legs more than I wanted air.

"Please, Tor," I begged when he skipped past the underwear and started exploring my legs.

There wasn't an inch of them he didn't caress or lick, and I was a puddle of desperate longing by the time he finally touched my underwear.

"I love the sounds you make," he murmured, pressing his lips to my clit through the material.

"I'll make more if you get on with it already," I panted.

He chuckled, a low sound that teased me with its vibrations. Thankfully, he didn't toy with me more. As soon as the underwear were off, he was on me. His tongue slicked over my opening and circled my clit. My fingers tightened in his hair, and I bucked against him, too far gone to care.

On the third pass, he paused to press the flat of his tongue against me. The heavy pressure sent me over the edge. With a cry, I ground against his tongue and rode out the orgasm.

Spent and boneless, I twitched under his hold as he nudged my legs farther apart and lapped at my opening. I drifted in languid bliss, my channel pulsing around him as he used his tongue to stroke me from the inside.

"That was incredible, Tor."

He made a low sound in response before pulling back with a final lick.

"I want to do that again." He slid a finger in me, setting off another wave of aftershocks. His thumb circled my clit, showing he was entirely serious.

"Again? I think I might need a minute or two. My heart is still racing." He slowly moved his finger in and out of me several times before adding a second one. The stretch of two gave me pause, and my thoughts went to the glimpse I'd gotten of him.

"I'm—"

"Hello?" a voice called from below. "It's Emily."

Eyes wide, I jolted, partially sitting up in bed, and I stared down at Tor, who was still between my legs, fingers slowly thrusting.

He exhaled heavily and removed them.

"Just a minute," I called before swearing under my breath. "Where's my shirt?"

He pressed a kiss to my inner thigh, sending an echoing jolt of pleasure through me.

"I will go talk to Emily while you dress," he said.

He stood, his massive erection straining against his pants.

"You can't go down there like that," I said, trying to pull myself together enough to slither from the bed.

He palmed himself, adjusting his length. It didn't do any good. Whether his bulbous head was trying to bust free of the waistband or touch his kneecap didn't matter. He was too big to hide.

"You stay here," I whispered. I stood on shaky legs and tugged my shirt over my head without bothering with a bra. The jeans went on next, without underwear.

Tor didn't try to stop me as I hurried downstairs.

CHAPTER NINETEEN

EMILY LOOKED UP AT ME, AND A SLOW SMILE SPREAD ACROSS HER face as I descended the steps.

"Did I interrupt something?" she asked, taking in my bed hair.

"No. You're fine. What's up?"

"I wanted to talk about today and the plans for tomorrow," she said. "But I can come back later if you think that'll help."

I shook my head and gestured to the couch, hoping she would stay. After the combustible experience I'd just undergone with Tor, I needed this break to calm my chaotic thoughts.

"Now's fine."

She removed her jacket and sat with a weary sigh.

"Everything worked exactly like you'd thought it would, only on a faster scale. People noticed us as soon as we arrived, and word spread. Matt fielded questions while I helped the fey figure out everything. A line formed before the fey even finished setting up. I could tell right away that we needed to make more soup than we'd thought, which was fine. We'd brought extra to make a show of taking the overages back. However, there wasn't any left. The fey made and served every single drop. We let people come back for seconds.

"The fey got to talk to people. Normal conversation. They were thanked and smiled at. And that's exactly what we needed because, as soon as word spread about the awesomeness of the fey, the haters descended. Caleb and Connor were outside to take down names of those who wouldn't come inside. And Taylor was sitting at a table, pretending to eat and listening in on conversations.

"There are twenty names on this list, June. The twelve in red either showed signs of physical violence or verbally threatened people or fey in a way that our helpers thought was more than an idle distrust of the fey. The yellow names made negative comments or refused fey-served food. Taylor, Caleb, and Connor also made a note of every person they saw eating.

"In all of Tenacity, the only people who didn't show up were the ones on the supply run or those unable to get there by themselves. The fey and I went to check on the ones who didn't make it and offered to hand-deliver tomorrow. Each person accepted with gratitude."

"So the list is complete, then, after one day?"

"I think so. I'm still planning on serving tomorrow, but considering today's volatility, I'm not sure we should try for a third day."

"What did Mya and Matt have to say?"

"They're both worried."

"Do they want to keep going, though?"

"Both said it was up to you since you're the one moving back. Matt's worried one fey won't be enough protection now, but he's not sure two fey would go unnoticed. He's very aware that we've taken an already powder-keg situation and turned it nuclear."

I stared at nothing for a moment, considering carefully what I'd likely face, and shook my head.

"It will never get better until we make a stand. I don't see any other way. Let Mya know that I'm packing my bag tonight. I'll publicly approach Matt tomorrow about living in Tenacity."

"He thought you might still want to go forward with the plan. He asked me to warn you to tread carefully."

A sardonic smile tilted my lips.

"Treading carefully is the last thing we need me to do. I'm moving back to incite hate. Maybe I'll be lucky and they strike the first day I'm back."

"I'm not sure if that'd be luck," she said, standing.

"Thanks for letting me know how it went. I'm glad it wasn't all bad for the fey."

"They loved the positive attention. And, for the most part, Matt kept the haters outside. Let me know if you have any other ideas like this," she said. "Well, not like this exactly. But stuff to bring both communities together."

After she left, my thoughts turned from the conflict between the two communities to the man who was remaking my world one day at a time. I glanced at the stairs, but Tor didn't appear. My pulse fluttered at the idea that he was waiting for my return.

So many emotions raced through me. Worry that I was jumping in too quickly. Fear that something would happen to Tor because I was determined to move back to Tenacity. Excitement simply at the thought of Tor.

Slowly, I climbed the steps and tried to rein everything in. I hated the thought of putting Tor in danger, but I wasn't foolish enough to think I could move back without protection. I also wasn't foolish enough to think that Tor would ever agree to stay here.

When I reached the bedroom, I found Tor where I'd left him. He sat on the bed, looking down at his hands.

Knowing what we both would need to do tomorrow, I approached him, standing between his legs so he would look up at me, and gently caressed his cheek.

"What are you thinking?" I asked.

"I'm worried for you."

That was all he said. He didn't try to talk me out of it or tell me that it would be too dangerous. In that moment, I saw just how different from Adam he was. Tor loved me with a single-minded devotion that would never confine me. No, Tor's love would set me free.

Smiling tenderly, I fully embraced what I felt for the gentle, yet incredibly fierce man.

"And I'm worried for you."

He grunted and leaned in to press a kiss to my covered stomach. He didn't try to start anything up again. Instead, he insisted on going downstairs so he could feed me.

We talked of nothing and everything as we made dinner together then headed out with another three roasts for Emily to level-up her cooking game for the next day. It didn't make much of a dent in the freezer but did give me an idea.

After packing up my things along with a healthy supply of canned foods, Tor and I went to bed. He didn't wait for me to fall asleep but pulled me on top of him right away. I sighed and snuggled in.

"I'm glad you're going to be there," I said softly. "I'd miss this too much."

"I would miss you, too," he said, smoothing a hand over my back.

I slept like that all night, partially waking only once when he started to snore beneath me. It wasn't loud. Just the deep, even breaths of a contented man with a woman lying on top of his chest. Smiling, I'd drifted back to sleep.

The next time I woke, a tongue was circling my clit.

"Are you awake, my June?" he asked before pressing his tongue against me.

"Very awake," I murmured, my hands already finding his hair.

"Good." He eased a finger inside of me, stroking deep as his tongue worked its magic. A second digit joined the first, building the pressure. He knew just where and how to touch me, and in seconds, I came apart. He didn't stop, though. He continued, curling his fingers and rekindling the fire until I was bucking against his mouth. The second orgasm ripped through me, and I clenched hard around his fingers.

Instead of pulling out, he eased a third one in. It stretched me, but not painfully. Only uncomfortably. He idly stroked me and trailed kisses along my thighs as my pulse gradually slowed.

"I saw the way you looked at me," Tor said softly.

Confused, I lifted my head to peer at him. His head rested on my thigh, and he watched his fingers as he slid in and out of me.

"You were afraid of my size." He lifted his gaze to mine. "That's why you didn't want me to touch you. That's why you weren't ready. Your heart is ready, but your mind wasn't because your body isn't."

"Humans underestimate the fey. You might not understand certain phrases or slang, but you understand us very well."

He flashed his teeth at me.

"We are learning. Females are so different, though." He eased his fingers out of me. "Will you shower with me?"

I glanced at the window and saw it was still dark out.

"Do we have time?"

"Yes. It won't take long."

I hesitated, feeling a nervous flutter in my stomach. Yes, I was ready to emotionally go all in with Tor, but the physical aspect did still worry me a bit.

"Are we going to have sex?" I asked, needing to know.

"No."

I exhaled my tension and managed a shaky smile. "Okay."

He moved enough so I could stand, then he watched me with hungry eyes as I crossed to the bathroom. When I glanced back, it was my turn to watch him as he stood, completely naked. I knew for a fact he'd gone to bed with shorts on.

His cock jutted outward, its impressive girth and length a thing of legends. Or maybe nightmares. I wasn't sure yet.

"No sex, June," he repeated, his knowing gaze taking everything in.

When the water was warm and we both stood in the steam, he handed me the soap.

"Will you wash me?"

Even as my soapy hands traveled over his impressive chest and abs, my thoughts were on the one place I feared to touch. The one place I knew he really wanted my hands.

Before I could go there, he turned so I could wash his back and groaned when washing changed into a back rub.

"My turn," he said, facing me suddenly.

I dodged his grab for the soap and shook my head.

"Wasn't the whole point of this so I'd be less afraid of your size?"

He hesitantly nodded.

"Then I missed an important part on your front."

He studied my face for a moment then nodded. I surrendered the soap, knowing both lathered hands would be needed, and I looked down at his thick shaft. His free hand twitched, and I knew he was fighting the urge to cover himself. Not wanting him to worry, I slicked my palm down his length. As I'd suspected, I couldn't close my hand around him. I added the second one.

A groan echoed in the shower, and his hand closed over mine, squeezing them, showing me the pressure he wanted and the speed. Letting him lead, I glanced up at him. His eyes were closed, and his head tipped back. The expression on his face was pure bliss. Because of me. Smiling, I leaned in and licked his nipple.

He grunted and jerked in my hands. The hot spray coating my stomach took me by surprise, but not in a bad way.

"June," he rasped, shuttling my hands along his length even faster.

I rode out his release with him, placing small kisses on his chest until he freed my hands and quietly washed my front.

He couldn't seem to stop touching me. Not when I dressed. Not when he made my breakfast for me. Not when I put on my jacket. Honestly, I loved all the contact. Touch was very much my love language.

Before opening the door, he pulled me close and kissed me hard.

"You will be safe today," he said, setting his forehead against mine.

"You too, okay?"

He grunted and took my hand. We strolled through dawn's early light to meet up with the rest of the group at the wall.

There was a new face in the gathered Tolerance crew. He smiled and gave us a wave as we approached.

"Hi, June. I'm Garrett. I'll be your spy handy-man today."

"My what?"

"I'm the one who will hook up all the cameras in the house to capture any evidence of break ins so Matt has what he needs to start giving people the boot."

"How do you—"

"Know? Word travels here. Mya, Emily, and Angel have been keeping me posted. Angel knew I had a few cameras and whatnot that could do the trick."

He pivoted slightly and pointed to the backpack on his shoulder.

"I'll have a laptop you'll need to keep plugged in and use every day to download the footage from all the devices. It'll be a manual process, obviously, but it's a decent computer and shouldn't take too long." He glanced at the duffle Tor was carrying in his free hand. "Looks like you're all set then?"

"I am," I said.

Garrett nodded and glanced at Ryan, who was speaking quietly with Drav, Mya's husband. The pair noticed our attention and headed toward us. Drav's eyes locked on my hand holding Tor's before lifting to my face. He looked almost angry.

"Spit and harsh words do not bother us, June," he said. "It

would be safer for you to stay here and let Matt handle the people in Tenacity on his own."

"Safer for me, maybe, but how many more people will be hurt if I choose to hide instead of face the problem. Matt needs our help. Emily is working hard to bring the two communities together. That won't ever happen if things don't drastically change."

His gaze shifted to Tor.

"Watch after her closely, my brother. She is too precious to lose."

"With my life," Tor said, releasing my hand and pulling me closer to his side.

"Uh, how about no lives lost? We're smart. This is a good plan. We don't want anyone to get hurt."

Drav blinked at me and glanced at Ryan. Ryan grinned.

"He wouldn't mind seeing a few people hurt if it meant keeping women and children safe. But, yes, we all hope that no one's unnecessarily hurt. How do you want to play this out?"

"Business as usual. After you talk to Matt, I'm going to request the house back on the premise that the freezer of my host is being cleaned out because of the freeloaders at Tenacity. Matt told one of the supply runners yesterday that he'll never take away the shares of the people who go out, so I'm going to use that as my angle. I'd rather get my own food than carry people too lazy to do their share."

Ryan nodded.

"Okay. Then, if you're set, we're ready too. And if you need something, we're here to support you in any way possible. There will always be a fey with you."

"I'm not worried." I glanced at Tor. "I'm in good hands."

After that, Tor carried me to Tenacity. The bag and all its

canned goods weighed on my stomach, but I didn't complain. Everything we were doing was nothing compared to what I'd already survived. I needed to do my part to make our world a better place. I wanted a brighter future than the one I saw for myself after those men hurt Adam.

I gazed up at Tor and set my hand on his throat, toying with his skin. He glanced down at me.

"It's not easy running when I'm hard," he said.

I burst out laughing.

"Kiss me before we reach the wall. Then have Hasten take me over while you walk it off."

He did as I asked, and Hasten shyly grinned at me when Tor said he needed Hasten to take over or Tor's cock might catch on the wall when he tries to jump. Although I'd done my best not to compare Adam and Tor, in that moment, one aspect stood out in complete clarity. Adam hadn't protected me; he'd sheltered me. And by sheltering me from everything, I'd missed out on so much. I enjoyed Tor's honesty. While it might seem crude to someone who didn't know him, I knew better. He was being himself. A true version of himself not stifled by society's expectations.

That thought triggered another.

He wasn't stifled yet. But if the people in Tenacity had their way, he slowly would be. All the fey would. They'd need to conform to human ideals in order to obtain the one thing they wanted most. A companion. And there was nothing wrong with them the way they were. In fact, I found their openness and slight naivety far preferable to what most human men offered.

Hasten set me down inside the wall and handed me the duffle bag as I scanned the area. The typical meeting place, near

Tenacity's supply shed turned soup kitchen, was crowded with people. Most of whom were lined up already, hoping for a handout. Those in line were doing their best not to make eye contact with the few who were grouped together to go outside the wall. That small group did seem a little miffed at the people standing in line. But, their display of disgust was nothing that I didn't feel myself. However, just beyond both groups, a gathering of angry men stood, their arms crossed as they glared at everyone.

The tension was palpable.

"I'll wait here for you," Hasten said softly. "Good luck."

I knew better than to flash him a grateful smile with so many onlookers. A tempest of emotions whirled within me as I started toward Ryan and Matt, who looked harried despite the early hour.

"…chance she might set up earlier than yesterday?" Matt asked.

"I don't know. I'm sorry. All I can tell you is that I didn't see her gathering any supplies when we left."

I cleared my throat loudly, the most universally rude way to interrupt a conversation in progress. Both men glanced at me. Matt's gaze flicked to my bag then back to my face.

"Something I can help you with?" he asked.

"I want to talk about moving back into the house I previously used here."

"There's nothing to talk about it. It's yours if you want it."

"I want it, but I'm tired of making all the sacrifices wherever I go. The food from the bunker, meant to feed me for months, was taken away and split up without my consent. I thought it would be better in Tolerance, but now all the meat's going here for handouts. I'm done busting my back for freeloaders and deadbeats. I want to keep what I find when I go out there. It's not like it's needed for splitting when everyone staying behind gets a free meal."

The people already committed to doing this supply run heard me easily.

"We're the ones risking our lives," Bram, the guy from yesterday said. "I don't mind sharing. But I'd like more of a say in what and how much."

Matt's eyes swept over us and then the malcontent group not far away.

"Everyone is upset about the scarcity of food. Now might not be the best time to—"

"If there's no incentive for risking our lives to gather food supplies, then what's the point of going out at all? We can all sit on our asses and watch each other starve," I said.

Matt shot me a look, and I shrugged.

"Why should I work my ass off and have nothing to show for it?"

"Fine. However much you can carry, you can take back to your homes to share with your people however you see fit."

That news made a lot of people happy. A few standing in line even left the line to join those waiting to go out. Meanwhile, the haters smirked. I understood very well why. People who hoarded got robbed and beaten. Cold anger clenched in my stomach, and I knew I'd need to make myself a bigger target than anyone else.

"That's perfect since I live alone," I said, just loud enough to be heard by those nearest. "Would you mind holding onto my things until I get back?"

Matt accepted my bag from me, and I turned my back on all of them. Tor was watching from near the wall. Seeing him there lightened the burden. As much as I wanted to go to him, I went to Hasten.

The announcement that we could keep more of what we found changed things a little. To keep up appearances that I was cutting ties with Tolerance, I rode in the back of one of the trucks on the way to wherever Ryan had selected. There was a notable tone of hope and worry from the others. And none of the humans stayed in the trucks when we pulled up to the subdivision.

I worked with my usual group, taking care not to show any familiarity when we were in the open. We worked quietly and quickly inside the houses. Our group wasn't the only one busting ass. There were a lot more supplies sent back to fill up the truck. So much so that some of us Tenacity folks had to ride in the cabs of the trucks.

Bram, a woman, myself, and Richard were squeezed into one.

"Heard you're leaving Tolerance," Richard said. "Can I ask why?"

I wasn't sure if it was a sincere, or staged question, but considering our company, there was only one answer I could give him.

"I moved to Tolerance because I thought it would be safer. The fey I was staying with was nice and had a freezer full of meat. Then Adam broke up with me. The fey started acting a little too interested. And now the meat's going to Tenacity. There's no reason to stay and every reason to move if Matt holds true to his word. I'm tired of worrying where my next meal will come from."

"Same," Bram said. He looked at the other woman. "What about you?"

"I like food as much as the next person," she said quietly. There was something about her that seemed off. She'd been quiet in the back of the truck, too, but had willingly gone with her group of fey and returned with a decent take.

"How many people do you two live with?" I asked.

"Too many," Bram said. "I'm not sure if you're lucky or screwed living by yourself."

"I'll go with lucky," I said.

The woman glanced at me, her gaze flickering with pity before Bram glanced at her for her answer.

"Too many, just like you." She looked out the window once more and didn't join the conversation after that.

When we returned to Tenacity, there was the same bevy of activity as the prior day. Rather than going inside, I stayed by the trucks and started tucking the food I'd found into my jacket. After it was full, I loaded up a tote with everything possible, avoiding the heavier canned goods. I wanted it to look like I had a lot and succeeded, even though my arms strained.

No one protested as I left with my haul, but I felt every eye on me as I walked down the street.

Matt called my name, and I paused, watching him jog my way.

"Since it looks like you have your arms full, give me a minute to grab your bag, and I'll follow you."

"She has food in her jacket," one of the haters said angrily.

I laughed.

"Thank you, Captain Obvious. He said as much as I can carry."

The man's gaze hardened on me and flicked to Matt.

"Things are getting out of hand here real fast, Matt. People are starting to wonder if you're trying to lead us into a better future, signing us up for death, or worse, bitches to those fucking devils."

I snorted.

"Are you actually saying death is better than getting help? You're a complete dumbass." I looked at Matt. "This is getting heavy."

His gaze flicked between the hater and me before he ran his hand through his hair.

"I'll be right back," he muttered.

The guy continued to stare at me. "If you need help with that, I'd be happy to carry it for half."

"No chance in hell. If you want food, get your lazy ass in one of those trucks."

"So those fey can lead us to our deaths? Not happening."

"Do I look dead to you?"

Something mean and ugly flickered in the depths of his eyes before his gaze shifted to the wall.

"They sure do have a fascination with women," he said. "I'm surprised they let you go."

I followed his gaze and saw more than half the fey watching us. Tor wasn't among them. Hopefully, he was already making his way to the house. I'd need to talk to him about letting the others know not to be so obvious, though.

"They don't run a prison camp over there."

He made a speculative noise and glanced at my food again.

"Eyes up here," I said. "Unless you're casing my haul."

He smirked.

"Not at all. You're the girl who was with that guy who was beaten, aren't you? How's he doing?"

"Don't know," I said with an indifferent shrug I didn't feel. "We're not together anymore."

"That's a shame."

"Why's that?"

"He could carry more."

A heavy weight lifted from my shoulders at what he was insinuating, and I did my best to look intimidated when he smiled coldly at me. I swallowed hard, playing along. Let him think he had his easy prey. This time, I wouldn't be the one held down and terrorized.

His smirk disappeared a moment later, and he nodded to Matt as he rejoined me.

"You ready?" Matt asked.

"Yes," I whispered.

The man grinned, thinking he had me cowed. I curled my shoulders, willing to play the part.

For now.

CHAPTER TWENTY

As soon as the door shut behind us, Matt turned on me, worry in his eyes.

"They've been quiet all day, just watching. I don't like this. I've made sure to post guards that I trust on the wall with a vantage point of this house. I'd feel a lot better if—"

"June is safe," Tor said, calling our attention to where he sat on the steps leading upstairs.

Matt looked truly conflicted when he glanced at me.

"I'll be fine," I said. "I trust Tor and the fey, and Garrett said he was going to set up cameras here while I was gone."

"He did," Matt said, pulling out a piece of paper and unzipping my duffle to hand me a laptop. "He didn't want to leave this in the house without anyone here to watch it. These are the locations of the cameras and how to download the data. If you have any questions, come to me and I can radio over to Mya."

I took the paper and the laptop from him.

"You're going to be the most vulnerable when you leave the house," he said.

"We will watch over her," Tor said. "We can move without being seen when we wish it. Your guards will not be the only ones watching the house."

"Who was the guy I was talking to just now?" I asked.

"Nat. He's one of the main troublemakers."

"One of or *the* main one?"

"It's hard to tell. He's the most vocal. Why?"

"Just something he said. I wanted to make sure he was one of the names in red."

"He is. His wife's name isn't on the list, though. Shelby was on the supply run today. She's quiet. Doesn't cause any trouble."

I described the woman in the truck with me, and Matt nodded.

"Sounds like her."

"How often does she go on supply runs?"

"Today was the first time in a long while. She joined the group after I changed the rule. I really hope that wasn't a mistake. Every person on today's run carried away enough food to tempt another break-in. And they don't have fey watching over them."

"No, but they don't live alone, either. Two or three people held me down when Adam and I were robbed. And it would have taken more than one person to overcome Adam. We're talking five to six people against how many in a full house?"

"Ten to twelve."

"Exactly. Who's the easier target?"

Matt nodded and glanced at Tor again. I put down the computer and nudged Matt toward the door.

"It's time for you to go before anyone gets suspicious. I'll see you in the morning."

"Stay safe," he said, looking at both of us before letting himself out.

As soon as he was gone, I turned the lock and faced Tor.

"Let's see where these cameras are," I said.

He watched me move around the house, inspecting Garrett's work. There were several cameras in the main living space, collectively angled just right to catch every possible point of entry. There was another at the top of the stairs, hidden on a shelf of knick-knacks that looked recently installed. Another was in the bedroom. It captured the area by the door, but not the bed. I blushed at Garrett's forethought.

As soon as I was done inspecting, Tor wrapped his arms around me from behind and pulled me close. I let the paper flutter to the ground and placed my hands over his.

"Is it crazy that we spent the day together and I still missed you?" I asked.

"No. I missed you, too."

I turned in his arms and looked up at him.

"Are you hungry?"

"Very."

I grinned.

"I meant for dinner."

He grunted and leaned in to steal a kiss that robbed me of the ability to think or speak for the next several minutes. I loved the way he kissed me. It alternated between all-consuming hunger and gentle brushes of his lips against my brow and eyelids, which made me feel like the most treasured thing in his life.

"I could do this all night," I said when he moved to nip my earlobe.

He growled his agreement.

"But if I do, then I wouldn't feed either of us."

He sighed and pulled away from me.

"You are right. This is selfish of me. You must eat." His gaze dipped to my lips, and I figured he was thinking of letting me go hungry a little longer. However, he surprised me with a completely different thought. "I will watch you move in the kitchen and think of how I will kiss you after."

My core clenched at the thought of him watching me cook and fantasizing about tonight.

"I like the way you think."

He sat on the stairs, out of view if anyone happened to try to look in through any of the curtained windows. I left the window in the kitchen open and turned on every light. The computer had music and a decent enough speaker, which I turned up. Anyone watching would witness me having a great time dancing around the kitchen in nothing but a tee-shirt and underwear while cooking way too much of today's food.

There was a purpose to everything I did. The lack of clothes showed both a confidence that I was safe and a vulnerability because what man would view a woman in her underwear as a threat? The music showed a blatant disregard of Nat's earlier threat and, hopefully, called attention to the house in an otherwise quiet neighborhood. The abundance of food was a throw down. If they wanted what I had, they needed to move fast.

I hoped it would be enough.

It sure was for Tor. His hungry gaze tracked every shake and shimmy I executed as I made our lavish meal. When I finished and turned off the music, I headed toward the stairs with one plate piled high with a ridiculous amount of food in my hand and two forks in the other.

He stood and retreated a step, making room for me to ascend but not taking his eyes off me for an instant.

"Any chance you'll help me eat some of this?" I asked.

His gaze flicked to the food, and I could see a hint of impatience in them.

"If you help me, we'll finish with the dinner portion of our evening faster so we can move onto the making out part."

His gaze heated further.

"I will help," he said finally.

Once we reached the bedroom, though, his version of helping was feeding me bites in between kissing any portion of exposed skin. Not even a quarter of the way through the mountain of food, I willingly set it aside in favor of Tor's far better idea.

His mouth set me on fire, suckling my breast through the shirt while his hand cupped me through my underwear.

"Turn over," he said huskily, stripping off his shirt while leaving mine in place.

Trusting him completely, I rolled to my stomach. He surprised me by using his hands on my back, applying the perfect pressure to rub out a knot I hadn't even realized was there. When it released, he leaned in and kissed the spot before moving on. I groaned, relaxing even as he turned me on more.

It all felt so good. I melted into the mattress as he worked his way down to my legs with his hands and his lips. The pressure on my calves and the way he used his whole hand to knead the entire muscle had me groaning again.

"This is just like the backrub that I had at Angel's house. He really shared every detail, didn't he?"

His hands paused briefly.

"I rubbed away your aches, June."

I jerked my head off the pillow and twisted to give him a horrified look.

"Twice?" I demanded.

He frowned in confusion. "Yes…this is the second time I have rubbed you. Is it not good?"

My annoyance melted, and I shook my head at myself.

"Tor, it's amazing. I'm upset with myself that there have been two times I haven't recognized it was you. No, not upset. Mortified. What is wrong with me?"

"Nothing is wrong with you," he said soothingly. "You are perfect. I purposely said nothing when I rubbed you the first time. I didn't want you to ask for someone else. I wanted to feel your skin and make you moan with pleasure."

He crawled up my body and dipped his head to lick my shoulder.

"Tell me I can keep touching you."

"Absolutely. Touch away. No areas are off-limits for you. But if I mistakenly don't recognize it's you again, I demand you get mad at me."

He snorted a laugh.

"I'm serious. It's not acceptable. I should know you by now."

"I will help you know me better," he said.

He tugged at my shirt, and I removed it in a heartbeat. He palmed my backside and used his fingers to rub deep. Angel's comment about the fey's willingness to rub anything made me grin.

"I never knew this would feel so good."

He asked me to roll over and worked my underwear down my legs. There was something about the way he settled my legs over his shoulders and looked down at me that stole my breath.

When he proceeded to take his time, licking me slowly while murmuring how pretty my folds were and how he wanted to taste them all night long, I was fully onboard for his education process. Threading my fingers through his hair, I held on tight as he brought me close to my first orgasm.

And let me hang there.

I squirmed and panted and begged.

"I want more than squeaky noises, my June," he said, sliding a digit inside to stroke my core. "Who is bringing you joy?"

"Tor," I rasped.

"Tor," he agreed before using his tongue on me again.

I writhed underneath him as he drove me crazy, purposely avoiding my clit.

"Please, Tor," I begged.

Rather than giving me what I wanted, he added another finger. I groaned, loving the stretch of it. He surprised me by reaching up with his other hand and tweaking my nipple. It sent the best kind of jolt between my legs, and I made a small noise.

"I like the way you clench around my fingers," he murmured, kissing my inner thighs.

The words alone were enough for me to clench around him some more.

"I'd clench harder if you put that tongue where I want it."

He chuckled against my skin then rewarded me with another round of slow licks that drove me crazy. I was panting and desperate with need when he slid a third finger in me. This time, I hissed out a breath at the stretch.

"No screaming, June," he said a moment before his mouth closed over me.

My mouth opened in a silent cry of both agony and delight as his tongue and fingers worked in synchrony to bring me to the edge. I tumbled over willingly, grinding down on Tor, trying to remember to breathe as my eyes watered from the intensity of the sensations. My core pulsed around his fingers, and he growled, not easing up. I squirmed, trying to escape the overload, and he thrust deeper.

Finally, he lifted his mouth and met my gaze. I could see the unquenched passion simmering beneath the surface.

"Tell me you're mine," he said.

"I'm yours."

He stood, kicked off his pants, his erection spearing the air, then he lay on the bed.

"Show me."

I could have played it safe and reached for him with my hand. He no doubt would have loved it if I had used my mouth on him. But I knew what he wanted most from me.

My legs shook as I leveraged myself up and straddled his hips. He drew a ragged breath as I slicked my wet folds over his length.

"I know what you were doing," I said, bracing my hands on his chest as I moved. "Three fingers were a tight fit, though. I'm still worried this is going to hurt."

"I will never hurt you. That is why I'm down here and you're up there. You're in control, my June. I will do nothing but lie here as you have your way with me."

He folded his arms behind his head.

"How long have you been thinking about this?"

His expression turned hesitant. I petted his chest and rocked over him more firmly.

"Tell me, and I'll do more than slide over you."

He groaned slightly and removed his hands from behind his head to grip my hips. To hold me still.

"When Adam severed his relationship with you, I couldn't stop thinking about his stupidity and how I wanted you for my own. I craved your taste. The sounds you made. The smiles you gave me. Your touch. Your hugs. Breathing in the scent of your hair as you sleep. I thought of holding you against the wall and thrusting into you while you made your little noises. Over the kitchen counter—it's the perfect height. On your hands and knees in bed. I thought of sinking my cock deep into your sweet pussy many, many ways." His eager expression turned troubled. "But then you looked at my cock with fear." He sighed gustily and lifted his hand to toy with my nipple.

"Some of my brothers had the same problem."

"What problem is that? Too big?"

He shook his head. "I am not too big, June. I only need to work harder to earn your willingness to see that truth for yourself."

I lightly shook my head at him. "You're a smooth talker, Tor. I like it."

Grinning, I gently kissed his lips.

He drank me in with his greedy mouth and groaned when I lifted my hips and reached between us. The bulbous head of his cock felt like a fist pressing at my entrance. The kiss helped distract me, but not enough. How did he not think he was too big? I broke away, gasping for air as I tried to lower myself onto him.

"Wait," he said. He reached between us, lifting me as his fingers delved into my folds before reseating me. The head slid in, stretching me, but not uncomfortably so.

Tor's pupils dilated so much they were round and very little green was left.

Inch by inch, I worked myself down his massive shaft until I couldn't go any farther. I was full. Too full. Stretched beyond anything I'd ever felt before.

"I think this is it," I said, moving cautiously.

"Up," he said, his hands lifting me several inches. "Again."

This time, I slid down his length more easily. He had me repeat the process twice more. On the final time, our hips met, and he growled.

"Do you trust me?" he asked, his voice tight and his jaw clenched.

"I do."

In a blink, I was under him. He dipped his head to tease my nipple with his tongue, pulling out of me in the process. My core clenched at the scrape of his teeth, and I groaned. He released my breast and gave a shallow thrust forward as he moved to lick the other side.

When he'd suckled that one into a hard point, he lifted his head and studied me, slowly easing into me. Tor was big. There was no getting around that. He filled me up to the point of aching. But it was an ache that built a fire inside of me. I could feel each inch of him, every slow thrust in and out.

My eyes kept drifting closed, and he would pause to kiss me senseless until I looked at him again.

"I love your eyes," he whispered. "They never saw a monster. Only a man."

"Because that's what you are."

I wrapped my arms around his neck and nipped his ear.

He went wild, bracing his weight on one arm and using the other to tilt my hips. Each deep thrust fed the fire. He trembled and shuddered above me, moving faster, our bodies slapping together.

Then suddenly, I was falling without ever standing on the precipice. My mouth opened in a silent scream as I clenched around him and arched. His hungry lips found mine, ravenous in their need to consume every part of me, even the pleasure he gave.

With one final jarring thrust, he came. The hot wash of his release coated my insides. I quivered around him with a gasp and collapsed.

He peppered my cheeks and jaw with little kisses, murmuring words I was too incoherent to understand...until he started moving inside of me again.

I opened my eyes to look up at him.

"Tell me to stop," he said softly.

"Never."

GROGGY, I left the house just before dawn and almost stumbled down the sidewalk. My legs were sore, and there was an ache deep inside. It twinged with each step.

Tor had asked me repeatedly throughout the night if I was tired and ready to stop. I'd loved what we were doing too much to deny either of us, though. I should have. Oh, how I should have. Instead, when he'd woke me up in my favorite way, I'd whispered that he needed to be extra gentle while I'd played with his ears.

At least, I would have today to recover. I could only imagine the greeting I'd get when I returned.

Ducking my head to hide my smile, I continued toward the

wall and waited with the group gathered there. It was a little bigger than the day before. But, I spotted a few familiar faces.

"Morning, Bram."

"Hey, June. You sure you want to go out again today?"

I gave him a fake-puzzled look.

"Why wouldn't I? Look around. People are getting braver now that Matt upped our take. Pretty soon we'll need to draw straws or something for a chance to go out for food. I'm going to stockpile while the getting's still good."

"I didn't think of it that way."

"What way were you thinking, then?"

He looked around and lowered his voice. "I heard what Nat said to you. Don't take him lightly, June."

That simple warning put him on the top of my nice list.

"Thanks. I won't."

Anything else we would have said was cut short by the arrival of the fey and Ryan. They came over the wall like a wave. I watched in awe at their agility and felt a pang of longing for Tor. The way he'd considered me as I'd gotten dressed this morning, and his lingering touches had conveyed an echo of what I felt for him. Somehow, someway, he'd become the air I needed to breathe. I craved the feel of his arms around me and his sweet kisses peppering my face. Despite the soreness a night of making love had created, I would willingly get back in that bed if it meant we wouldn't need to be apart for the day.

Ryan's gaze swept over the gathered humans and briefly paused on me. I ignored it and side-whispered to Bram.

"Make sure you stuff your jacket today with supplies. As much as you can carry."

He grunted in acknowledgement in a very fey-like way that

made me grin. He caught on and chuckled while shaking his head.

"I'm spending too much time with them," he said.

"Better to hang around the people who help you find more food than the people who take it away from you."

"Words of wisdom."

We waited while Ryan and Matt did their usual information exchange then moved out to load into the trucks.

"Who knows how to drive?" Ryan called.

I was the only one who raised my hand.

"We could use you if you're willing."

"Sure."

I went to the truck he indicated and wasn't surprised to see Richard in the passenger seat.

"How'd it go last night?" he asked.

I flushed scarlet and pretended to check the mirrors as I answered.

"Fine. No attempts to break in. I'm guessing they'll try today while I'm gone. No witnesses. Less risk to them."

"Makes sense."

"Which is why I emptied all the bagged food into a box for Tor to drop off at the storage shed and left the wrappers in a pile in the kitchen along with a note."

Ryan gestured to start up the truck. It rumbled to life under my feet.

"What's the note say?"

I glanced at Richard and grinned.

"Fuck you. It's my food. Go get your own."

"Are you sure that's wise?" he asked as I shifted into gear and eased the truck forward without choking it.

"Yes and no. Provoking them is dangerous. But it's also the

best way to flush all of them out. My guess is that they'll find the note today, get mad, and make a plan to grab everything I have tonight before I can eat it."

Richard looked out the window.

"How does *he* feel about that?" he asked.

I followed his gaze and spotted Tor running along Richard's side of the truck. My mouth dropped open, and I almost swore before I realized this was a good thing. I'd been nervous about leaving him in the house alone, knowing that he'd likely have unwanted visitors. This way, he was out of danger. But there was also a better chance that the people would ransack the place in a fit of rage and discover the cameras.

"Based on your silence, I'm guessing he's not a fan of the plan, either."

"He's supposed to be watching the house while I'm gone. Honestly, I'm glad he's not there. The idea of leaving him behind while knowing someone was going to break in wasn't easy. I know he's big and stronger. But I was still worried something might happen."

Richard made a humming noise.

"You sound a little like my daughter with Drav. Protectiveness isn't a bad thing for someone you love."

The flush that had faded reignited slightly.

"I'm struggling with it, you know? How can I possibly love someone this soon? I've only known Tor a few weeks, and part of that time I had a boyfriend, a person I thought I'd spend the rest of my life with."

"The world is a crazy place. Don't worry about what could have been or should have been. Focus on what is. If you love him, you love him. Let it be that simple."

I gave him a grateful smile.

CHAPTER TWENTY-ONE

It took us two hours to reach Ryan's chosen location. Driving that long wasn't without its risks. The noise of the trucks drew attention. However, fey watched and listened for any signs of infected and often split off to deal with any that noticed us. Their diligence was usually enough to ensure we didn't have too many surprises once we reached our destination.

We weren't so lucky this time.

As soon as the trucks rolled to a stop, infected swarmed us from nearby houses.

Richard swore under his breath as the fey were swallowed up by the number. We both slammed the locks on the doors at the same time.

"Start backing up real slow," Richard said. "The fey will get out of the way."

Hands shaking, I tried to do as he said. The truck lurched underneath us, almost dying when I let out the clutch too quickly, and I thought of the people in the back. Slowly, I inched us backward as infected climbed up the sides of the truck and hit the windows. Soon, I couldn't see through the windshield.

"The road was straight. Keep the wheel straight," Richard said.

His calm helped me keep some of my own.

Suddenly the bodies were ripped from the windshield and Tor's blood-smeared face stared back at me.

"Stay inside the truck, June," he said before pivoting to rip away the infected trying to break off my door handle.

I flashed Richard a quick grin despite the seriousness of the situation.

"Tor always knows exactly what to say to lighten the mood," I said.

Richard chuckled next to me. "I didn't know they had a sense of humor."

"Tor does, and I love it."

Tor, still close to my door, looked up to flash a quick smile at me. Infected spatter got in his mouth, and I made a face.

"You're not kissing me until you brush," I said through the window. "That's gross."

He scowled at the next infected like it was its fault, which I thought was hilarious.

"I think we can stop backing up now," Richard said.

I scanned the infected still trying to get to us. There were too many fey for them to reach the trucks anymore.

"I hope everyone in back is okay," I said.

"We don't make a big deal out of it, but the fey lock the passengers in with a padlock. The infected wouldn't be able to open the door."

"Yeah, I'm glad I didn't know I was locked in when I was riding in the back."

He winked at me and continued watching the infected until the remaining ones scattered. A few fey took off after them, and the rest of us waited. Eventually they returned bloodier than before. Those who'd remained behind had started moving bodies into one large pile, clearing the road. Once done, they broke off into groups to clear nearby houses.

A fey stopped by Ryan's truck for a moment then jogged back to mine.

"Ryan would like to know what Richard's thoughts are," the fey said through the window.

I looked at Richard, who thoughtfully scanned the surrounding houses.

"I doubt there's another group of infected this size waiting to spring a trap, but it's better to be cautious in case we missed any. Tell Ryan we need to be in and out in thirty minutes."

The fey grunted and returned to Ryan's truck while a few fey emerged from the houses, clean and hair dripping wet.

Tor was one of them. He came to my door and helped me down as someone else opened the back of the truck.

"We only have thirty minutes," I said softly. "We'll need to work quickly to bring back enough to stand out."

I heard some of the Tenacity people swear when they spotted the pile of headless bodies and looked at the mass piled close to the back end of our truck. So many infected. I shuddered to think what would have happened if the infected had waited until we'd been out of the trucks.

"Come," Tor said.

He picked me up, and my usual team of fey fell in around us as he jogged farther down the road. The Tenacity people tended to converge on the closest houses then returned to the truck, too afraid to venture any distance. Typically, I wasn't overly concerned due to the fey presence. After our current greeting, though, I would be a liar if I said I wasn't more anxious.

Fallor already carried a stack of totes, which he set outside the first house.

"Food is the focus today. If it looks even remotely like food, toss it in the tote. We clean out the kitchen and move to the next house. We don't have time for full cleanouts," I said.

My team grunted in acknowledgment, and I divided them unevenly into three groups. The main group would stay with me. Two teams of two would go to the next pair of houses under the guise of sweeping for infected when, in reality, they would be prepping the supplies. To the Tenacity people, it needed to look like I was doing the gathering so they wouldn't question the hopefully big haul I'd go home with at the end of the day. The reality was that I would be inside the house, safely held in Tor's arms, while my team packed everything into totes for me.

I was using the fey in the exact way they weren't supposed to be used. But they all understood what the end goal was. Heck, even if the goal wasn't to make Tenacity a fey-friendly settlement, I knew they would have still helped me. They were simply that nice, which was why Mya had established the rules in the first place.

Thirty minutes later, I was back in the truck and behind the wheel.

"You did good work," Richard said. "I counted twelve totes of food from your houses."

I nodded. "Did anyone question anything?"

"No. Ryan suggested the humans only focus on kitchens while having the fey check for obvious overstock locations elsewhere in the house. One of them got lucky and found a shelving unit stocked with canned goods. They'll think you were lucky, too."

Ryan gave the signal and climbed back into his truck.

"Let's hope we have a quiet ride home," Richard said.

I started the truck and eased forward behind Ryan's, checking the mirror to make sure I didn't clip the body pile. An arm moved.

"I think one of the infected is still alive in the body pile," I said.

"Unlikely. They only pile them up once they're headless."

Frowning, I glanced at the mirror again. Nothing moved this time.

"They give me the creeps on so many levels," I said.

"Agreed."

The drive home was relatively uneventful with only a few car blockades and infected to clear. I spent a good deal of the time watching Tor run. The man was droolworthy, and he knew it, too, because every time he caught me looking, he winked and flashed his teeth at me. However, when the truck stopped, he wasn't the one to help me down.

My gaze swept the surrounding fey who unloaded the supplies, but Tor was already gone.

The chaos inside Tenacity's walls was greater than the day before since we'd returned much sooner than usual. The long line of people waiting to be fed stunned me, and I hoped the fey inside the soup kitchen were managing all right.

I hurried to fill a tote with everything I could carry from my take. There was a lot to choose from. This time, I made sure to weigh it down enough that I would need to stop and take breaks. My back would hurt tomorrow, but I knew someone who would willingly rub it for me.

Nat's group of men was a lot smaller than the day before. And he wore a fairly impassive mask compared to the hateful one he'd previously sported. Wondering if he'd found my note, I started forward with my heavy burden while he watched the people line up for fey-prepared food. My forearms started to ache before I reached him. Unwilling to be too obvious in my provocation, I didn't set the tote down.

When I'd almost reached him, his gaze found mine and dipped to the supplies I struggled to carry.

"Lose a few people to the soup kitchen line?" I asked with a smirk, not stopping my progress.

"Unlikely. I'm sure they'll show up soon. Looks heavy. Need help?"

"No. I'll manage fine. I always do." I passed him and didn't look back. However, I didn't make it much farther before I needed to stop for a break.

The people in the line eyed the supplies while I shook out my arms.

"How was it out there?" one woman asked.

"A little nerve-wracking," I answered honestly. "But the fey handled everything the infected threw our way. It's worth going out there."

She glanced at the food near my feet and nodded slightly before her gaze shifted over my shoulder. I glanced back and saw she was looking at Nat. Did she know he would be a potential problem if she went out? If so, how did so many people know and let him continue his stealing?

I reached into the tote, plucked up a can of something, and tossed it to her.

"Give it a try tomorrow. I'll be going back out."

"If you're giving handouts, I'll take some," a man behind her said.

"It's not a handout. It's proof that you all can do something to feed yourselves if you stop letting fear rule you."

He blustered and tried making excuses. Bad back. Bad knee.

"The fey carry you. All you have to do is grab the food from the cupboards and put it in the totes. They carry the totes out."

"I ain't letting some man carry me around."

I shrugged and picked up my food.

"Hope your pride keeps you company while you slowly starve to death."

He flipped me off and would have likely come at me if that wouldn't have meant losing his place in the handout line.

I managed to give away five more cans of food, which didn't seem to lighten my burden much before I reached the end of the line. They all went to people who were curious about going outside the walls. Hopefully, they would join tomorrow's group of supply runners.

By the time I reached the house, my arms were burning. I set the tote down, opened the door, and pushed my haul inside, too tired to try lifting it again.

Tor and another fey were speaking quietly by the stairwell as I shut the door and dragged the tote to the kitchen.

"They are in Matt's basement. He will watch over them until we have the rest," the other fey said.

"What's going on?" I asked.

"Five men came here, looking for yesterday's supplies. They were angry when they saw no food and the paper with writing. They read it and left again. Turik was watching from outside and followed them to their homes. When they came out again, he took them to Matt. Matt is keeping them."

"What do you mean 'took them?' Turik grabbed them off the streets in front of everyone?"

The other fey flashed his teeth at me, showing me his humor.

"Turik made sure no one saw. He said that others are looking for the men and are angry that they can't be found."

I wasn't sure I found it as funny. Especially when those men disappeared after coming here for food. Although, maybe this is what we needed to push the haters into acting rashly.

"Tell Turik thank you for me. Did any of the men see you when they came in?"

The fey shook his head. I asked him to wait while I downloaded all the footage from the cameras. The men were clearly visible from several angles, including when they snuck in and their reactions to the missing food. As soon as I had it downloaded, I gave the memory stick to the fey to deliver to Matt. He left through the back door.

"How often do the fey sneak around Tenacity?" I asked.

Tor grinned at me then pulled me into his arms to hug me close.

"This is where most of the single females are."

"That's not really an answer."

"Isn't it?"

I shook my head, looking up at him.

"You guys need hobbies."

He kissed me thoroughly, giving me an idea of what hobby he would like to have.

"We need to be more careful," I said, pulling back. "We've kicked the hornet's nest now. They're going to respond."

Tor grunted in acknowledgment, and I eased from his embrace to put the supplies away. If I were someone out to steal food, I'd wait until dark. Leaving all the supplies in the tote would make it too easy to grab, and I wanted to make sure that the cameras caught everything. Most of the food went into the cupboards. I opened a bag of chips and set it on the couch. Then I randomly placed a tower of canned goods on the coffee table like a work of art.

Tor's gaze grew hungrier as he watched me move around the room. I knew what he was thinking. He wanted me up in the bedroom so we could have a repeat of last night. I wanted that, too, but wasn't sure how smart it would be.

"What do you like for dinner? I could make spam and rice again," I said, looking through the supplies.

"I want you."

I glanced up and shook my head at him.

"I'm aware. But it wouldn't be smart to be caught with our pants down." I set the spam and canned veggies on the counter along with the rice I'd grabbed.

"I very much want to catch you with your pants down." He started to stand, his moves taking on a predatorial edge that made my heart race.

I held up a hand.

"Sit, Tor."

The words barely left my mouth when there was a knock on the door. I glanced at Tor, and he moved up the stairs, just out of sight, as I went to answer.

Matt and Nat stood outside.

"Can I help you?" I asked.

"We'd like to come in if that's all right," Matt said.

"Do I have a choice?"

"Is there a reason you don't want our fine leader inside the house?" Nat asked. "You hiding something?"

"No. Protecting something. I just walked through town with a tote full of food and two men show up at my door. I'm not stupid. Why else would you be here?"

"We're not here for your food, June. I promise," Matt said, pulling my attention from Nat. "We're looking for some missing people."

"And you think they're here? Why?" Even as I asked it, I stepped aside to let them both in. Nat's gaze went straight to the food on the counter.

"It's mine," I said. "Stop drooling and start answering my questions. Why would you think your friends are here?"

"Someone said they were seen near your house," Nat answered.

I glanced at Matt. "Well, if that isn't a sign they were looking to break in, I don't know what is. I'm glad you came to check up on me. If the men did break in, though, they were likely disappointed." I met and held Nat's hard gaze. "I made sure to eat yesterday's supplies before I left."

His jaw ticked, and I knew Matt's presence was the only thing keeping him from crossing the room and beating me like they'd beaten Adam.

I glanced at Matt again. "If they are here, shouldn't you have brought more people to check over the house and not one of their friends?"

"That's not why we're here. Nat thinks you did something to them."

My surprised laughter wasn't faked.

"Me? Against…how many are missing?"

"Five," Matt said.

I faced Nat. "This is bullshit and you know it. I was gone all day. Why are you really here?"

"He thinks you're hiding a fey to protect your supplies."

I rolled my eyes and waved a hand at the house.

"Go look. Make sure to check under the bed. I hear that's where imaginary monsters like to hide."

Without acknowledging the jab, Nat left to search the house. While he looked, I started dinner as if I wasn't panicking on the inside. It didn't matter if the fey were good at hiding outside. There was no way Nat would miss a huge grey man hiding in my closet, or wherever else Tor might have hidden.

The water for the rice had just started to boil when Nat returned to the kitchen. He looked seriously pissed.

"Find any fey?" I asked.

He didn't answer. He walked right out the door, slamming it behind him.

Matt, who hadn't said anything, shared a look with me.

"Be careful, June."

"What's life without risks?"

He shook his head and left. I locked the door behind him then continued making dinner, waiting for Tor to reappear. It didn't take him long. A brush of noise on the stairs alerted me.

"Where did you hide?" I asked.

"On the roof."

"You went out a window?"

He grunted.

"Tell me what you're thinking," I said as I started cutting up the spam to fry. I didn't like that Nat suspected I had a fey with me. Did that mean he and his gang wouldn't come tonight?

"I'm thinking about licking your pussy again."

I jerked my head up from what I was doing to stare at him.

"Tor, be serious. It's not good that Nat thinks a fey is staying with me."

Tor shrugged.

"Vorx said that the men left and went to other houses. The human knows they didn't disappear here. He used that as an excuse to get inside and see how quickly you were eating your food. He and his men will be here soon after dark. Cook faster, June, and I will have enough time to lick you the way you like before they arrive."

I slowly shook my head, in awe of his thought process and his ability to obsessively focus on sex while still being very aware of everything else happening.

"Twenty minutes, and I'm yours," I said, anticipation shooting through me.

As soon as everything was finished, I plated dinner and carried it upstairs with Tor stalking behind me. And if I'd forgotten the direction of his thoughts, he thoroughly reminded me by smoothing his hands over my hips with each step I took. When I reached the hallway, he stopped me, pressing his erection into my back as he wrapped his arms around me to fondle my breasts through my shirt.

"Are you very hungry, my June?" he asked, the question rumbling against the side of my neck where he trailed kisses.

"Let me put this plate down, and I'll show you how hungry I am."

He growled, his hips arching into me briefly before he released his hold. I could feel him behind me as I hurried into the room and set the plate on the dresser. The moment it was out of my hands, he picked me up and tossed me onto the bed.

I laughed as I bounced. That laughter died, though, as he

fell onto me like a starved man. He had my pants off in seconds and buried his face between my legs, inhaling deeply.

"I thought of this all day." He kissed me there, then rid me of the thin barrier. There were no more words after that. Only long licks and rumbles of satisfaction. I was panting and making small sounds of my own.

He growled and used his fingers to prepare me. My core clenched around him at the first touch. I knew what was coming, and that only made my need climb higher and faster. He'd barely inserted the third finger before I came apart with a gasp, falling into the abyss. The pace of his wicked tongue slowed in time with the waves of pleasure pulsing through me.

Sighing, I ran my fingers through his hair and played with his ears. He grunted and placed a light kiss on my clit before rising to fetch the plate.

"Eat, my June."

While I struggled to hold the fork, he stripped off his clothes and settled his shoulders between my legs again. The tender kisses he placed on my inner thighs graduated to light nips. My insides clenched even as I struggled to focus on eating.

I tried to put the plate aside, but he wouldn't let me. Crawling up my body, his muscles temptingly undulating with each move, he insisted I hadn't had enough. He fed me a bite then dipped his head to take my nipple into his mouth.

The slow assault was killing me. How was I supposed to eat? There was no way.

I swallowed and let my head fall back to arch into his mouth.

"I can eat later," I said. "Please, Tor."

He grunted and took the plate from my hand, setting it to the side before returning to his favorite spot between my legs.

"Once more," he said. He held my gaze as he leaned down and circled my clit with his tongue. "No screaming."

"I'm not a screamer. Never have been."

He grinned wickedly at me. "The noises you make tell me you are, my June. You're only waiting for the right moment. That is not tonight, though."

The warning barely registered as he lapped at my core, drinking me in with long curling strokes of his tongue. I gripped his head, pushing and holding him in place at the same time.

He teased me, bringing me to the edge, one finger at a time, until he gave my clit a final kiss and withdrew. In the room's fading light, his gaze held mine as he positioned himself above me.

"Will you tell me if it's too much?"

"It won't be," I said.

He looked doubtful and tipped his head to look down between us. I did the same and watched him position his thick cock at my entrance. He eased in, one inch at a time. I clenched around him, still tender from last night's use, but it felt too good to tell him to stop.

After a few shallow strokes, he fully seated himself with a growl and lifted his head.

"My June," he said tenderly.

I peppered kisses across his face and arched up to meet his careful thrusts.

"I won't break, Tor. You can go a little faster."

He grunted, slipped a hand under my hip to change the angle, and picked up speed. I climbed higher. Reaching for that long tumble.

Before I could get there, he clasped a hand over my mouth and stopped moving, buried to the hilt.

"Stay here, my June. I will be right back."

He kissed me lightly and gave one more quick thrust before he left me spread out and alone on the bed.

Pulse racing, I lifted my head and watched him slip from the room.

It was then that I heard the murmur of voices downstairs.

CHAPTER TWENTY-TWO

My gaze darted to the windows. It was barely dusk. The realization that the men had already come sent a jolt of panic through me. Before I could move, I heard a series of thuds and rustles of noise. Then, there was silence.

When Tor suddenly reappeared, I almost screamed.

"You are safe, my June," he said, striding to the bed.

My mouth fell open when he climbed back onto the bed and reached between us to position himself. I pressed both hands against his shoulders. He paused and looked at me with a heated gaze.

"What's going on?" I demanded.

He blinked at me, glanced down at the hand he had wrapped around himself then back at me.

"We are having sex?"

"No, we are not. We *were* having sex, and then you left. I heard noises downstairs. What happened?"

"The men came to take your food. Vorx and Turik helped me put them to sleep. They will watch them for us. We will take them to Matt as soon as you and I are finished." He nudged my entrance, sliding in an inch before I pushed at his shoulders again. He immediately stopped and gave me a puzzled look.

"Should I lick your pussy some more?"

I sputtered as I tried to process everything that was wrong in this moment. His gaze shifted to concern, and he immediately withdrew.

"I hurt you. June, my heart. Forgive me." He shifted us so we were both lying on our sides and he had me cradled in his arms. "I thought your beautiful pussy would remain wet and ready. I didn't—"

He blinked at the sudden press of my hand over his mouth.

"Tor, I love you. And I need you to be quiet for a minute."

"You love me?" he mumbled behind my hand. I could tell by the look in his eyes that I was about to lose him.

"Stop." He stilled. Confusion clouded his gaze.

"Just listen for a minute. Okay?"

He grunted, and I removed my hand.

"You didn't hurt me. Yes, I love you. No, we're not picking up right where we left off. We are not having sex when there are people in the house. Please don't talk about doing things to my private parts when there are other people around. I find it embarrassing. Now, you can talk."

"Hannah and Merdon have sex with Emily in the house. Vorx and Turik will not care. And why can I not talk about your sweet pussy or your beautiful breasts around others but I can talk about your pretty eyes and your soft, silky hair? They are all parts of the female I love so much it hurts to breathe when I am not touching you." He dipped his head and trailed kisses along my jaw. "Everyone should know why you are the best female on the planet."

His hand stroked over my hip, and I rolled my eyes.

"You know what? You're right. There's no reason you can't talk about all my parts. But we're not having sex right now, Tor." I slipped from his hold and stood. "I need to know who showed up and if there are still more people we need to find."

His expression was pure, disgruntled disappointment as he looked from me to the erection jutting from between his legs. Slowly, he wrapped a hand around himself and winced.

"You'll live," I said, already grabbing my clothes and tugging my shirt on.

"I will live," he agreed. "Walking will be difficult."

"Nice try. You beat up intruders without a problem. I think you can manage a few steps."

He grunted, released himself, and stood. But he didn't get dressed. His hungry gaze zeroed in on my untethered breasts as I gave a quick jump to pull up my jeans. I didn't miss the way he clasped a hand around himself and winced again.

"I promise I'll make it up to you," I said, feeling a little sorry for him. I told him I loved him, but I wasn't really acting like it.

"Now? Three strokes in your pussy is all I need to make you scream and give you my Mr. Happy juice."

I shrieked, part laugh and part disbelief.

"Your what?"

He frowned at me.

"My baby batter? My love liquid? My scream cream?"

I kept shaking my head to each offered term.

"You know that's not what it's really called."

"Yes, it is. Angel says those are the fun names for my seed and women like hearing the fun names. It makes them happy." He flashed me a sly smile. "Maybe happy enough for a quick ride on my pony express?"

"Angel and I are going to have a long talk," I said, heading for the door. He was right on my heels.

"She said my pickup game was strong."

"Are you going to put on clothes?"

"No. Pants will hurt. Besides, I like when you look at my cock with hunger in your eyes."

Since I was leading the way down the stairs, he knew I wasn't looking at him. But darn if I didn't glance his way when my gaze swept the living room for our would-be assailants. Tor smirked at me. I shook my head and focused on the four men slumped on the couch and the two fey standing over them.

"Are they unconscious?" I asked.

Vorx and Turik shared a look that worried me.

"Are they breathing?" I asked, instead.

"Yes," Turik answered. "Matt showed me how to check on the last batch of humans."

I cautiously edged closer to the couch and peered at their faces. Nat wasn't there.

"This isn't all of them," I said softly.

The three fey grunted, and I considered what we should do.

"Did you see anyone else?" I asked.

Both shook their heads.

"It's early yet. There's four of them, one of me, and not a lot of supplies to gather up. I'm guessing someone will come looking when they don't show up in the next hour to two. Let's leave the lights off and see if we can't get a few more."

The fey agreed then bound and gagged the men so they wouldn't be able to raise an alarm if they woke.

"It would be safer if you waited upstairs, June," Turik said.

Nodding, I told the fey to be careful and started for the

stairs. Tor silently followed and closed the bedroom door behind us. I turned to give him a curious look. The unchanged state of his arousal told me his intent.

"Can fey hear through closed doors?" I asked.

He palmed my breast, kneading it with his big hand before rolling the nipple between his fingers.

"I will be very quiet."

As he tugged my shirt over my head, I briefly wondered how often in our relationship he would get his way. I grasped his thick length and stroked it firmly, enjoying his hissed inhale. Probably as often as I got mine, I decided, sinking to my knees.

An hour and two orgasms later, I fell onto Tor's chest, a puddle of loose muscle, as he continued to arch into me. With a groan, he came again. I think we were tied now. Four to four. I ached in the best possible way as he washed my insides anew, and smirked when I thought of his Mr. Happy juice.

His hand stroked my back while he continued to pulse and twitch within me. I loved how big he was and that I could feel every inch of him. Funny how things changed.

"Are you tired, my June?"

"Aren't you?"

The unwavering hardness filling me answered that question.

"I'm not sure I'll ever be able to face Vorx and Turik again," I mumbled against his chest.

"Why not?"

"We haven't stopped since we came up here." I lifted my head to look down at Tor. "Isn't this rude? You said you all want women of your own. Isn't having sex where they can hear like rubbing it in their faces?"

"No. My brothers are truly happy for those of us who have found females of our own. Hearing you with me gives them hope that there is a female waiting for them. And now, they will know what true happiness sounds like."

I buried my head against his chest. I wasn't naïve enough to believe the culture I grew up with was the only "right" way to behave. Public nudity hadn't been frowned upon in many parts of the world. And there had probably been many cultures with family-unit living where sex would have been heard. It was just hard to set aside what I knew and the shame that tried to pull me under at going against what I'd been taught.

"Rest, June," Tor said. "We can have more sex when we are home and no one can hear."

Lifting my head, I gave him a tender kiss.

"I love you, and you love me. There's no shame in sharing that love with each other behind closed doors. As long as they don't mind, I don't mind either."

Tor gave me a heated look, his hands sliding down to grip my butt tightly as he ground into me.

"I have no words to describe how I feel when I look at you," he said.

"Desperate?"

He nodded and withdrew enough to thrust up into me.

"Obsessed?"

His agreement was more adamant, and I grinned. My next suggestion was cut short when he rolled us, pinning me under him.

"Quiet, my June," he said softly. "More men are here."

My eyes widened.

He grinned at me and kissed me ravenously. And I didn't just let him. I kissed him back. By the time he pulled away, I was breathless and considering rolling my hips. He made the decision for me, though, by withdrawing.

"I will be back."

Like last time, he disappeared downstairs without putting any clothes on. There were a few grunts and some scuffling before everything quieted once more. I didn't wait for Tor to reappear before hurrying for my pants.

"You can come down now," he called, surprising me.

What surprised me more when I rejoined them was Shelby, Nat's wife. Unlike the men who were all unconscious, she stood silently crying between Vorx and Turik. All three fey watched me expectantly. Their gazes darted between me and Shelby, who was watching the floor at her feet. Was that due to guilt or Tor's nudity?

I decided it didn't matter and went to check the faces of the newcomers. Her husband lay among them.

"The fey don't want to hurt anyone," I said, facing her. "They only knocked these men out to prevent them from hurting me."

She nodded and quietly sniffled. The tears weren't coming fast. The slow trails were more resignation than fear or panic.

"Is anyone else going to come? Or is this everyone willing to steal food at the risk of exile?"

She dropped her head a little more but not enough to hide her pained expression.

"This is everyone."

"Why are you here?"

"He wanted a lookout." She lifted her head. "He knew something was wrong when the others didn't come back. He meant to beat you like he did your man and shoot whatever fey he found trespassing." She swallowed hard and glanced at Turik. "My husband's words. Not mine."

Turik looked like he wanted to comfort her. And maybe he was right to want to. She didn't strike me as the violent type. More of the domestically abused type. But her fate wasn't for me to decide. That was in Matt's hands.

"Go get Matt," I said to Turik. "Don't let anyone see you, okay?"

He grunted and reluctantly tore his gaze from Shelby. She didn't watch him leave or she would have seen how he'd looked back three times. I glanced at Tor.

"Matt might need your assistance carrying these guys wherever he wants them. You'd make a better impression on the people here if you had clothes on while you helped."

Tor flashed his teeth at me and stalked closer.

"It will be painful, but for you and my brothers, I will force Mister Boopsy into pants."

"Nope. You don't get to call it that."

"Would you like to name it?"

"You're stalling. Go put pants on, Tor."

"Tell me if she looks at my tight backside," he said to Vorx before winking at me and strutting his way upstairs.

I shook my head, watching him with a smirk like I knew he intended.

"I thought you were with a human," Shelby said hesitantly.

"I was. But it didn't work out." I gave a small shrug. "It happens sometimes."

The look she gave me was full of understanding.

"I'm glad you got away then."

Her comment revealed so much about her relationship with her husband.

"Why don't you sit down? It might take Matt a while to get here. Are you hungry?" She shook her head, but I was already moving to grab a bag of chocolate candies I'd found. The festive red and green colors had probably been intended for some kind of holiday baking. Comfort food was comfort food, though, no matter the form.

I held up the bag and lifted my brow. Shoulders slumped in defeat, she resolutely sat.

"I'm not angry," she said, watching me open the bag. "You don't need to feed me."

"Why would I think you're angry?"

"Because I was caught helping them try to steal food and hurt you. I know I'll be kicked out now. It's not your fault. I made my own choices."

I took a handful of candy and pushed the whole bag toward her. She needed it more than I did.

"Sometimes the choices we make are the ones we feel obligated to make." As I said it, I thought of Adam and his blind insistence to leave me. How he'd thought he wasn't enough to keep me safe.

"I don't think your husband was a good man and can't imagine he was ever kind to you. But you're right; you made your own choice not to stand up to him. You also chose to be nice to me when we were out on supply runs, and while you might have been here when they hurt Adam, I doubt you laid a hand on either of us. Because of all of those actions, I don't hold a grudge that you're here tonight.

"Eat up. It might make you feel a little better."

She took a few pieces of the candy and stared at the counter as we waited. Tor's expression wasn't as playful when he joined us, and I knew he'd been listening to our conversation.

He looked at Shelby with pity in his gaze. Vorx hadn't stopped looking at her. The conflict in his eyes seemed to be tearing him apart every time he glanced at the ring she wore. They knew married women were off limits and respected the rule. But their need to protect all females was just as strong. I wondered how they would react if Matt decided she would be exiled with her husband. Even if she weren't, that wouldn't negate the ring she wore.

The door opened, and Matt entered, followed by Turik. Matt scanned the room, taking in the scene, and exhaled heavily.

"Looks like we have everyone on the list, plus a few," he said, his gaze flicking to Shelby before settling on me. "Are you all right?"

"Perfectly fine. I had more than enough protection. None of them got close to me, and Shelby says this is all of them."

He faced her.

"I really wish you weren't here."

"I know, and I'm sorry for putting you in this position. But, we both know you can't make exceptions. People here will lose faith in you. Besides, Nat will find a way to cause problems if I stayed behind."

Matt's weary expression as he nodded pulled at my heart. Everything rested on his shoulders. Over in Tolerance, at least Mya had Drav.

"He'll try to find a way to cause trouble even if you don't stay," Matt said. "That's why I made sure to have proof of what he meant to do first." He looked at me. "Can you download all the footage while we start moving everyone?"

"Absolutely."

Shelby laughed, a bitter, sad sound. "Cameras? You're all a

lot smarter than he gave you credit for. I'm guessing you're going to publicly show some of it?"

"We have a projector we can use against the supply shed," Matt said.

"I'll go through the footage and clip pieces together," I offered. "You have enough on your plate."

"June, make sure I'm in it," Shelby said.

Although I didn't want to do it, I knew she was right.

Carrying the first four men, Tor and Turik left with Matt while I got to work. Shelby quietly watched the footage with me until it was her turn to go with Matt. Turik and Vorx accompanied her.

"You need sleep, June," Tor said, watching me work.

"And I'll get some. But I need to finish this first. Did you see how tired Matt looked? It wasn't from lack of sleep but the stress of having all this pressure on him. If I can do a little to help ease that, then I should. Tolerance is a thriving community because everyone is working together there. That's why I came back here. I want to help make this place more like Tolerance. Isn't that worth a few hours of sleep?"

He kissed my brow and rubbed my back while I pieced together the footage, saying nothing more until it was finished.

Tomorrow, Tenacity would lose fourteen of its citizens.

I STOOD BESIDE MATT, my gaze fixed on the video loop projecting on the shed wall. The footage glowed brightly in the predawn light and made it easy to see the men, who were now bound and kneeling in front of us, as they broke into my house. Even better was the audio I'd picked up and laced in.

The first group of five men didn't say much when they broke in and found nothing. But what they did say was damning.

"Nat's going to want her beaten for this."

The second group of four was chattier.

"Take everything. The bitch deserves it."

"I hope Matt reassigns her to one of our houses. She's good at getting supplies. We could use more women like her."

The third one, though. That was the cherry on top.

After making his lackeys go inside first, Nat strode through the front door and saw his men bound and out cold on the couch.

"I'm going to enjoy beating the shit out of her," he said.

"We should have done it the first time," one of the others said.

Behind them, Shelby remained by the door, peeking through the window and casting worried glances back at them.

I'd made sure to remove all footage of the fey kicking their asses. Although it would be clear they were responsible since they stood off to the side now, I didn't want to spread any more fey-fear or hate.

At first, it was just us silently watching the loop. But as the sky lightened, and the time to meet for a supply run approached, more people gathered. The size of the crowd gradually grew to include those who came to stand in the soup kitchen line as well. Finally, Ryan and his fey arrived. He didn't go to Matt as usual but hung back with the fey to watch the footage.

Through it all, the men in front of us remained hatefully aware but quiet. Shelby knelt beside her husband. She'd insisted on being bound and gagged like the others. She finally got her way, despite fey protest, after saying, "It'll be easier on me out there if I'm treated the same in here."

My heart went out to her.

"It's time," Matt said quietly.

I nodded and stepped forward. After a long discussion with him, I'd gotten my way as well.

"When the fey found me and Ryan told me about the settlements that had been created, it sounded like a dream. A safe place where I wouldn't be alone anymore. People living and working together to survive what the world threw at them. That's what I expected it to be. What it needs to be. Not the nightmare I experienced when a group of these men broke in and stole our food only to return the next day to beat the man I was with to the point he couldn't walk anymore.

"This isn't the community it needs to be if we want to survive. We have to help each other. We need to work together to bring food in so we don't starve. We have to stop the hatred."

Matt stepped forward.

"Change starts today. You will no longer be assigned to houses. You know your neighbors well enough to know who you want to live with by now. Choose wisely."

There was a murmur through the crowd at that.

"That's not fair," someone called.

"Why not?" Matt asked.

"All the people who go out for supplies are going to group together."

"Then become one of the people who leave for supplies," Matt said angrily. "What's not fair is living off of someone else's hard work. Which leads me to change number two. Everyone over the age of sixteen will leave on a supply run once a week."

There was more outcry.

"My knee's shot. I can't run. You'll be sending me out to die."

"No, he won't," I said, speaking up. "I've gone on supply runs. The fey do all the leg work. They carry us when infected are around and jump to the roofs to keep us out of harm's way. All I have to do is pack the food I find into totes. The fey even carry out the weighted totes. Don't throw out excuses before you even try going on a run. It's fear holding you back, not physical limitations."

"I'm not letting one of them carry me around," someone shouted.

"That's your choice," Matt said. "But those who refuse to do their share are saying loud and clear that they do not want to be a part of this community. From this day forward, this community will be open to the fey. If you can't sit at a table with them, eat the food they're generously preparing, and offer a word of thanks for their part in making this the safe haven it's meant to be, then this isn't the place for you.

"The group of men, and woman, before you are hereby exiled from Tenacity for their parts in stealing or intent to steal food. They will leave with the clothes on their backs and nothing else. But if anyone would like to join them, I will not hold you in the same contempt. I will provide you with provisions and an escort to the bunker June once used as a refuge. You can forge your own way of survival as you see fit and without fey influence."

"The fey hate ends today," I said. "Set aside your biases or leave. Stealing food and spreading hate are equally unacceptable. We're not saying you need to like them, but you must have the ability to willingly work with them."

The crowd was completely silent, finally understanding the

seriousness of the message. A few men made their way forward.

"We had nothing to do with stealing food, but I don't want to live in a place where our freedoms are being taken away from us."

"Yeah, the freedom to hate without reason is an important one," I said. "Good luck out there."

CHAPTER TWENTY-THREE

I WATCHED WITH THE RESIDENTS OF TENACITY AS NAT AND HIS group were escorted out of the gates. It surprised me that he had nothing to say about Matt's decision. Having the footage play in an irrefutable loop had probably helped kill any plea of innocence he might have voiced. I hated seeing Shelby leave, though. She walked a step behind her husband, a resigned vacancy in her gaze.

Turik glanced at me, and I shook my head slightly. He'd made it clear to Matt and me before anyone else had arrived that he intended to follow. It didn't matter to him that Shelby was forever banned from Tenacity. She was a female, and the fey were determined to save each and every one of us.

After the exiled group left, Ryan offered to take those who were leaving by choice to the bunker.

"There's a radio in the bunker. Can you bring it back with you, Ryan?" I asked. "People are still out there, and they might be interested in knowing about this place."

Mostly, I didn't want to give anyone the means to communicate and steal from the other preppers still out there.

"Of course," Ryan said.

"Thank you for doing this," Matt said. "I'm hoping if they leave on good terms, they might mention this place in a positive light to any other survivors they eventually come across."

Emily arrived, pulling the attention off of us with the vast amounts of food she and her fey were carrying. The shift in mood was immediately obvious. People stepped forward and volunteered to help carry things for the fey. They even smiled and voiced words of appreciation. Emily looked positively giddy as she took a few people, mostly women, up on their offers of help.

The young mom with the little girl broke off from the line and went to Noru, who had the doll sticking out of the waistband of his pants.

With everything going on, I almost missed Turik slipping away and leaping over the wall.

Tor wrapped his arms around me and kissed the top of my head.

"Do you think he'll be okay?" I asked softly.

"He will be fine. Shelby will be safe."

I didn't comment on how he made no mention of the rest of them. They'd made their choices. Now they needed to deal with the consequences.

A few men approached Matt to ask how he planned for the housing reorganization to work.

"I'm asking everyone to hold off on making any changes for the next few days. June and Tor are working on a supply run schedule with an equal weekly rotation. Once I have that, I plan to distribute it house by house and talk to the households about the reorganization."

"You're serious about requiring everyone to go out on supply runs?" a man asked.

"Yes. Very. I'm aware that some in this community have been using others for their gain. That ends now. We work together; we survive together."

The men seemed content with Matt's answer.

"You're quiet. Are you tired?" Tor asked softly.

I tipped my head back to look up at him.

"No. I'm happy that things will be better now, but I'm sad they weren't like this when Adam and I arrived. It would have saved him so much pain."

Tor studied my face, tenderly gliding his fingers along my throat.

"You still love him."

"I do. But it's not the same love as it was. It changed. Honestly, I think it'd been changing long before we got here. I'll always care about him. He's a good man. But I don't love him the way I love you."

Tor grunted.

"Does that upset you?"

"No. I care about Adam, too. He let me have you."

I made a face. "He didn't let anything. He was a stubborn man. I might have forgiven him for his stupidity, but you are not allowed to thank him for it."

"I'm sorry he hurt your heart and made you cry. I promise to be very careful with it." Tor dipped his head and nuzzled close to my ear. "Just like I was careful feeding my cock into your very small pussy."

My eyes nearly popped out of my head, and my gaze wildly swept over the nearby fey. A few of them flashed a grin at me before looking away.

"Tor," I whispered. "Knock it off."

"Merdon spanks Hannah when she misbehaves. Sometimes she likes it. Sometimes she does not. Would you like to spank me? I might not like it."

I snorted, not believing him for a minute.

Then, I understood what he was doing and turned in his arms.

"You're a sweet man, Tor, but I don't need you to distract me from thinking of Adam anymore. He made his choice, and I made mine. I chose you, and you healed my heart."

He grunted and gave me a playfully sly look.

"You can still spank me."

"You're ridiculous."

"Excuse me. June?"

I turned toward the sound of the voice and found a woman watching us. A light blush painted her cheeks, and I wondered just how much she'd overheard.

"Sorry about that," I said. "Can I help you?"

"Hi, um, maybe? My name's Sam. I was wondering if you two would consider letting me live with you when Matt rearranges things. I'm not looking for a free ride," she said quickly. "I just…" Her gaze flicked to Tor then back to me. "I'd like to know what it's like to live with a fey without having to commit to one."

I struggled to keep the grin off my face at the number of fey who were avidly watching her now.

"Honestly, Tor and I have a house in Tolerance and weren't thinking of staying here." Her expression fell. "But it's not a bad idea," I added, glancing back at Tor. "What do you think?"

"Matt would need to—"

"I think it's a great idea," Matt said, having overheard. "You're both welcome to live in the house June's been using."

I focused on Sam again. "You should talk to Emily about what it's like living with a fey and human couple before you decide anything," I said, thinking of how she'd been wearing her headphones to block out the sounds Hannah and Merdon were making. "The fey are very open people."

She nodded thoughtfully. "Thanks. I'll talk to her."

Matt joined us as she walked away.

"Do you mind staying here?" he asked.

"No," I said, speaking for both Tor and me. "We started the change, and we said fey were welcome here starting now. It's the best way to show that we're serious."

"I like how you keep saying we. I wouldn't mind the help."

I looked at Tor. "What do you think?"

"I don't care where we live as long as I'm with you."

I tilted my head, offering my lips. He kissed me hungrily, and I heard Matt chuckle before walking away.

Since Ryan was taking the deserters to the bunker and there was no supply run going out, the usual gang returned with us to help us move our things from Tolerance. Not that there was a lot, but what Tor had accumulated I didn't want to leave behind. He'd spent time collecting the games, food, and clothes, and things that were once easy to purchase, but now required hours of searching and potential risk. Each item he had mattered.

"Can I live with you, too?" Scath asked as he carried a tote filled with blankets downstairs.

"I'm saying this with love, Scath—"

"She doesn't mean sex love," Tor said, interrupting. "She means mom love. Mom explained it to me."

I grinned, hoping I'd get to meet Mya's mom soon.

"As I was saying, no, you can't live with us. I know the only reason you want to is because Sam asked to live with us, too."

He grunted. I could tell he was disappointed, but he wasn't upset by it.

"However, I still want to do game nights with you guys. It's fun, and I think it would be a great non-pressure way for Sam to spend some time around you single fey."

After that, I had to field at least a dozen questions about the next game night while keeping an eye on Tor. He liked standing behind me and stroking a hand over my backside whenever I bent over to pack something into a tote. The guys didn't miss a thing and thought the game of cat and mouse Tor and I were playing was completely hilarious.

I was so wrapped up in the contentment of the moment that I didn't hear the commotion outside at first. The fey did, though. They all paused what they were doing and watched the front door.

"What's going on?" I asked.

"They're back," Tor answered.

I didn't need to ask who he meant. Uan, Adam, and the rest had returned.

Tor wrapped his arms around me. I pressed myself close, sliding my hand under his shirt and stroking my fingers over the skin of his lower back.

"I love you. Let's go check on your brothers and Adam," I said.

We joined the throng of fey moving toward the south wall. The shouts and good cheer were contagious, and I was smiling by the time we joined the masses. There were so many fey. Some of them had hair as short as Adam's had been, which wasn't a typical hairstyle. I couldn't remember seeing it before.

"Did some of your brothers cut their hair?" I asked.

Tor flashed his teeth at me, his joy radiating from him.

"No. Those are my brothers who stayed in the caves. They returned with the others."

I recalled my conversation with Turik about those they'd left behind and returned Tor's smile.

"I'm glad you're all together again."

Drav lifted his arms, and they all went quiet.

"Welcome, my brothers. Your eyes will adjust to the light. Until they do, there are dark glasses you can wear. What news do you have of Uan?"

"I am here," a low voice called, stepping from the masses. The large fey had no hair whatsoever. None on his head. No eyebrows. And I would be willing to bet no eyelashes.

Drav strode forward.

"It is good to see you well, my brother."

"Uan? Uan!" The shrill voice rang out, and the crowd parted, revealing a middle-aged woman furiously pushing at the wheels of her chair to propel herself forward. As soon as she saw the bald fey, she started crying.

He rushed to her, fell to his knees, and embraced her tightly.

"That is Nancy," Tor said softly. "Uan's female."

I glanced back at Tor.

"Do you see Adam?"

Drav heard me. "Where is Adam? Was he reborn?"

Uan whispered something to Nancy and pulled away from her.

"He chose to remain as he was and not risk the pools. We stayed in the caves only long enough to gather our brothers.

The crystals had already started to make Adam's head ache as we made our way to the surface. But he recovered quickly." His gaze moved from Drav to me. "We were many and attracted much attention from infected and hellhounds. We kept Adam safe. But during one attack, he disappeared. We searched for him, but he was gone."

I couldn't stop the tears from falling. Tor tugged me close to his side and stroked a hand over my back. His worry helped ground me in the moment.

"I understand," I said to Uan. "Thank you for trying to keep him safe. He knew the risks he would be taking going with you."

"I am sorry, June."

I nodded and managed a weak smile of reassurance.

"We killed twelve hellhounds and many infected," Uan said, talking to the crowd now. "But we saw no sign of Molev."

"Rest," Drav said. "Spend time with your family." His gaze locked with mine. "Mya would like to speak with you."

Swallowing down the dull ache of my grief, I nodded and made to follow him. Tor allowed me one step before picking me up and hugging me tightly to his chest. I buried my face against his shirt and shed a few more tears for Adam. It didn't seem real that he was gone. But mostly, it didn't make sense to go all that way and change his mind at the end. He'd risked his life for nothing.

By the time we reached Drav's house, I'd managed to dry my tears. There would be time later to grieve for Adam. Mya needed to know how things went clearing the haters from Tenacity.

"June is here," Drav said, the moment he opened the door.

"Good," Mya called from the kitchen. "Get in here and try

one of these cookies, June. Did you find out what all the yelling was about, Drav?"

Drav glanced at me. Though his expression didn't give anything away, I knew he wasn't sure what to say. She didn't know. Any of it.

I patted Tor so he'd put me down and walked into the kitchen. Mya took one look at my face and her cheer fled.

"Uan and his group have returned. Uan's safe and healthy. Adam disappeared on the way back. There's an irony in that. He chose not to die in the caves and died anyway."

"June, I'm so sorry," she said, hurrying to hug me.

There was nothing to say, so I hugged her in return to reassure her the best I could that I didn't hold anyone to blame for it. No one had forced Adam to go.

"I'll take a cookie if you're still offering," I said, "and tell you about our success in Tenacity."

Mya released me, gave me a searching look, then fetched a cookie. They were lemon.

I took a seat. Tor stood behind me and gently played with my hair as I spoke for us. Mya listened to the recap and admitted she'd heard a bit from one of the fey who'd run back with the news once the group of men was booted. I told her about our plans to move into the Tenacity house on a more permanent basis to help support Matt's message that things were going to change.

"The timing couldn't be more perfect," I said. "It looks like you have a lot of new fey to house. Matt has humans cohabitating about ten to twelve to a place. I know fey are bigger, but you should be able to fit that many in Tor's house."

Drav shook his head.

"My brothers know it is difficult to find a female and even

more so when there are many of us together. It is better they have their own homes. We may need to start another community."

"After Matt announced his intent to rearrange the living assignments, a woman asked if she could live with Tor and me. She was clear that it wasn't to freeload. She wants to live with a fey and a human couple to get a feel for what it would be like. It doesn't free up houses necessarily, but it might reshuffle the numbers enough here that a place could open up."

"I like that idea," Mya said. "I know Cassie and Kerr wouldn't mind a helping hand. Nancy and Uan probably wouldn't be a good fit since they're focusing on Tasha. But maybe Thallirin and Brenna?" She looked at Drav.

"I will speak to Thallirin and the others. Many will defer to their women."

"Perfect. I know I can talk Angel and Eden into it. It's like an exchange program for potential brides," she said with a grin. "But you're right, Drav. We should still look into starting another community. Is there anything within the same distance as Tenacity?"

A heavy knock on the door interrupted the conversation. Drav went to answer it.

"The infected have returned," the fey said.

Since coming to Tenacity and Tolerance, I hadn't seen or heard an infected nearby. We saw plenty of them when we went out for supply runs, but never any nearby the settlements.

"What does he mean?" I asked Mya.

"We used to see infected outside the walls all the time. The lights drew them in," she said, standing and talking as she moved.

I followed her to the door.

"A few weeks before you arrived, they used ladders and breached the walls. That was before Tenacity was finished," she continued as she shrugged into the jacket Drav handed her. "We were overcrowded, and it was complete chaos. We lost a lot of people that day. But after that, the infected just disappeared from around here."

"So why are they back?" I asked.

"Exactly."

We must have been walking too slowly because Drav and Tor scooped us up at the same time and took off at a run for the wall. They didn't need a ladder to jump to the top.

Just below us, a line of fey waited. Beyond them, a line of infected stood, some swaying slightly, side to side, in a creepy predatorial way. At their center stood a familiar decaying man in a blue jacket.

"I've seen him before," I said. "He was at the bunker. He's the one who seemed to coordinate everything. The hellhound, the horses, killing the cows. Adam said that everything that thing did reminded him of when he and his father used to hunt. Baiting the prey."

"Well, that just gave me future nightmares," Mya said under her breath.

"Sorry."

"No. It's okay. That's exactly what this feels like." She glanced at Drav. "We need to watch everywhere, not just here."

"We are," the fey who'd knocked said. "As soon as we spotted them, we doubled the watch and sent a group to Tenacity."

I only half-listened while I watched the blue coat man. There were only eight infected with him. Why so few?

"I'm not the only one imagining a pack of hellhounds

hiding in the trees behind them, am I?" I asked, glancing at the sky. It was almost at its zenith.

"It's the wrong time of day for that," Mya said. But I could hear the doubt in her voice.

It wasn't hellhounds that emerged from the trees, but Adam, led by another infected. His mouth was gagged, and his hands were tied behind his back.

A choked sound escaped me.

"What are they doing?" I asked.

Tor didn't wait to find out. He leapt from the wall, running impossibly fast. The other fey from below joined the charge. The blue-coat man let out an unholy bellow but didn't flee like he had last time. His eyes flashed red, and he charged at the oncoming fey.

"What the fuck?" Mya breathed, seeing the same thing I was seeing.

The infected behind Adam let out an answering call. Adam tried to run. I could see in his eyes that he knew what was coming for him as the infected behind him lurched forward. They went down in a heap, and Adam used his legs, the only thing that was free, in an attempt to kick the infected away.

Tor leapt over the leader, leaving him for the others as he raced to reach Adam. Adam rolled and kicked and did his best to avoid the snapping teeth. I lost sight of him behind Tor.

The blue-coat man let out one final call before his head was ripped clean off his shoulders by one of the fey. The field went silent.

Tor tossed a head and bent to pick up Adam.

Tears streamed down my face as he raced back to me. The hope and joy I felt faded when I saw Tor's devastated expression a moment before he leapt onto the wall and landed in front of me.

"He was bitten, my June."

"No," I gasped in denial.

Tor set Adam down and carefully removed the gag. Drav nudged Mya and me back a step.

Adam's face was pale as he looked up.

"Listen to me, June. There's not much time. They followed us from the bunker. They watched this place. They waited for us to leave and followed us to the caves. They're watching, June. They're smart. And they're changing." He looked at Tor. "I was with them when your brothers were looking for me. I watched the fey kill a group of them. They're not all dying when you take off their heads."

Adam made a pained sound, like someone was torturing his insides.

"You need to figure out what's happening, and you need to stop it. We won't survive if we can't kill them." His gaze swept over everyone but me. "Let me become one of them. Study me."

Now it felt like my insides were being tortured. A sob escaped me, and his gaze found and held mine.

"I have no regrets, June, except for hurting you. I'm sorry. Please be happy. Live. Love. Have a huge family like you always wanted." He grabbed Tor's hand and gripped it tight. "Figure this out, Tor. Keep your promise. Keep June safe."

Adam threw up all over himself, and Tor looked up at me then at Drav.

"Go, Tor. We will care for Adam."

Tor stood, and another fey picked me up.

"Wait," I said, struggling from his arms. I fell to my knees beside Adam and gripped his hand.

"I will always love you. Thank you for saving me."

He smiled at me.

"I love you too. Go."

CHAPTER TWENTY-FOUR

A SHAKY EXHALE ESCAPED ME, AND I UNFOLDED THE BLANKET ONLY to refold it a different way.

Tor's hand settled on my head, the heat warming my hair and seeping into my skin. I closed my eyes and absorbed the comfort of that simple touch.

"I'm sorry I failed you, June," he said. "I ran as fast as I could."

I twisted away from the tote I was packing to look up at him, shock on my face.

"Failed me? You didn't fail me." My gaze swept the other fey in our home helping us, and I saw their gazes all reflected the same guilt. "None of you failed me."

I rose and threw my arms around Tor.

"You tried to help him, Tor. You did everything you could. I know that. I don't blame you for Adam's death."

Tor hugged me close.

"But your heart still hurts."

I nodded, leaning my forehead against his torso.

"It does. I don't agree with all the decisions that Adam

made, but I know he was trying to take care of me. I think that's why I hurt. Even though I know he was the only person in control of his decision, a part of me feels like his death was my fault. It's going to take me some time to accept everything that's happened." I lifted my head and looked up at Tor. "I think the best thing I can do right now is focus on moving us to Tenacity. Helping there will be a good distraction from the hurt."

Tor blinked at me.

"You want distractions?" he asked.

Despite everything, I laughed because I knew right where his thoughts had gone.

"I'm very willing to let you distract me after we're moved into the new house."

He looked at his brothers.

"We can carry everything in one trip."

I rubbed my face against his shirt, drying my tears and hiding my sad smile. I loved Tor so much and knew he would do his best to keep me from dwelling on the past. I also knew he wouldn't begrudge me the occasional quiet moment so I could reflect.

Tor really was perfect.

He took the face rubbing as the signal I was ready and picked me up. Considering recent events, more fey joined us when they learned we were going to Tenacity. Many of them were from the newly arrived group. They wore sunglasses, no shirts, and leather pants and boots. If not for the ears and grey tint to their skin, any woman with a libido would stop to drool.

They ran with us through the fields and trees, but we didn't see any other signs of infected.

When we arrived at Tenacity, the soup kitchen line was still going strong, and Matt was nearby to greet us. He encouraged the new fey to stand in line for something to eat then walked with my group as we made our way to the house.

Staying true to how fast news traveled, he'd already heard what happened in Tolerance and extended his condolences.

"Part of me wishes I'd had the chance to tell Adam what we've done here," I said as the fey moved our things in. "He would have been proud, I think."

"He would have. Then he would have pushed for more," Matt said.

I smiled slightly. That was exactly Adam. He liked to push for improvement in everything.

"So, what should we do next?" I asked.

During the next several hours, Matt and I worked together at his place. We combed through the list of Tenacity residents and where they were living. He noted the ones who'd gone on supply runs and those he thought had never left the walls. We planned. We brainstormed. We worked together to come up with something that would push Tenacity and its people toward a better future.

Tor and his group were great support, volunteering to help with some of the ideas we wanted to set into motion.

By the time Ryan returned from the bunker, I felt hopeful for the next day.

"The deserters are all settled in," he reported.

"Were the fish still alive?" I asked.

"A few were. I think they were eating each other. They'll be fine now, though. The group was pretty excited that they were there. They weren't happy about the radio going, though. But after seeing the cameras and the power sources they were getting, they didn't complain too much."

"They shouldn't," I said. "It was a decent place to hole up. However, we should check on them every now and again."

"I already told them we would, but I also told them not to expect supplies from us. They chose to be on their own."

While he talked, a fey came in with the radio and the supplies.

"We can probably go back to the base and dismantle one of the towers. We'd get better range than what we'll have now," Matt said, removing parts from the bin and setting them up next to his existing radio.

I looked around his house as I leaned into Tor.

"Matt, you need to make some changes, too."

He glanced up at me in question.

"Well, I'm sending the message that fey are great, and everyone should have one. But I think you need to be the other side of the coin. Did you lose someone in all of this?"

He messed around with some wires and connections for a bit.

"I did," he said finally. "I'm not sure I…there's a lot going on here. Romantic distractions aren't something I can afford right now."

I studied the man as he turned on the radio. The familiar sound sent me back to the bunker for a moment and the loneliness I'd felt there.

"We've all lost people, Matt. I'm sure that's why many of the women aren't willing to consider a fey. But in order to move forward, we also need to move on."

He sighed heavily.

"I know you're right. I'll talk to Emily."

"Nope. Emily needs to stay focused on her current projects. You'll be Tor's project."

Tor grunted.

"What type of female do you want? One with big breasts and wide hips? One with a sad smile? I saw one with purple hair. She scowls like you do."

Matt shot me a worried look, and I smiled.

"You'll be in good hands. Trust me. Tor knows what he's doing, and he knows how to be subtle."

"...comprised. The eastern barrier is gone. There are no lines to hold. Relay on all channels."

We all turned to look at the radio.

"God help us all," the voice said. "Is anyone out there?"

Matt got on the radio.

"This is Matt Davis from the Tenacity settlement. Please repeat the message."

"Holy shit," the voice said. "I'm glad to hear your voice. The guy that sent the message isn't on the channel anymore. That was more than a week ago."

"What's the message?" Matt asked.

"I wrote it down. Message received on the east coast. The western barrier has been compromised. The eastern barrier is gone. There are no lines to hold. Relay on all channels. God help us all."

There was a moment of silence.

"Listen, I don't care if you're a bunch of supply stealing survivalists. I'm done doing this alone. You can find me at—"

I was across the room and taking control before the man could get more out.

"Wait," I said. "Just wait. We're not supply-stealing survivalists. And we don't want to see you or anyone else killed by any assholes listening. Don't give us your location. Let's set a meetup point instead."

Matt's gaze met mine, and he nodded.

"You aren't alone," Matt said to the man. "There are hundreds of us here. Enough to protect anyone looking for communities working together to survive. We'll take anyone in. But you should know—the world isn't what it was."

I returned to my seat and listened as Matt talked to the man about the infected, hellhounds, and the fey. He laid it out plain and gave the man an option of three places and asked if any of them were doable.

The man said two were but suggested we go to all three at set times just in case other people who were as done surviving alone as he was were out there listening. Matt readily agreed.

Yes, we'd all lost so much. But now it was time to start putting the world back together.

EPILOGUE

Tor ran his hands up my sides and palmed my breasts, growling in pleasure as I rode him. He always seemed to know when we needed to change up positions during our sex marathons so I didn't get too sore and end the fun sooner than he'd like. He'd like forever. Even after four weeks of almost non-stop sex, he showed no signs of flagging interest. It only took a look from me for him to get hard. I didn't know how the man had the stamina.

He pinched my nipple, and I clenched around him.

"Are you ready to scream, my June?"

I clenched again, harder, and ground down on him in greedy anticipation just the way he liked. He chuckled and rolled us so he was on top but then lifted me and got to his knees while I still straddled his hips. There was something about this position that hit all the right places when he thrust hard and fast. It made the orgasms explosive to the point that I passed out afterward.

But not before I screamed my release.

He grinned wickedly at me then dipped his head to suck my

nipple hard into his mouth. I gripped his shoulders and held on for dear life.

Five minutes later, my scream echoed off the walls, followed by his fierce growl. Tor held me when I fell forward and continued his delicious thrusting until he was spent.

"Sleep sweet, my June," he said, kissing my temple as I went under.

When I came to, Sam was lying next to me, reading a book.

"You need to tell him no, Sam," I said, struggling to sit up and keep hold of the sheet Tor had used to cover me.

Sam snorted.

"He bribed me with food. Do you really think I'm going to say no to sitting next to you so you don't wake up alone? Oh, and he told me to tell you he loves you and will lick your pussy until it weeps into his mouth."

I made a face, and she grinned at me.

"Don't even try to lie to me. I can hear how much you love what he does to you."

"Has it convinced you to try a dinner date yet?"

She shrugged lightly and held up her book.

"I still like my men fictional for now. Although, I don't think I'll be able to hold out much longer. Emily is persistent."

"She is. It's her best quality." I smoothed my hand over the sheet. "I'm awake and know I'm loved. You can go now."

Laughing, Sam sat up and started from the room. Over the last three weeks, we'd grown pretty close. I'd be sad when some fey finally won her over, and she moved out.

Sam paused in the doorway and looked back at me.

"There's a present in the bathroom from Tor. He wants you to put it on and come downstairs when you're ready. I added a present, too. Have fun." She left before I could ask questions.

Curiosity piqued, I hurried out of bed. A pretty sundress hung on the back of the bathroom door, and I smiled, already guessing what Tor was up to. He'd been talking about taking me on a dinner date for days now. I fingered the soft material, melting a little bit more for the man. He was a romantic, through and through.

I turned on the shower and spotted Sam's gift to me. A pregnancy test. I frowned, thinking back to my last period. It had started the day after we moved into this house. They were always light and never lasted long, but I'd always been regular. Like clockwork.

Slipping into the shower, I washed between my legs and thought of how often Tor and I had had sex. My gaze slid to the test in disbelief. No…I couldn't be pregnant that fast.

Thoughts of Adam slipped in, and I felt a sharp pang. Guilt. Hurt. Sorrow. But those quickly fled, and my eyes watered with hope. Adam would've wanted this for me. He knew how much I'd wanted a family. Almost as much as Tor did.

Smiling through the tears, I finished my shower, used the test, and slipped into the dress while I waited. The positive sign was almost immediate.

A baby.

Tor was going to go crazy. I couldn't wait to tell him.

My light steps barely made a sound on the stairs. It didn't matter, though. Tor was watching for me from his place beside the candlelit table. The moment he saw me, he got to one knee.

A lump formed in my throat as he held up a ring between his thumb and forefinger. I drifted closer, everything feeling more dream-like than reality.

"I love you, June. Will you wear my ring and never leave me?"

Tears started falling, and I quickly nodded before tackle-hugging him. He grunted and wrapped his arms around me.

"You're supposed to put the ring on, June."

"I'm going to have your baby," I sobbed in his ear.

He made soothing sounds and rubbed his hand over my back.

"It will be okay. My cock is big, and your pussy isn't as tiny anymore. The baby will come out without hurting you. Too much. Hopefully. I will keep trying to make your pussy bigger."

I jerked back and gave him a 'what the fuck' look. He opened his mouth to say more, but I clapped a hand over it.

"Nope. We're going to talk about what you just said and how it might be taken in a heart-hurting way later. But right now, we're going to focus on happier things. Yes, I will be your wife, Tor. And I just took a test." I lifted my other hand, which was still gripping the pregnancy test. "I'm already pregnant Tor. In nine months, I think, we will be saying hello to a little boy or girl."

His expression flitted through a myriad of emotions before settling on complete elation. He lifted me and pressed his ear against my stomach. He stayed there for a second then turned his head.

"I can't hear you, yet, little one. But I am here. I will keep you safe and feed your mother well. You will grow big and strong." He hesitated and glanced up at me before lowering his voice. "But not too big. Your mother is very small. Don't hurt her, okay? I promised to keep her safe, too."

I threaded my fingers through Tor's hair, loving him more with each word he said.

"The baby and I will be fine, Tor."

He grunted and nuzzled my stomach. Then lower. I grinned down at the top of his head. The man was insatiable.

"Let's go tell Molev the good news," I said. "I think he could use it. When we're done, we can come back and have dinner. Maybe cuddle on the couch and watch a movie."

Tor grunted but continued to nuzzle.

"This will be the first of many, my June," Tor said, confirming the direction of his thoughts. "I will fill you again and again with my love juices."

"We talked about this…"

"Our babies will be perfect."

I shook my head and bent down to kiss him tenderly.

"Our babies *will* be perfect because they'll be half you."

AUTHOR'S NOTE

Oh, Adam. Poor, poor Adam. What can I say? I'm a sucker for good guys. He really did love June. A lot. Enough to see that he wasn't the one who could give her the future she deserved. With him, she would have lived in fear every time he left for supplies. He understood the moment he was hurt that there was every chance he would die and leave her alone. He didn't want to put her through that pain. But, by leaving her, he ultimately did just that.

We can make all the wrong choices for the right reasons, and it'll still hurt the people we love.

June understood it was self-sacrifice. She was mad at him for it, but wasn't going to fight him. In her mind, she was either worth fighting for or she wasn't. That he didn't want to try was on him. However, she didn't hate him for it because she knew he was doing it out of love, no matter how misguided.

And, honestly, she got Tor out of the deal. He was the overly-affectionate fey she needed. With him, she can have her family and net of safety in an ever-changing world.

Speaking of ever-changing…how creepy did those infected

get? And what the heck was that Molev mention in the Epilogue? I can't wait for you to find out. And no, I'm not telling you more here. LOL. All good things come to those who wait!

(Don't worry, I have the patience of a gnat, too.)

The next book will be Molev's, and as of right now, it will be the final book in the series. I know. It's sad, but this has been a really long series. An author's worst nightmare is writing past the point of interest. I'd rather close with everyone loving what we have than thinking I'm just stringing them along.

But for those of you in love with these adorable dark fey, I have a hidden cache of stories (maybe not so hidden if you're already signed up for my newsletter) on my website under the book extras. I wrote them as a thank you to all the loyal Resurrection fans. I hope you'll stick with me to see what I come up with next, after the final Resurrection book.

Hugs and books!

Melissa

WHAT WAS ADAM THINKING?

Adam's first thought wasn't to pawn June off on Tor. He truly did love her. However, once they got to Tolerance and he realized he was seriously hurt, he started doing some thinking. What would happen to June if he never walked again? How long would Tor be willing to host them if they couldn't pull their weight? Adam knew Tor was a decent guy and wouldn't just kick them out. He didn't want to be a freeloader, though, either. The start of his epiphany came in chapter 8 when they were talking about how his uncle went after the strongest bull. He knew he wasn't the strongest any more. That went to the fey. As innocent as the thought was, the seed was planted. It grew further when he snapped at June in his frustration and pain and Tor very politely told June to go for a walk so he could ream Adam out. But even then, when Tor was truly upset with Adam, he wasn't an ass about it. He was a good guy. A guy who wished he could have a girl as amazing as June.

It was Adam's need to secure June a place no matter what the future might hold for him that had him sharing information he knew he shouldn't be sharing. Under the guise of an apology, he told Tor, in vivid detail, June's favorite way to be woken up. Now take a moment to imagine that conversation and all the questions Tor probably asked. (Yep, all the questions!)

Go back and read the beginning of Chapter 9. That's where you get to see Tor acting all sorts of shy around June because now he knows. He knows about the little sounds she makes when she's turned on and how much she likes her "pussy" being licked. And Tor wants a woman like that with every fiber of his being.

Now, Tor's happily educated, and Adam's smart enough to know he just helped Tor fall a little more in love with June. And it hurts him. He doesn't want to take advantage of Tor, but he knows how dangerous the world is for June.

When she comes home and starts talking about these miracle caves that could reincarnate a person, everything changes. He's excited at first, but the more he learns about it, the more he knows it's as dangerous as limping around with a bum leg for the rest of his life.

Then, Tor drops the bomb. Sleeping with the fey brings immunity from infection. Adam doesn't see anything beyond his burning need to give June the life she deserves.

So, Adam cuts out his own heart. To keep June safe for life and give her a real chance at a happy future, he decides to let her go. That's why he said he wanted to go to the caves. He never had any intention of making one of the fey kill him. He only wanted to get himself out of the way so Tor and June could have a test run. He needed to make sure she'd be happy. But he knew it would take a lot more than him going to the caves for June to willingly try a relationship with someone else.

Everything from that point on was to get June to see Tor for the amazing person he could be. Adam knew what he was doing was wrong, and he also knew he had to play his hand carefully to bring them together.

Adam may have thought he loved football more than June, but he never did. It was always June.

THE RESURRECTION CHRONICLES

Humor, romance, and sexy dark fey!

Book 1: Demon Ember

In a world going to hell, Mya must learn to accept help from her new-found demon protector in order to find her family as a zombie-like plague spreads.

Book 2: Demon Flames

As hellhounds continue to roam and the zombie plague spreads, Drav leads Mya to the source of her troubles—Ernisi, an underground Atlantis and Drav's home. There Mya learns that the shadowy demons, who've helped devastate her world, are not what they seem.

Book 3: Demon Ash

While in Ernisi, cites were been bombed and burned in an attempt to stop the plague. Now, Marauders, hellhounds, and the infected are doing their best to destroy what's left of the world. It's up to Mya and Drav to save it.

Book 4: Demon Escape

While running from zombies, hellhounds, and the people who kept her prisoner, Eden encounters a new creature. He claims he only wants to protect her. Eden must decide who the real devils are between man and demon, and choosing wrong could cost her life.

Book 5: Demon Deception

Grieving from the loss of her husband and youngest child, Cassie lives in fear of losing her remaining daughter. To gain protection, Cassie knows she needs to sleep with one of the dark fey and give him the one thing she isn't sure she can. Her heart.

THE RESURRECTION CHRONICLES

The apocalyptic adventure continues!

Book 6: Demon Night

Angel's growing weaker by the day and needs help. In exchange for food, she agrees to give Shax advice regarding how to win over Hannah. If Angel can help make that happen, just maybe she won't be kicked out when her fellow survivors find out she's pregnant.

Book 7: Demon Dawn

In a post-apocalyptic world, Benna is faced with the choice of trading her body and heart to the dark fey in order to survive the infected.

Book 8: Demon Disgrace

Hannah is drinking away her life to stanch the bleeding pain from past trauma. Merdon, a dark fey with a violent history, relentlessly sets out to show her there's something worth living for.

Book 9: Demon Fall

June never planned to fall in love. She had her eyes on the prize: a career and independence. Too bad the world ended and stole those options from her. Maybe falling in love had been the better choice after all.

Beauty and the Beast with seductively dark twists!

Book 1: Depravity

When impoverished, beautiful Benella is locked inside the dark and magical estate of the beast, she must bargain for her freedom if she wants to see her family again.

Book 2: Deceit

Safely hidden within the estate's enchanted walls, Benella no longer has time to fear her tormentors. She's too preoccupied trying to determine what makes the beast so beastly. In order to gain her freedom, she must find a way to break the curse, but first, she must help him become a better man while protecting her heart.

Book 3: Devastation

Abused and rejected, Benella strives to regain a purpose for her life, and finds herself returning to the last place she ever wanted to see. She must learn when it is right to forgive and when it is time to move on.

Becareful what you wish for...

Prequel: Disowned

In a world where the measure of a person rarely goes beneath the surface, Margaret Thoning refuses to play by its rules. She walks away from everything she's ever known to risk her heart and her life for the people who matter most.

Book 1: Defiant

When the sudden death of Eloise's mother points to forbidden magic, Eloise's life quickly goes from fairy tale to nightmare. Kaven, the prince's manservant, is Eloise's prime suspect. However, when dark magic is used, nothing is as simple as it seems.

Book 2: Disdain

Cursed to silence, Eloise is locked in the tattered remains of her once charming life. The smoldering spark of her anger burns for answers and revenge. However, games of magic can have dire consequences.

Book 3: Damnation

With the reason behind her mother's death revealed, Eloise must prevent her stepsisters from marrying the prince and exact her revenge. However, a secret of the royal court strikes a blow to her plans. Betrayed, Eloise will question how far she's willing to go for revenge.

www.ingramcontent.com/pod-product-compliance
Lightning Source LLC
LaVergne TN
LVHW041059080826
845145LV00007B/1634

* 9 7 8 1 6 3 8 6 9 0 1 2 2 *